Conquering Shadows

This is a work of fiction. Names, characters, places, and incidents either are the product of the author's imagination or are used fictitiously. Any resemblance to actual persons, living or dead, events, or locales is entirely coincidental.

Cover Design by Lesia T.

Map by Thiago Liuth

ISBN (paperback): 979-8-9895166-2-9

ISBN (ebook): 979-8-9895166-3-6

www.lcyruswhelchel.com

This book is dedicated to Moona, my partner and better half. Even with all my faults, she still shows that she loves me every day, and I know I'd be much worse off without her at my side.

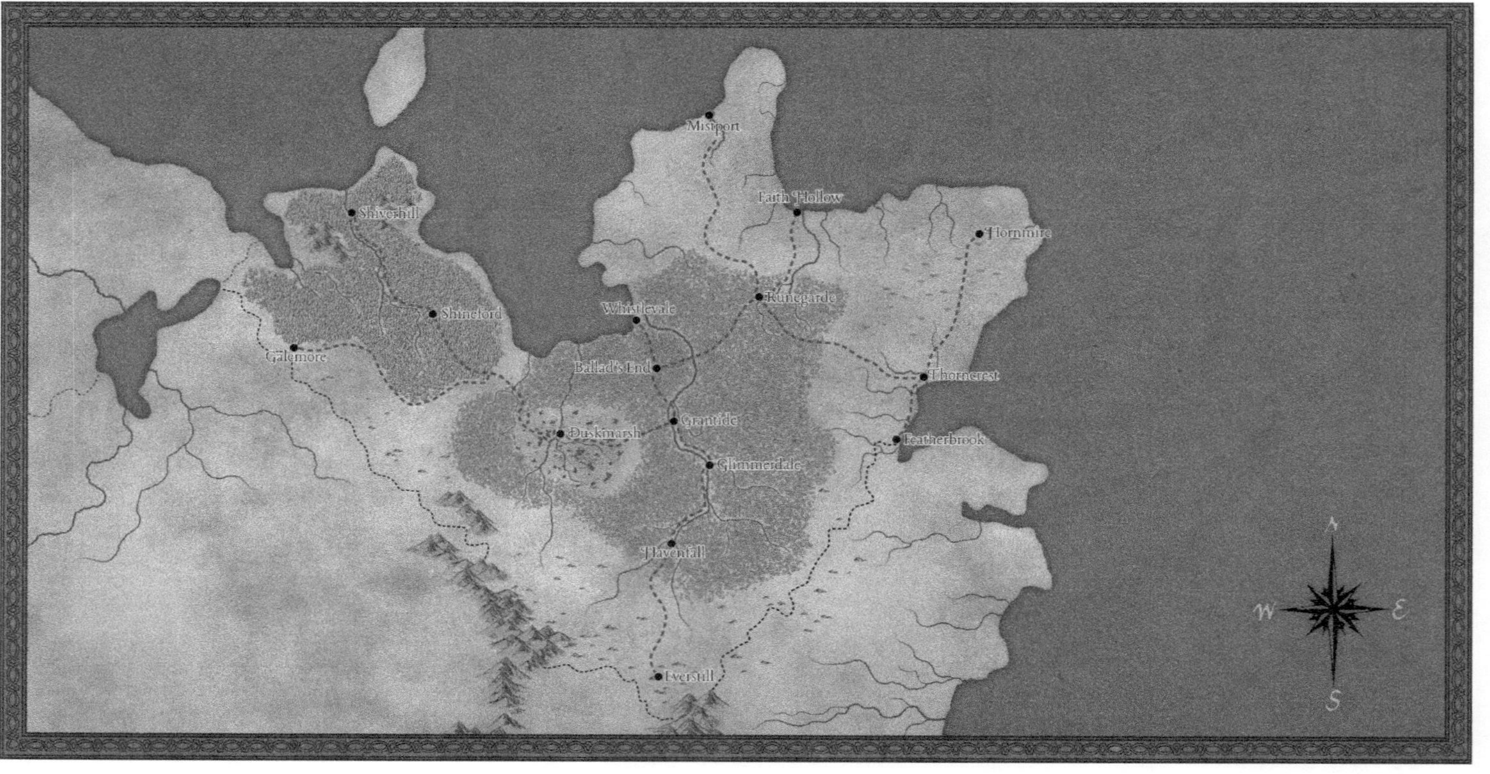
Mistport
Faith Hollow
Hornmire
Shiverhill
Runegarde
Whistlevale
Shineford
Galemore
Ballad's End
Thornerest
Grantide
Duskmarsh
Featherbrook
Glimmerdale
Havenfall
Everstill
N
W
E
S

Chapter I

It was truly amazing how so many nobles in Whistlevale waltzed through life as though nothing was wrong. In their eyes, the war raging over the past half year was a faraway inconvenience with no bearing on their lives.

Never mind the fact that the prices of many goods were rising throughout Livoria due to the enemy's decision to raze any field and town they came across. That was a problem for the common folk. The nobles had better things to do with their time, expecting others to deal with the Liberation Army for them.

Standing among the Royal Palace's rooftop gardens overlooking Whistlevale and the lines of nobles walking along the streets below, Kai reflected on the events leading him to this point and his frustration at the court for dragging their feet. If they bothered pulling their weight, the Grand Duchess wouldn't be so overworked in keeping the duchy from falling apart. The aroma of the surrounding roses and gardenias drifted across his nose, soothing his anger and lulling him into a peaceful calm.

Considering its status as the largest city in the duchy, Whistlevale was without a doubt the most beautiful, renowned throughout Alezon for its many gardens, resplendent half-timbered architecture, and views of the Great Ardei River. Kai found himself grateful for the surrounding greenery that reminded him so much of home.

After their most recent battle at the Royal Archives in Runegard, Kai and his companions were swept up by Lady Fusette and brought back to the capital at her insistence. In hindsight, Kai appreciated the woman's willingness to press them into joining her, as he knew they needed rest desperately with the ordeals dogging them since the war's beginning.

Of course, hearing Fusette argue with the nobles of late infuriated Kai to the point he worried he might slip into a Frenzy Haze.

"How did I know I'd find you out here?" a familiar musical voice trilled from behind.

Kai was unable to restrain the smile stretching across his face as he turned to see Maple approaching. Seeing the Aerivolk merchant was always a bright spot of his day. No matter how much he tried suppressing it, he couldn't stop his heart from racing when she gifted him one of her lopsided, cheeky smiles. Or the tingling shock that spread from his head to his fingertips when her feathers brushed against his skin.

He heard his adoptive mother wax poetic about such things often as a boy, but hearing it paled in comparison to the physical reality of the situation. Kai Travaldi was many things, but a fool wasn't one of them. He grew up learning to apply logic to any problem, but this was an arena where logic was scattered to the winds. Regardless of what the Order of the Windbringers said about it, he knew precisely what happened to him over the past few moons, since his disastrous mission in Mistport.

Kai had, against the teachings of his faith, fallen in love with the cheery Aerivolk.

"Hello? Nixtral to Kai! Are you okay?" Maple tapped the stunned Norzen on his nose, jarring him from his thoughts.

He shook his head to clear the gentle haze muddling his thoughts. "Yeah, I'm fine. Sorry, Maple. Just had a lot on my mind lately."

"Oh? And what were you thinking about, Sir Gravebane?" she asked, leaning forward and purring his Exarch Brand in an alluring lilt that sent a spark down his spine.

You, he thought. Not that he would admit it aloud.

"Too much, to be honest. I understand what Fusette wants, but I worry about letting you all get dragged into this mess. Traveling to Havenfall won't be easy."

"Oh, pish, not this again," she muttered. She wrapped her wings around him in a warm embrace. "For the last time, we're joining you of our own free will. Well, maybe not Lucretia, but you know how she is. Now quit with the lone knight act, or I'll send Orelia up here to give ya a few good whacks with her staff."

"You wouldn't dare!" While he adored Orelia and appreciated the priestess' soothing manner in most cases, he also knew she wouldn't hesitate to bash him on the head if she thought he was being stupid.

"You know I would, Kai, and I damn well will if I hear any more of that nonsense. Stand tall and proud, like Fusette says." Hearing that sent a shiver through Kai's body, and not just because he loved her voice. Being told to stand proud of himself was a phrase beaten into his head multiple times over the three moons since their arrival.

Kai smirked and turned to face Maple, who clicked her tongue and sauntered away with a sway in her hips. The apothecary found his eyes locked on her tail feathers fluttering in the breeze.

Wait, what am I doing? Damn it all, that woman doesn't realize what she does to me. Kai fought the urge to slap himself, knowing if he did, it would result in questions he had no intention of answering.

"I reckon we should head to the throne room," said Maple. "Saredi says we're supposed to receive directions on our new mission."

"Understood. Shall we?" Kai held out his arm, allowing Maple to hook hers around his elbow with a shy smile.

"Indeed we shall, good sir. Thank you, for putting up with me, that is. I know some of the others find me a bit much, trying to be cheerful all the time."

Kai rolled his eyes, pinching the merchant on her cheek and drawing a surprised chirp. "Now who's talking nonsense? I think it's refreshing to have that kind of optimism. It makes my heart feel like we can do this, even when my mind tries to say otherwise. Don't ever lose that."

With a huff, Maple swatted him on the mane. "You really know how to cheer someone up, ya know? Let's go, before Lucretia comes up here and starts accusing us of impropriety." Kai allowed himself to be pulled back inside, suppressing a contented sigh when he caught a hint of appleberries and honey; since they began traveling together, Kai came to recognize Maple's unique scent as easily as the cappara pepper he enjoyed sprinkling on his meals.

For now, he needed to quash those thoughts before they got him in trouble. The mission came first.

"Thank you very much for coming, everyone," said Fusette as the party settled into a comfortable silence in the throne room.

Kai stood at the head of his group, with Maple standing directly beside him. The scholar Lucretia Dineri stood on Maple's other side just behind her, wearing the bright blue overcloak announcing her as an Archivist of the Citadel. Towering behind Lucretia was the party's Soltauri member, Teos, standing tall in his scruffy sailing clothes and rounded hat. To Teos' left stood Morgan Cauzet, a quarter-Wasini sellsword from Corlati. His armored breastplate looked freshly mended and he wore a Cadist monk's habit in reddish brown beneath it. On Kai's left was the half-Vesikoi priestess Orelia Basner, wearing her clerical vestment and leaning on her trusty cudgel with a smile on her face. Filling out the group was the tavern maid Ione Rasina, standing behind Orelia. She looked to be the most nervous of the group, her eyes downcast as she fiddled with the apron of her dirndl.

Despite being the ruling monarch of Livoria, Kai learned fast that Fusette Ardei was an oddity in her aversion to standing on ceremony. It was hard to ignore the years of etiquette lessons driven into his skull by his parents, but Fusette was a bull in her refusal to acknowledge anyone in the party calling her by 'Your Grace.'

The same could not be said for the Vesikoi man standing beside her: Saredi Bastion, the Lord Chamberlain. As head of the palace staff and Fusette's chief advisor, he more than made up for the monarch's lack of decorum by having it in abundance.

"Your Grace, everything is ready per your instructions," the noble commented. His eyes roamed over the party with a discerning eye, his expression darker than the muddy green skin of his neck. Kai couldn't help but feel like a sailor being inspected by an officer for the slightest infraction.

He liked Saredi on a professional level, but the man's earnestness to serve the duchess could do with being reined in at times. Then again, that might explain the intensity of his recent lessons.

"Excellent work, Saredi. Now, let's go over to particulars once more." Forgoing her traditional veil and robes, Fusette concealed her ears beneath a sage green silken shawl and wore a flowing cerulean dress that did well to hide her figure. In the time since the party reached Whistlevale, Kai soon learned that Fusette only wore dresses when she absolutely had to, which often meant Parliament was meeting. Kai noted the pinched smile Fusette gave as she fiddled with the lace trim around her waist, to Saredi's visible irritation.

"As you know, the Liberators are growing more brazen in their attacks. Despite their reduced numbers, many of the smaller villages and towns of the east have fallen victim and the resulting destruction is having a profound effect on the duchy's food supply. What's worse, their numbers are swelling every day as new conscripts arrive from the west. Admiral Larimanz has informed me the enemy also seems to be breaking off into smaller units on the march to make tracking them more difficult.

"As a Hunter, Gravebane already knows this, but due to parliamentary decree, I am unable to muster the Hunter Corps for our war effort via carrier hawk. Otherwise, I would've already sent for Commander Petro. I swear, those fools have been enjoying themselves too much in passing these inane laws to limit my authority. It does nothing but make getting things done as difficult as possible."

Even though it was clear she was frustrated, Fusette did her best to hide her irritation behind a warm smile. "In short, Sir Gravebane, I must ask you to travel to Havenfall and deliver this edict to Petro in person. As an Exarch Knight, your authority in this matter holds the same weight as my own. Though I would love to join you on this journey, I must remain and await word from our allies in Galstein. Can I trust you to accomplish this to the best of your ability?"

Kai dropped to one knee and pressed a closed fist to his chest. "Yes, Lady Fusette. No matter what, we will not fail you."

"I know you won't." Fusette's eyes sparkled with elation as she stepped forward and pulled the apothecary to his feet. "In order to make the journey as easy as possible, I shall supply you with an envoy steamboat named *Senberg*. I understand Sir Teos is a qualified helmsman?"

The smuggler tipped his hat. "Aye, milady. I might need a day or two to get used to the vessel and learn all her quirks before setting sail, but nothing beyond that."

"That is acceptable. We shall provide all necessary supplies, including a personal stipend for each of you to spend as you see fit. Do try not to overindulge." Everybody's eyes swung to Morgan, who refused to meet their gaze and looked to the side, whistling to himself. Since their arrival, the sellsword made it a point to clear several courses worth of food at every meal, much to the women's disgust.

"Lastly," Fusette said, "I would like you to take this." She held up a spherical bottle filled with a blue concoction that seemed to be *glowing*. Whatever the liquid was, it was unlike anything Kai had ever seen.

"What is it?" the apothecary asked.

The duchess turned the bottle in her hands, examining the contents with a critical eye. "I'm not certain. Sir Hanblum delivered it as a gift from Her Majesty, Queen Isolde. According to the letter it came with, it's a purification concoction crafted with ingredients acquired from a sacred land."

"With all due respect, milady, why are you giving this to us?" Lucretia inquired. Saredi nodded his agreement, stating the mixture was better off staying in the capital.

"My instincts tell me there's no better place for this potion than with Gravebane. Perhaps it shall come in handy on your journey." Stammering his thanks for her confidence, Kai accepted the bottle and tucked it into his satchel.

"Excellent! I'll have the port master take Sir Teos down to the docks. Did anyone else wish to join?" The rest of the party shook their heads. "Very well. You're all dismissed for the time being."

Bowing, Kai led the others out into the main hall, followed by the two nobles.

"I wish you all a wonderful day. Sadly, Saredi and I must venture forth onto our own battlefield: The Parliament floor." The chamberlain chuckled, nodding his head to the party in respect before following Fusette down the hall. Teos shook Kai's hand before trailing after the port master, a long-bearded Vesikoi in scruffy clothes with a pipe hanging between his lips.

Kai faced the rest of the party. "Alright, you heard the lady. As soon as Teos says we're clear, we sail for Havenfall. Unless you have any questions, I suggest you take the time to hit the markets to grab anything you think you'll need. We'll only be making two or three stops along the river to refuel and restock supplies."

To the apothecary's surprise, it was Ione who asked to speak with him. Before he could respond, a small body burst from a nearby room and slammed into Kai's legs, almost toppling him.

"Mr. Kai!" a young, blonde Norzen girl shrieked, throwing her arms around him in a happy embrace. Tuvi was quickly becoming a common sight within the palace following Fusette's decision to take the young orphan in after the Runegard incident.

"Now Tuvi," Orelia said while peeling the girl off Kai's leg, "you really ought to be more careful."

"Yes, Sister Orelia. I'm sorry," she replied, allowing the priestess to envelope her in a loving hug. Seeing her downcast expression, Kai heard an almost imperceptible sniffle from Tuvi and kneeled down to stroke her cheeks. The girl's eyes rose to meet his warm gaze.

"You know we're always happy to see you, Tuvi. I'm not sure if Lady Fusette told you, but we'll be leaving on a trip soon to visit my hometown.

Can you promise us to keep on top of your studies and behave until we return?"

"Yes, sir." Tuvi's sniffles grew louder, prompting Kai to take her in his arms and plant a gentle kiss on her forehead. Tuvi's sweet yet mischievous nature reminded him of his younger sister at times. He whispered in her ear, asking if she wanted to show him anything before they left. She nodded and drew her right arm across her eyes to wipe away the tears. Seeing the stump where the Liberators had cut off her hand sent a tremor of anger through Kai.

"Can you and Sister Orelia come see my painting? I finished it yesterday."

"Of course we can," Orelia answered. She pulled Tuvi into a tight hug and begged her to lead the way. Bowing to Ione, Kai swore to come talk with her after they were done with Tuvi.

"Oh no worries, you three take your time," the tavern maid said. "I'll find something to do while I wait. Just meet me at the palace entrance once you're done."

Allowing Tuvi to lead them to her room, Kai and Orelia shared a smile as the girl gushed about how much she was enjoying her lessons since coming to Whistlevale. Kai couldn't help but feel grateful to Fusette for the monarch's decision to take the younger Norzen in. After her terrifying experiences at the Liberators' hands, he felt that Tuvi deserved a bit of happiness and stability in her life more than anyone.

"Lady Fusette is always so nice," she exclaimed as she threw open the door to her room and dragged the two adults inside. The room was large enough to provide the girl plenty of space to play, but still small enough to feel secure. A child-sized bed sat perpendicular to the wall halfway on the right side, with a sturdy wardrobe and mirror set along the opposite wall.

On the far side of the bed was a small desk with an easel and supplies set up for Tuvi to practice her art. At the moment, the canvas sitting on the easel was covered with a cloth tarp, hiding it from view.

Since their arrival, one of Kai's greatest joys was the time he spent teaching Tuvi the finer skills of painting, his preferred pastime outside of work.

"She even gave me a room where I can see the flowers from my window!" Sure enough, the window opened out into one of the palace's many gardens. The one outside Tuvi's room was bursting with color, as many bundles of flowers showcased their early spring blooms in varying shades of pink, blue, red, yellow, and white.

"It does look quite lovely," Orelia agreed, turning and giving Kai a slanted smile that reminded him of Maple's signature grin. "Wouldn't you agree, Kai?"

A sudden thrum echoed within Kai's chest. His eyes pulsed for a moment, unsure of what to think of the sensation. *What in the winds was that,* he wondered.

Shaking the thought from his head, he returned her smile and nodded. "I'd say so. The gardens here remind me of the one my mother keeps back home, just much larger."

"Look, look!" Tuvi pleaded as her tails twitched about, rushing to her desk and tugging the tarp away to reveal her work. Kai couldn't restrain a grin from stretching over his face. While certainly not of master quality, it was still an impressive piece for something made by a child of thirteen.

It was a landscape. Depicting the rolling hills outside the capital at sunset, if his assessment was correct. Waves of dark purple and blue near the top shifted to a beautiful sea of orange, yellow, and red surrounding an image of Nixtral's twin moons, the pale blue Eoria and Bucheron, in its muted pink, peeking over the horizon. The hills were done at a scale that showcased their massive size in real life. Tiny trees dotted the slopes and varying lines shaded in green marked the fescue grass common in the Livorian hills. A few curved lines depicting birds were scattered across the sky and an image of the golden sun dipping behind the hills completed the image.

Resting a hand on Tuvi's head, Kai ruffled her hair with a broad smile. "It's beautiful," he murmured. "This is Ballad's End, right?"

"Yes," Tuvi confirmed. "Lady Fusette took me outside the gates last moon to get a closer look. Why do they call it that, anyways?"

"It's a name the bards came up with ages ago, long before any of us were ever born. Back in the old days, those hilltops were said to be the first place where you could see Whistlevale on the horizon. After a while, they called the area Ballad's End because, in their minds, the hills marked the beginning of the end of a long journey to the capital."

Tuvi tilted her head to the side, as if ruminating over Kai's explanation. The movement produced an adoring coo from Orelia. "Bards are silly," the young girl finally declared.

Both adults gave out sputtering laughs. "You know," said Orelia, "the Archbishop, Mr. Jovanni, was a bard for years when he was a young man. You've seen how he still likes to perform tricks during service some days." Kai bit on one of his knuckles to stifle the mirth threatening to explode from his gut. He looked over and noticed Orelia was close to losing her composure as well. The two emitted muffled snickers and Kai felt a spark of *something* when the Vesikoi mixblood leaned against his shoulder while giggling under her breath.

"Oh, I know," Tuvi retorted. "He hasn't changed much since then, if you ask me. It just proves they're still silly."

Erupting into another wave of laughter, Kai couldn't help but agree with her as he brushed the odd sensation aside. Jovanni was one of the most amicable priests he'd ever met outside of Orelia, but the man did at times display a ludicrous sense of humor which hinted at the antics he enjoyed during his youth.

Maybe Tuvi was right. Bards *were* rather silly.

Upon finishing his talk with Tuvi, Kai and Orelia split up. The priestess admitted to wanting to grab a few personal items from the market square before they left. As she brushed her hand against Kai's arm, the soothing chill of Orelia's skin caused a tingle that arced through his body. He shivered at the brief contact, his fur bristling.

With a fleeting thought about why his body reacted so intensely, Kai hurried downstairs to the palace vestibule. There, Ione stood talking to a pair of palace guards while she waited. The moment she saw him, she gave a cheerful wave and removed herself from the guards' company, clapping her hands together and bowing low.

"Sorry I took so long," Kai muttered.

"It's no trouble at all," Ione soothed, wringing her dirndl apron in her hands with a nervous grin. "I know your time with Tuvi is important. That girl just adores you, ya know. I did have a favor I wanted to ask you for."

"Hmm?"

"I was hoping that, along the way, we could stop at Grantide for a spell?"

Memories of their talks while traveling flitted across Kai's mind. "That's right, you hail from Grantide, don't you?"

Ione nodded, gripping the skirt of her dirndl. "Yes. I want to see my little girl again. I haven't seen Larina or my parents since after my husband's disappearance."

Kai's gaze flickered to the older woman. "I almost forgot you mentioned having a daughter. How come you don't talk about her much?"

Her hands clenched, rumpling the heavy cotton. "Shame, mostly. When Athos vanished, my mind was in a constant fog. I loved that man, but then he was gone without any warning. Like a spirit in the wind. After that, it felt like everything we built together came crashing down. I began drinking. I refused to eat. I couldn't even bring myself to take care of my little girl, and Larina was at an impressionable age. Somehow, she sent a carrier hawk to my parents back in Grantide. As you can imagine, they weren't happy." Ione's eyes glistened with fresh tears. Her body shuddered as she fought back sobs.

Biting his tongue, Kai knew he needed to let her get everything out before saying anything. Instead, he pulled the distraught woman into a one-armed hug.

"When my parents arrived and said they were taking Larina, I barely reacted. I let myself get so lost in that fog, I told myself I didn't deserve to keep her. And so, they left, taking my daughter and swearing I would never see her again until I fixed myself up. After that, the only reason I didn't lose my house too was because Athos' parents willed it to him when they died and all I had to pay was the yearly taxes."

"What brought you out of it? You seemed cheerful enough when I first met you."

"I've never fully escaped the fog, but I learned to cope with it. The only reason I even got that far was because my foolishness almost got me killed one day."

Kai's face wilted. He had a hard time believing the doting woman before him being in such dire straits. "What happened?"

"I was drunk, as usual. All I remembered at the time was being hungry, so I stumbled into the port market to find something to eat. Instead, someone bumped into me and sent me tumbling into the water. With how drunk I was, I couldn't swim or stay afloat. I thought for sure I was going to drown. But Luopari looked out for me that day. A Vesikoi woman jumped in and pulled me out; a merchant captain who happened to be unloading her ship when I fell.

"After we got back on dry land, she brought me home and we started talking along the way. She asked how I ended up in the harbor, and I suppose I was so drunk, all my troubles came spilling out like a waterfall. I told her everything, from Athos disappearing to my parents taking Larina from me. She snapped me out of it in the most unusual way."

"What did she do?" asked Kai. His curiosity screamed for more.

"She slapped me."

"Eh?" Kai was taken aback but knew from their adventure in Runegard the effectiveness of a well-placed slap. Morgan still bore the scars Lucretia gave him from that incident.

Ione giggled at the befuddlement on Kai's face. "Believe me, I was as shocked as you, but it worked. That woman made such a ruckus, I was terrified she might start smashing up my house! She lectured me the whole evening, telling me I was meant for so much more than dying drunk in a harbor. I reckon she was a merchant for a reason because she had this way about her. When she spoke, you listened. By nightfall, she had me believing I could turn things around. I stopped drinking myself into a stupor every day and kept busy working at the *Sunken Anchor* while fixing the house into a tolerable state. After that, I kinda fell into a routine until the war started."

"And then we showed up," Kai finished.

She smiled, patting the scar on his left shoulder. "Indeed, and the rest is history."

After hearing Ione's story, Kai realized how little he knew about his friends. Sure, they talked and shared amusing stories over the campfire, but Maple was the only one whose past he had any deep insight to. He resolved to fix that.

"Well, don't worry. I was already planning on stopping at Grantide as part of our supply route. It *is* the largest city between the capital and Havenfall. In fact, we'll make a full trip of it and see about spending a few days there to show your family just how far you've come. Lady Fusette said we have until the end of the moon to complete our mission. It's the second day of Palemond, so if we include today that gives us 23 days to deliver the missive, and getting to Havenfall by steamboat should only take maybe eight or nine days."

With a squeal of happiness, Ione threw her arms around Kai, staggering him. She showered him with gratitude, swearing to work extra hard to make it up to him.

Grabbing her by the shoulders, Kai held Ione still and gestured to his eyes, helping her focus. "Don't even think of overexerting yourself, understand? We're doing this because you're our friend. Besides, you do enough work in this party helping me make sure everyone is fed. If you exhaust yourself before we get there, I swear I'll tie you to a bed and let Morgan sing you drunken lullabies."

Ione smirked. "You'd dare subject a lady to that kind of torture?"

"I would if it taught you to take better care of yourself."

They chatted about various topics as they left the palace, making their way towards the city's central market while enjoying each other's company. Kai was glad he took the time to speak with Ione. The older woman was a calming influence in his life, always making sure the party took care of themselves and doting on them in a way only a tavern maid could.

Their boots clacked along the cobblestone streets weaving through Whistlevale. Made of spotted granite, the stones sparkled in both sun and moonlight, giving the streets a constant ethereal glow. Many of the streets were lined with laurel trees and sunflowers common in the central forests, their blossoms creating an explosion of color. The trees also helped fill the city with a calming fragrance. Since coming to the capital, Kai found himself wandering the streets at all hours for the sole purpose of breathing in the aromatic air.

Seeing a fresh bundle of sunflowers nearby, Kai plucked one with a flick of the wrist. Turning towards his companion, he nestled the flower into her wedding ribbon.

Ione flushed. "Sweet Luopari, Kai, what are you up to? You really shouldn't be getting an old gal like me flowers."

Scratching behind his head, bit back a chuckle. "First of all, you're not *that* old, Ione. Second, consider it a gift. I know I haven't been the greatest friend in the world and we haven't talked as much as I would like, but I want you to know I do appreciate everything you do for us. For me." Ione quirked an eyebrow.

"I think it's a bit much if I'm being honest, but thank you, Kai. And you've been a wonderful friend. Ever since we met, we were just trying to survive, so I don't blame you for us not being able to talk. Shucks, I wouldn't even be alive right now if it weren't for you. I don't ever want to see you doubting yourself like that, understand?"

Kai gave a shy grin but said nothing. Sharing a laugh, the pair ventured into Whistlevale's market to prepare for the next leg of their journey.

Chapter II

Kai learned early in life he was not a fan of surprises. Standing in the throne room with Fusette alone the day after receiving their orders, he expected to report the party's readiness to set sail. What he *didn't* expect was to receive a sudden offer from the Grand Duchess that brought all thoughts of Havenfall to a halt.

The apothecary was grateful for Saredi's absence at that moment. He was certain the chamberlain would have terse words for both of them if he knew about this.

"Forgive me, Fusette, but let me ensure I'm hearing this right. You want me to visit Ambroz in the palace dungeons and speak with him. Why?"

"Correct. I know it's a strange request, but my men say none of their methods thus far have gotten him to speak of what happened. The entire war could rest on what Ambroz knows, yet he refuses to talk to anyone. It's my hope that, as someone with personal experience in the war, you might be able to convince him to share his story."

Pacing back and forth, Kai regarded her with hesitance. He admitted to a certain level of curiosity about the incident which sparked the entire war, but he was unsure of his ability to get the information Fusette sought.

"Did you wish to bring one of the others along?"

He shook his head. "No, I'd rather not drag them into this. I'll speak to Ambroz alone and see what I can find out, but I can't make any promises."

"Thank you. That's all I ask."

With that, Fusette strode past Kai, brushing her fingers over the ivory tundra wolf fur of his apothecary robe. Bowing his head, Kai followed her through a side door in the throne room's corner, which opened into a spiraling staircase.

Staring down into the darkness, Kai shot Fusette a side-eyed glance. She shrugged and led the way, plucking a lit torch from its place on the wall to light their way. Kai bit back a sneeze as a wave of dust assaulted his nose. "I can tell the palace cleaning staff doesn't come down here often. I assume your guests don't get top-notch trout for dinner every evening?"

The duchess stifled a giggle. "Hush. It's a prison, not a noble's inn."

Kai allowed his eyes to wander as they reached the bottom of the stairs and pushed open the thick, heavy door leading into the palace gaol. The pair entered a long hall lined with dingy iron-barred cells every five yards. A single breath told Kai the air was stale and dry. Cobwebs were strewn along the ceiling from one end to the other and a liberal coating of dust gave the brickwork a gray shading.

"How many prisoners do you keep down here? And where are the guards?" Kai whispered. From where he stood, the gaol was large enough to contain a small company of people.

"Very rarely do we have more than five prisoners, so we don't bother keeping a guard on constant watch. Usually, they'll send someone down twice a day to feed the prisoners and clean their facilities," answered Fusette. "This area is meant to keep the most important prisoners relating to the realm's security. As of now, there's only two: Ambroz and a Liberator scout captured shortly before our arrival."

An unfamiliar voice echoed from one of the nearby cells, raspy and hoarse, "Do my ears deceive me or is that the Grand Duchess herself I hear?"

Undeterred, Fusette cleared her throat and ambled forward at a brisk pace, stopping in front of the fifth cell on the left before facing its occupant. "That's correct, Ambroz. I see the guards haven't taken to heart what I said about your treatment. I swear those fools prefer listening to the nobles more than me..."

Lips pursed, Kai sidled alongside the duchess and peered into the cell. His eyebrow raised at the ragged figure lying within.

Pale of skin and covered in dirty brown feathers, Ambroz looked the spitting image of an Aerivolk vagrant. His tunic was ratty, caked with dust, and barely covered his thin frame. It was obvious the man was whipped; his arms, neck, and talons were covered in thin scars lined with dry blood. Until now, Kai didn't think it possible for him to meet an Aerivolk who looked worse than Locke, an infirm traveler he often crossed paths with on his journey.

"Aye, Your Grace. I've come to expect it, though. Not everyone thinks the way you do. I must confess, I am curious as to why you brought a Norzen here."

"This is Kai, an apothecary in my employ. He's also someone with first-hand knowledge of the war. I brought him here ask you a few questions." Ambroz gave a grim chuckle, eyeing the duchess with a smirk.

Kai wondered if the guards were starving Ambroz as well. He spoke at a snail's pace, and his voice grew hoarser with every word. "Fusette, is there a well nearby? This man clearly needs water."

"There is. I'll fetch a pail. In the meantime, I shall leave you gentlemen to talk." Without another word, Fusette marched deeper into the gaol, leaving Kai alone with Ambroz. She said there was another prisoner within the gaol, but there were no other sounds. Perhaps he was asleep. Or listening in.

Ambroz regarded Kai with suspicion. "I don't know what Her Grace is thinking. No matter how many times those brutes of hers try to beat the information out of me, I can't tell what I don't know."

Now Kai's curiosity was stoked. It was clear that Fusette needed to reign in her guards' treatment of their prisoner. He may have been accused of a heinous crime, but he was still a citizen. "Perhaps they haven't been asking the right questions," the apothecary replied.

Another chuckle came from within the cell. "A Norzen with logic. Now I've seen everything."

A deep rumble echoed from Kai's chest. "I'm not like the Norzen you've likely encountered, so mind yourself. I'd like to keep this respectful, if possible. Besides, I'm an apothecary first and foremost, so my oath is to heal others. Seeing you in this condition against the duchess' wishes rankles my fur."

"Fair enough. I apologize. As for Her Grace, I've heard the guards mention she and that Lord Chamberlain of hers are kept busy dealing with the nobles in Parliament. With all that business, it's no surprise she can't give any attention to us lowly prisoners. So what questions do you have for me about that wretched day?"

The longer this conversation went on, the more Kai pondered over how Fusette could have allowed this to go on. Then again, she had plenty on her mind with focusing on the war effort and Parliament's irritating power struggles. "For starters, I'd like to know what you remember. Even the slightest detail could be important."

"Now *that*, my boy, is a good question, and it's one nobody else has bothered to ask in the entire five moons I've been here. All they keep demanding is to know how I managed to kill a man from that distance. Can't tell them a damned thing about that, cause I ain't a murderer. I was part of the everyday crowd outside the palace. We were celebrating the new trade treaty with Galstein, and their minister was meeting Her Grace to make everything official. It was a heck of a commotion, let me tell you. Even though it was the end of summer, everyone braved the heat to come join the celebration."

Nodding, Kai jotted down notes on a spare bit of parchment he always carried around. He asked Ambroz to describe what occurred just before the attack. Their voices carried well in the sprawling hallway, echoing in the empty space. It made hearing Ambroz easier, despite his raspy speech.

"There was a lot of noise, as you can guess. So many people wandering around trying to get a good look at the ceremony. I was up on a raised platform they provided for Aerivolk. I never really fit in with the others, but with our height, it offered the best vantage point. I remember there being a lot of folks with different colored feathers around. Black, blue, red, white, yellow; the whole mix. We looked like a rainbow."

Kai's eyes flicked to Ambroz for a moment before returning to the parchment. The man's voice and breathing were steady, though still hoarse. "What about the attack itself? I know what the official report says, but Lady Fusette has confided that she believes there is more to it. Would you be so kind as to share what happened from your perspective?"

"You're a smart lad; nobody ever asked about what I saw. And you have manners to boot. The guards here are a bunch of pissants, but Her Grace has always been kind. Despite her orders, she can't always watch them to ensure we get enough food. I think half the guards are in the nobles' pockets, so they're always making up loopholes to get around Her Grace's commands. Things like giving us rotted food or claiming I was being belligerent and thus needed a good beating.

"Anyways, right before it happened, everyone was jumping and cheering when the minister came out of the palace with Her Grace. The platform was quite wide with everyone standing in a circle around a big open spot in the center. I'm not sure why no one moved into the area. It would've made things less crowded. All I remember was this strange sound, like a muffled whistle or a flute that went out of tune."

Pausing his quill, Kai lifted his gaze to stare at the prisoner. "A whistle? Do you know where it came from?"

"I believe it came from around the open space, but there wasn't anything there, so I reckon it was a nearby child behind me trying to whistle and not quite getting it right. Next thing I know, there's this loud bang from a flintlock going off right next to my bloody ears. Hurt like Nulyma, let me tell you! I see the minister go down and drop to my knees to make sure I'm not the next poor sod to get shot. I feel this painful tug on my wing and turn around, thinking that someone's trying to pull me off the platform. Instead, I look down and see this odd flintlock laying in the open space with a couple of *my* feathers stuffed down the barrel!" Kai's gaze flickered to Ambroz's wings, where several of his pinion feathers were indeed missing.

"What was strange about the flintlock?"

Ambroz lifted his arms, holding them about a yard apart. "Damned thing had a longer barrel than any pistol I've ever seen."

Kai felt his grip on the quill tighten. *A musket.*

"Do you know what happened to the weapon after you were arrested?"

"Not a clue, lad. I reckon the constables made off with it after they trussed me up like a hen for slaughter. Now that I think about it, there was something else that felt off about the whole thing."

Rather than speak, Kai gestured for Ambroz to continue.

"Right after the gun went off and I looked over, I swear to the Winds I saw the air in that open space moving. Almost like ripples in the water."

Kai's blood ran cold, his face paling to an alabaster sheen.

The soft clacking of Fusette's boots on the stone floor echoed as she returned. Kai's fingers tensed. He felt the quill feather bend in his grip until it snapped, falling to the floor in two pieces.

"Are you absolutely certain about that last statement?" asked Kai. He turned his wide eyes on Fusette, who carried a small bucket and ladled some water from it into Ambroz's bowl.

"Aye. I didn't think much of it until you said that bit about small details. And it seems something about what I said has you spooked."

Rising to her feet, Fusette shot Kai a concerned glance. "Is everything alright? You look as though you've seen a vengeful spirit."

"You may not be far off, Lady Fusette. Do you know what happened to the weapon they found near Ambroz after Minister Falber was killed?" Kai had no intention of explaining his second theory until he had more evidence.

The duchess tapped her chin with an intense look etched on her face. "Now that you mention it, I don't recall. I remember hearing a weapon was found, but never thought to inquire of its whereabouts after the incident."

"You and Saredi need to investigate and find that weapon. From Ambroz's description, it sounds like one of the muskets the Liberators are using."

Fusette nodded with a frown and turned to Ambroz, thanking him for his time.

"Thank you for the water, Your Grace. Much appreciated." The thin man struggled to his feet. Hobbling away from the wall towards them, his tunic caught on a crack in his wooden cot and tore along the side. The sound drew Kai's attention to Ambroz, his eyes bulging when he saw the man's bared torso.

And the set of four thin gills hidden behind his frayed wings.

"What in the name of Tapimor?" Kai muttered. Fusette followed his line of sight and gasped.

Ambroz frowned at the pair but murmured a curse when he saw them staring at his exposed side. Crossing his wings, he fell to his knees and curled in on himself. Kai saw the man's entire body tense up, as if trying to brace himself against something.

A chill ran down Kai's back when he recognized the position. He'd seen it in more than one Norzen he met during his Hunter career.

He's expecting us to beat him.

"Ambroz," Fusette whispered, squatting into a crouch and flashing the prisoner a timid smile, "is there something you want to tell us?"

"Why bother?" he spat. "You can see it, plain as day. I'm a bloody freak. An abomination in the eyes of the church, even among mixbloods. My father was a Vesikoi who my Aerivolk mother had a brief fling with. They were both exiled and excommunicated when the townsfolk discovered my existence. Neither one lived long enough to see me grow up. Now you know why I don't get along with other Aerivolk. Most of the ones in this city know about me. About what I am."

"All I see is a man given a rotten shake in life, who believes he has no one to turn to," Kai declared. Ambroz raised his head and met the Norzen's stare.

"Why would you care? I told you everything about what I saw and heard that day. The law needed a scapegoat, and I was in the right place at the wrong time."

The duchess' eyes swung to Kai. "Do you believe he might be innocent?"

Kai gave a single nod. "If Ambroz is telling me the truth of what he saw, and I have little reason to believe he's lying, then it's likely he was framed for Falber's murder. My first suspects would be either a Liberator sympathizer trying to pin the blame on a faumen or a Corlatian assassin looking to drive a wedge between Livoria and Galstein. We also can't rule out a Windbringer zealot trying to get a mixblood executed."

Clapping her hands together, Fusette embraced Kai, an action which caused him to seize up. "I knew it! Excellent work, Kai. This gives us a few more questions, but at least now we're pointed in the right direction! We need to keep our investigation in the shadows for the time being, but with any luck, we can dig up the evidence needed to clear his name."

Ambroz scoffed, reminding the two that even if they cleared his name of the murder, he still had to answer for his existence.

"That is absolute balderdash of the highest order!" Fusette hissed. "You are still a citizen of this duchy regardless of your lineage and deserve as much respect as anyone else, even as a prisoner. In fact, the guards who patrol this gaol are about to receive a harsh reminder of that."

Spinning on her heel, she leveled a hardened glare at Kai. "We have work to do, Kai. Please finish your preparations and gather your party. I shall locate Saredi and...impress upon him the severity of our situation. Mark my words, we will locate that weapon if I must have this entire city inspected to its very foundation!"

As he walked through the palace halls, Kai mulled over everything he learned in the gaol. Despite his initial concern about speaking with Ambroz, he was glad Fusette convinced him to do it.

Then again, the potential implications of what he heard left an anchor of worry settling in the pit of his stomach. Especially the comments about the air rippling around the platform where the musket was fired.

Is it possible? Kai wondered. *Was Grimghast inside the capital that day? If so, why didn't it attack? That doesn't make sense given its previous behavior. Perhaps it was a heat wave of some form.*

A muffled chattering came from behind, but Kai was so engrossed in his own thoughts he didn't think to turn around. The thought of that monster being in Whistlevale chilled him to the bone. He'd faced Grimghast on multiple occasions, and to this day he still wondered how he left each encounter alive.

The beast was a ferocious ambush predator, able to blend into its surroundings. Combined with its massive size, comparable to an adult elephant, killing it seemed a tall order. But he had personal reasons for wanting to see Grimghast take its last breath. That monster had slaughtered his squad, and he would bring it down if it was the last thing he ever did.

Kai was yanked from his thoughts when something struck him behind the head, not enough to truly hurt, but more than enough to grab his attention. Frowning, he rubbed the spot and turned to see Maple glaring at him, a short club clutched in her hand. The club's owner, a female Soltauri guard, was standing at attention behind the merchant, doing a poor job of concealing her mirth.

"Now that I have your attention, Sir Gravebane," Maple snapped in her western drawl, "what in Finyt has you so spooked? The last time I saw you like this was on the *Fallbrook*." Beneath the obvious irritation, he noticed a hint of concern in her eyes.

Kai remembered the day she mentioned well. It was the party's first battle with Grimghast together, near the remains of a wrecked river pirate vessel.

Taking a deep breath, Kai tried to give Maple a soothing smile. It was unsettling to see her face scrunched up in anger. He wanted to tell her his theory; the merchant was an excellent listener and had earned his trust several-fold, but the guard's presence stayed his hand. "I'll tell everyone the full story later, but for now all I can say is I've learned some disturbing things that make little sense on their own. Kinda like putting a puzzle together when you don't have all the pieces."

Maple huffed. "Pish, that's just what we need. More puzzles. I'm sure we'll figure it out though. We always do."

The distinctive click of talons on stone echoed in the cavernous hall. The three turned to see an ornately dressed Aerivolk, with a hawkish face and narrow mauve eyes, promenading towards them with an upturned chin. His feathers were a bright mix of moss green and maroon, with intricate gold chains draped over his wings. He wore a lavish blue noble's waistcoat, specially tailored to accommodate his wings, and a silken kilt. His dorsal feathers and hair matched the maroon shading of his upper feathers and were slicked back, the sheen gleaming in the lantern light. Two soldiers marched astride him in full plate armor, swords tied to their waists.

A bubble of frustration swelled in Kai's chest. He knew the man, and this was the last noble he wanted to see in his current state. Dealing with nobles was never enjoyable, and this particular one had a habit of infuriating him more than the rest combined. Still, he should've expected to run into him at some point. With Parliament meeting today for its first spring session, this was the first time the realm's highest-ranking nobles were gathered together since the party's arrival.

It was bad enough the nobles kept taking advantage of certain legal powers in the Livorian Codex to band together and veto many of Fusette's preferred laws. Kai also suspected them of conspiring to erode the Grand Duchess' authority even more than they already had since her ascension to the throne. At least, that was the impression he got from overhearing Saredi's constant rants to Lady Bidelga, the Minister of State.

"Out of my way, peltneck!" the Aerivolk barked, prompting Kai to wordlessly pull Maple and the guard out of the way. Ignoring the twitch in his eye, Kai knew better than to respond to the man's goading.

Maple, on the other hand, had no such qualms. "Well that was rude," she muttered. The guard regarded her with stunned silence.

The noble stopped walking mid-step before turning to face the trio, indignation plain as day on his face. "Excuse me? Who in Finyt do you think—?" his rant sputtered out when he spotted Maple. In moments, his face shifted from an imperious sneer to a confident smirk. He ambled towards them, a haughty chuckle rumbling from his throat.

Kai felt a jolt of nervousness spike within him. That type of look from a noble never meant anything good. "Apologies for disturbing you, Lord Kendela," he grumbled. "Maple, we should go. We need to find the others and finish our preparations."

The lord shoved himself between Kai and Maple, pushing the Norzen aside with a shoulder. "Yes, yes, begone with you Gravebane," said Kendela, "I don't much care to listen to your drivel. This lovely creature, however, may stay." Reaching out, he brushed a wing against Maple's cheek.

The woman's eyes widened. Kai bit back a grin when he saw her nostrils flare and eyebrows pinch together. Maple's cheeks puffed out as Kendela flashed her what Kai assumed was supposed to be a saucy smile, though the apothecary thought it only made him look constipated.

I should probably stop this, Kai thought. *But the last time Maple was that pissed, she tore Grimghast's ear clean off. Sorry, Kendela. You're on your own.*

"What did you just say?" Maple asked, her body shaking.

"My dear, I don't believe I stuttered. I said you will stay. I assume you must be new to the capital. I would've remembered seeing someone like you when I was last here half a year ago. A woman of such remarkable beauty as yourself deserves better than to be seen in the company of this filthy peltneck."

Kai's eye twitched again.

"Why," Maple inquired, "would I want to be anywhere near you?" Looking at her hands, Kai saw them clenched together in tight fists. Her talons raked against the floor.

Kendela's eyebrow rose. "Why ever would you want to be anywhere else? I am one of the most successful merchants in Livoria, with the wealth and title of Margrave to prove it. Aerivolk women desperately seek my affection, hoping to become one of my wives. I have three currently, and can provide for many more if needs be. Now let us be off. We need to discuss your new duties in my household. Come quietly and I'll be generous enough to ignore your earlier tone."

A familiar crimson fog blended into Kai's vision as the noble continued blathering. He bit his tongue, hoping to stall the Haze until he could remove Maple and himself from the lord's presence.

"I think your waistcoat is a bit too tight, if you believe I'm going anywhere with you. I have my own duties to attend under Lady Fusette's orders."

"Silence!" Kendela snapped. "I will deal with any issues concerning Her Grace. I have decided that you will be my wife, and that's all there is to it. Now follow your orders or I'll be most displeased."

Kai felt his control slipping. His hand twitched towards the mace on his sash. He needed to get them out of there before he ended up thrown in the cell next to Ambroz.

The Haze sputtered out of existence when he felt Maple press into his side, wrapping her arms around his elbow to keep it from his weapon. The sensation of her soft hands on his arm sent a quiver through his entire body. Kai froze and glanced at Maple, who flashed her signature tilted smile before turning on the noble in anger.

"If that's how you approach women, then it an honest surprise that anyone would marry you at all. I don't trust you and have no intention of going anywhere with you." Maple flaunted a cocky grin at the sputtering noble. "And for the record, there's only one man I respect enough to allow giving me any type of order, and he's right next to me."

If he didn't already know doing so would land him in trouble, Kai would've cackled at the way Kendela's face looked like a ripe tomato. Then again, he was certain his own face was the same shade, if the burning in his cheeks was any indication.

"You dare refuse a titled lord of this realm?!" Kendela shouted. Kai heard whispered mutterings as several of the palace staff poked their heads into the hall to investigate the commotion. The guard who had come with Maple looked unsure of what to do. Interfering with a noble of Kendela's stature was often considered foolish at best; the four Margraves were the highest ranking nobles in the duchy, responsible for the realm's largest provinces, and had enough influence and authority to *discipline* most people who annoyed them. "And worse yet, you do so in favor of some dirty peltneck with delusions of adequacy! I don't think you understand—"

Releasing Kai's arm, Maple stomped forward and yanked Kendela's head forward by his dorsal feathers, giving him a fierce glower. Her voice tight with each word.

"Call him that slur again. I. Dare. You."

Fighting back an audible gulp, Kai felt his heart pounding. Whether it was from worry about what Kendela might do to Maple, or the fluttering in his stomach at seeing her defend him, he wasn't sure. Kendela was frozen, his eyes wide in fear over the look of rage in Maple's eyes. His guards reached for their swords but hesitated in drawing them, instead looking to their lord for direction. Kai, as an Exarch, was among the few able to challenge a Margrave's orders. Fusette was limited by laws imposed by the nobles of Parliament except in specific circumstances. The Exarch Knights were not, given their unique status as guardians of the royal family and the realm as a whole.

Kai considered it a blessing the man seemed too stunned to do anything. He didn't fancy the idea of fighting a noble's guards in the middle of the palace. Saredi would have his head! Easing forward, Kai took Maple by the elbow and pulled her back. "Thank you. Now let's go grab the others."

Her gaze flickered to his. "But..."

Kai shook his head and tapped her on the nose. "You've made your point, and we have a mission to prepare for. Tell you what. Once Teos finishes briefing us, we'll sneak into the kitchens, and I'll whip up some appleberry pies."

The change was immediate as Maple shifted from confused frustration to unadulterated glee. Grabbing Kai by the arm, she tugged him down the hall, the Soltauri guard following in their wake. "You know me too well. Come on, we've got boring stuff to hear and delicious pies to bake!" Kai chuckled and allowed himself to be pulled along, happy to see her smiling again.

"Don't think you've heard the last of this, Gravebane!" Kendela exclaimed. Despite his earlier fear, the man was quick to regain his pompous bearing. "I always get what I want. One way or the other!" Rather than allow Kendela to goad him, Kai focused on the glimmering smile of the woman dragging him through the palace.

He had more important things to busy himself with than the rantings of a snooty margrave.

Chapter III

The sounds of industry filled the air as Razarr lumbered through the labor camp at a sedate pace, his hood drawn up to conceal his face. The sunlight gleamed off a pair of curved blades attached to the outside of his gauntlets. The journey from his manor had been long, with several important stops along the way. However, he was glad to have a chance to inspect this specific camp. Despite his failure in major battles thus far, General Doulterre was proving he could at least follow simple instructions.

If the officer had somehow managed to bungle this, Razarr was more than ready to send Obram specific orders to...deal with the issue.

He noted the Norzen captives' wretched condition with pinched eyebrows. Many were covered in thin scars from the frequent lashes of an overseer's whip. All but the most recent arrivals wore tattered clothes and thin overcoats which offered little protection from the elements. He also doubted they received fresh water for bathing; the entire camp was rank with the stench of sweat, blood, and feces.

It was the smell of death.

By comparison, the camp warden walking alongside him was clean shaven and wore a washed cotton tunic beneath his woolen vest. Though spring was in full swing, the air still carried a chill that bit into Razarr's exposed cheeks.

"How is everything proceeding?" asked Razarr.

The warden, a lanky square-faced man named Quatto, rubbed his hands together and spoke in a low, raspy voice. "I must confess we're a touch behind schedule, milord. The winter was harsher than usual this year, so we ran into complications."

"I see. Thank you for being honest. And the workers?"

"We had a few who attempted to escape on the outset. Needless to say, we made it clear any further foolishness of that nature carried severe consequences. Haven't had a single problem since." Quatto's face slipped into a sneer as he observed the Norzen hammering and sawing at the large trees brought into camp on wiroch-drawn carriages. Several large hunks of metal sat piled in the corner of the camp, covered in a light layer of dust.

Razarr turned to face the warden, an unreadable expression on his face. "Am I to assume that you killed the ones who tried escaping?"

A short, hacking laugh erupted from Quatto. "Of course we did! What else are you going to do with a bunch of dirty peltnecks who don't listen?"

"Perhaps my instructions weren't clear when I relayed them to General Doulterre. Either that, or you're ignoring them on purpose," Razarr muttered, his lips pursed and eyes blazing. "I ordered these captives to be kept alive at all costs. The work won't get done if you continue putting them in an early grave, Quatto!"

"The work won't get done either if they all pack a carriage and flee into the night, milord. I know what I'm doing. These peltnecks, they need a firm hand to get any useful work out of them."

The sound of heavy breathing reached Razarr's ears. Turning his head, he spotted a blonde man dashing towards them; huskier than the warden with a thick mustache covering his upper lip. Razarr recognized him as Fedrin, Quatto's deputy.

Fedrin slowed his approach, bending over to catch his breath when he came within earshot. "I apologize for disturbing you during the inspection, sir, but we have a slight problem."

The warden's eyes hardened. "What kind of problem? I swear, if those damned peltnecks are trying to escape again—"

"It might be worse than that, Quatto," Fedrin interrupted. "We've got a bunch of them laid up in Barrack Three. None of them can hold down food. The guards refuse to go in and check the situation; they say it could be an epidemic."

"I don't give a bloody damn what the guards think! Tell those peltnecks they better get up and start working unless they want a legitimate reason to be in bed."

Razarr put himself between the two bickering men. "That is quite enough." His eyes swung to Quatto; the warden's face was flush with anger. "Do you have an apothecary on hand? Suppose your guards are correct. If you have an outbreak of disease, it could wipe the entire work-force out. At that point, nothing will get done; and worse for you, *I* will be rather upset."

"We do have an apothecary among the staff, but I fail to see why we should waste his time catering to a bunch of worthless vagrants. What's so important about this project anyway? I've been trying to make sense of the pieces you've been having these peltnecks build and it's impossible. Just what in Nulyma are you trying to—"

Anything else Quatto had to say was cut short when Razarr backhanded the warden across the cheek, sending him to the ground. Fedrin backed away, eyes bulging as Razarr grabbed Quatto by the collar of his tunic and hauled the man up. Without a word, the forge master gripped Quatto's hair and pulled his head back before drawing a bladed forearm across the warden's throat. Quatto gurgled as a bloody slit stretched across his neck, struggling against Razarr's unyielding grip.

Blood flowed down the man's front in waves, staining Razarr's arm crimson. Fedrin shivered, seeing a gleam of silver within the man's cloak. Giving a dark chuckle, the forge master slammed Quatto's face against the cliff wall looming over them and buried a dagger into the small of his back. The warden hissed in pain, which turned to choking cries when Razarr pulled his head back and struck it against the stone once more.

None of the guards moved, too stunned by the sudden attack to do anything but watch in morbid fascination as Razarr reduced Quatto's face to a bloody mess on the crags. The Norzen workers were in much the same condition. All work ceased as everyone watched the brutality unfold.

By the time Quatto stopped moving, Razarr's arm halfway to the elbow was covered in blood. He tossed the corpse aside, remaining silent while walking towards a nearby water trough and using it to wash himself. Ignoring the sting of the wind on his wet skin, Razarr used the fur of his coat to dry his arms before turning towards the crowd.

His eyes landed on the assistant warden. Fedrin's body shook under Razarr's blank stare. "I suppose congratulations are in order, Mr. Fedrin. You've been promoted to chief warden, owing to your predecessor contracting a lethal case of stupidity. I trust you understand the importance of knowing when not to ask foolish questions?"

Fedrin wordlessly nodded. He staggered forward, bowing at Razarr's feet. "I understand, sir! I'll do my best to accomplish your vision."

"Excellent! Your first order of business should be getting that apothecary down to the barracks to see what is wrong with our Norzen. Despite my firm approach, I find treating one's employees with a modicum of decency can have profound effects on the quality of their work. Take that to heart, Fedrin."

The new warden stroked his mustache, pondering Razarr's words. "Milord, I hope you don't consider this a stupid question, but are you suggesting we be *nice* to the Norzen?"

Razarr smirked. Fedrin may be a coward of the highest caliber, but at least he was willing to defer to his obvious betters. "I believe asking for clarity in certain matters is never a stupid question, Mr. Fedrin, and I'm willing to admit I may have been a tad vague just now. I know I can't force you to treat them with respect, nor am I asking you to. However, what you can do is lessen the beatings. Reserve them for your worst offenders. Provide adequate food and water. Allow them to bathe on occasion. Don't force them to work when ill or injured. This is all common business practice in Corlati. Many of those in power feel free to ignore these rules with their slaves, but I find it provides incentive to perform better. My mentor used to say it's easier to catch flies with honey rather than vinegar. Think about it. Now return to your tasks. I shall continue the inspection on my own."

Fedrin bowed once more before hustling off in search of the camp apothecary. The rest of the crowd returned to what they were doing before, excepting a few guards who dragged Quatto's corpse away for disposal.

Rubbing a finger into his temple, Razarr wondered if allying himself with the Liberation Army was the right call.

These belligerent fools are proving to be more trouble than they're worth.

His muscles tensed when he heard the soft shifting of gravel nearby. Razarr spun on his heel but relaxed when he saw a familiar young woman approaching, the neck-length black hair framing her square, youthful face fluttering in the breeze . "I must admit, Mirabell, I wasn't expecting you so soon. I trust your assignment was a success?"

"Of course, Master. Everything went according to your predictions. I could do with a bath, though. My body feels rather sore after all that work."

"Understandable," Razarr agreed, "once we finish here, we'll have a chance to clean ourselves at the next inn. For now, I must finish inspecting the camp and ensure everything is going to be finished on time."

"I'm curious, Master," Mirabell continued, her brown eyes sweeping over the guards, many of whom eyed her like a piece of meat. "How long will it take before they realize the truth?"

"My dear Mirabell, with these fools, I doubt they'd understand the full magnitude of my plans even as it unfolds before their eyes. They're so focused on this crusade against the faumen, they don't bother considering the consequences of their actions."

Mirabell tilted her head. "Consequences?"

"The faumen may have their origins in the Belomas Highlands, but they have been found in the farthest reaches of Nixtral. There are even tribes native to the other continents many here have never seen before. I would not be surprised if many realms beyond Alezon, should the Liberation Army win, decide to take drastic measures in making life difficult for them. There are even nations made of nothing *but* faumen, some of whom would rethink their current trading treaties with Livoria should a government assume control who actively hunts them down."

The maid bowed her head with a thin smile. "You speak with wisdom, Master. This was something I never knew or considered, so thank you for the insight."

"Consider it a free lesson, my dear. I'm a merchant, after all. It's my job to know potential threats to my business." Razarr gestured for Mirabell to follow as he led her to a cave near the camp's edge. The entrance was guarded by three fully armored soldiers, who stepped aside as they strode into the cavern. One of the guards handed Razarr a lit torch, prompting a nod of thanks from the forge master.

Once the pair was out of earshot, Mirabell asked, "If they're such a problem, why make this deal with the Liberation Army in the first place? Why give them the means to defeat the Royalists?"

"Any wealthy merchant will tell you the best way to make a profit is to let others do most of the work at little to no cost. Right now, the Grand Duchess and her allies are an obstacle I cannot deal with alone. They're too powerful. The Liberation Army, on the other hand, is a problem that will take care of itself without me needing to lift a finger."

Understanding bloomed over Mirabell's face. "I see. Now everything is coming into focus. But what's so important about this cave for you to have so much security? If it's okay to ask, of course," she inquired, raising her hands.

Razarr waved off her concerns. "I don't mind explaining it to you. You are a valuable confidant, unlike that worthless twit, Fedrin. As for why this cave is so important, it's because of *that*."

Lifting an arm, Razarr pointed at a lavender glow coming from around the corner. He led the way, bringing Mirabell into a large open room. It was easy to see the glow's source: a mountain of small purple crystals, each growing from a chunk of slate.

"They're beautiful," Mirabell whispered. "What are they? I've never seen gems like these."

"It's a rare mineral ore called lekrite. Livoria used to mine it for various purposes from the days before the Desolation Wars, but all the mines went defunct perhaps a hundred years ago. I wouldn't recommend you touch them, though."

"Why is that?"

"Because the crystals are quite temperamental and formed from energy drawn directly from the Origin ley lines. A severe enough shock will make them explode. Even the smaller ones produce a force greater than our largest cannons."

Paling, Mirabell shuffled back while peering at Razarr. "What exactly are you planning to do with them, Master?" she asked.

The forge master chuckled. "You'll see soon enough."

Chapter IV

It was rare for Kai to see such a cheerful look on Teos' face, but he was happy for his friend. On occasion, the apothecary still mulled over the battle with Grimghast that left Teos' original barge, the *Gulley*, on the bottom of the Galen river.

Still, watching him direct the dockworkers in loading their supplies was impressive. Kai respected Teos. The Soltauri was almost twice his age, with a vast wealth of knowledge and experience. Barking orders in his gruff brogue, Teos looked comfortable in a position of command. More so than the Norzen himself did, at any rate. Kai guessed it came from helming a ship for so long. In a matter of days, Teos became so intimately familiar with the *Senberg* that, had he not known the man, Kai would've believed he owned it for years.

Standing next to him, Maple nibbled on an appleberry pie clutched between her fingers. While admitting greater familiarity with the larger circular variants, the merchant gushed over the handheld pastries Kai baked up in the palace kitchen; a style he learned from his adoptive father.

"Kai, you have *got* to teach me how you made these," she mumbled, taking another bite. A rust-colored piece of appleberry dribbled down her chin. "The filling has this spicy tartness that's so delicious!"

The apothecary laughed, lifting his finger and wiping away the stray filling to her embarrassment. "I appreciate the compliment. It's a trick my Da taught me. I add a pinch of nutmeg and anise when making the filling on top of the cinnamon."

Maple's eyes widened. "I never thought of that. Nutmeg is hard to find back in Shiverhill, so Papa and I rarely got to use it."

A soothing voice from behind the pair carried over the workers' cacophony. "What in the winds are you two making such a fuss about?"

Kai and Maple spun around, coming face to face with Orelia. The priestess smoothed out her temple vestment with a bright smile. Reaching into the pouch on her hip, Maple retrieved another pie and handed it to Orelia. "I want Kai to teach me how to make these. I've been making appleberry pie for years, but these are the most delicious things I've ever eaten! Try one."

Orelia lifted the pie to her face, giving it a cursory sniff. Humming, she took a big bite out of the corner.

It took all of Kai's will to suppress his laughter at the throaty moan coming from the priestess. "Is it safe to assume you like it?"

She nodded and took several slow chews before swallowing. Opening her eyes, she cast a saucy grin towards Kai and poked him in the chest with the rounded head of her cudgel. "All I can say is some lucky woman will be a very happy wife one day. With how charming you can be, maybe even more than one."

Whatever Kai expected to hear, that wasn't it. His cheeks burned red as his eyes instinctively flickered to Maple, an image of her in a lace wedding dress flashing through his mind. His eyes twitched to the bronze-skinned Vesikoi, lingering on her before shifting back to Maple, who continued munching on her pie with a cheerful smile. In his heart, he hoped Orelia didn't notice the movement of his gaze, but that dream was dashed when he met her eyes again and spotted her shy grin.

Oh, Tapimor's hairy ass, that's not good. Kai didn't enjoy invoking the name of his trade's patron in such a way, but he felt it appropriate in the moment. Seeing the way Orelia tucked her head between her raised shoulders, both eyes cast downward, sent a shiver down his spine.

Rather than allow the younger woman to fluster him, Kai cleared his throat and settled for thanking her. He watched her finish the pie and continue walking towards the *Senberg* with a clear skip in her step.

"She seems happy," Maple murmured, giving Orelia a curious glance before hurrying after her. Kai agreed but said nothing about the grin he saw. The last thing he wanted was either woman learning a hint of his true thoughts before he was ready to bring it up. If he ever felt ready, that is. He shuddered at the thought of what the church would have to say about that, regardless of his status as an Exarch Knight.

Why in Finyt am I such a mess, he wondered. *Of all the women in the duchy I could've fallen for, it had to be the one who would get me in the most trouble.*

A loud bellow startled the apothecary from his thoughts. Looking up, he spotted Teos glowering while tapping his hoof against the *Senberg*'s deck. Giving the smuggler an embarrassed smile, he decided boarding the ship was his best option.

They wouldn't reach Havenfall just sitting there, after all.

"Wait up!" Maple called out as she rushed after Orelia.

The priestess turned and smiled at Maple, giving the merchant a shoulder bump as she sidled beside her. "I would've figured you'd want to get on the ship with Kai," she teased. As they approached the *Senberg*, they watched as the dock workers used pulleys and ropes to haul a variety of barrels and crates onto the ship. Some were lined up along the edge of the deck wall, while others were lowered into an opening leading to the cargo hold. A pair of Soltauri men were walking along the deck, the larger one pointing at each item brought on board while his smaller companion jotted notes down on a sheaf of parchment.

Maple blushed and gave Orelia a gentle shove. "Oh, don't you start," she grumbled. "It's too damn early in the morning for that sort of talk."

Emitting a soft giggle, Orelia apologized. "You have to admit, though, this will be an interesting trip. You've never been to Havenfall, have you?"

The Aerivolk shrugged. "I passed through there once on the way to Everstill years ago, but didn't stay. The people seemed nice enough, if a bit excitable."

"I'm definitely interested in meeting Kai's family," said Orelia, pressing a long finger to her chin. "With how he turned out, it makes you wonder about the people who raised him."

"They can't be all that bad," Maple replied. "Then again, I've heard him mention his sister is a bit of a prankster."

The two women shared a giggle as they boarded the ship and made their way up towards the upper decks. The entire time, they whispered wild theories amongst themselves in hushed tones about what Kai's family would be like.

After receiving a thorough lecture from both Teos and Lucretia, Kai led the party in finalizing their preparations. One last surprise arrived when Fusette strolled towards them, surrounded by guards. An older man in an intricate vestment and scarlet stole around his shoulders accompanied them: Jovanni, the Archbishop and leader of the Windbringer church in Livoria. Kai felt a twinge of nervousness. Why was the Archbishop seeing them off? His eyes chanced a peek at Orelia, who regarded the older man with an expression of deep respect. The party stood along the deck's edge, bowing in deference as the duchess and priest returned the greeting.

"It brings me great joy to see you all prepared to embark on this journey," Jovanni declared. Despite being in his sixties, the old priest had a youthful vitality in his voice that Kai found refreshing. It was common knowledge that, in his youth, Jovanni had been a bard plying his musical talents across the realm, and his voice retained the crispness of a storyteller. Even now, he liked to showcase his talents in playing the pipe organ every week before service. "I expect to see all of you return in good health once your mission is complete."

"May the winds guide you all safely," Fusette declared. "I expect routine reports via carrier hawk, Sir Gravebane. You have three hawks on board for both personal and official correspondence. Good luck!" Kai and the others thanked the two for their blessing and waved as Teos clambered into the pilot house.

Saredi hired a crew to help Teos run the ship, given its larger size compared to his old towboat. At thirty yards in length, the *Senberg* was a single-masted stern-wheeler triple the size of the *Gulley*, requiring an additional seven crew members outside the party to operate.

A pair of Soltauri men were hired as deck hands to handle most of the menial labor tasks such as moving cargo and tying the boat down in port. Fusette offered the services of two of her own palace maids, both Norzen, to clean and maintain the ship's living quarters and the offices on the upper decks. Lastly, an older Aerivolk from the seaport was brought on as engineer, with two young human men assisting as his fire crew.

Following Teos to the pilot house, Kai heard the boiler churn to life below, puffs of smoke pouring from the smokestack. A slight rumble ran through the ship as the paddle began spinning, sending the ship on its way down the Great Ardei to the applause of the crowd lining the docks.

"And we're off," Kai declared, a wide smile stretched over his face. This would be his first trip home in over a year. His body trembled in excitement at the thought of seeing his family again. He guessed his parents would make more of a fuss compared to his sister, but he also knew Serafina liked defying expectations. It would be a gamble on whether she'd try knocking him over or ignoring him entirely. "I trust you can handle this floating boulder, Captain Teos?"

"Oh, I can handle her alright," replied Teos, "but I ain't the captain on this voyage, my friend. That'd be you."

A fog of confusion brought the rest of Kai's thoughts to a halt. "Wait, what are you talking about? I don't know the first thing about sailing."

"You could say it's a title of convenience. You're the leader of our merry band of misfits, so overall command of the ship falls to you, Gravebane." The way Teos drew out Kai's Brand sounded like one child taunting another in the play yard.

"I can handle any sailing-related issues, but officially I'm just the helmsman. It helps that, while I may be from Hornmire, I've spent most of my life on the rivers and know how to run a boat. I had to submit a report to Lord Saredi detailing who filled which roles on the ship in order to get our crew. I figured we wanted as small a group as possible, so some of our friends also fit into those official positions."

"That makes sense. Anything vital I should know before we get too far?"

"I better give you the beginner's lesson, so you know the basics. I've already gone over our roles. Thanks to her knowledge of cartography, Lucretia serves as our navigator; her job is to keep us on the correct path. The Great Ardei has several major branches along the way, so she needs to ensure we take the correct forks. Next is Maple. As a merchant, she has experience with supply orders and inventory, so she's the clerk. Whenever we dock for additional supplies, her job will be to procure what's needed and get it onboard."

Kai had seen Maple's negotiation skills in action. He couldn't think of a better role for her. "She'll definitely enjoy that."

"You ain't wrong there. The last two major roles are Ione and Morgan. Ione is taking over as the crew's cook, and she's already turned the kitchen into her own little queendom. That woman is scary when she puts her all into something."

Images flashed through the apothecary's mind of their run-in with some Norzen bandits after fleeing Mistport. "Pray you never do anything to make her swing a pan at you. Ione would make a hell of a paddlepod striker if we put her on the field."

"Duly noted. I don't envy Morgan's job, but he's got as much sailing experience as me, so I reckon he can handle it. He's the ship's mate, in charge of the deck and cabin crews. He'll have the deckhands and cabin maids working in shifts."

Kai nodded his understanding, his quill flying over parchment once more as he took detailed notes. Not for the first time, he was grateful for the breadth of skills his friends brought to the party.

"Other than that, we've got three members on the boiler crew: an engineer and two firemen. Their job is to keep the boiler running, and thus us moving."

"Excellent. I'll go ahead and have a look around. I may as well learn as much as I can while we're still early on." Teos gave an approving hum, flashing a grin.

"One last thing before you go, Kai." Turning back, the apothecary almost froze in place at the heated glare Teos was sending him. "I'm sure you know the rules about impropriety and all that rot, but it's clear you don't take full stock in them. Plus, I saw how a certain pair of ladies were looking at you earlier while we were loading. So I'm giving you one warning: Don't you dare hurt them. Otherwise, Exarch or not, they'll never find all the pieces."

Gulping, Kai could only nod as he left the Soltauri at the massive wheel and descended to the main deck. Halfway down the stairway, he froze as the entirety of Teos' words hit him full force.

What in Finyt did he mean by a pair*?!*

Letting his eyes roam over the ship, Kai admired the workmanship that went into its construction. The outer hull was painted bone white with the duchy's official seal engraved at the bow. A royal flag fluttered in the winds from its place atop the mast. The smokestack sat halfway between the mast and the ship's rear, clouds of smoke now pouring from it. The sounds of splashing water came from the stern, where *Senberg's* wide paddle wheel churned.

At their current speed, Kai was able to leisurely gaze towards the horizon while the crew bustled about their duties. He found the scenery helped distract him from Teos' earlier comment. It was early enough in the day for him to inspect the ship before lunch. Deciding to start from the bottom, Kai passed by the Soltauri deckhands on his way to the boiler deck, their stubby horns poking through wide-brimmed straw hats as they moved barrels of fish into storage. The men waved, prompting a smile from the apothecary, who returned the gesture. Kai thought he saw a flash of irritation pass over one of them but attributed it to wishing their roles were reversed. He remembered seeing the work deck crews put in at the many port cities he'd visited, and Kai could see himself thinking the same way if he were in the man's boots.

Poking his head into the engine room, he greeted the boiler crew and had a quick chat with the engineer, a scruffy Aerivolk with dull orange feathers named Dekel. The man gave off the same gruff air Kai sensed around Teos and Morgan at times, which made him wonder if it was a common disposition among older sailors. Then again, after hearing Dekel gripe about the work he and his crew did just to keep the *Senberg* moving, Kai figured he'd be just as grumpy if he had to do what they did for over twenty years.

After returning to the main deck, he almost collided with the younger of the two cabin maids. The girl, a petite redhead with a thin mane named Kerta, looked barely older than his own sister. Her companion, an older brunette with bushy fur named Annika, tugged Kerta back while offering a contrite bow to Kai. The apothecary waved it off with an apology for not looking where he was going. He dipped his head in a respectful bow as he continued on his way, not noticing the pair eyeing him with intrigue.

Making his way back to the central stairwell, Kai was waylaid by Lucretia. His association with the scholar was tenuous at best, and he still wasn't sure if that had changed, or how, in the wake of their trials in Runegard. Since that day, she spent a vast portion of her time with her nose buried in the unassuming tome tucked within her arm.

She regarded him with a timid frown, her body tense. "I-I need to speak with you. Alone, if possible. Do you have a moment?"

Kai shifted his gaze skyward for a moment and nodded. "Sure, I've got some time to spare. Lunch won't be for a while yet, and I can inspect the ship later. Let's go to the navigator's office. There shouldn't be anyone there."

Casting a furtive glance, Lucretia led him to the other side of the ship before ascending to the observation deck beneath the pilot house and entering the room that served as her new office and sleeping quarters. Kai stepped in and wasn't sure if he should be impressed at the room's efficiency or concerned at the minimal contents. Three bookshelves were nailed into the wall over a small work desk in the far corner, all filled with tomes of varying sizes. In the center of the room was a large table littered with maps and scattered documents. The only other thing in the office was a small cot nestled against the corner opposite the work desk.

"Is everything alright? You wouldn't come to me unless it was important."

Lucretia chuffed, waggling the tome in her hand at him. He recognized it immediately.

While investigating the royal archives in Runegard, they had discovered the forgotten travel log of Kai's suspected ancestor: the fallen Wind Saint, Cacovis. Lucretia had been tasked by Fusette with translating the tome from its original High Norzen script into Centric. When asked why she wasn't remaining in the capital, Lucretia grumbled that Fusette demanded she go with the party. According to her, the duchess' entire reasoning for the command was so Lucretia would actually get some fresh air, for once!

Kai remembered biting back a chuckle when he heard that. He knew from experience Lucretia wouldn't hesitate to spend an entire day with her nose buried in a tome if given half the chance.

"I wanted to report on the translation before we discuss other matters. I already spoke to Her Grace about this, but she asked me to share it with you as well. I would say I have completed half of the journal's translation. Some of the words are a tad archaic, so I asked Lady Fusette to lend me additional tomes written in High Norzen for reference. Remember what we learned about the warlord Berelmir?"

The name stoked a sense of unease in Kai. He couldn't readily describe it, but something about that name gave him the heebies. "Isn't he the one Cacovis destroyed in the Desolation?"

The scholar nodded. "Indeed, but it seems there were deeper personal reasons for Cacovis to join the Wind Saints. She began writing in this shortly after her handfasting to her husband, Matthias. According to the journal, she led a Norzen farming town named Littlehope in what is now the Voidlands, earning coin as a carpenter. When Berelmir first rose to power, she regretted not doing anything to stop him."

"Why would she worry about that? Was he a member of her village?"

"Worse. It appears Berelmir was, in truth, Cacovis' younger brother."

Kai blanched. That changed everything. "Her *brother*? Merciful Galen."

"Indeed," Lucretia replied. "In addition, Cacovis had a reputation as a powerful warrior. Most thieving bands refused to go near Littlehope for fear of inviting her wrath. Berelmir was among the few to not fear her, though in hindsight he probably should have. He asked her to join him and serve as his right hand. From what was written, it appears Cacovis took offense to the offer and told her brother to pound cobbles, though in much more...foul language."

A deep chuckle reverberated from Kai. "I can imagine. What happened next?"

"Berelmir decided to take revenge on his sister, and in doing so, set her on the path that led to the Desolation. His minions captured Matthias, and he murdered his brother-in-law in a public execution. Cacovis witnessed it all from the shadows, and from her description, it was a bloody and horrific act."

Kai paled even further. *That* was Berelmir's response to being spurned? The more he heard, the more he empathized with Cacovis. "By the winds, this sounds like some long-lost fairy tale."

"It may as well be, considering how little we know of the Desolation Wars. Many of the records from those days have been lost for decades. I will let you know more once I translate the next section. There was one other thing I wished to ask."

"Sure, what is it?"

Rather than speak up, Lucretia shifted in place, her fingers interlocked and gripping the edge of her blue overcoat. She finally spoke after a few moments of awkward silence. "This has bothered me since we left Runegard. I know we have not gotten along well since we met."

Kai suppressed an amused snort. He couldn't disagree with that. He still remembered the look of panic in her eyes when she first saw him sitting with his old Hunter squad.

"Why would you go to so much trouble to help me when I was barred from the Citadel? After everything I said, no one would have blamed you for leaving me to fend for myself. You could have disbanded the party and gone about your business as we planned. So why? What possessed you to go to such lengths for someone who doubted your trustworthiness every day? Who questioned what you were capable of?"

Thinking about it, Kai wasn't surprised by Lucretia's confusion. From the day they met, the scholar made it known she didn't trust him and tolerated his presence at best. In those early days, it was Ione who formed the mortar holding their group together, as Lucretia expressed constant aggravation with both Morgan and him, though for different reasons.

Now, seeing Lucretia try to make sense of his actions when they contradicted everything she assumed about him, Kai knew he had a chance to, at least, make her consider the possibility that he wouldn't betray them or do whatever else she believed him capable of.

"Listen," Kai began, leaning against the wall with arms crossed. "I won't pretend to know why you feel the way you do about Norzen, and that's not my concern. I can't expect or force you to change your beliefs on my word alone. What I *can* do is explain how I see things as a Norzen who doesn't fit in anywhere.

"Growing up in Havenfall, I didn't meet another Norzen until I was ten, and he was both a traveling drunkard and mad as a hatter. Regardless, I know nothing of how a typical Norzen from Duskmarsh is raised or how they're supposed to act. I only know what I learned from the family that raised me. Everything Duarte said in the archives that day, it doesn't change who I am. I never knew anything of my birth parents, like what kind of people they were."

Seeing Lucretia nod along, Kai hoped what he was saying made sense. "It's like what I told Lady Fusette. The circumstances of one's lineage have little effect on their future. It's our choices that determine who we become. I consider myself an apothecary before all else, and I like to think the beliefs I developed in Havenfall made me a better man.

"The reason I put all my effort into helping you is because it was the right thing to do. You're right, of course, in saying I could've left you be after reaching Runegard. But that's not who I am. I promised myself to guarantee you made it home safe. Even with our disagreements, you are still a member of this party and my comrade. And no matter what, I never abandon a comrade. Hunter's cardinal rule."

Silence reigned as Kai took a deep breath and awaited Lucretia's response. It was hard to judge her reaction based on the intensity in her eyes. Before long, he heard her sigh and meet his gaze.

"I should not be surprised to hear this from you. In all my years, no Norzen has ever given me reason to believe there were good people among them. I should explain my history for this to make sense.

"I was born in Runegard as the elder of two children. My father was a minor baron who earned his title shipping farm goods between Runegard, Faith Hollow, and Hornmire. Before then, he'd been a schoolmaster, so there were often books in the house. Even as a child, I was fascinated with Father's tomes and learned to read at an early age. In those days, books were my only companions besides my younger brother, Evodio. It was no surprise to my family when I declared I would seek an apprenticeship at the Citadel.

"Sadly, my parents never got to see me follow that dream. While making a routine delivery to Faith Hollow eleven years ago, they were ambushed by a Norzen thieving band. According to the reports, there were perhaps thirty bandits against my parents and five guards." Lucretia's eyes glistened with tears and Kai already knew what she would say next.

"There were no survivors. The Navy informed my brother and me days after I received a letter of acceptance for my apprenticeship. I was fourteen then and my brother eight. As you can guess, I was unable to care for him. Evodio went to live with our mother's brother while I left for the Citadel. I sent money to my uncle every moon after attaining certification, to assist with expenses until my brother reached adulthood. The last I spoke with them was two years ago, when Evodio decided to join the Navy after turning seventeen. I have not seen them since."

The scholar wiped her eyes and apologized for losing her emotions. Chuckling, Kai remarked that he would've been more concerned if she *wasn't* crying after reliving those memories. The two stood in awkward silence until Lucretia clutched the journal against her chest.

"Please do not mention what I have said to the others," Lucretia pleaded. "I would prefer to admit my history to them on my own time."

"Of course. I'll consider it private information related to your health. By my apothecary's oath, I'm forbidden from sharing information that could cause a severe negative impact on someone under my care."

"Thank you. I am not sure if we will ever truly be able to consider one another friends, but I shall endeavor to put my prejudices against your tribe aside when dealing with you and Her Grace. Lord Saredi suggested I test my boundaries if I am to heal from what happened to my parents, so I figured this was as good a chance as any to try his advice. If nothing else, you and Her Grace have shown me that there are at least some good people among the Norzen."

Kai's smile broadened from ear to ear as he stepped forward, offering his hand towards the scholar. "I can agree to that. And I appreciate you keeping an open mind."

Gripping his hand, Lucretia gave a firm shake and watched as Kai reached for the door, the smile never leaving his face. Mulling over their words, he was surprised to hear the scholar titter behind him and whisper a sentence that made little sense.

"This explains so much. At least now I can see a little of what they do."

Chapter V

Kai released a contented sigh as the wind caressed his mane. It was nights like this when he was grateful for the thick pelt on his upper chest. The wind was crisp and chilly, intensified by the river's moist air.

He loved the way the forest looked on spring nights. The sporadic golden flickers of airborne lightning bugs gave a splash of color to the moonlit trees. The winds swept through the branches, creating a soothing whistle. Kai's ears twitched at the occasional splash of a fish. To the apothecary, he wondered if the paradise of Finyt could surpass the prevailing peace he felt in that moment.

He wanted to savor the calm while he could. His eyes flickered to the vial of translucent purple fluid hanging from his robes. Grimghast's venom. With a frown, he remembered tipping the vial's contents into his tea that evening and knew it'd come back to bite him later.

"Why am I not surprised to see you out here?" a voice came from behind, jolting him from his thoughts. Twisting his head, Kai spotted Orelia striding up with an amused smile and a fur overcoat around her shoulders. Instead of her normal vestments, she was wearing a tight-fitted cream blouse and pleated purple skirt that stretched to just below her knees.

Shifting to the side, Kai greeted the priestess as she sidled next to him. His gaze roamed over her new outfit, appreciating how attractive she looked, though he averted his eyes the moment he realized her blouse afforded him a generous peek at her cleavage. Orelia was beautiful for sure, but Kai refused to let himself disrespect her by staring. He said nothing else, unsure of why she would seek him out now. As a Vesikoi mixblood, her human lineage kept her from drying out as easily as a fullblood, though that came at a cost of increased vulnerability to the cold.

"You sure you want to be outside? I'd rather you not take ill."

"Oh hush, Kai, I'll be fine out here for a short while. I'm not a delicate flower." Her gaze pinned him in place, flashing with a steely determination.

Holding his hands up with palms out, Kai gave a nervous chuckle. "I wasn't suggesting you were. It is my job to take care of you all, though."

"And you've done a wonderful job so far, which we appreciate. I did have another reason for coming out here, though. I think you already know what I'm talking about."

Kai couldn't hold back a wince. Of all the things he *didn't* want to talk with the priestess about, that was at the top of the list. "Listen, Orelia, you shouldn't have to worry about any problems there." Noticing her curious glance, he continued. "I already know the ramifications of taking things further, and I'd rather not put you or anyone else in an uncomfortable position."

The apothecary's confusion grew when he heard her laugh. "Well if I'm being honest, what I meant was discussing our plans for when we reach Grantide, but this is definitely more intriguing."

A burning sensation spread across Kai's face as his cheeks turned crimson once more. With a disgruntled huff, he turned away from the giggling priestess. "Let's not talk about it and say we did. I've already put my foot in it deep enough."

He flinched when Orelia rested both hands on his shoulders, massaging the tense muscle. "Kai, I was already aware of this. Even a blind man can see the adoration in your eyes when you look at Maple."

"Wouldn't you need to report it, though? Isn't it part of your priestess' oath? I don't want to get you in trouble." Kai bit back a satisfied groan at the woman's ministrations. Her fingers slipped beneath his robes and the cool sensation of her skin on his bare shoulders produced a contented purr from his chest.

Gazing at her, he suppressed a blush when he found his eyes transfixed on her lips as they curved into a sly grin. He fought to keep his breathing under control, wondering why Orelia seemed to be having such an effect on him.

I'm starting to think I put a few too many drops of venom in my tea tonight. It's making me delirious.

"I suppose you could say that. But at the same time, my duty is to offer advice and comfort to those who need it. In a way, my duties as a priestess aren't much different than yours as an apothecary. Reporting this to the church would cause unnecessary harm to multiple people under my care, as it were. People who I consider as good as family, or even more." Kai tensed when he saw her eyes scan him from head to toe with a smug expression. "Thus, it's my discretion to decide whether I say anything to those in power. And, as you can probably guess, I intend to say nothing of the sort."

Threading his fingers through his mane, Kai felt immediate relief at Orelia's words, but he couldn't shake the nervousness welling in his chest. It was a sensation he had grown accustomed to since the war started, though he didn't enjoy it.

"I'm scared," he muttered.

"I can imagine. It's a frightening position, and one I've found myself thinking about more often."

Without thinking, Kai's head turned, his eyes locking on the window to the dining hall where the rest of the party, sans Teos, sat around enjoying their dinner. "I don't even know how this happened. Nothing makes sense, and it's growing more complicated by the day. By the moment, even."

"From what my father tells me, love never makes sense until you're willing to grab it with both hands and never let go. I suppose I never really thought about what he meant until recently."

A soft creak echoed around them. Kai glanced down to see his fingers gripping the deck wall hard enough to crack the wood. "How could I even hope to grab this with both hands? She deserves better. Nulyma, *anyone* would deserve better than what I have to offer."

"Only because you're short-sighted about your own worth. Even if you fail to see it in yourself, you've proven to be loyal, compassionate, brave, intelligent, and above all else, honorable. This may be shocking to hear, but many women would find even *one* of those traits attractive, regardless of your tribe, let alone all of them at once. Myself included."

Kai blinked, feeling the wood splinter beneath his fingers as the two shared an uneasy glance, their faces burning in embarrassment. "Is this really a discussion we should be having?"

"You started it. I'm just saying the truth of the matter. I'm beginning to wonder if your Brand should've been Ironskull instead of Gravebane." Orelia spun on her heel and giggled, rapping the head of her staff against Kai's rear. "I may not be experienced in affairs of the heart, but I do know one thing. If you allow life to pass you by, it's possible you may never get another chance at what true happiness could be. Think about it." With that, she trailed a finger over his cheek and, before he could blink, leaned in and brushed her lips against his ear. Orelia bustled away and ascended the stairs towards the cabins, leaving a blushing Kai to wallow in his thoughts.

W-what was that?! Kai asked himself, his face lighting up like a beacon as dozens of questions raced through his mind. *That was dangerously close to a kiss, wasn't it? Orelia can't possibly think that way about me...could she? I mean, she is pretty, but I've got enough on my plate dealing with Maple. I hate to admit it, though, but she's right. Still, what can I possibly say? Damn it. Of all the things Ma and Da taught me, they could've spent more time explaining this. I can't just go in swinging, either. What if Maple says no? And how do I handle the situation with Orelia?*

It was those last two thoughts which sent tremors through Kai's body. His breath hitched and sweat greased his palms like oil. An image flashed before him, of Maple glaring with wings crossed and disgust written in her eyes. It only lasted a moment, but it was enough to drop the Exarch to his knees. A similar image, this time of Orelia cackling in his face while boasting that only a fool would love him, had the apothecary clutching at his mane. His breathing came in short, heavy gasps, and he could feel his heart pounding against his chest. He didn't know if he could handle such a look directed at him. Seeing it in his mind was horrible enough.

A loud splash rang out. Startled, Kai leaned over the deck wall to scan the river. Seeing nothing, he marched towards the stern wondering if something fell overboard.

"We better not have lost any important supplies," Kai mumbled to himself. The last thing he wanted was to lose anything belonging to Fusette. Striding onto the rear deck, he saw both deckhands peering into the murky water below. "So you both heard it, too?"

The pair jumped and spun to face him, looking relieved. "Aye, sir," the older and larger of the two replied. "We were checking to if anything fell off, but ya can't see a damned thing. Maybe it was just a big fish. Oh, we never got a chance to introduce ourselves. I'm Montagru and this is my nephew, Yasso."

Shaking the men's hands, Kai introduced himself. "Everyone here knows you, Sir Gravebane," Yasso admitted. "Lord Saredi mentioned your accomplishments when we took the job. He wanted to make sure we were properly respectful. Gotta say I like this work a lot more than plowing the fields back home, that's for certain."

Unable to hold back a laugh, Kai scratched behind his neck. "That sounds like Saredi, but don't trip over yourselves trying to be too respectful. I'm not one to stand on formality. So long as you complete your work to the best of your ability and help protect the ship and crew, that's what matters."

The two Soltauri regarded him with curiosity. Yasso looked unsure of how to respond to Kai's statement.

A loud creak cut through the silence, causing the three men to jump. Kai plucked the mace from his sash and gave it a test swing. "Please tell me you heard that."

"Aye," Montagru answered, reaching for an iron rod sitting on the deck. Yasso removed a gaff hook from the cabin wall, gripping it like a spear.

"Who's there?" Kai called out. Nobody responded. He heard the rest of the party chatting in the dining hall, unaware of the situation. Turning to the deckhands, he asked if it was the boiler crew.

Yasso shook his head. "I don't think so. They would've answered you. I think we got a stowaway on our hands."

"Brilliant," Kai grumbled. Signaling to the other men, Kai whispered for them to check the port side while he went starboard. They gripped their makeshift weapons and slunk off. Kai considered ducking into the dining hall to rally the others, but he wasn't comfortable leaving the deckhands alone and vulnerable that long. A brief thought flitted through his mind, wondering how much worse the night could get.

He soon got his answer when a flash of steel nearly blinded him. Dropping to one knee, Kai felt a rush of air as a sword flew overhead and clanged against the stairway railing. He thrust his mace forward and heard a satisfying *thunk* when it struck armor, his assailant being knocked backwards.

Blinking the spots from his eyes, he stepped back and hissed when he saw Agosti scrambling to his feet. "Oh bloody Nulyma, not you again!"

"You didn't think I was done with you yet, did you, peltneck?"

Kai's eye twitched. The more he heard that abrasive slur, the less patience he had for anyone vulgar enough to use it. He reached down and grabbed a small iron fishing weight, rolling it in his hand. "I'm not sure which of you bastards I hate more: you or Duarte. You're both more annoying than a splinter under my nail."

"I'll consider that a compliment. Now maybe you should just come quietly, and your little band of freaks won't be harmed."

"Duarte gave me the same spiel, and I told him to fuck off before beating him like a drum. What makes you think I won't do the same to you?"

Kai felt a shiver go through his tails at the malicious grin Agosti wore. "Oh, I already knew you'd decline," the Liberator snapped, "but at least now I can tell the general I tried it his way first when I bring your corpse back. That and my men have a legitimate reason to kill your friends as well."

"You're welcome to try. Maybe this time you'll finally—" Kai's voice trailed off as he looked past Agosti, his eyes widening. The captain's eyes furrowed when a board creaked behind him. He spun with sword raised to strike whoever was sneaking up on him. His anger turned to confusion when he came face-to-face with another Liberator, this one wearing a lieutenant's bars.

"What the...? I thought I told you to board on the other side, Lieutenant!"

Kai smirked, flinging the fishing weight upwards to strike the ship's bell with a deafening gong.

"All fighters on deck!" Kai shouted. "We're under attack!"

Swearing, Agosti shoved the lieutenant backwards and brandished his sword. The rumble of multiple footfalls shook the deck as the party barreled out of the dining hall, weapons drawn. Kai heard more curses erupt from his friends moments later.

"This fool again?" Morgan asked, drawing his falchion. "I think he likes you," he shouted at Kai.

Rolling his eyes, the apothecary slid into a battle stance. "He likes me about as much as I like your jokes, Morgan."

"You really know how to hurt a guy, 'pothy. That was just mean."

"You can insult each other later," Orelia snapped. "Get these asses off our ship!"

Kai grinned. "You heard the lady! Search the whole ship. There's bound to be more of them around," he shouted while twirling his mace. He rushed forward and met Agosti's attack, their weapons colliding in a spray of sparks. The others scattered, searching for the Liberator's men.

Ducking under a wide swing, Kai chanced an overhead strike at Agosti's wrist. The officer leapt back, leaving Kai to crack the deck under the force of his blow. Glancing up, he caught the kick Agosti aimed at his nose. With his opponent's ankle clutched tight, Kai rotated his hips and swung the Liberator back-first into the wall.

Agosti staggered to his feet with a groan, eyes blazing with fury. He rushed forward, thrusting his blade in quick successive jabs that forced Kai to back away.

Using his mace to parry, Kai brushed aside the next jab and stepped in close. He grabbed Agosti by the back of the head and hammered the Liberator's temple on the railing. Agosti stumbled backwards cradling his head. Kai was ready to rush in again when a familiar burning sensation erupted in his gut.

Taen, not now! I knew I shouldn't have had so much! Kai berated himself as he collapsed to his knees, the venom sending a boiling sensation through his torso. The mace clattered to the deck with the apothecary nursing his stomach. The pain felt worse than before, somehow. Any attempt to move his arms triggered another wave of agony. Lumbering to the deck wall, Kai leaned over and retched into the river.

"What do we have here?" Agosti taunted, stalking towards the prone Norzen. "You don't look too good. Perhaps I should end your misery." The officer grabbed Kai by his robes and hauled him back. His skull rang when Agosti returned the favor and slammed his head into the wall several times in quick succession.

The sounds of battle echoed from all around, leaving a throbbing ache in Kai's head. He tried crawling away to gather his bearings, only for Agosti to yank him back and stab him through the shoulder, pinning him to the wall.

"Looks like it's the end for you, peltneck. Seems rather silly to see you laid low by stomach pains. Any last words before you die?"

Kai settled for glaring at Agosti. He refused to give the bastard the satisfaction of seeing his true emotions. He hissed at the tug when Agosti removed the sword from his shoulder. He just hoped the others would be safe and find a way out of this.

A familiar clomping sound resonated through the floor. Kai looked to see Teos crash next to him, having leapt from the pilot deck.

"Kai, what in Finyt is going—" Teos began, his voice trailing off when he spotted Agosti. "You?!"

Agosti was similarly stunned, his face paling at the sight of the Soltauri smuggler. Within moments, he broke out into hysterical cackling.

"Oh this is beautiful," he brayed. "I had no idea *you* of all people were with the peltneck. This must be fate at work. It seems Lord Galen is smiling on me today."

It was taking all of Kai's focus to not vomit all over the deck, though he wondered how Teos knew the Liberator.

"Here I thought you drowned in the river all those years ago," Teos murmured. Twirling his halberd, he dropped into a stance.

Agosti lifted his sword and gave Teos a confident smirk. "I ain't that easy to kill, you stupid goat, you know that. What say I take the other one and make you match?" To both men's shock, Agosti reached into his pocket and removed a long, spiraling object. After glancing at it for a moment, Kai's eyes widened.

It was a perfect match to the single horn remaining atop Teos' head.

Kai bit back a wince. He knew Teos was sensitive about his horns. He was rendered speechless, however, when the smuggler's eyes darkened to a blazing crimson. With a bellow, Teos charged like a raging bison and was on top of Agosti before the Liberator could blink. The halberd flashed in the moonlight, Teos swinging it into Agosti's raised sword with a blaring ring.

The impact sent Agosti flying across the deck to land hard on his back. Kai struggled to rise, using his free hand to put pressure on his injured shoulder while trying to ignore the painful pulses in his gut. He watched Teos preparing to attack again, but a sudden flash of cream entered his vision with Orelia wrapping her arms around the furious smuggler. The sound of tearing fabric reached his ears as one of her sleeves was torn by Teos' halberd.

"Teos, calm down! You need to fight it," the priestess begged. A thin line of blood was visible through the ripped sleeve, flowing down the side of her arm. The smuggler's eyes swung towards her, and Kai grabbed his mace through the pain. This was his first time seeing another faumen in the throes of a Frenzy Haze, though he hoped he wouldn't have to jump in and stop Teos from hurting Orelia. He wasn't sure how much help he'd be in that case, though he was ready to force his body to listen if need be, if it meant it would keep Orelia safe.

His concerns were unwarranted, though, as he saw Teos visibly calming in the woman's arms. He collapsed to the deck floor in her embrace and locked eyes with Kai, who swore he saw a hint of anger.

The brief peace was shattered when Agosti's lieutenant jumped out from around the corner, grasping a small sphere in his right hand. With a deranged cackle, the young officer pulled a sparkstone from his pocket and struck it against the railing, lighting the small fuse jutting from the sphere's top.

Kai hissed when he saw sparks flying. "He has a bomb! Fall back!"

"Let's see you faumen bastards survive this," the lieutenant exclaimed while waving the sphere around. "Now you'll see the true might of the Liberation—"

A thunderous clang reverberated when a dark shape burst from the window next to the lieutenant, smashing into the side of his head. He staggered sideways a few paces, his body toppling over and collapsing against the deck wall. The sphere fell from his hand and rolled to a stop near his feet.

Kai, baffled by the sudden attack, blinked at what he realized was an iron pan sticking out of the window. When Ione poked her head out and turned to face Kai and the others, the pain in his stomach and the bomb were forgotten in the moment in favor of side-splitting laughter. Teos and Orelia joined in, leaning on each other as they howled in mirth.

Agosti groaned from the other side of the deck, easing himself up. Kai's ears twitched, drawing his attention back to the injured Liberator. Agosti cursed at seeing his lieutenant lying prone and threw himself overboard.

Noticing the sphere's fuse nearing its end, Kai's face turned sallow. He shouted a warning, watching Teos pluck Orelia off the ground and retreat with the priestess squawking to be put down. The smuggler darted past Kai while Ione ducked back into the dining hall, shutting the window with a bang.

The lieutenant emitted a tired moan of pain and tried clambering over the wall but proved too slow when the sphere exploded next to him. The blast, smaller than Kai expected, threw the soldier sideways back onto the deck alongside a spray of crimson blood.

A thin, dark mist spread over the area, covering the lieutenant before he could get back up. Kai stepped back when the Liberator's body seized up and began twitching. He took a tentative sniff, but the mist was too far away to discern any unique smells. To his relief, it looked to be dissipating fast, scattered about by the winds swirling over the river.

Several more splashes broke the budding silence. Kai heard footfalls coming from behind and turned to see everyone else approaching, including the deckhands and boiler crew. Ione was with them, leaving Kai to assume she left the dining hall from the opposite side.

"Merciful Ausrina," Maple gasped, seeing Kai's injuries. "What did that bastard do to you, Kai?"

An angry huff drew everyone's eyes to Teos. "I'd say our illustrious Exarch got his bell rung, and by a river pirate, no less."

A haze of confusion stopped Kai's thoughts cold. "River pirate...what are you talking about, Teos? Do you know that damned pain in the ass?"

"Aye, more than I wish to. That whoreson is the one who broke my horn off fifteen years ago." Gasps rang out from the group. "You saw his trophy yourself, remember? His name is Valdis Agosti, and he used to be the first mate of the pirate known as Bloodbeard."

Kai flinched when Orelia began swearing like a sailor. "That bastard was the right hand of *Bloodbeard*? His crew was responsible for wiping out whole villages along the border! He's probably the most infamous pirate since Aina the Bonebreaker."

"I know. Truth be told, I was in a pirate crew myself back in my youth. I started out as a deckhand under a Livorian pirate named Captain Hahns. He considered himself Bloodbeard's rival, and our crews' skirmishes were how I met Agosti. By the time he snapped my horn, I had worked my way up to helmsman." Everyone backed away from the smuggler, eyes wide. Unperturbed by their shock, Teos turned his ire on Kai. "You're supposed to be an Exarch, one of the duchy's most skilled defenders. How in blazes did he come so close to killing you? I've seen you fight, and he's good, but there's no way he should be *that* good."

Biting back the pain, Kai eased himself up only to cry out when the burning intensified. He clutched his abdomen and leaned against the wall, taking slow methodical breaths. Orelia rushed forward and wrapped his arm around her shoulders, helping him to his feet. She turned a stern glower on Teos, warning him that he was being too harsh on Kai.

"I freely admit I wasn't at my best tonight, Teos. I don't know what else to say. My gut feels like it's being fried in oil at the moment, so moving hurts like Nulyma."

Lucretia's eyebrows furrowed. "This is not the first time you have had these stomach pains. Are you suffering from an illness you failed to tell us about?" she asked.

"No, it's not a disease. It's from a trial concoction I've been testing."

He bit down on his tongue when Maple grabbed his mane, pulling him close. "You're testing unproven medicine on yourself? Are you mad?!" she screeched. "What could be so important you had to do something so risky?"

"My specialty as an apothecary is in treating poisons, so I often research ways to improve current concoctions. It's not uncommon for a new antivenom to require thorough testing, but I refuse to test my experiments on others. It goes against everything I stand for. I'd never use a concoction on someone I wasn't willing to take myself. On a normal day, I can withstand the cramps, but tonight was worse than expected. Besides, I didn't think we would be attacked by a pack of Libbies."

Her lip quivering, Maple's eyes glistened with tears as she threw herself into his arms. "You stupid fool!" she bemoaned, striking his chest with a fist. "Please, for the love of the Saints, promise me you won't take that medicine anymore. We *can't* lose you."

The desperation in her voice was palpable. Looking around, he noticed the concern in the others' eyes. Ione and Orelia had both joined Maple in shedding tears, with the priestess wrapping her own arms tight around him. Morgan, Lucretia, and Teos all wore grim frowns with pinched eyebrows. The rest of the crew stared in confusion. Yasso and Montagru in particular were frowning as they trussed up the dead bodies of two more Liberators before dumping them overboard.

A soft thump against his chest caused Kai to glance down and see Maple burying her face in his mane. Her stammered cries of "Please," cut through his heart quicker than any blade.

He flushed red and pulled a vial from its hook on his robes' fur collar. Popping the cork, he downed the contents in one gulp. "Okay, I promise I won't take it anymore. The tonic I just took should ease the cramps. I'll be good as new after some rest."

Maple tilted her head up, whispering, "You promise we won't have this conversation again?"

Kai felt his lips curve into a cheeky grin. "You of all people know how I am with promises. I swear to Tapimor, it won't happen again." The merchant mumbled her approval and pulled away.

"Oi, what happened to that fool?" Yasso asked, pointing at the lieutenant, who lay immobile on the deck where he fell.

Kai frowned and slid forward at a snail's pace, not wanting to aggravate his gut further. Kneeling next to the body, he wrapped a spare cloth around his fingers and pressed them to the man's neck, feeling for a pulse. Considering a huge chunk of the man's torso was blown off, he didn't expect much, but he'd seen crazier things happen.

There was nothing. Stranger still, the muscles in his neck felt hard and unyielding to the touch, like metal. Not many ailments could produce such a symptom, let alone so quickly. Pulling his fingers back, he noted a dark substance on the cloth.

He asked for a light. Dekel stepped forward with a torch. Looking again, he noted a dark blue powder, finely ground. He took a quick sniff, detecting a pungent odor he only encountered once before. One that explained the sudden stiffness in the muscles.

"Well, this moron is as dead as one can get, and if this powder he's covered in was in that bomb, then we have a new problem to worry about."

It was Lucretia who asked the question on everyone's minds. "What problem?"

"The Libbies have somehow created bombs filled with stonehood pollen."

The scholar hissed a curse. "You are certain it is stonehood?" Kai nodded.

"What's the big deal, 'pothy?" Morgan asked. "For that matter, what's stonehood? I've never heard of it."

Kai answered the sellsword, "That's shocking since stonehood is a popular ornamental flower native to southern Corlati and Galstein. It usually grows on riverbanks. It's not rare, but also not very common, so nobles like to put it in their gardens for the prestige even though it's dangerous to handle. Most parts of the plant are toxic, and its pollen is infamous for causing a condition called ironleg if ingested or it meets open wounds. It causes the body to seize up and the muscles to harden like iron, hence the name."

"And the Liberators created a bomb with it? Or to be more accurate, they received it from their Corlatian benefactors?"

The apothecary nodded. This war was becoming more dangerous the longer it dragged on. Fusette would have to be notified of this first thing in the morning. He allowed Morgan to help him back to his cabin as the others wandered upstairs. As he was carried away, he watched Yasso donning gloves before pulling the dead Liberator's body away for disposal. Reaching into his pocket, Kai removed the vial of Grimghast's venom and flung it into the river as the others watched with curiosity. He never told them what he used that caused his cramps, and the thought of admitting to what he was drinking filled him with trepidation. His friends had enough to worry about.

If the Liberators surprised the Royalist Navy with this new weapon, however, it could shift the war in favor of the enemy.

Maple felt the air leave her lungs as she collapsed on her bed the moment she entered her cabin. To her surprise, the other ladies followed her and set themselves along the wall facing her. Even Kerta and Annika joined them as she nestled into the bed linens.

"I already know what y'all want to talk about, but I ain't in the mood," Maple groaned.

Lucretia scoffed, tilting her head towards the cabin door. "Care to explain what that was out there? For Dolmaru's sake, you were practically draped over him. And Orelia! You weren't much better!"

"I panicked, alright!" Maple shouted. "Hearing him admit he was testing unproven concoctions on himself, without any thought for what it could do to him...it *terrified* me. Ausrina be damned, you have no idea how scared I was when he said that."

Orelia nodded, admitting that Kai's confession rattled her in a way that she hadn't felt since she was a child being bullied by her schoolmates.

"Do you truly believe he will keep his promise?" Lucretia asked.

Ione sent the scholar a stern frown. "I think we all know Kai well enough to realize he wouldn't break a promise if he could help it. Besides, we all watched him fling the vial into the river, and I doubt he's crazy enough to try swimming after it in his condition. I don't know about the rest of you, but I saw the look in his eye when he made that promise."

The others stared at her with puzzled expressions.

"Maple, honey, I'm only gonna say this once, so listen close: You have no idea how lucky you are. Kai looked at you like the brightest diamond in a pile of gems. Most of us here know how you feel about him, and I'd wager my whole stipend from Lady Fusette that he feels much the same about you. Then again, I'd also wager you're not the only one harboring a torch for our reckless leader, at least from what I've seen."

The Aerivolk's face flushed crimson as she covered herself with a pillow. From the corner of her eye, she saw Orelia eyeing the tavern maid with a pinched expression. The cabin girls were gazing at Ione in confusion, though it was understandable considering their lack of experience among the party. "You don't know that for certain, Ione," she answered, her voice muffled.

"Take it from a gal who was married for nine years and spent most of my working life being flirted with by every type of man you can imagine. I may not know for certain if it's love or not, but the spark is there. I can see it when his eyes light up every time he sees you. You hold a special place in Kai's heart."

Orelia giggled, drawing all eyes in the room to her. "Good to know I'm not the only one who sees it. Finyt knows I wish someone would look at me like that. Let me just add that, while I was chatting with him, Kai may or may not have revealed some juicy thoughts of his own."

The pillow came flying at Orelia so fast, one would have thought it was fired from a cannon. Maple propped herself into a sitting position, her eyes locked on the priestess full of worry. "Are you serious? What did he say? He saw how clingy I was and thinks I'm too much trouble, right? I know that's what it is..." Her rambling was cut short when Orelia launched the pillow back, thumping against her face.

"Perhaps I could finish if you'd refrain from letting your mind go on a wild stampede. Now, I can't say exactly what he said, but there are plenty of hints. If you want my advice, Maple, you'd best make your move, before someone else does. Kai isn't the type to assert himself and he clearly has trouble with his self-worth. The untested concoctions were just an extension of that. I can see it in his eyes. He's desperate for someone to love him for who he is and wants to see where things would go, but it seems he's terrified of either disappointing you or being rejected, never mind the church's official stance."

Maple blinked back tears. "Why would he think I'd reject him?"

"It does make sense if you think about it," Lucretia commented. "He was found abandoned on the riverbank as an infant. Even ignoring the idea of being descended from Cacovis, he grew up alone in a village where he was different from everyone else. It would not be surprising for him to have abandonment issues, wondering for years whether his parents loved him or if he was set adrift because he was not wanted."

A loud groan came from the merchant. "I never even considered that. How could I be so *stupid?*"

"Nobody ever said love was smart...or easy," Ione replied.

Laying back, Maple considered her options. Knowing what she did, she didn't want to make Kai feel pressured. But if she let this opportunity slip by, there was no guarantee she'd get another chance to reveal how she felt. The thought made her consider what would happen if Kai found someone else.

Her heart pounded at the images her mind conjured up, of Kai holding someone else in his arms as she looked on from afar. Shaking her head, Maple's face settled into a hard determination.

Absolutely not, she grumbled to herself. *I'm not letting him slip away like that. Even if he says no, at least I'll know I tried. I have to say something.* A brief thought of asking him to dance came to mind, but she also wondered if doing so would be skipping a few steps. A formal dance request was akin to declaring an official courtship, from what she remembered.

She cast a tired smile at the others. "Thanks for talking with me. I think I know what to do now." The women bid Maple goodnight and told her not to worry too much before leaving the merchant to her thoughts.

One, however, remained.

"Did you need something, Orelia?" asked Maple.

The priestess emitted a heavy sigh and cast a solemn expression towards her. "I'm going to be straight with you, Maple, because you're my friend. Ione wasn't wrong about what she said earlier. You're not the only one interested in Kai."

Launching herself off the bed, Maple grabbed her friend by the blouse with a frantic look in her eyes. "Are you serious? I thought she was just trying to convince me to get off my tail feathers and confess. But who would—wait," she muttered. Meeting the younger woman's stare, Maple could see the steely conviction beneath Orelia's ocean-hued gaze. Her lips parted in a whispered gasp.

"It's you, isn't it?"

She nodded, her expression wavering to a hesitant smile. "Yes. I can't deny it, nor do I wish to. I've found myself thinking about Kai more and more since Runegard. After what happened at Stahl Granz..." she explained, her voice catching, "Kai was the one who kept me from spiraling into despair. He offered me comfort when I desperately needed it. The children in the orphanage were my life, Maple. Seeing them butchered like that was like having my heart torn from my chest. Despite my desire to kill Adalbard, if it hadn't been for Kai holding me in place, I might have jumped into that tidal wave on the river during our escape."

Hands flying to her mouth, Maple rushed forward and drew the priestess into a tight hug, now shedding tears herself. "Don't you ever think like that again, understand?" she whispered.

"I won't. Regardless, I wanted to make my intentions clear. It wouldn't be fair to you if I snuck in the shadows trying to come between you and him for my own benefit. No matter what happens, I want us to still be friends. Do I sound crazy?"

Maple wiped a wing across her tear-stained eyes. "Not at all. If anything, I appreciate the honesty. Would you even be allowed to marry him though? I'm not sure about the rules for clergy."

"It's not a problem. Clergy members are permitted to marry and have children, though obviously the fact we're from different tribes would cause a ruckus. Sweet Finyt, I believe Archbishop Jovanni is a grandfather three times over, and he's served the church for over thirty years."

"Makes sense to me. I'm glad we could talk about this without tearing each other's hair out."

"Agreed. I'm a firm believer of justice in every form, so I wanted us to be on equal footing going into this." Orelia held out her hand, which Maple grasped with a firm grip and a wide smile.

"That poor man isn't going to know what hit him, is he?"

"Definitely not," Orelia declared. "I did tell him he should've been Branded as Ironskull earlier. He's certainly dense enough, though that's part of what makes him so cute. Still, it wouldn't be near as much fun if he did, would it?" The two women burst into giggles, sharing a quick hug before Orelia bid the merchant goodbye and left for her own cabin.

Thinking of what was in store, Maple perched herself on the headboard and wrapped a blanket around herself. She drifted off to sleep with a thin smirk on her face. She had to let Kai know how she felt, no matter what happened.

Orelia might be her friend, but she wasn't about to let the younger woman catch up to her so easily.

Chapter VI

Fusette Ardei considered herself an even-tempered woman. She always sought to be fair and honest in her decisions as Grand Duchess and took time to consider both sides of an argument before choosing the option that best benefited the duchy and its people. There were days, however, where she toyed with the idea of abdicating and taking early retirement on a nice peaceful beach somewhere.

Staring at the letter she received from Kai that morning, she knew the war was reaching a point where choices would have to be made. Choices that could scar her realm and its people. Fusette's eyes flickered to the throne room doors, knowing Saredi would soon return with Hanblum.

The Aerivolk envoy was pleased to hear about the Royalists' victory in Faith Hollow. When she shared their suspicions regarding the Corlati Federation assisting the Liberators, Hanblum was more than happy to pen a message to Queen Isolde requesting military aid.

Perhaps, with the Galstans at their side, they might be able to quell this rebellion. The word left a bitter taste in her mouth, but Fusette couldn't dispute the facts laid bare.

The Liberation Army was in full rebellion against the duchy. Worse, they seemed intent on turning their beautiful realm into a copy of the Federation! Whether they rose on their own or were incited by Corlati, she didn't know for certain. All she knew was her people were in danger and the rebels needed to be put down as soon as possible.

A loud groan from the doors startled the young duchess. "Your Grace," Saredi's voice echoed through the cavernous throne room, "I've brought Hanblum. He received a missive this morning from Her Majesty, Queen

Isolde." True to his word, the dignified envoy strode in moments later, a scroll of parchment clutched in his hand.

"That's wonderful to hear. And Hanblum, I do hope you've enjoyed your time here."

Hanblum took a knee and bowed. "Your hospitality has been exquisite, Your Grace. I am truly grateful for the steps your staff have taken to make my stay feel like home. Her Majesty has responded to my request for aid. You may read it at your leisure." The envoy held the scroll out, allowing Fusette to take it.

Hands shivering in anticipation, she unfurled the parchment and took care to read at a slow pace. She remembered Queen Isolde as an eloquent woman, if a bit verbose, and the letter matched her style of speaking. More than once, she needed to stop and consider the context of a sentence to understand the other monarch's meaning. The more Fusette read, though, the higher her hopes soared. Despite her strong vehemence towards Corlati in regard to their potential involvement, it was apparent Isolde was not about to let her realm's staunchest ally weather the storm of war alone.

"This is the best news I've heard since the war started," she declared. "I'll confess, I expected to receive limited aid. Her Majesty must look after the well-being of her own, after all. This is far beyond what I imagined."

"How many men are being sent, Your Grace?"

"A full fleet of five thousand, headed by Admiral Basner himself."

Saredi took an involuntary step back. "Basner? As in Ottoten Basner, the hero who brought about the end of the Fifty-Years War?"

"The very same. Now that I think about it, it's probably for the best that Admiral Basner be the one leading our allies. His daughter happens to be in the thick of everything, and I'm sure he'll be concerned."

Hanblum paled. "His daughter? Are you insinuating, Your Grace, that Lady Orelia is involved in the war?"

Fusette regarded the Aerivolk with confusion. Then she remembered. "I forgot, you spend much of your time in the southern wing, attending your duties. Sister Orelia came back with me from Runegard, and I'll confess I never once considered the thought you might know each other. She left a few days ago as a member of our envoy party sent to marshal the Hunter Corps for battle."

"Wait, why would she submit to your service? From what I remember, Orelia's always been a rebellious child. That was her entire reasoning for becoming a priestess. Ottoten tried pressing her to join the Navy alongside her older brothers, but the girl up and fled like a spirit in the night. What brought her out of her temple?"

Fusette and Saredi shared a look. "Stahl Granz was put to the torch by Liberator allies during the Battle of Faith Hollow. Sadly, one of them turned out to be Adalbard, the very bishop overseeing the temple, and he committed horrific acts which drove Sister Orelia to pursue him." Hanblum's face paled, his spectacles sliding down his face.

"One of my Exarch Knights assisted her in this matter. Adalbard was among the group who attacked us in Runegard, alongside a faumen working under a man we suspect of backing the Liberation Army. My Exarch and his party drove them off, and the same knight is leading them towards Havenfall as we speak."

"This Exarch must be rather exceptional if Orelia is willing to follow his lead," said Hanblum.

"I like to think so, though he does have moments of putting others before his own health," replied Fusette with a cheerful smile. "Speaking of which, I received a letter from him today. It appears a Liberator scouting squad attacked their ship last night. Thankfully, they drove the attackers off, though they did discover worrying information."

Tilting his head, Hanblum asked what the party found out. Saredi adjusted his stance, moving into an easier position to hear.

"Either the Liberators are getting more inventive, or their Corlatian benefactors are more vicious than I thought. An enemy soldier was carrying a new type of bomb and fell victim to it himself. One capable of spreading stonehood pollen."

Both men's faces turned a pasty grey. "Stonehood?" asked Hanblum. "Are we sure of that?"

"I'm more than willing to defer to Gravebane's expertise. He may be an Exarch, but he remains one of the continent's most renowned young apothecaries, with extensive knowledge of Alezon's deadliest flora and fauna."

Saredi began pacing back and forth, mumbling under his breath. "This poses a serious problem. It's bad enough they use those new muskets. If the Liberation Army has access to weapons capable of spreading ironleg among our forces, we could be seeing a reversal of the tides. This could easily put us on the defensive."

Fusette couldn't argue the point, and Saredi's words reminded her of another pressing issue. "Saredi, do we have any news on locating the weapon responsible for Minister Falber's murder?"

"I'm afraid not, Your Grace. We may have to interrogate every guard in the city."

The duchess frowned. "We don't have that much time. Check the records and contact the constable offices with men on security duty that day. I want every officer who was anywhere near the event questioned. And Saredi...let the constable chiefs know that, considering the urgency, I'm not above tearing their offices and homes to the ground in order to secure this weapon."

Hanblum inquired if Fusette would truly follow through on her threat.

"Sir Hanblum, I'm amid retraining my guards because they allowed personal prejudices to blind them. Thanks to a proper questioning, I have reason to believe Ambroz was made a scapegoat to hide the true murderer. We are quite certain Gerhardt Falber was killed with a Corlatian musket." The envoy's eyes widened. "However, I can't prove anything without the gun. If it provides proof the Federation is even indirectly responsible for this tragedy, I'll do what I must."

"If it truly was a Corlatian weapon, it would imply—"

Saredi cut in, "Indeed. The mere implication might be enough to draw Rodekan and Belomas into the conflict. As odd as it sounds, I doubt President Harmod would be careless enough to risk his entire realm like this. He's too fastidious. The Empire hasn't seen war since the Federation won its independence but interfering with another realm's internal affairs is expressly forbidden by the Fulano Pact. Emperor Kabuji would be furious!"

Fusette slumped into her throne, massaging her throbbing temple. This war was spiraling out of control, with the potential to plunge the entire continent into disaster. Never in her entire life had Fusette wanted a drink so badly.

"Saredi," she muttered, drawing the Vesikoi's eyes to her. "I believe we must consider every available option. I think I'll pen a message to Harmod requesting correspondence while we search for the musket. As you said, he's never struck me as a risk taker, so perhaps a direct approach can give us answers."

The chamberlain's eyes shifted to the doors, gesturing a guard to step forward. "I had a feeling you'd say that, Your Grace. I'll send a guard to fetch Lady Bidelga."

Fusette released a sigh of relief. If anyone knew the best way to phrase her inquiries to the Corlatian leader, it was her Minister of State. She thanked Saredi for his suggestion and turned back to Hanblum.

"Do we know when Admiral Basner will arrive?" she asked.

"If I know Ottoten, I'm confident he's already on his way and will arrive before the end of the moon, perhaps even within the week. The man was never one to dally about."

The duchess emitted a soft chuckle. "I see his daughter takes after him in that regard. Sister Orelia is a woman of action if I've ever met one. She forced several of my guard captains to teach her some new fighting techniques while she was here. I hope my inquiries to President Harmod will shine some light on this situation." As she spoke, Fusette muttered a prayer for good luck.

Livoria would sorely need some if it hoped to survive.

Chapter VII

The sparkling lights ahead sent a wave of memories flooding through Kai's mind. The apothecary remembered traveling to Grantide with his Da many times growing up, helping deliver carriages of sweet rolls and other goods from his bakery.

As the *Senberg* sailed into the riverport and prepared to dock, Kai made his way to the main deck hoping the memories of his father would keep him from thinking about their trip thus far. Following Agosti's attack, the party settled into a routine of patrolling the ship at night in pairs. They were relieved when the cantankerous Liberator failed to make a reappearance. Kai was forced to suppress a scoff one night after overhearing the ladies muttering amongst themselves in the dining hall that perhaps Agosti finally learned to leave them alone. The apothecary seriously doubted it, considering the man's history with them.

No, he was certain they'd run into him again somewhere after the man finished licking his wounds.

"It's beautiful," he heard Ione say from beside him. Turning his head, he saw the telltale signs of tears at the edges of her eyes. He agreed. The sun was nearly gone from the horizon as Eoria and Bucheron loomed over an early night sky. The encroaching darkness gave an ethereal glow to the flickering flames of the torches lining Grantide's piers.

"To think I haven't been back here in so long. What will I say to my little Larina? What *can* I say? Will she even remember me? My parents are probably still furious with me. What if they—"

"I'll hear none of that, Ione," Kai replied, brushing the tears away and flicking the distraught woman on the nose. "You've come a long way since then. Don't forget that. It's possible they're still upset, considering everything that happened. Just remember, you've got our support, no matter what comes."

"Kai's right," an enthusiastic Maple declared, running up from behind and wrapping her wings around Ione's shoulders. "We're your friends! Better still, we're as good as family. Besides, we already knew we'd have to stop here for resupply anyway, so it works out." Giving the tavern maid a passing hug, Maple skittered off to wait for the boarding ramp to lower, a polished wooden board with a sheaf of parchment on it clutched in her hands. Kai looked over her shoulder and nodded approvingly when he saw that it was a supply inventory.

Montagru and Yasso were hard at work, leaping onto the dock to secure the ship, the mooring ropes flung over their shoulders. Once everything was tied down, Yasso clambered back up the hull and pushed the gangway into Montagru's waiting hands. The moment the two deckhands gave their approval, Maple dashed down and towards the port market.

"I swear we need to nail that girl to the deck," Teos grumbled as he descended from the pilot house. Glancing at the youngest members of the party—Kai, Lucretia, and Orelia—the smuggler asked how they could all be younger than the energetic merchant and yet so much more mature.

Threading his fingers through his mane, Kai pondered the question. As far as he knew, he was still the only one in the party to know many details of Maple's childhood. "I don't think it's a matter of being more mature, as Maple has her own type of maturity which manifests differently than ours. For example, she handles finances better than any of us. Heck, she does it better than many older merchants I know. She also has a mental fortitude I'd wager outstrips over half the Exarchs."

"He's right," Lucretia added. "She's also more in tune with both her own emotions and the feelings of others. I've noticed she can build amicable relations with almost anyone. That's something I have little skill or experience in."

Giggling to herself, Orelia tapped her staff against Teos' leg. "You're just jealous she has so much energy, old man."

"O-old man?!" Teos gasped. "I'll have you know I'm only 43, you little whelp. I've still got a few decades left in these bones!"

The party shared a chuckle as they disembarked, following Maple's trail towards the market. They were surprised to find the Aerivolk stopped at the end of the pier, chatting with an older human man as she handed her inventory to a nearby broad-shouldered Soltauri who gave off the authoritative air of a dock foreman. The human watched their approach and regarded them with a suspicious eye, prompting Maple to turn and face them.

She rejoined the party and flashed her brightest smile at Kai. "Oh fearless leader, this gentleman is the town port master and has some questions."

The man stepped forward, his face lined with wrinkles and the smell of pipe smoke wafting from him. "We weren't expecting any other ships today. You lot here for the festival?"

"I must confess I forgot the Spring Festival was occurring this time of the year," said Kai, pressing his hands together at chest height and bowing. "We're merely stopping for several days to restock our supplies and rest. We're traveling to Havenfall."

One of the surrounding men grumbled. The stench of alcohol on his breath was so powerful, Kai could smell it from yards away. "Havenfall, eh? What's a Norzen like you going there for? Best watch yourself, boy, or the Hunters might mount you over the mantle." Several others joined the man's uproarious laughter.

A quick glance showed most of the party ready to rebuke the drunk. He stayed their comments with a raised arm. "I think we'll be fine but thank you for your concern."

The drunk burst into a high-pitched cackle. "Concern? I'm hoping they nail you to the wall and skin you while you're still breathing, ya damned peltneck!"

Kai's eye twitched as he heard a heaving growl from the party. "Kai, turn around," Orelia warned, her hands clenched tight around her staff. "I'd rather you not see this."

"I appreciate the support, Orelia, but I've seen a lot worse than a drunkard getting a well-deserved thumping. Also, you probably shouldn't beat the fool unconscious. He'll suffer enough once the hangover hits."

"Are you *sure* we can't smack him a few times?" Maple asked. She and Orelia shared a mischievous grin. "I was hoping to vent some frustration from dealing with that damned noble from the capital. Kendela, or whatever his name was."

The port master turned to Maple with sunken cheeks. "You've met Lord Kendela?"

"Unfortunately. How do *you* know him?"

"He's the province's Margrave; the senior noble in these parts. His reach stretches from Grantide to Havenfall and eastward towards Mosswell. I hope you didn't provoke him. Lord Kendela is not someone you want as an enemy."

"The only reason I didn't punch him in his pretentious beak is because Kai bribed me with food." The crowd stepped back, gasping. "That windbag had the audacity to demand I marry him. Didn't even ask, just said I was his."

Yasso piped up from behind the party, "And you turned him down? Sounds like you could've been set for life, miss."

Turning to the laughing deckhand, Maple quirked an eyebrow. Kai was impressed when her flat stare unsettled Yasso enough to quiet him down. "I prefer a man who's compassionate and open-minded," Maple answered, "not some haughty noble who thinks he's better than everyone else because he has money."

A frowning Montagru cuffed Yasso behind the head and asked, "Aren't you both merchants, though? Wouldn't it be good business to marry someone who can provide for you? Besides, what if he forces the issue? He wouldn't be the first noble to do so."

As much as Kai wanted to dispute Montagru's claim, he couldn't. Despite Fusette's best efforts, Livorian nobles were known to exercise their authority over the people in ways that disgusted and unnerved him. There were good men among the throng, like Saredi, but just as many deserved to be left to rot in the dankest, foulest gaols of the continent. The thought of Maple being subjected to Kendela's 'mercies' sent a rumble of anger through his chest.

"I may be a merchant but love and marriage are not the place for business sense to take precedence," she responded. "If I marry, it'll be because I love the man in question for who he is, not what he can afford. A man may buy my wares, but no one can buy my heart." Maple's eyes darted among the party as she said it.

Kai thought her gaze lingered on him longer than the others but dismissed the idea almost immediately.

The women cheered, while Kai noticed the crowd looking amongst themselves with worry. He wondered what kind of life they led under Kendela to gain such a look. The man had only gained his current title four years ago, so Kai was settled into his Hunter career and rarely stayed in the province long enough to see the impact of Kendela's policies. It reinforced his concerns about Maple drawing the noble's attention.

The drunk who insulted Kai pitched a fit when he realized he was being ignored, spewing a plethora of vulgarities which left the crowd gaping. Mothers covered their children's ears and ushered them away. At least one elderly woman fainted from shock. Several words the drunk was spouting were things Kai never heard in his life, and more than one phrase had him questioning if the acts described were physically possible.

I can guarantee a body won't bend in that direction, Kai thought. *Not without ample screaming, anyway.*

The apothecary's gaze met Orelia's. He was tempted to let the furious priestess deal with the man as she wished, when a loud clang cut off the fool's inebriated ramblings.

Everyone's eyes swung to the drunkard, now splayed face-down on the dock as an older woman dressed in dusty farming clothes towered over his unconscious body. She carried a wide iron pan in her hand.

Well there's a familiar sight, Kai thought.

The woman had a heart-shaped face and appeared youthful for someone with so many wrinkles. Her hair was done up in a bun adorned with several pins.

"Which of you damn fools set this idiot off?" the woman asked in a husky voice Kai thought sounded familiar. "I swear, I could hear him blabbering from the market."

Kai heard a gasp behind him and saw Ione staring at her.

"Mom?" she breathed. Her words stilled the other woman, who turned and scrutinized the maid until releasing a choked gasp of her own.

"Great merciful Galen. Is that you, Ione?"

Rather than speak, Ione nodded with tears in her eyes. She stepped forward, raising her arms to embrace the other woman.

A shiver rushed from Kai's neck down to the tips of his tails. Dilating his pupils, he noticed a scowl growing on the older woman's face. Several townsfolk stepped back with fearful expressions, allowing her to stride towards Ione while raising an arm.

The one carrying the pan.

With a deep growl, Kai waited for the pan to rise level with the woman's chest before acting. The rest of the party shouted a warning, causing Ione to skid to a stop. She gaped in horror as her mother prepared to swing at her, demanding to know why she dragged her drunken hide home without warning.

The utensil started arcing towards Ione's head when Kai appeared from nowhere, batting it away with his mace and sending it flying into the river with a splash.

He heard Morgan mutter, "Bloody hoarfrost, did any of you see him *move?*"

The crowd staggered back, though Ione's mother turned on him with a fierce glare. Staring the woman down, Kai knew Ione would throttle him if he harmed her. A jingle in his chest pocket gave him an idea, though he didn't like invoking his status.

Still, she attacked my friend without provocation. Not the best impression.

"I hope you have a good reason for that," he began.

"Shut your mouth, boy! You don't know the shame this girl's brought my family."

One of the townsfolk called out, "You tell him, Nerea! We don't need some dumb Norzen—"

Nerea spun and jabbed a finger towards the interloper, "What *I* don't need right now is any of you pebblewits opening your gobs when they're better kept shut." The man snapped his mouth closed as everyone backed away.

Kai bit back a chuckle at the crowd's immediate withdrawal. "No questioning who wears the breeches in this town," he muttered under his breath. Instead of letting her turn on the innocent bystanders, the apothecary stepped in. "I know more than you think. As it stands, you just attempted to assault my friend."

Running her eyes up and down Kai's body, Nerea scoffed. "The stupid girl has lost the plot if she's making friends with your type."

The sound of weeping rendered Kai immobile, as if turned into stone. Turning his head just enough, he saw Ione sobbing from the corner of his eye. In all the time he knew her, Ione always put up a cheerful and kind front. Always doing what she could to help everyone else. He had watched her share stories and provide a consoling shoulder to the others.

Now, hearing her grief-filled wails, he sensed the red shadow of the Frenzy Haze encircle him. Through sheer willpower he formed a fist, digging his nails into the palm, and forced himself to snap his fingers twice. He heard Maple curse behind him and soon felt the pinch of her talons burrowing into his thigh. The Haze broke, his vision clearing as the crowd observed from afar.

Shooting the merchant a grateful smile, Kai took a moment to calm his breathing. A deep inhale brought the scents of the port to the forefront, giving him a focus.

Reaching into his pocket, he revealed his Exarch watch. Forged of brass, with a crystalline cover bearing the seal of the royal family, it was a relic every Livorian would know of. Sure enough, the sight of it sent the crowd into a furor. Many were calling for Kai's head, labeling him a heretic.

"Enough!" Lucretia bellowed. The scholar's shout brought the clamor to a sudden halt. Raising the emblem from her overcoat, she continued, "I am Lucretia Dineri, certified Archivist of the Citadel. Furthermore, I am willing to swear on my crest the watch you see was legitimately earned. This man is the Exarch known as Gravebane. Should you still doubt me, then I demand you fetch the local chief magistrate to have him verify its authenticity. Otherwise, you will all settle down and keep quiet!"

Not a person spoke. Instead, many took the opportunity to scramble back towards town. Peering at the scholar, Kai emphasized with them. Lucretia looked ready to shoot flames from her gullet, her eyes burning with fury. He wondered if she was really a mixblood fallen into her own Frenzy Haze.

"Thank you, Lucretia." Facing Ione's mother, he cleared his throat. "I'm not aware of all the circumstances regarding Ione's past. *However*," he stated, pinning her in place with a hardened glare, "one of the reasons we stopped here was for her to make amends and show you how far she's progressed. I cannot force you to do much, but I suggest you at least listen. Ione has been a wonderful friend and received a blessing from the Grand Duchess herself."

The woman frowned at him before casting her gaze downward as she mumbled to herself, sending a furtive look at the party every few moments.

"May I ask the priestess a question first?" Nerea asked.

Kai felt a hand on his shoulder and relaxed. He didn't need to turn his head to know Orelia was there. "Of course," she said, "I'm more than happy to assist. I'm Sister Orelia Basner, formerly of Stahl Granz Temple."

"Listen, Sister, I'm asking you because I figure if you can't trust a servant of the winds, who can you trust?" Kai bit back a wince. He hoped Orelia wouldn't mention the glaring exception to that comment they were acquainted with.

"I understand your reasoning. What would you like to know?"

Sending a withering glare at Ione, Nerea snapped at the priestess, "I wanna know if she's still the same lush she was when my husband and I left her in Mistport. Did she clean herself up finally?"

Blinking, Orelia stood flabbergasted. She turned to Kai, who let out a brief chuckle before gesturing for her to answer. "I must confess, I wasn't expecting such a question. I can say I've never seen Ione drink anything stronger than mead as long as I've known her. Even then, she only has one before switching to water or juice."

The change in the woman's attitude was so sudden and counter to what Kai had seen thus far, he was left dazed. Nerea's face melted into pure relief as she rushed forward and drew Ione into a crushing embrace. The party skittered back, confusion plain on their faces.

"Oh, thank the Saints!" Nerea proclaimed, now sobbing on her daughter's shoulder. "When I first saw you, I didn't know what to think. All I could see in my mind was the wretched mess you were in the day we left."

Rubbing her mother's back, Ione gave an awkward laugh. It was clear the tavern maid was unsure of how to approach the drastic shift in demeanor. "No, I understand. I really was a ruin after Athos disappeared. I lost myself in the sorrow and forgot what I still had. But I like to think I've learned a lot, and I can thank my friends for that." Backing away, Ione introduced everyone.

Scratching her head, Nerea fiddled with the hem of her apron, an action that reminded Kai of Ione. She apologized for her foul attitude, saying she assumed her daughter was trying to force her way back into Larina's life before she was ready. "Guess I never thought she'd clean up so well. I've always been the 'strike first, ask later' type."

"No fooling," Morgan whispered to Teos, jerking a thumb at the river where her pan had flown. The smuggler bit back a laugh.

"That reminds me," Ione spoke up, looking around, "where is Larina?"

"Oh, the poor thing ate too many sweets at the festival, I reckon. She's back home with your father sleeping off a bellyache."

Ione wilted. Her mother assured her not to worry, saying it was common during festivals for children to indulge where they shouldn't and that Larina was far from the only one to be having trouble.

"Dozens of children in town have been eating themselves sick," Nerea said.

A tingle arced down Kai's spine, his tails coiling together like a corkscrew. Something about Nerea's statement sounded off.

"You said *dozens* of children are suffering the same ailments?" he asked. The woman nodded.

Pushing her spectacles up the bridge of her nose, Lucretia cast a veiled smirk at Kai. "You suspect there's more to the issue, don't you?"

"I'd wager my watch on it. Having a few children come down with bellyaches is one thing, but so many? No, there's something else in the currents."

"If it's alright," said Ione, staring at her mother, "I'd like to have Kai examine Larina. He's an apothecary; a good one."

"How good?" Nerea asked. "Old Grasol is still working the town dispensary even if he doesn't make house calls anymore, plus there's a traveling apothecary assisting for the festival."

"He's good enough for Her Grace to retain his services whenever he sets foot in Whistlevale." Her mother gawked. "I wouldn't be surprised if the only reason she hasn't been able to convince him to settle in the capital is because he can't stand all the city noise."

"Well," Nerea replied while scratching her neck, "if he's good enough for Lady Fusette, I suppose it wouldn't hurt to get another opinion. Grasol is getting on in years and he can't work so fast anymore, so we had the new fella examine Larina. She was up and running around this morning after taking some medicine last night, but tonight she said she was feeling a bit tight in the belly again."

Bowing low, Ione thanked her mother and suggested they go now. Kai held his laughter at her visible excitement. She looked like a young hound ready for its first hunt.

Taking the lead, Nerea led the party into town. Teos shouted orders to Dekel, leaving the engineer in charge of the crew until they returned. Maple handed a scrap of parchment to Montagru, instructing him and Yasso to follow the dock foreman and ensure all the supplies were paid for and loaded onto the ship.

They followed the older woman into the market plaza, where the festival set up shop in an explosion of vibrant color and riotous sound. Stalls filled with steaming pots of food from around the duchy enticed Kai's nose. Troops of performers dazzled the crowds with tricks and dances. A loud clang rang out from a nearby stall where an older Wasini blacksmith displayed his craft, hammering away at a glowing red sword and sending sparks through the air.

The sounds sent a dull throb through Kai's head but, at the same time, he missed the exhilaration of seeing so many people come together in harmony to bring a town joy. Casting his eyes over the party, he saw them gazing in wonder at the celebrations. Even the oft-serious Lucretia was enjoying herself, a spark of happiness visible in her eyes.

So engrossed in the sights and smells, Kai was surprised when another body collided into him, almost knocking him off his feet. Feeling Teos grab hold of his shoulder, he righted himself in time to see a human pushing themselves up and brushing the grass from his robes.

Gangly and pale, the man had stringy, noodle-like arms. Kai's eyes widened when he noticed the man wearing bright yellow apothecary robes, which hung from his thin frame like a cloak. His eyes were baggy but alert, covered by a set of round spectacles perched on an aquiline nose that reminded Kai of Lord Kendela.

"So sorry, friend," the stranger apologized. "I'm afraid I wasn't watching where I was going. You're not hurt, are you? Do I need to examine you?"

Holding his hands up, Kai assured the man he was fine. "By any chance, are you an apothecary?" he asked.

Nerea hustled back when she realized she wasn't being followed anymore. "Aye," she piped up. "This is the traveling apothecary I mentioned. The one helping out with the festival who treated Larina."

The stranger's eyes swept over the party, flickering between each member. "Yes, I remember you. I hope your granddaughter is doing better. Though I suppose I should introduce myself to your companions. My name is Josep, a wandering healer from Galemore."

Kai held out his hand. "Pleasure to meet a fellow tradesman. I'm Kai, an apothecary hailing from Havenfall."

Josep regarded the offered hand with curiosity. "Really, a Norzen apothecary? I must say, we don't see too many of your tribe in the business." Kai chuckled and rubbed the back of his head, unsure of how to answer. What the man said wasn't wrong. Outside of Duskmarsh, Kai wasn't aware of any other Norzen in Livoria plying the trade.

They were interrupted by a happy couple who stopped to shake Josep's hand. "Oh thank you so much for coming by yesterday, sir," the blonde woman praised. "Our little boy is doing much better after taking your tincture. How can we ever repay you?"

"Oh, don't worry. My first exam is always free. I'm just glad to hear your son is doing better." Josep replied, bowing to the couple as they sauntered away. He rubbed one hand over the other in a circular motion, as if applying a salve or cream. Turning back to the party, he gave a weak smile. "I must confess it's rather intimidating to have so many seek my services during an event of this size. Galemore is a hamlet compared to Grantide, so I'm not much used to the crowds yet. I've heard there is an older gentlemen serving as the town's apothecary, but they say he's being pressured to retire by the guild. Still, I'm happy my skills can provide succor to those in need."

Kai laughed and said he often thought the same. "I know Grasol and heard the guild's been wanting him to hang up his robes, but he's a stubborn old buzzard, for sure. Maybe we can have a chat sometime before my group moves on. It's been a while since I last talked to a fellow apothecary. We could even share recipes."

"Oh, that sounds grand. However, I'm afraid I must decline, at least to sharing recipes."

Quirking an eyebrow, Kai tilted his head in confusion. "Eh? Why is that?"

"You see, I have some tinctures I've developed which I'd prefer to keep to myself as professional secrets. A trademark, if you will."

Thinking about it, the Norzen understood the benefit of such an action. Several concoctions in his own repertoire were personal recipes passed down by the master apothecary he apprenticed under. Kai apologized for his assumption, which Josep waved off.

"I understand your eagerness," said Josep. "Such a intense drive to learn will serve you well. Sadly, I have a few more patients to see before turning in for the evening. I bid you farewell." With a wave, the man continued on his way, vanishing into the crowd.

Kai stroked his mane while feeling one of his tails coil around his upper leg. Ignoring the itch, he asked Ione's mother how much longer it would be before they reached their home.

She replied it wouldn't be much longer, leading the party to the plaza's edge, where the roads gave way to shadows. Covered by passing clouds, the moons gave little light to the thin roads weaving between the wooden buildings. Teos lit a lantern and held it high, illuminating the path as they stepped into the darkened streets of Grantide.

"It's not much, but it's home," Nerea commented as they approached a quaint house nestled at the far end of a street still within eyesight of the festival lights. A row of lanterns along the path were lit, casting a faint glow over the thin road. Though clearly aged, Kai could tell the home was well-maintained and sturdy. Several children's toys littered the space surrounding the front door. The sounds of the festivities were muffled by distance, leaving the dim light accompanied by the chirps and buzzing of insects.

"Amazing," Ione gasped. "It looks just as I remember." Her quivering grew in intensity the closer they got to the house. Morgan had to grab the tavern maid by the elbow to prevent her from charging through the door. Nerea strode forward and opened the door, gesturing for the party to follow.

The inside looked plain and unassuming. Simplistic furniture took up much of the living area, with a long desk set against one wall covered in sewing materials. A wood-burning stove was visible in the kitchen, set close to the corner with a smokestack extending out the window. Kai spotted several dolls near one of the furthest doors; he assumed it led to Larina's room.

A man wearing a grungy tunic and overalls stepped out from the kitchen, wearing a disappointed scowl behind his round spectacles. His face and arms were tanned and gnarled, though still filled with wiry muscle. "What in Finyt is all this, Nerea?" he hissed. "Who are all these people?"

Turning to the others, Nerea gestured to the man. "Everyone, this is my husband, Massio. We own one of the berry farms outside of town, so I apologize if we're always covered in dirt." She looked back at him and snapped, "As for you, are you really so blind you haven't realized your daughter's home?"

The man's eyes bulged, swinging to look over the party before landing on Ione. "Bloody Nulyma, is that really...?" Nerea nodded.

Tucking her hands behind her, Ione regarded her father with clear apprehension. "Hi, Dad. It's nice to see you again."

A sense of trepidation trails down Kai's tails at the look of fury on Massio's face. "What in Finyt made you think you had any business coming back here?"

Ione's face sank. "But Dad—"

"I don't want to hear it! Didn't we tell you not to drag your sorry hide back here again?" Massio brandished a closed fist at his daughter, prompting Kai to stick himself between the two, to the older man's shock. "Huh? What in Nulyma is a damned Norzen doing in my house?!"

"Shut it, Massio!" Nerea hissed. "I already came close to butchering things with Ione earlier, so muffle your gob before I do it for you." The two glared at each other as Ione glanced between them with fear in her eyes.

"That doesn't explain *him*," Massio argued, pointing a thick, calloused finger at Kai.

Her face settling into a frown, Ione stood at Kai's side, resting a shaky hand on his arm. "I don't care a whit if you're still angry with me, Dad, but leave Kai out of it. Mom said Larina was feeling sick, and I asked if Kai could treat her since he's an apothecary."

"You expect me to believe such hogwash?" Massio retorted. He flinched back when Nerea strode up and thumped him behind the head, her eyes blazing.

"Did I not just tell you to shut it," she muttered. "Ione is telling the truth, whether you believe her or not. I agreed to let the man check our granddaughter. A second opinion never hurts, after all. Now try not to make any more fuss. If we're lucky, Larina will still be asleep." As if to prove the older woman wrong, a hacking cough came from the rear. The party spun, startled by the sudden noise.

Blinking, Kai saw a girl that, were she in better health, would've been a copy of Ione in her younger days. They shared the same heart-shaped face, thin frame, and brown eyes. Larina even had her mother's button nose.

"Grammy, wha's going on? Who are these people?" Larina choked out. Leaning against the wall, the girl staggered forward at a snail's pace. Even in the dim light, Kai could see mucus flowing from her nose and a faded red tint in her cheeks.

"Merciful Galen. Are you alright, Larina?" Nerea asked. She ran forward and grabbed the child before she collapsed. "Listen, sweetheart. I know this is sudden, but your mother is here. She's home at last."

Despite her illness, Larina's eyes reminded Kai of Maple with how bright they shone at those words. "Mama? Mama's home?"

Unable to hold back any longer, Ione rushed forward with a gasp. Kai noticed Massio clenching his fists, struggling to suppress his anger despite his wife's stony gaze. Dropping to her knees, the tavern maid clutched her daughter tight. "That's right, baby, Mama's home. I'm so sorry!"

The rest of the party stepped back and seated themselves on the floor, watching from a respectful distance.

Tears gushed from Larina's eyes as she embraced her mother just as tightly. "I'm sorry too, Mama! I didn't want Grammy and Grampa to make you stay away. I promise!"

"I know, Larina," Ione replied, wiping the girl's tears away. "I think I needed it, though. I know it's just an excuse, but when your Papa went missing, my heart was not in a good place. I needed time to learn just how important you and your grandparents are to me. I also made quite a few new friends since you left."

Wiping her tears away, Larina nodded and buried her face in Ione's neck. After a few sniffles, she glanced up and met Kai's gaze. The girl gave a hacking cough and backed away from Ione, looking at the Norzen with fear in her eyes. "M-mama...why is a Norzen here? All the kids in school say they're bad people."

"Well your schoolmates are wrong. I reckon all your schoolteachers talk about are the bandits everyone hears of. Not all Norzen are bad, and especially not this one. Kai's a good man." A wheezing scoff sent everyone's eyes flickering to Massio, who continued to silently glare at Ione. "He saved my life when the war started. Without him, I never would've made it here to see you." Looking at Ione in awe, Larina let the woman draw her back into a hug. "Now listen, Larina. I know it might seem scary, but Kai is an apothecary. I asked him to help you feel better. Is that okay?"

Erupting into another coughing fit, Larina's eyes switched between her grandparents and mother, as if unsure of what to do. Finally, she nodded and let Ione guide her forward. Kai asked for some blankets to spread over the floor and directed Ione to lay Larina back. Grabbing a strip of cloth, he wrapped it around his lower face, covering his mouth and nose.

"Mr. Kai, what are you doing?" Larina asked, taking slow breaths while emitting the occasional cough.

“Some illnesses can be passed from person to person through the air. This makes sure I don’t breathe any air from your coughs. Now, your grandmother said you were feeling better this morning after taking some medicine. What made you feel bad in the first place?”

Turning her head aside, Larina blushed. “I think I ate too much. There so many yummy sweets at the stalls, especially this one really nice lady, but I ate so much it gave me a tummy ache.”

Shifting his eyes to Nerea and Massio, Kai asked for their thoughts. The couple agreed, mentioning that the lady Larina spoke of specialized in pastries and sweets for children. Most of the adults avoided her stall’s wares themselves, citing an overpowering sweet scent.

They were interrupted when Larina broke into a wheezing cough. Kai helped her sit up, watching as the girl expelled all the air in her lungs until she had to take a deep breath. The raspy sound she exuded sent a shiver down Kai’s tails.

“It couldn’t be…” he murmured. He pressed a palm against Larina’s forehead, noting a heavy fever. Pulling his parchment out, he jotted down his thoughts and observations.

“Kai, what is it? What’s wrong with her?” Ione begged.

“There are a couple possibilities, but I need more information. This stall where she got the sweets is a good start. Nerea, do you know how many other children complained of belly aches after eating this woman’s food?”

“I think most of the children who fell ill had eaten at least one thing from her stall. Now that you mention it, the Tolsons next door didn’t let their daughter have anything from there, and last I saw she was hearty as a wiroch. How could her food made them sick, though?”

“It’s possible, depending on what she put in the food. My Da is a baker and says some ingredients to enhance sweetness can cause stomach cramps. I want to investigate the stall before making an official diagnosis. Once I learn what’s in the food, I can better determine what Larina and the other children are suffering from.”

The party rose to their feet and offered to help. “Thanks, everyone,” Kai said. “We need as many eyes on this as possible. Let’s go.”

Before leaving, the apothecary asked Massio to stay with Larina while Nerea showed them where the stall was. He instructed the cranky man to ensure Larina drank plenty of water and stayed in bed except to eat or use the privy. Massio brushed Kai's words off with a huff, grumbling under his breath.

Their goal set, Nerea led everyone back towards the festival. Kai's tails twirled in anticipation, which told him he was on the right track.

There was something odd going on with that food stall, and he had every intention of unveiling the truth.

CHAPTER VIII

Approaching the dazzling lights of the festival once more, the party marched in synch behind Nerea as she led them towards their destination: the stall where Larina got her treats. Kai went over everything he knew in his mind.

"You okay, 'pothy?" Morgan inquired, patting Kai on the shoulder and jolting him from his thoughts. He assured the sellsword he was fine, just thinking about the puzzle.

A shout of triumph from Nerea drew Kai's attention, as she pointed at a brightly colored stall stocked with various candies and pastries. Seeing the cart reminded him of when his Da set up a similar cart at festivals.

Shaking his head, he took a deep breath and pushed the memories from his mind. He needed to focus. No time to reminisce and lose sight of the objective.

Kai strolled up to the stall. A young woman was behind the counter, thin and pale with soft features and piercing blue eyes. She smiled as the party approached.

"Why hello!" she exclaimed, opening her arms. "Welcome to my humble stall. My name's Gema. I don't see any children; are you still interested in my treats? I should warn you, they may be strong for an adult palette."

"I think I'll take my chances," Kai replied to the others' silent shock. "My Da is a known baker in these parts, so if it's stronger than anything he makes, I'll be impressed."

"Oh, we've got a brave one," said the woman. Kai ignored the jab and selected three different pastries before handing Gema a handful of coppers. Securing his prizes, he offered to share his thoughts later before wandering away with his friends in pursuit.

Dazed, Maple asked why he bought the food if he suspected it was dangerous.

"Simple misdirection," Kai answered. "If we asked for answers up front, she'd get defensive and refuse to say anything. It's also possible, though unlikely, she doesn't know or realize her food is causing a problem. Either way, this lets me inspect the materials without arousing suspicion. If there were any chicanery involved and she thought someone suspected her, she'd pack a carriage and bolt quicker than a tree ferret."

Nerea stared at her daughter. "You were right, Ione. He *is* good. Where did you find this boy again?"

Once they were out of sight, seated at a large table near the edge of the festival grounds, Kai laid the pastries out and pried the first one open. A reddish amber jelly pooled from within. Kai dipped a fingertip into the jelly and took a sniff. He frowned at the aromatic scent.

Wiping the jelly onto a spare cloth, Kai broke open the next pastry and found it filled with chunks of what looked like apples slathered in bright red sauce. He sniffed the contents and ran the sauce between his fingers. The scent carried a heavy aroma of apples, but Kai detected a familiar tart sweetness.

A theory began forming in Kai's mind. Opening the final pastry, he was surprised to see it filled with ground meat. Beef, if the smell was any indication. Like the second pastry, it was covered in a dark red, almost purple, sauce with visible pieces of chopped leaves mixed in. Knowing what to expect, Kai performed his test a third time. The same tart smell from before assaulted his senses, and he knew the ramifications.

"Have you figured anything out, or are you going to spend all night sniffing pastries?" Lucretia snapped. The others looked on, worry etched on their faces.

Casting a firm glance at the scholar, Kai released a heavy breath. "No, I think I've figured it out. But the real question is—"

A loud ruckus rising from the festival grounds cut him off, drawing everyone's attention back to the plaza. A crowd of people was gathering near the center, where Josep was surrounded by unruly adults.

"What in the winds is going on now?" Kai muttered, pushing himself up and venturing towards the throng, the party on his heels. Josep looked overwhelmed by the furor, with dozens clamoring for his attention. By the time the party reached the scene, the crowd quieted to a manageable level and Josep asked what was going on.

"Please, Mr. Josep, it's my daughter," an Aerivolk woman cried out. "She's come down with a horrible cough and her face feels like it's aflame! Can you please do something for her?"

Several others broke into shouts, citing similar ailments in their own children. The parents looked ready to riot when Josep held his hands up, calling for silence.

"Please, I understand your plight. I truly do. I've noticed several children the past few days with these symptoms. Don't be alarmed, but I believe we may have an outbreak of hearth lung on our hands. I witnessed a similar epidemic in the west last year, so I know how to treat it."

Everyone broke into worried whispers. Kai heard several asking amongst themselves if anyone had heard of hearth lung. The apothecary's eyes furrowed, and he knew his friends were watching his reactions closely.

A couple hurried to the front of the crowd, the same parents that shook Josep's hand when the party first met him. "Mr. Josep, I'm begging you," the father pleaded, "our son came down with a hellish fever. If you can treat it, we humbly ask for your aid again."

The thin man patted the distressed father on the shoulder, a grim smile lining his face. "I feel for you. If this truly is hearth lung, I do have several bottles of tincture almost ready. However, the ingredients are not only rare and difficult to harvest but must be added at a specific point during preparation, so I will have to charge for this particular medicine."

"Of course, I understand. How much is the treatment?" Kai swiveled his ears forward and listened in, his muscles tensing.

"Considering the work involved to produce the tincture and the rarity of the ingredients, I'm afraid the lowest I can charge per vial is a hundred."

"One hundred marks?" the mother asked, her blonde hair growing frizzled and unruly in her distress.

"One hundred *golds*."

Josep's response sent Kai into a swearing fit. Next to him, he heard his friends choking on their own spit while the crowd erupted into a frenzy. He couldn't blame them. It was an outrageous amount. To his shock, there were several offering to pay the ludicrous price.

"D-did he just say a hundred golds?!" Morgan asked while burying a finger into his ear to clean it out.

"That's trail robbery!" Teos added. The smuggler's face was flush with anger, his fists clenched tight. Lucretia carried a similar furious look.

Ione swayed in place at Kai's side before leaning against him. "Twenty thousand marks a vial? How in Nixtral could anyone afford something so expensive if they're not a noble?"

"That's just it," Kai muttered, "they can't." The Norzen's eyes swung to Nerea. "You said Larina took medicine you received from him last night?"

The grandmother replied, "Aye, he gave us a tonic to fix her aching belly. It seemed to work because she was fine when she woke up."

"Do you still have the bottle it came in?" She nodded, saying it was back at the house. "Good. I need that bottle."

As they prepared to head back to Nerea's house, Kai noticed more than half the group slinking away in tears. Others were asking where the town apothecary, Grasol, was. Kai's eyes narrowed when he heard a voice from the mass reply, "That old buzzard isn't as good as he used to be. He can cut herbs just fine, but his mind's too damn addled from age to mix his tonics! Even if he had the right ingredients, I doubt he could do it properly."

The ones who stayed were pushing and shoving each other in a struggle to be the first to beg for the yellow-clad apothecary's medicine. Around them, the festivities continued without pause, with many people ignoring the sorrowful crowd as if it were another show.

In fact, he even heard a nearby group of men praising Josep's acting ability, one of them muttering, "A hundred golds...what will these bards think of next?" He saw the couple from before clutching each other, the woman wailing into her husband's chest.

A tightness enveloped Kai's heart as he watched the pair. He knew nothing of being a parent, but he knew nobody deserved to be put in such a position. Sweeping his eyes over the masses, he spotted many in similar straights. Some had collapsed to their knees, sobbing uncontrollably.

"I apologize, everyone, but I must be off," Josep exclaimed to the crowd still surrounding him. Kai's ears twitched. "I shall be back soon, but I do need to finish preparing the tincture for those who will be paying. It won't take long, I assure you."

Clapping his hands, Josep bowed and rushed southward, towards the road leading into the forest. Kai cast a final glance around the festival and spotted the woman from the food stall, Gema. She watched Josep's retreat with an indifferent look, her lips set in a thin line. Turning back to Nerea, Kai asked where to find the city headman.

The woman scoffed and grumbled some choice curses about how the headman rarely left his house. "Half of us have wagers on whether he's dead or not. What do you need that fool for?"

"Is there a large enough building to keep the children who have taken ill?" the Norzen inquired.

"I reckon we can use the old warehouse at the riverport's edge. Why?"

"We're going to need it very soon. First, I must inspect the medicine bottle you got from Josep. Please fetch it and bring Larina while we rally the parents."

Without a word, Nerea bustled back towards the house as quickly as her legs allowed. Kai gestured for the party to follow and asked them to goad the parents into gathering their children at the warehouse. No one spoke but followed their orders with curiosity plain in their eyes.

Spinning on his heels, Kai rushed to meet the couple from his earlier interaction with Josep. The pair skittered away when he approached, fear overriding their worry.

"Easy, folks. I swear to Tapimor, I mean you no harm," said Kai, raising his hands in peace. "My name is Kai Travaldi, an apothecary working for Lady Fusette. I saw everything that happened and wanted to offer my own services. Before the Lifeweaver himself, I promise I won't charge for my diagnosis."

"And what of your medicine?" the father spat. "Will you charge a king's ransom for it like the other man?"

The words of the guild's laws came as easily to him as though he read them just that morning. Kai answered, "In accordance with guild bylaws, apothecaries may ask a fair fee for concoctions and in fact are required to do so. However, what Josep demanded is excessive for even the rarest ingredients in my opinion. I will likely need to charge for my concoctions, but I'm willing to swear on my own head it will be affordable. At the moment, my best estimate would be sixty marks a vial if the ingredients are as rare as Josep suggested."

The couple shared a glance before agreeing to Kai's offer. Three silvers a vial sounded much easier to swallow than a hundred golds. A bitter voice in the back of Kai's mind wondered if the reason they were so willing to listen was because he offered his own life as collateral. Ignoring the voice, he instructed them to take their child to the port warehouse as they gathered the ill. The father ran to retrieve their son while the mother waited with Kai. Several others who overheard converged on the Norzen, asking if he would be willing to tend to their children as well.

Kai was happy to see his friends leading small groups of families towards the port. A shout from the opposite way caused him to turn and see Nerea bustling back with a bottle clutched in her hand and a fuming Massio following behind, Larina in his arms.

"Here ya go," Nerea declared, slapping the bottle into the apothecary's outstretched hand. Kai thanked her for the assistance before leading his group to the warehouse. A sudden rush of movement in the corner of his eye pulled Kai's gaze to Gema, who looked to be running away from the furor.

Towards the southern forest.

The warehouse wasn't hard to find. A throng of people rushed for a wide building nestled between the port and the market plaza. Numerous people still attending the festival watched the scene with curiosity. Asking the parents to take their children inside, he rejoined the party where Maple was waving her wings and revealed the bottle.

"Will you be able to tell what he used?" Orelia asked, leaning on her staff.

"There's enough residue remaining for me to determine the type of concoction by sight, smell, and touch alone." Lifting the open bottle to his nose, he took a short sniff, only to reel back in a sneezing fit. The contents gave a harsh, musky scent he hadn't come across in some time. Asking for a lantern, he used a cloth square to dip his finger inside and remove a maroon paste.

Pulling an empty vial from his satchel, Kai poured a dram of water from his canteen into it before adding the paste. Corking it, he shook the vial vigorously for a few moments and held it up to the lantern.

Floating in the translucent pink water were the distinct curls of dried red moss.

Kai's fingers curled around the vial as white-hot rage boiled in his chest. Tossing the vial into his satchel, he spewed every curse he knew in High Norzen.

Lucretia turned a disappointed expression at the apothecary. "You'd best be glad I'm the only one who understands you, Kai, because that was unnaturally vulgar for you. What did you find?"

"If I catch that rat, Josep, I'll crush his head like a melon." The party staggered back at the declaration of violence. "There's no way in Nulyma he didn't know what he was doing."

"What do you mean?" Ione asked, her own face settling into a scowl. "What did that man do to my daughter?"

"His medicine contains witherbell moss. It's a potent herb from the western mountains which saw common use hundreds of years ago due to its pain suppression properties. However, it was outlawed by every apothecary guild on the continent in the year AR 640 because it was found to contain irritants which caused a severe cough in those who imbibed it. Most call it the witherbell whooping cough. The effects are worse in children, often resulting in high fever and a burning in the lungs from the amount of coughing. I reckon that's why Josep told everyone it was hearth lung; the symptoms are similar enough no one outside of an apothecary would know the difference."

By the time Kai finished his explanation, the entire party gaped in horror. "That monster..." whispered Orelia, her eyes pulsing in a storm of rage. "H-he poisoned the children!"

"As good as," said Kai. "It's possible things could be worse, but I want to confirm a theory first. All I know is, if those kids don't receive a proper healing tonic soon, the fever alone will be enough to kill them." Every member of the party paled. Morgan asked if there was a cure.

"We're lucky this idiot used the moss in Grantide. Da brought me here all the time as a sprout, so I know this place like the back of my hand. There's an herb called woderam that grows in the forest south of town. A tonic of woderam, elderberry, and ginger should be enough to diminish the whooping cough."

"Then let's go get it," Orelia declared. "There's not a moment to waste."

Kai warned her that if they all left at once, the crowd could fall into panic. "I'll take three of you to gather the woderam. The rest will stay behind to help the families and keep them calm. Feel free to decide amongst yourselves who goes and who stays."

The party huddled together and whispered. After a short while, it was decided: Maple, Teos, and Orelia would accompany Kai into the forest while Ione, Lucretia, and Morgan stayed and tended to the sick.

Ione pleaded for Kai's group to stay safe, clasping her hands in prayer. Everyone, even Morgan, copied the gesture. Maple hugged the tavern maid close, swearing they would be back soon.

"Come on," said Kai. "I saw Josep and the pastry seller heading for the forest."

"Gema?" Lucretia asked. Her eyes were pinched together in a deep frown. "Why in the winds is she going out there?"

"I don't know, but I suspect she's involved. If they're both venturing into the forest, we may end up having to deal with them."

Teos cast a sly smirk. "And what do you plan on doing if we encounter them?"

"If my suspicions are correct, they're both on borrowed time. Attempted murder of a single child carries an automatic execution order, as you well know. At the very least, I've got Josep red-handed on using illegal medicine to poison *dozens* of children with intent to allow those not willing or able to meet his demands to die. The fact that he's an apothecary makes his crimes worse, as he both knows the law and is willingly breaking it for self-enrichment."

Morgan winced. "Put like that, it's no surprise you wanna kill the bastard."

Rather than respond, Kai settled for a single nod and told his group to travel light. "We won't have to go very deep into the woods, so we'll go on foot. Make sure you're ready for a fight. There's no telling what awaits us in there."

A loud, screeching voice rang out from the port. "What in the winds is all this?" The party turned to see Lord Kendela marching towards them, a full retinue of guards and attendants following in his wake. The Margrave's resplendent river cruiser, bedecked in gold plating with numerous jewels lining the trim, sat docked several piers away from the *Senberg*.

It took all of Kai's restraint to not groan aloud. Dealing with Kendela was the last thing he needed. Without a doubt, the apothecary knew he'd need to lean on his Exarch status to stop the pompous Aerivolk from interfering. He spotted Maple concealing herself behind Teos' towering body.

"Gravebane!" Kendela shouted. "Why in Ausrina's holy name are you gathering so many of *my* commoners in the port warehouse? Men, remove them and send them home." Several guards moved to storm the warehouse but stopped short when Kai planted himself in front of the door. His eyes simmered in fury as he retrieved his watch from its resting place.

"Lord Kendela, unless you want me to charge you with impeding an official Exarch investigation, you and your men will back off. I'm afraid we have a potentially fatal epidemic afflicting the children of Grantide. There are enough ill that the warehouse is the only building large enough to contain them all."

"Balderdash!" the noble retorted. "I am the Margrave of this province, and I say they're gone. Now get of our way!"

Before Kai could respond, Morgan shoved his way forward and bodily threw the guards backwards, tumbling them over. Now free to address the noble, Kai pinned Kendela in place with an icy glare.

"I'm warning you," he hissed. "If even one child in this town dies due to you preventing me from harvesting the herbs needed to save them, I shall hold you responsible. Which means I'll take your *head* as restitution for the victim's family. Do not press me on this. You know the law, and not even Lady Fusette is immune."

Stumbling back, Kendela looked at Kai with unrestrained fear. It was clear the noble was unused to being reprimanded or threatened, but the law was clear, and Kai was more than willing to take advantage if it kept the snob out of his way.

He refused to allow any of these children to die because of Kendela's overbearing pride.

Allowing a small smirk to cross his lips, Kai warned the team staying behind to keep watch and prevent Kendela pushing anyone around. "Remember," he added, "you're all sworn officers of the court. Do whatever it takes to protect these people from anyone who would harm them." Turning to his group, Kai gestured for them to follow.

"Where are you taking my fiancée, Gravebane?" Kendela demanded, pointing a long, ring-adorned finger at Maple. Kai was impressed at how fast she turned on him, eyes burning in rage.

"I never agreed to marry you, you arrogant ass!" Maple snapped. Lucretia couldn't hold back her snicker at the perturbed look on Kendela's face. "Furthermore, I will never marry you, and that's a promise I'll stand by till the end of my days."

"You're making a mistake, girl," the noble replied. "I can take this all the way up to Parliament if you'd prefer. You can fight it all you want, but it won't end well for y—"

In a flash of silver, Kai's mace was so close to Kendela's eye the party was stunned by the distinct lack of blood spraying from the man's head.

"Finish that sentence. I dare you," Kai snarled. His voice was hitched but firm, every word spoken in a steady tone that left no argument as to the rage roiling beneath the Norzen's volcanic stare. "If you ever threaten any member of my party again, you won't get a second warning. I will return to Whistlevale and declare Blood Feud."

Lucretia choked, hands flying to her throat as Ione thumped the scholar's back. Orelia and Maple both stared at Kai in silence, their cheeks crimson.

Staggering back, Kendela gave a heaving gasp with his guards keeping him from toppling over. He jabbed a finger towards Kai. "You have the gall to threaten me with Blood Feud?! You mistake your place, peltneck!"

Kai shrugged. "At this point, I don't care what you call me. I've been insulted by better men than you. But listen closely. Don't ever gamble on threatening someone precious to me unless you're ready to wager with your *life*."

Whispering to the recovering Lucretia, Morgan asked what was going on.

She regarded him with confusion before realization flashed through her eyes. "Right, Corlati does not use the concept of Blood Feuds. It is essentially a declaration of war between families. This is a big deal in Livoria and Galstein because pushing someone to make a vow that serious means you have insulted the declaring family so deeply they are willing to slaughter you for it. Blood Feuds must be declared before Parliament and are only considered over once one side's entire family is destroyed to the roots. All of the losing family's property and holdings go to the victor. It is a brutal method of settling differences, but Parliament is very selective about allowing them. Otherwise, we would have wiped ourselves out years ago."

Teos stroked his beard. "Wait. If Parliament has to approve them, would they even allow Kai to declare one? I doubt they're fond of Norzen."

"From what I learned in Whistlevale," Lucretia continued, "Kai's status as Exarch trumps his tribe in regards to Parliament affairs. Then you must consider that, among the Exarchs rotating in and out of the capital while we were there, many have told me Kai is their least aggressive member. For someone to infuriate him to the point of Blood Feud would cause such a shock, I would not be surprised if Parliament approved it just to protect themselves from his retribution."

Ignoring Kendela's enraged blabbering, Kai slid his mace back into its loop and met Maple and Orelia's eyes. His gaze softened seeing their red cheeks and he gave them a calming smile, which they returned. Releasing a sigh, he ordered his team to follow as he began trekking towards the southern gate. Maple and Orelia fell into step on either side of him, with Teos following along. The two women grinned and bumped their fists together behind Kai's back, sending a ripple of confusion through him.

The apothecary muttered a silent apology to the Wind Saints. He knew, in the depths of his mind, a part of him hoped they encountered Josep and Gema, if only to vent his frustrations with Kendela. He allowed the noble to get under his skin, and he overextended. He hoped his actions wouldn't cause trouble later on.

If luck were on his side, the forests would calm him. Until then, he needed to focus on finding the woderam. He prayed the cave where it grew was undisturbed.

Chapter IX

Ione knew she was at her best when her mind was occupied. Wringing water from another band of cloth, she passed it to a waiting mother who pressed the rag against her child's forehead. She did her best to ignore her father leaning against the far wall, glaring at her with an unapologetic scowl.

"It still baffles me as to why an apothecary would attempt to harm so many innocent people," Lucretia muttered as she sat beside the tavern maid, a dripping cloth in her own hands.

"I don't know," Ione answered, "but I'm rather confident in saying Josep won't be returning alive." Her eyes flickered to Morgan, standing guard at the door with his sword ready, on the chance Kendela decided to test Kai's warning.

"You truly believe Kai would kill him without sending him before a magistrate?"

"You saw the look of fury in his eyes, Lucretia. I know the law says we're supposed to send all accused before a magistrate, but I'll tell you here and now I wouldn't bat an eyelash if that man died resisting capture."

The silence following Ione's statement sent a chill through the woman's body. She turned to see her friend staring with unabashed shock. "By the winds, I do not believe I could ever imagine you saying such a thing, Ione."

Turning to face the crowd of families skittering through the warehouse, Ione spotted her mother tending to Larina nearby. She took a deep breath and pointed at the pair. "Were I younger, I'd be just as shocked as you. However, I have a reason for thinking this way. I know my parents are here, but Larina is all I have left of my husband and the family we built together.

It took me five years to reach a point where I wasn't trying to drown myself in ale every night, and another two before this war gave me an excuse to leave Mistport.

"I thank the winds every night for bringing you, Kai, and everyone else into my life. I wouldn't be here if not for you. And now that I've gotten to see my little girl for the first time in years, some bastard is threatening to take her from me again. I won't apologize for wanting to see him brought to justice any way possible."

"I cannot say I know exactly what you are going through, since I do not have a child," said Lucretia, "but I believe, were I in your position, my thoughts would be much the same. All I have to do is imagine how I would feel if someone did such a thing to my younger brother. You actually remind me a lot of Evodio; you both have kind hearts but are not afraid to step in to protect others. Josep has committed an atrocious act and, one way or another, I know Kai will see him answer for it."

The two women shared a smile and continued with their work as several other parents offered to set up buckets of their own to help.

In the darkness of the forest outside Grantide, Kai and his team opted for a small lantern to light their way. They knew Josep and Gema were hidden somewhere in the area and wanted to avoid alerting them to their presence.

Very little moonlight penetrated the tops of the numerous beech and walnut trees filling the forest. More than once, Kai heard the crunch of fallen walnuts under his boots. The usual cacophony of the forest resounded around them, from the chirps of crickets to a lone owl hooting somewhere to the west. The grass shifted as a tiny snake slithered away.

"Kai, you really upended a hornet's nest, you know that, right?" Orelia asked as they weaved through the trees.

The apothecary bit down the urge to scoff. He'd heard numerous warnings on the dangers of upsetting nobles, but he preferred to face that battle with his head held high, rather than abdicating his convictions. "I'm aware, but as much as I wish I kept my temper under control, I stand by what I said. I won't let Kendela harm any of you."

He felt a soft touch as Maple ran the tips of her feathers over his back. A moment later, there was the cool sensation of Orelia's fingers stroking his arm. The brief contact sent a shock through his body. He was grateful the two women were behind him, and thus unable to see his reddening cheeks.

"I think it was rather sweet," the merchant admitted. "That bastard is obviously used to getting what he wants and having people fall over themselves to appease him. Even a blind man can see he can't handle someone telling him to pound cobbles."

"Kai, would you really declare Blood Feud against him? It seems like a drastic way to handle things," Teos asked.

"Before Fusette brought us all back to Whistlevale, I would agree with you." Kai's body shuddered as memories of his time in the capital returned. "But that crazy woman forced me to take lessons with Saredi on standing up for myself and finding my pride as a Norzen. I respect the man and everything he's done for us, but Tapimor's hairy ass is he a brutal taskmaster."

"What did he do?"

"If I told you, you'd have nightmares." The others shared a concerned look. "Regardless, he did knock some sense into me I sorely needed in my life. Not only would I declare Blood Feud against Kendela if he hurt any of you, but I'd drag his feathered carcass into the Coliseum and settle it before the whole capital."

"Well let's avoid that," said Maple, hooking her arm around Kai's elbow and pulling herself close. "The less we have to worry about you, the better. And I have no intention of being Kendela's toy. Now where's this cave?"

Coming to a stop, Kai spun in place while holding the lantern higher. His eyes focused on the spaces between the trees. Finally, he gave a pleased hum and strolled towards a moss-covered rock with several holes scattered across its face. His eyes flickered upwards, spotting the moons through openings in the canopy.

With one last sweep of the area, Kai turned and pointed to a path on the left. "This way. We're very close."

"Hey Kai," Teos spoke up. The apothecary turned his head and saw his friend glancing about in fear. "Am I imagining things, or did it get quiet all of a sudden?"

Frowning, Kai swiveled his ears and listened. He swore under his breath when he realized Teos was right. All the sounds from before were gone. The forest had gone silent as a grave except for the whistle of the wind. It reminded him of both the day he first saw Grimghast and his Trial.

"You're not imagining it, Teos, and it's not good. There's danger here."

He felt a tug on his other arm when Orelia grabbed him by the elbow. "Is it Grimghast?" she asked, her bronze skin paling to a sickly shade.

Kai fought back a wince as the priestess' fingers dug into his skin. "Let's pray it's not. But whatever it is, I doubt it's friendly."

A soft sound prickled Kai's ears, causing them to twist in the direction of the path. "Wait, I do hear something." Focusing, he recognized the sounds. "Someone's talking in that direction. Two people, from the sound of it. It could be our errant suspects. Stay alert."

The others readied themselves as they pressed forward. Approaching the cave, Kai felt a sinking feeling in the pit of his stomach. It seemed like Josep located the woderam, though Kai wasn't certain whether he was using it for his overpriced tonics. Either way, it looked as though they couldn't harvest the herb without confrontation.

The muttering of their quarry became clearer as the quartet approached. Kai's eyebrows pinched together when he recognized the other apothecary's voice.

"I think this may be our best haul yet, Gema," said Josep.

Holding a finger to his lips, Kai gestured for the others to follow him behind a large boulder. Peering around it, he spotted the pair sitting on a log near the cave entrance, a wide opening into a rocky outcropping jutting from the ground. Kai remembered the cave being a known bear den in his youth, at least until the bears were forced to seek shelter elsewhere. A thicket of interconnected trees loomed over the far side of the cave, looking like a massive, woody net. There was an odd sound coming from inside, like heavy breathing, though Kai didn't recognize it.

Somehow, he doubted the bears had returned.

"I tell ya, these fools get stupider with every town we go to," Gema replied, a wide grin stretched across her face. A soft rumble echoed from Kai's chest when he saw her smile. It reminded him too much of Kendela's cocky smirk.

"You hear that?" the woman asked. Kai's breath hitched, wondering if they heard him. "Didn't you feed that thing before we went into town?"

Quirking an eyebrow, Kai felt a wave of confusion. What were they feeding, and why was Gema so concerned about it?

"For the last time, dear sister, yes I fed it. Poor fella is probably snoring." The party's eyes bulged hearing Josep reveal his relation to the pastry seller. Kai, realizing what the pair's connection meant, couldn't hold back his own grin.

There's our missing piece.

"How will we get inside?" Orelia whispered. "They're both right by the entrance."

"I doubt we can sneak in together. But what we can do is distract them so one of us can slip past and get the herb."

"Oh, and who will be going inside? You?" Teos asked.

"I was hoping Maple could do it."

The merchant looked askance at Kai. "Are you trying to keep me out of a fight, Kai Travaldi?" she asked in an unamused tone.

Beads of sweat trickled down the apothecary's neck and pricked his mane. Even the most brainless of idiots would recognize that tone of voice coming from a lady. "The thought never crossed my mind. My line of thinking was that, since you're the smallest among us, you'd be the hardest to spot."

Turning his head just enough, he noticed she was giving him a flat stare. "Damn it all, I can't be mad at you when you make sense."

"When does he not make sense?" Orelia asked.

"When he tests strange medicine on himself."

"Fair point."

Kai winced when he heard Josep jump to his feet. "We were followed," the man snapped. "Who's there?!" Jerking his head in the opposite direction, Kai nodded for Maple to ready herself. He inhaled deeply before stepping into the open with Orelia and Teos close behind, their weapons at the ready.

"Well what do we have here, Gema? It's the Norzen apothecary I met on the grounds, and he's brought some friends too," Josep pronounced. Holding his arms wide open, the man asked Kai if he was out doing some late harvesting.

"Cut the *bulskein*, Josep. We both know why I'm here. You're a disgrace to our trade and will answer for it."

Releasing a sigh, Josep turned on Kai with a malicious smile. "What a pity. I was hoping we could come to an understanding, but it seems as though you already have your mind made up."

"Unlike you, I take my oath seriously. What possessed you to do this to *children*?"

"You can't possibly be this blind. Money, you damned fool, and lots of it! You probably don't understand, but parents are the most desperate pack of idiots ever. So many are willing to throw obscene amounts of money at any problem threatening their bundles of joy."

"So you decided to poison them?"

"It's much more intricate than that, my friend. If you want to build the right mindset to part a fool from their money, you need a proper foundation."

His eyes shifting to Gema, Kai clenched a fist. "And that's where your sister comes into play. She did the initial poisoning, allowing you to swoop in and put on your gracious savior act."

His companions spun towards Kai with shouts of surprise. "Wait, she poisoned the children too?" Teos demanded. "What exactly did she do?"

"The pastries. Each one had a red sauce inside with a distinct sour scent. Rhubarb. The stalks themselves are harmless and common enough in jellies and pies. She took it a step further and mixed chopped or powdered rhubarb leaves into the food. The leaves contain a toxin which induces stomach cramps and vomiting."

Orelia's face turned ashen. "Then the medicine Josep provided—"

Kai gave a single nod. "Was meant to cure the stomach pains caused by the rhubarb poisoning while also infecting the children with witherbell whooping cough, a rarer condition more difficult to treat."

The siblings began cackling. "Well I'll be damned, you figured out the entire thing!" Josep admitted. "Impressive."

Now it was Kai's turn to smirk. From the corner of his eye, he spotted Maple creeping towards the cave. With the siblings focused on him, they had no idea she was there. "You two underestimate me at your own risk. My specialty is in the study of poisons and toxins. If you surrender now, you might be able to reach a magistrate and plead your case."

The siblings cackled, sending a twinge of worry through Kai's gut. Neither of them looked built for fighting, so their confidence was unsettling.

"If you think we'll give up so easy, then you're stupid even for a peltneck. I already know death awaits us if we're brought before a magistrate," Josep answered. Raising two fingers to his mouth, the man blew a shrill whistle that left Kai flinching. His gaze flickered to Maple, who stared back in confusion.

A loud thump echoed from the cave. Kai's tails coiled around each other, deepening the unease in his gut. Orelia trembled next to him with Teos standing protectively in front of the group.

From the shadows of the cave, a huge shape emerged. Whatever it was, it towered over the group. Kai's blood ran cold, his skin clammy. The figure was much too large to be a bear, but too broad to be Grimghast, which the Norzen decided was a small favor. He was not prepared to face the beast again after their last encounter with it.

"It's amazing, isn't it?" Josep questioned. The ground rumbled and trees quivered under the thunderous boom of the figure's steps. "Most people see animals as mindless beasts good for nothing except food and parts. In most cases, they'd be right. Then again, there are some creatures that have evolved into something...more."

Drawing his mace, Kai slid into a stance. A curse flew from his lips when the creature's massive head passed the cave opening and it stepped into the light of the surrounding torches.

The beast was a colossal deer with a thick mane reminiscent of a lion covering its chest and shoulders. Kai estimated it at four yards tall at the shoulder and five yards from snout to tail. Its legs were thick with muscle, ending in wide hooves ringed with short, curved spines. The shoulders were broad and powerful, and a pair of stately six-point antlers stood atop its head.

Orelia almost collapsed, Teos' arms being the only thing keeping her standing. "Kai," she whispered.

"Yes, Orelia?"

"What is that thing?"

The trio turned to Josep, who broke out into hysterical laughter. "You must not be from Livoria, my dear, if you can't recognize this majestic creature."

Seeing the priestess' eyes on him, Kai nodded. "It's a bulwark deer, one of the six Great Beasts, and the sole member native to Livoria, though this one seems a bit too far east for its normal range. They normally inhabit the hills and highlands to the west. The Great Beasts are unnaturally intelligent compared to other animals, enough that it's been theorized they can understand human concepts."

"Oh, he understands so much more than you think," said Gema. "It turns out they're smart enough to understand the concept of payment. If we provide it with foods it finds pleasing, the deer guards this cave for us and keeps nosy fools like you out."

Kai gave a grim chuckle, regarding the siblings with exasperation. "You can't possibly think you can control something so dangerous completely. Domesticating a bulwark deer is impossible!"

"You think so?" Josep asked. "Then let's test your theory." Turning to the deer, the other apothecary snapped his fingers. Its head twisted towards Kai's group, both large eyes locking on them before releasing a deafening bleat and charging.

Kai felt the strange sensation of wind blowing through his mane before his back struck the ground hard. Clambering to his feet, he realized that Teos had thrown Orelia and him aside before twirling his halberd, using it to parry the deer's antlers. One look at the cave entrance and he saw Maple ready to jump in to help. Meeting her gaze, Kai shook his head and gestured for her to continue into the cave.

He whispered for Orelia to swing around and keep the siblings occupied.

A pained shout drew their attention to Teos, sent flying when the deer lashed out with its hind legs and caught him in the chest. Slamming into a tree, he flopped motionless to the ground as the beast charged again with a grunt, its head bowed.

"Teos!" Orelia cried out. Josep and Gema cackled in glee, shouting for the deer to skewer the prone Soltauri.

Kai swore under his breath and took off towards Teos in a full sprint. His mind raced, hoping to get him out the way before the deer could gore him. He quickly realized he wouldn't make it in time. Teos would die unless he did something crazy.

Hearing the sibling's raucous laughter in his ears formed a pit of rage in his chest. They were clamoring for the smuggler's death, Gema shrieking for the deer to pierce his heart. The apothecary begged the Saints for the strength he needed.

An audible snap erupted in Kai's mind as the scarlet fog of the Frenzy Haze flooded him like a wave. The last time the Haze overcame him was when Grimghast was moments from devouring Maple. Like before, his body trembled with power. His first few experiences with the Haze left an odd, uneven feeling in his skin, but now he sensed a breadth of control not there before.

His heart hammered in his ears, both eyes focusing on Teos' body. The tension in his legs grew, as if all his muscles were pulled taught. Breathing deep, Kai pushed off the ground as hard as he could, and everything became a blur.

He covered the distance between him and Teos in the blink of an eye, causing a momentary instance of tunnel vision. Disconcerted by his speed, Kai couldn't stop in time to avoid colliding with the tree. To his surprise, he felt no pain in bouncing off the trunk. Teos looked up at Kai in befuddlement, holding back a pained groan long enough to ask where he came from. Instead of answering, Kai grabbed him by the tunic, hauling him up.

The bulwark deer bore down on them, its yellow eyes pinched together. Kai's tails lashed about. Without thinking, he dove aside, dragging Teos along as the deer hit the trunk head-first. The blow split the tree like a dry twig across the base, knocking it down with a vociferous crash.

Scrambling to their feet, the two men shared a hesitant look, then eyed the downed tree. The deer snorted, shaking its head around to find them. "I'm pretty sure we're dead if we get hit head-on," Teos muttered.

Noticing the lack of weight in his left hand, Kai spun around, spotting his mace lying near the boulder where he started.

Blast, he thought, *I must've dropped it when I took off.*

Grabbing Teos by the shoulder, Kai pushed him in the direction of the siblings. "Help Orelia. I'm confident you two can take those idiots together."

"What about you? You can't possibly fight a bulwark deer alone."

Clenching his fist, Kai flexed the forearm inward. The muscle felt heavier than normal, but the movement was smoother. "I think I'm in some strange kind of Frenzy Haze. I have more control over it than before."

Am I in control because of my desperation?

Blinking, Teos asked how that was possible.

"I'm not certain," Kai replied, "but whatever it is, I'll make use of it while I can. There's no guarantee it'll last. Now go!"

With a forlorn scowl, Teos barreled towards the siblings. Josep shouted for the deer to attack as Orelia and Teos advanced with weapons raised. The beast bellowed in defiance, cantering in a wide arc.

Kai's eyes swept the forest floor, spotting a large rock. Thinking back to their battle against Grimghast on the *Gulley*, he hoisted it, testing the stone's weight by lifting it up and down. He curled his arm around it and spun his whole body. After building up speed, he hurled the rock like a discus, striking the deer on the rear flank with a thud. It screamed in pain, its body tumbling to the ground.

He couldn't hold back a grin when Josep stumbled backwards trying to avoid Teos' halberd. Blood sprayed from Gema's mouth after taking a hit to the jaw from Orelia's cudgel, which knocked the woman off her feet. The siblings were doing a poor job of evading their pursuers and their lack of fighting ability was blatant; neither could mount any kind of defense.

The deer eased itself up, whirling to meet Kai's stare. "Your fight's with me, you overgrown rug!" the apothecary roared, bending at the knees and spreading his arms in a clear challenge. Growling, the deer stomped its hooves and reared up with a bellow before charging again.

Orelia shouted for Kai to move, but her voice seemed like a faint buzzing in his ears, so intent was he on the charging beast. Muscles ready, he waited. The bulwark deer thundered along, its head lowering.

Josep's voice broke through his concentration, "Get back here and kill these two first, you stupid animal! Protect us!" The deer ignored the order, its eyes set on Kai blazing with fury.

Power surged through Kai's body, the thought of his friends being trampled beneath the beast's hooves hardening his resolve. The Norzen snarled, reaching out as the deer bared down on him. To everyone's shock, Kai grabbed both antlers while digging his feet in. His stance held firm, bringing the deer to a sudden and complete stop. The massive animal stalled from the unexpected resistance and slipped, crumpling to its knees. Teos spat a curse when Kai twisted his hips, dragging the bulwark deer across the ground by its head and flinging it aside.

"That's not possible!" Josep shrieked, frozen with his mouth gaping. "There's no way a peltneck is that strong!"

"I think he just proved you wrong," Teos quipped.

The deer staggered to its feet, lowing at Kai but refusing to attempt another attack and backing away. Kai chuffed and turned around, marching towards the others.

"Great merciful Galen," Orelia breathed. "If I didn't know any better, I'd say the beast is *afraid* of him."

"Can you blame it?" responded Teos. "He just tossed it around like it was made of straw."

Each step Kai took felt like his foot was made of lead. The Haze ebbed away, leaving his muscles sore and throbbing. His face settled into a thin line, refusing to show how much pain he was in.

A loud snort sounded from the deer, which paced and thrashed about. Throwing a backwards kick against a tree, it gave another bellow and charged.

Kai bit back a groan when he heard the thundering of its hooves again. Reaching into his pocket, he pulled a vial with a light blue concoction within. An energy tonic.

"I'm *so* gonna regret this later," he grumbled, downing the mixture with a grimace. He saw looks of triumph on his friends faces and fought to hold his composure. If they knew how much pain lanced through him at that moment, they wouldn't look so confident. Closing his eyes, Kai swiveled his ears and allowed his tails to sway behind him. The beat of its steps thrummed in his head, gaining volume with every second.

"Kai, what are you doing?" Teos screamed. "Move!" He and Orelia fell back to the cave entrance where Maple was emerging with Kai's satchel in hand, filled to the brim with bundles of plants bearing bright magenta flowers. Woderam.

Bending his knees, Kai threw himself aside in a roll, tucking himself into a ball. The deer blew past him like a powerful wind, his robes fluttering.

Josep brayed with glee. He turned to Teos, swearing that his pet would smash Kai into a pulp. Spotting Maple, the yellow-clad apothecary sputtered in confusion. Teos smirked and jerked a thumb towards the deer, which hadn't stopped its advance.

"Wait, wha—" Gema began, only to be cut off when the deer slammed into them. The antlers pierced the siblings' bodies like spears, spraying blood across the ground as it carried them forward before crashing into thicket of trees next to the cave. Josep and Gema cried out in pain, struggling to free themselves to no avail. With its antlers stuck in the mire of branches, the beast thrashed about in a desperate attempt to free itself, sending spatters of blood and flesh everywhere.

Slowly rising, Kai ambled back to the boulder and retrieved his mace, regarding the weapon with stoic respect. His gaze flashed to the deer, gripping the weapon's shaft.

"And we find ourselves here once again, old friend," he murmured. The deer's predicament reminded him of his Trial, six years ago.

Maple led the others to Kai's side, her eyes blazing. "Kai," she hissed. "What in the winds happened? Teos said you fell into some kind of coherent Frenzy Haze."

"It's true. I think I'm starting to understand how these Hazes work, but only a full investigation can confirm my theory. Damned if my body doesn't hurt, though."

"I can imagine," Orelia piped up from beside Maple. "You look like death warmed over. But what do we do about the deer?"

Everyone's eyes swung to the exhausted beast, now laying at an awkward angle and still trapped in the branches. Josep and Gema were both dead, staring blankly into the abyss while impaled on the deer's antlers.

"We can't leave it here," Kai answered. "It's too dangerous for a Great Beast to be so close to town."

"How do we get rid of it?" Teos asked. The smuggler met Kai's glance, frowning when the apothecary began walking towards the prone animal.

"Kai?"

"This should never have happened. Those two brought this creature to a place it wasn't meant to be and took advantage. As a Hunter, I must end this to ensure it can't endanger anyone else."

The others remained quiet, bowing their heads as Kai stumbled forward. Hunter and beast stared at each other. Emitting a weak bleat, the deer gave a final, futile pull.

Thoughts of his Trial flashing through his mind, Kai raised his mace overhead. He muttered a short prayer to Tapimor, asking the Saint to provide solace to the fallen beast on its journey to Finyt. With a pained shout, Kai brought the mace down between the deer's eyes, the flanges crushing its skull in a burst of blood and bone. The Great Beast gave one last shudder before stilling.

Kai said nothing, simply gazing at his dead opponent. He raised two fingers and tapped his neck, nodding in respect. He jumped a bit when he felt Maple's wings encircle his waist and her chin dig into the middle of his back.

"You're going to make me worry myself to death."

Chuckling, Kai turned and returned the merchant's embrace as Teos and Orelia joined them. "I apologize. I never meant to make any of you worry. Is there anything I can do to make it up to you?"

Maple shared a quick look with Orelia, the Aerivolk's face stretching into a grin.

"Well, there is one thing, but I'll ask later. Consider it a favor I can trade in. Now then, we got what we came for. Let's go back. The children need us."

Chapter X

Upon their return to Grantide, the quartet met with worried glances and questions on whether the children would be okay. Kendela was nowhere to be found, a fact Kai was grateful for. The margrave was the last person he wished to see.

Ignoring the prickling stings wracking his body, Kai appropriated a spare table and spread his equipment across it. He commanded the party to bring five cauldrons of water to a boil and provided a list of additional herbs to acquire, including a large bundle of tea leaves. When asked why he needed so much tea, he explained it was to dilute the concoction's pungency, as woderam had an overpowering scent when boiled. The others split off into teams of two to carry out their orders.

While waiting for the water, Kai began preparing the woderam. He separated the flowers and buds from their stems and set them in a separate bowl. Then he did the same for the roots, grinding them into a fine powder in the mortar. His arms twitched with every motion, but he took steady breaths to focus on his work rather than the pain. He knew once the energy tonic ran its course, he would collapse wherever he sat.

Next, he chopped the stems and leaves into a shredded mass. Kai heard Lucretia state the cauldrons were almost ready. Morgan and Ione brought the requested herbs, placing them on the table while Orelia and Maple set up a line of bowls. To his pleasant surprise, everything was already prepared, sliced to perfection.

"How did...?"

"Been a while since I've seen you, ya furry sprout," a gravelly voice came from nearby. Kai swerved to see a grizzled Aerivolk man with dark brown wings walking towards him, leaning against a gnarled cane and wearing grey apothecary robes.

"Well I'll be damned. Grasol! I thought I heard you were still running the dispensary. Didn't the guild tell you to retire years ago?"

"Bah! You know me, boy. The day I listen to those stuffy fudders is the day you have to put me in the ground. One of my neighbors came and told me what happened with that brat who was supposed to be helping out."

"If you haven't died yet, you old buzzard, you'll probably outlive me." The party watched the two banter in confusion.

Shutting the journal in her hand and tucking it away, Lucretia cast an amused look at Kai. "I assume you know this man?"

The aged Aerivolk broke out into a hacking laugh. "Know me? I taught this sprout most everything he needed to know about being an apothecary. Helped him get his apprenticeship too once he learned to tell a tea leaf from an acorn."

"I wasn't quite that bad. Still, it's good to see you, Grasol. I assume I have you to thank for the diced herbs. It looks like your handiwork."

The old man nodded, offering his help in preparing the remedy. Kai accepted, directing Grasol to add the herbs to the cauldron. The party watched as the older apothecary used cheesecloth to wrap the herbs before steeping them in the cauldrons.

"So how did you two meet?" Ione asked, carrying a basket of ginger to the table.

Kai gave a nervous laugh. "I'd already known Grasol for years. My Da used to bring me up here from Havenfall once a moon on delivery runs and whenever he wanted to sell his baked goods at festivals like this one. Once I passed my Trial and decided to take up apothecary training, Grasol was the one to teach me the basics while I sought out a master to apprentice under."

"Why could you not apprentice under Grasol, then?" Lucretia asked, her eyes flickering between the two men. "I apologize if my question is too personal."

Grasol broke out into a wheezy laugh. "Nah, you're fine, lass. The truth is, I'm forbidden from receiving a mastery certification. The guildmaster and I got into a hell of a tiff years ago and he banned me from ever taking on an official apprentice. Still, I've been in this business long enough to know a lot of folks. Even if I couldn't be the brat's master, I introduced him to a friend of mine from Everstill named Gerardo Fallone. He was one of the few masters willing to take the kid on. Most are under the guildmaster's thumb and refused to teach a Norzen. The guildmaster said if he wanted to join the trade, he should apprentice under one of his own kind. Gerardo didn't care a whit about that; to him, the only thing what matters is whether you're willing to learn."

As they talked, the group worked together, adding herbs and stirring until an aromatic fragrance rose from the fumes. Removing the cheesecloth, the leftover herbs were discarded while leaving the finished concoction. Everyone organized the parents in lines and assisted with doling out bowls of the remedy. They settled into a smooth pattern and ensured at least one bowl was provided for each child.

"We still have so much left," Lucretia commented, peering into the cauldrons after they were done. Of the five pots they started with, two were still filled to the brim and a third was just over half full. "What shall we do with the remainder?"

"We'll keep it on hand to provide additional treatments to those who need it. That's why I made extra. Better to have too much than too little. Anything left over, we can bottle up some for our own use and leave the rest for the townsfolk. Woderam is good for most types of breathing afflictions."

Ione bustled over with a light sheen of sweat covering her face, having come from the warehouse. "All the children are sleeping. The good news is most of them have stopped coughing."

"Good, that means the woderam is working. It should repair the damage to their lungs caused by the witherbell. Thankfully, the moss's irritants are susceptible to heat, so warm tea will make the herbs' job easier."

The tavern maid emitted a soft sniffle before throwing her arms around Kai. "You have no idea how grateful I am for this, Kai. And I'm sure many of the other parents feel the same. If you hadn't been here, there's no telling what may have happened."

Patting the woman's arm, Kai reminded her that he was happy to help and grateful to hear the children were already doing so much better.

The sound of a throat clearing drew the group's attention to the couple from before. They gazed at Kai with worry, the mother clutching her apron. The father's eyes were full of confusion, sweeping over the party.

"I apologize for coming when you likely have other pressing issues, but I had a question," the father said. Kai motioned for him to continue. "I know you said you would charge a fair price for this concoction, but why would you provide treatment before anyone has paid?"

The others frowned at Kai. "What's this man talking about, Kai?" Ione asked. "You can't possibly be thinking of charging the people of this town for our help?"

"The guild requires all member apothecaries to charge what they believe a fair fee for any treatment rendered," Kai explained. "This is so they can deduct the appropriate taxes when the apothecary files their expense reports. I typically send my expenses back to guild headquarters in Whistlevale as a bundle every moon. However, they never put an exact price on any specific concoction because each apothecary prepares their medicine differently. The system gives us leeway to set whatever prices we wish, something Josep took advantage of." Turning to the couple, he flashed a toothy smile. "But you are correct in saying I haven't mentioned a final price yet. Please gather the parents and I promise to explain."

The two shared a pinched stare before going to do as asked. Soon, a wave of people emerged from the warehouse and encircled the party. The couple came forward and promised everyone was there.

"Many thanks. You have my gratitude." Casting a sweeping glance at the crowd, Kai raised his hands. "Everyone! I hear your children are all doing better, which is wonderful news. Should the medicine work as intended, I expect to see most, if not all, of them to be back to normal within a day or two. Now, I'm sure you may have heard that I'm required to charge a dispensary fee, per the guild's bylaws."

The tension in the air thickened to the point Kai could feel it in his tails. "Please, do not worry! I already swore to several of you I would be fair. I never renege on a promise if I can help it. To this effect, I'm offering a singular charge to each family, regardless of the number of children. Whether you have one child or ten, every family will pay the same amount: One single coin."

"One gold?" a man from somewhere in the crowd asked. "That sounds much more reasonable." Titters of agreement echoed from all around, with several couples releasing sighs of relief. The couple who spoke with him earlier looked on in worry, knowing his earlier estimate had been three silvers.

Kai broke into raucous laughter, drawing the crowd's eyes back to him. "No, no, I think you misunderstand, sir. When I say one coin, what I meant was...you'll only pay a single copper mark. No more, no less."

The crowd burst into confused babbling. More than one asked if Kai was playing a trick on them. The party gaped as if he had lost his kettle.

"Calm yourselves, everyone!" To Kai's relief, they were quick to quiet down. The noise was brutal on his ears. "I find what Josep did to be a disgrace to our trade and he has already been appropriately dealt with, along with his accomplice. As apothecaries, our duty is to provide succor to all, not unlike the clerics serving the Windbringer church. I know many of you look at me and see the tails and ears of a Norzen, but know this: To me, tribes mean nothing.

"Yes, many times we are defined by our differences, but we still have much in common. We share the same air, the same rivers, the same ground upon which we walk. At the end of the day, we all bleed red. It matters not a whit whether you are noble or commoner, human or faumen; we are all children of nature. For that reason, it has never been my intention to make my services unreachable for anyone."

A young woman stepped forward, her eyes brimming with tears. She inquired why he would offer them so much relief for so little. "Who are you?" she asked.

Tilting his head back to stare at the moons, he pondered the question. It was one he often asked himself. "I suppose you could say I'm many people in one body. An apothecary. A Hunter. An Exarch. But those are just titles and jobs. I like to think I'm also someone's friend. A protector. A teacher. A student. When I think about it, I realize I'm all of these. But I'm also just one man. A man who wishes for our little corner of Nixtral to be a better place for everyone in it. Does that make sense?"

The crowd mumbled amongst themselves once Kai went silent. Maple sidled next to the apothecary and gave him a sideways smirk. "One copper, eh? You know, any merchant with an eye for gold would be shrieking for all that wasted profit."

"It's a fair point. Are you saying I did the wrong thing? I noticed you all looking at me as though I were mad."

She scoffed. "Absolutely not. I think we were more surprised by your generosity. Also, you should already know I'm not a typical merchant. I don't sell wares for the money. I do it to see the smiles on people's faces when I can provide them what they desire with all their heart. The money is nice, true, but it can't beat the feeling you get when you see their looks of unrepentant joy. Maybe that's why it makes me so happy to see this. Look at them."

Blinking, Kai turned and watched as each family stepped forward to a collection table and offered their copper to Lucretia and Morgan. In each parent's eye, he saw the glistening tears cascading down their faces. This was different, though. Where their tears were accompanied by looks of despair before, now they were filled with bright, happy smiles and words of gratitude.

A muffled cough brought the pair's attention to a Soltauri man standing just behind them. He loomed over them, dressed in a priest's vestments with a dark blue stole signifying dedication to Edeval the Bandit Lord, Wind Saint of Loyalty, draped over his shoulders.

"I heard your little speech," said the priest, eyeing the two of them with curiosity. "You seem rather well-spoken for a Norzen."

With an indignant scowl, Maple ruffled her feathers. "And for a priest of the winds, you seem remarkably *rude*," she snapped.

Kai rested a hand on her shoulder, an act the priest noticed at once; his gaze locked on the apothecary's hand. "I am only here to ensure my congregation is taken care of. For that matter, it behooves me to inquire as to why the two of you seem so close. I'm sure you know the consequences of impropriety between the tribes."

"If you're telling me my best friend and I can't support one another, sir," Kai answered, his gaze turning frigid as he met the priest's stare, "then I suggest you find a new profession before you offend someone with a shorter temper than myself."

The two men matched glares as Kai felt Maple shift against him. He could sense she was trying to refrain from drawing him into a hug. If he was being honest, Kai would admit the priest's scowl unnerved him. As if he could detect the apothecary's true thoughts without hearing them spoken aloud.

"May I help you?" Orelia asked, stepping between the other cleric and her friends.

The priest's glare shifted. "Stay your hand, Sister. I am attempting to ascertain whether these two are having illicit relations against the will of the church."

Kai fought to hold back the laugh yearning to burst free when Orelia jabbed the head of her staff into the man's gut, nearly folding him in two. "These two are under my personal jurisdiction, Brother. I can attest to their faith myself, and I'm insulted you would accuse them of committing any sort of crime after all they've done in service to this city. Your attitude reeks of tribalism just because one of the two happens to be Norzen, and I refuse to tolerate it. Leave, lest I report you to the provincial High Priest."

Casting a final glare at Kai, the priest rubbed his tender stomach and fled. Orelia gave the pair a knowing smile and wrapped her arms around both of them in a warm embrace. She whispered something into Maple's ear before striding back to the others.

A shiver shot down Kai's spine, the soft touch of Maple's feathers gliding across his arm. The sensation helped distract him from the throbbing pain pulsing through his body and the chill in his mind from their encounter with the priest.

"I'm pretty sure I owe Orelia a boon now. With the windbag gone, I have to speak my mind. You're a good man, Kai Travaldi," she whispered. "That's why we follow you. You have a presence that can sooth even those who feel all hope is lost. Bloody Nulyma, you even made a believer of Lucretia! None of us would be here if not for you. Take pride in that."

"I do. Thanks to Saredi, I've learned to accept I'm good at this, though I'll always strive to be better. So what exactly did you want for your favor? I saw the way you looked at Orelia back in the forest, so I imagine you already had something in mind."

"Never miss a trick, do you? I suppose I should come out and say it. Once we get back on the river, I'd like you to dance with me. Just the two of us."

Kai was grateful he wasn't drinking anything at that moment, otherwise he would've sprayed it all over the grinning Aerivolk. He stammered incoherently, unable to form a lucid thought. He knew that, between them, Maple was the more outgoing and daring of the two. Her request was the last thing he expected, though. "Maple, are you certain that's what you want? I mean, you know what it would signify, right?"

"Of course I do. Is an official courtship really so bad?"

Kai held up his hands. "No, not at all! I'm just...surprised you would make the offer to me of all people. Especially after we just got accosted by that priest." Kai felt a tremor of fear wrack his body. He knew how to dance, of course. His parents never would have let him leave Havenfall otherwise. It was the shock of hearing *Maple* asking him to do so which sent him reeling. Particularly considering his own feelings.

"You shouldn't be. Listen, I know what this means going forward, and I've spoken to Orelia. She has no problem with us beginning an official courtship and promised not to bring anything before the church. Then again, I suppose she has her own reasons for taking such a stance. Assuming, of course, you're willing to accept. So I ask again, may we share a dance?"

The question, asked in her throaty western drawl, sent a chill down his spine. He never considered the idea of being physically affected by someone's accent, but Maple's natural voice did things to him he didn't believe possible. Her comment about Orelia's reasoning also brought a slew of questions to his mind, along with renewed thoughts about the kisses he'd received from both women thus far. Thinking of that brought a new, unusual sensation to his body. His face felt as though it was burning, while the rest of him felt colder than ice.

Having Maple ask him for a dance was already intimidating. The thought of both women potentially expressing an interest in him was enough to turn his face a shade more appropriate for an apple. Non-monogamous relationships such as polygamy and polyamory were technically permitted within Livoria. However, the financial constraints associated with it, imposed by Parliament, often limited the practice to the nobility or wealthy merchants, as they were the only ones able to produce enough income to support a larger family.

No matter which path he chose, overcoming years of instilled values and lessons was not easy, even knowing how he felt. Despite his own talk with Orelia a few nights ago, hearing that she had a similar conversation with Maple was mind-numbing. Everything Kai learned from church slammed into his mind at once. Promises of an eternity in Nulyma called to him, swearing vengeance for going against the precepts. What unsettled him was that the voice in his mind matched the Soltauri priest they just encountered. To hear the clergy talk about it, Nulyma was said to be a hellish, painful way to spend the hereafter, no matter which of the five levels you were damned to.

However, the moment Maple's eyes met his, her violet globes flush with eagerness, the concept of such a punishment seemed like nothing in comparison to the thought of seeing her in tears. If accepting her feelings meant he would spend an eternity in the void, then damned he would be.

He already knew what he wanted: To see those eyes glow with the same happiness that drew him to her in the first place. He just never believed he would be lucky enough for her to reciprocate.

Reaching out, he took her hand and gripped it tight. Using his other hand, he brushed the bangs from her eyes and gave a tender smile. "I would be honored to dance with you, Maplyne. To tell the truth, nothing would make me happier."

Maple's entire body trembled with obvious excitement. The pair cast a look at the others, though they were all occupied with tending to the crowd. Kai felt Maple's arms loop around his elbow, pulling him closer. Seeing her smile now, it filled him with an explosion of joy he didn't think was possible.

Sitting back down and resting his head on the table, he returned her smile and allowed sleep to claim him, her happy grin the last thing he saw before darkness enveloped him. One final thought crossed his mind as he drifted into slumber.

No matter what, he would do everything in his power to protect that smile.

CHAPTER XI

Thorncrest was no more. Vizent Doulterre and the Liberation Army saw to that with brutal efficiency.

The smell of blackpowder engulfed the ruins of the once-peaceful city. Very few buildings remained standing, and those that did were mere husks of what they once were. Fires spread through the wreckage, consuming everything in their path. Thousands of bodies lay where they had fallen.

Few residents of Thorncrest survived, and those who did were in one of two groups: The ones who fled days before the Liberation Army's arrival, and the faumen captured and thrown into crates once the attack was over. Everyone who stayed placed their faith in the Royalist Navy battalion quartering on the outskirts of town.

Sadly, their faith was not enough to prevent the enemy from overrunning the battalion and putting Thorncrest to the torch.

The Liberators themselves set up camp in a small valley outside of town, surrounded by hills. They used the hills as a cover, taking advantage of the respite to celebrate their success.

His uniform covered in dust and smelling of smoke, Vizent stood at the top of the tallest hill, overlooking the results of his men's handiwork. After the disaster of Faith Hollow, it filled him with pride and relief to conquer a decent-sized town.

The soldiers were coming together as a unit at last. Nowhere near perfect, of course, but capable enough to compete against the more disciplined Royalists. As concerning as Razarr's aura was, Vizent could admit the forge master was a fine weapon smith.

They utilized the newest variant of Razarr's muskets during the Thorncrest campaign, and the upgraded flintlocks were a smashing success. Set against traditional bows and even pistols, the muskets had better piercing power, though they remained unable to punch through a shielder's namesake armor. They also had a longer range compared to the original models and were less likely to malfunction. That last benefit was Vizent's favorite, if only because his men didn't injure themselves as much from a barrel exploding in their faces.

Even more impressive were the bombs filled with a mixture of blackpowder, glass shards, and stonehood pollen. At first, the concept confused him. His opinion of the weapons did a complete reversal once he witnessed them in action. With the amount of damage soldiers gathered on the battlefield, the pollen was quick to find open wounds, rendering anyone unfortunate enough to be in range immobile and thus easy prey.

Memories of things he saw during the battle brought a cruel smile to his lips. And to think, Razarr had plans for even more weapons in mind. Vizent was excited to see what new methods of destruction the forge master could devise.

"It's a tad disturbing seeing you smile," a deep voice resonated behind him. Vizent turned, tilting his head back to meet the looming gaze of Duarte. One of Razarr's enforcers, Duarte was an ordained Cadist monk with years of battle experience, a fact Vizent made use of in having the Soltauri teach his squad leaders training drills. Despite hating each other's tribes, the two men developed an odd bond over a shared contempt for formality.

Vizent allowed himself a rare chuckle. "You are not the first to tell me so, Duarte. Even before I joined the Royalist Navy, my friends always used to say my smile frightened small children."

The monk erupted into braying laughter. "I have heard many in this realm say the eyes are the windows to one's soul, which does make some sense. Back in Corlati, they say the smile is a window to the mind."

"Interesting idea. If it were true, what does my smile say about me?"

Duarte stared for a moment, scratching his chin. Crossing both arms across his chest, the monk finally answered, "I would say it shows you are determined. Strict. Not afraid to take what you want, regardless of the consequences."

The general smirked. "Well I'll be damned. That does sound like me when I think about it. The Corlatians may be onto something."

Afterwards, the two discussed their plans for the immediate future. With Thorncrest destroyed there were several options. Vizent knew of other small towns to the south able to provide them with ample supplies. With their recent advances and the weapons available to them, the general was confident the Liberation Army was ready to take another crack at a more skilled opponent.

"I'm curious about one thing," said Duarte, "wherever did that new commander go? Agosti, I think was his name."

Thoughts of Agosti's last report brought out a frustrated groan from Vizent. "If that idiot ever makes it back, I swear he'll be on latrine duty for two moons!"

An amused smirk lined Duarte's face. "Pleasant. What did he do this time?"

"He grew too eager to punish any mistakes the men committed during drills, so I ordered him to do reconnaissance around Whistlevale. I figured the experience would cool his heels. At least then, he could so something useful in locating weaknesses to exploit when the time comes. The information would be invaluable when we're ready to besiege the capital."

"Is it safe to assume he failed?"

"Worse, he let himself get sidetracked. He spotted that blasted Norzen you and he have been quibbling over and diverted his entire squad to chase after him. Not only did he fail to gather any useful intelligence, but he lost most of the squad in a botched nighttime raid. Only two of the six men with him survived. The one bit of good news was that he injured the Norzen, though from his description the peltneck may have been ill."

Duarte's hand reached up to grip his shoulder with a wince, an act Vizent couldn't blame him for. The general was aware of Gravebane's reputation and skill from the reports, on top of his own investigation into the Exarch. Duarte's last encounter with the Norzen was wholly unpleasant and didn't even account for the injuries their ally Adalbard, a former bishop, suffered at the hands of the Aerivolk with him.

The monk's broken shoulder, severe burns and scarring to both eyes, heavy bruising, two fractured ribs, and multiple lacerations didn't lie. Gravebane was dangerous. The fact he managed to fend off Agosti long enough to receive aid while ill said more than enough. Vizent prayed to Galen he wouldn't be forced to confront the Exarch with anything less than a full company.

Then again, he was never able to prove or disprove the idea of Gravebane being behind the disaster at Faith Hollow. He knew Hunters and the more he mulled it over, the more he realized the Royalist defense in that battle reeked of a Hunter's trap.

Without thinking, Vizent reached into his pocket and pulled out the warped piece of metal he kept there. Running his fingers over the dried slag, his mind drifted to Havenfall. He knew he would have to face the Hunter Corps one day. If he had his way, though, that day would be a long time coming.

"So where is the fool now?" Duarte asked.

"He and the remains of his squad are following them from a safe distance, though it's a gamble on how long it'll take for Agosti to grow impatient and try again."

"Then why let him continue? Such insubordination in the Federation would result in being censured. Hoarfrost, execution wouldn't be a surprise either!"

"Which is why I sent Obram. The man is efficient, if nothing else, and is under orders to bring Agosti back under any means necessary."

A sense of foreboding crawled up Vizent's spine. He spotted Duarte staring with a deadpan expression. "You just wanted an excuse to get the man out of your camp, didn't you...?" the monk drawled.

"It may have played a small part in the decision. Have you seen him *eat*? Half my rations for the moon are gone! Where does he even put it?"

"I sympathize with you. How he consumes so much without bloating like a pufferfish is a mystery I will never fathom."

The rapid thump of running footsteps reached Vizent's ears. Turning, he saw a young sergeant approaching, a large black carrier hawk on his shoulders. The general bit back a groan. He recognized Razarr's personal hawk.

"General Doulterre, apologies for interrupting," the man bowed, "but this urgent message just arrived at the command tent. I figured you'd want to see it."

Vizent thanked the man for bringing it and removed the scroll from the hawk's leg. He dismissed the soldier with instructions to ensure the hawk was fed and watered while he penned a reply. Whatever missive Razarr was sending now, his gut was saying he wouldn't like it. Unfurling the scroll, he began to read.

Silence reigned as the soldier hurried back to camp, leaving Duarte to watch Vizent grumble the further he read. The general's face flushed red as his eyes trailed down the parchment. He forced back a groan, wondering for a moment if his army's benefactor could detect thoughts.

He understood that, to some extent, Razarr could be a risk taker. It wasn't a surprise, given the power he wielded among the wealthiest merchants in Corlati. Only someone who knew how to make calculated risks could achieve such prominence. The parchment in his hands, outlining the forge master's next plan, seemed less a risk and more an instrument of the Liberators' self-destruction.

"Duarte?"

"Hmm...what is it?"

"Pardon my candor, but has your master lost his damn kettle?"

The monk frowned, asking what was so distressing about the letter that he felt compelled to ask such a question.

"Razarr has made his intentions clear, though I'm unsure if our men are ready to commit to such a dangerous mission. He's ordered us to begin marching to our next target. A target of his own choosing."

"And where is he having us go?"

"Havenfall."

Duarte blinked. Plucking the letter from Vizent's fingers, he read the entire parchment from beginning to end in silence. Vizent waited patiently for the monk's reaction. While he spent much of his life in Corlati, Duarte remained a native Livorian, and thus aware of Havenfall's significance.

Pinching the bridge of his nose, Duarte heaved a sigh. "As much as it pains me to admit, you may have a point. This army is hardly ready to take on the Hunter Corps. While we have numbers on our side, we would be cut in half at a minimum."

"Did you see where he wrote that he would meet us there?"

"I did, and it makes me wonder what the final goal is. The only thing I can think of is that he's finished a major project and plans to test it during battle. He could also be bringing reinforcements to improve our chances."

Stroking his beard, Vizent wondered aloud if it was the weapon Obram mentioned to him after Mistport. Seeing Duarte's curious stare, he explained the strange faumen's promises from Razarr of a weapon capable of turning the entire tide of the war in the Liberators' favor.

"It very well could be," Duarte answered. "I like to believe that Master wouldn't issue such an order unless he was confident in our ability. He takes risks, but not impossible ones."

Staring down the hill at the encamped army, Vizent knew he had to make a choice. If he followed Razarr's orders and marched on Havenfall, there was a good chance he'd take significant losses. The Hunters' numbers were small, but he knew from experience their ability to make up the difference through skill. A company of two hundred Hunters was more than capable of wiping out a force three times its size with minimal effort.

On the other hand, he could ignore the order and continue building up the army at the expense of infuriating Razarr. The forge master already made it clear further failures would result in more than just a loss of their supplies. It didn't take a Citadel scholar to see the underlying threat.

Vizent was never the most intelligent man, but he did have an innate sense of self-preservation. He never would have lived this long otherwise.

"We should head back," he finally muttered. Duarte asked if the general decided on their next move.

"I have. We'll drill on the march. We head for Havenfall at first light."

Watching Mirabell work always filled Razarr with a calm sense of peace. The young woman was methodical and focused, both traits the forge master found admirable. The recent reemergence of her sass was an annoying problem, but one easily dealt with. After so many years in his service, it didn't take much to realign Mirabell's attitude to Razarr's expectations.

Seeing her stooped over in those grungy cleaning clothes she preferred, wiping away the blood from the most recent recipient of Razarr's ire, churned thoughts in his mind he believed long dormant at his age. Still, he could appreciate the view of her—

"Are you going to stand there and stare at my ass all evening, or don't you have important documents to review?" Mirabell snapped, not bothering to meet his eyes.

A tired sigh escaped Razarr's lips. Perhaps he eased up on her too soon. Rather than let her goad him into losing his temper, he offered a brief warning to mind her tongue. He returned his gaze to the pile of parchment littering the desk he seized. The manor they were using as a temporary base was luxurious, though Razarr found he preferred the more diminished tones in the ornamentation back home. The tapestries and ceramic decorations here were much too vibrant for his aging eyesight.

In the time since his visit to the labor camp, Fedrin had taken the forge master's words to heart. Production on his project improved several-fold, to the point that Fedrin's last letter suggested they might finish ahead of schedule. It was an unexpected boon Razarr had every intention of milking for what it was worth. With the project almost complete, he could deal with one of his biggest obstacles: Havenfall.

Fedrin's good news helped relieve some of the sting from hearing what happened to Duarte during the Runegard mission. However, at least one good thing arose from his defeat: the Soltauri monk as good as confirmed his second target survived that damnable night 22 years ago.

The line of Erklaus still lived, though not for long. By Berelmir, he would enjoy watching the life fade from that boy's eyes one day.

"Master, do you believe Doulterre suspects what we've been doing?" Mirabell asked. She tossed the bundle of crimson rags into a corner and used the nearby basin to wash the blood from her hands.

Leaning back, Razarr emitted a dark chuckle. "My dear, the fool is too busy doing exactly as I tell him. If he suspected anything, I reckon he would've gone rogue moons ago. Besides, thanks to a little duplicity on my part, I wouldn't be surprised if the blithering idiot still thinks everything is going according to his plans."

Mirabell quirked an eyebrow. "Do tell...how have you been pulling the wool over his eyes? The man earned his reputation for a reason."

"By showing him precisely what he expects to see, courtesy of Obram. I will admit Doulterre is a formidable man. Stealthy, powerful, and ambitious. He would be the perfect subordinate, if not for the fact his hatred of the faumen blinds him in ways which make him more liability than asset."

Looking up, Razarr's gaze met Mirabell's for a split moment before the woman turned away. He watched her bend down to grab the legs of the dead man in the middle of the floor and drag the body to the study's cavernous fireplace. Razarr never understood why nobles enjoyed having such large fireplaces. The weather in Livoria was balmy enough even in winter to discourage the thing's use, so why bother?

Cramming the body inside at an awkward angle, Mirabell took a sparkstone from the mantle and used some spare kindling to set it and the bloody rags ablaze.

The young maid clapped her hands together with a smile. "Well, I suppose that's finally done. How many of these do we have left, Master?"

"He was actually the last one, if my dossier notes are correct."

"Truly? Oh, thank goodness! Disposing of these bodies was growing irksome."

"I suppose so. Regardless, it's one less thing to worry about. Let's visit the manor hawkery. I'll send a message to my trump agent and have them meet up with Obram. Doulterre sent him to retrieve a rogue scout, but this will work in our favor."

"So what will we do now with every member of the Conclave dead?"

Razarr tapped his chin, a diabolical grin stretching over his face. "With the Liberation Army's so-called 'leaders' out of the picture, Doulterre is the one standing at the top of the heap. And the man is, if nothing else, an easily manipulated pawn. We'll get what use we can out of him, for now."

Turning his eyes on the crackling flames consuming the body, Razarr allowed himself to burst into laughter. Things were beginning to slide into their proper place. So long as Fedrin did as he was told, there was little stopping the forge master.

And to improve matters, if his minions could weaken that brat of Erklaus' bloodline, his ultimate goal will be close enough to taste.

Chapter XII

The sounds of the *Senberg* paddling along the river were oddly calming. Kai was never one to be entranced by modern technology like steam engines, though he would admit they made life easier for people. Still, the groan of the ship's engine alongside the rhythmic slapping of the paddle on the water had a hypnotic effect on the young Norzen. Combined with the soothing melody of the surrounding forests, Kai wondered if he might fall asleep as he waited on the ship's main deck.

He still felt exhausted from the Grantide incident. Thankfully, none of the children died. The party stayed an extra three days, for the remainder of the festival, to ensure every child made a full recovery before continuing downriver. During that time, Kai was surprised to see his friends manning their own little stall on the grounds where Maple sold her handmade accessories and other trinkets she bartered for while in Whistlevale.

Many tears were shed when Ione confessed to Larina she would be leaving with the party to complete their mission. When the girl begged her mother to stay, Ione held her tight, promising to return to Grantide for good after the war. Just as pleasant was seeing a contrite Massio apologize to his daughter for his previous behavior. Thinking about the bone-crashing hug the two shared after the children were fully healed still sent sparks of joy down the apothecary's spine.

Though Kai asked where Lord Kendela ran off to, nobody would admit to knowing the man's whereabouts, which he found concerning. With luck, the noble would stay out of their hair until after they reached Havenfall. Margrave or not, Kai doubted even Kendela would be so brazen as to try pulling rank on an Exarch in their own hometown.

Tugging at the uncomfortable pine green waistcoat he wore, he weathered the itchy sensation the silken garment formed in his mane. While wearing a low-cut shirt underneath to keep the fur on his upper chest exposed to the cool air, his clothes covered both shoulders, leaving the rest of his mane stifled. The waistcoat's copper buttons gleamed in the moonlight. The trousers, loose-fitting but comfortable, were the shade of polished brass with slits tailored into the rear for his tails. It was much more formal attire compared to his apothecary robes, but he felt it appropriate for tonight.

He never expected actually having a reason to wear this outfit after Fusette forced him to have it custom-tailored during their time in the capital. Come to think of it, he remembered Saredi telling everyone to make sure they had presentable formal attire, on the off-chance they needed it for handling any issues requiring them to exercise their authority as royal officers. He bit back a snicker at the thought of Morgan or Teos being forced to wear anything the court deemed 'presentable.'

The rest of the crew, save for the firemen at the boiler and Teos at the helm, were supposed to be asleep in their cabins on the observation deck above.

Well, there was at least one other awake...

"You're really here," a voice chirped from behind. Turning around, Kai's breath caught in his throat the moment his eyes landed on Maple.

It was the first time Kai saw the merchant in anything besides her nightdress or her handwoven vest and skirt. Instead, she opted for a more flowing garb that complimented her figure. Her shoulders and neck were bare, save for a plain silver choker around her throat with an oval-cut citrine embedded at its center. The top was a simplistic, apple red chest wrap with cloth fringes, leaving her midriff exposed to the chill air. She wore wide-bottomed pantaloons in a darker burgundy with open slits in the sides exposing her slender legs, tied with a cord just above the ankle. Completing the ensemble was a hip sash around the waist in misty blue with long ribbon-like strips that draped over her right leg like a veil.

The apothecary's eyes were drawn to the long, branching scars covering Maple's left side from just above the breast until it disappeared beneath the cover of her hip scarf. She turned away with a blush, using her wing to cover the scar. Kai ran the fingers of one hand along her feathers, using the other to interlock his fingers with hers.

Her violet eyes flickered to him. "I know it's hideous. I try not to show so much of it, but I really wanted to wear my tribe's traditional dancing dress for this."

Kai forced himself to hold back the chuckle bubbling in his chest, instead pulling her close and tapping her on the nose. "Nothing about you is hideous, Maple. I'm quite flattered you chose to share this with me. If anything, I should apologize for staring. I was struck dumb by how beautiful you look."

A sly smirk grew across Maple's face. "Are you just naturally this charming, or am I special? Also, you look quite handsome. This is a good look for you."

"Thank you," he replied with a light tint to his cheeks. "I knew you were special from the day we met, though I never could've imagined us in this position. Oh, that reminds me..." Reaching into the small pouch tied to his belt, Kai revealed a small wristlet made from rope and adorned with bunches of small white flowers.

Maple gasped as Kai tied the accessory to her left wrist and pressed a finger against her palm. "Kai, it's beautiful," she whispered. Raising the flowers, she inhaled their fragrance with a contented smile. "And the flowers smell divine. It's like vanilla with a touch of almond."

"They're called heliotropes. Most people put them in their gardens due to their pleasant smell. Now, I believe I owe a lovely lady her dance?" Despite the show of confidence, Kai's mind raced, and he could feel sweat beading on his temple.

As a Hunter, he had faced some of the most dangerous creatures to grace the continent, including Grimghast. And yet, none of those beasts were able to instill the same terror in him as the thought of disappointing the young woman in his arms. Gulping audibly, he allowed Maple to grasp his wrists, guiding them into place. He fought back a flinch when his left hand rested on the bare skin of her hip. The way her other hand slid up to meet his was slow, almost sensual in its tenderness. Weaving their fingers together, he felt her other hand clutch his arm in a firm grip. Taking a final deep breath, Kai stepped forward and led Maple into a simple waltz.

Without music, Kai was forced to rely on muscle memory to keep to the steps, something he wasn't as confident in. To his relief, Maple was an adaptable partner, able to adjust to his choppy steps and avoid having her talons stepped on in the process.

He blushed when he heard her emit a small giggle. "Nervous?" she asked.

Knowing he couldn't deny it, he nodded. "Very much so. I've never danced with anyone outside my mother's lessons."

"You're not the only one. I don't think I've ever been so terrified in my life."

"Really? You always seem so cheerful and confident. Then there's the fact that *you're* the one who approached me about this."

Maple burst into a trilling laugh, a sound Kai thought sweeter than the tune of a professional musician. "To be honest, I was scared to ask you. I'm still scared. I don't think I've ever been this nervous, even during a thunderstorm."

The apothecary's eyes twitched to the large scar. "I assume it has something to do with how you got injured?"

"Yes," she answered after a brief silence. "It happened the day I got into that big fight with Peppra. While chasing her down, a thunderstorm swooped in out of nowhere. I didn't even stop to consider the danger. I was so angry at what she and her drones did to my friend, I wanted them to feel the same pain. Well, once I caught up with her, we began tussling mid-glide when a bright flash came. My whole side burned like fire and felt like I got punched in the rib by a Soltauri. Knocked me on my tail feathers, it did."

Kai winced. He knew what Soltauri were capable of. His chest still stung with shadow pain at times thinking of the kick Duarte landed on his ribs back in Runegard. "That sounds painful, but at least you survived."

She responded with a smile, reminding Kai to focus on his steps. His body twitched trying to time everything right. The pair stayed silent as they continued dancing, savoring each other's company. The only sound came from the clicking of Maple's talons on the deck.

Neither noticed several pairs of eyes watching them from the shadows.

Kai's blush returned full force when he felt Maple's head rest against his mane. "As scary as this is," she whispered, "I'm still so happy you're here with me."

"Aye," Kai replied, "I feel the same way. My heart is pounding like a drum, yet I've never been so excited."

"I can certainly attest to the heart pounding. It sounds like the poor thing is trying to burst from your chest. Am I that terrifying?" Maple quipped with a soft giggle.

"I'm not scared of you. It's the thought of messing this up. I don't know the first thing about romance and courtships. All I know is I want to make you happy."

Kai fought the instinct to flinch back when Maple reached up and laid both hands on his cheeks, tilting his face down to meet her gaze. "I don't know what I'm doing either. I just do what feels right. And I'd say you're doing wonderfully so far. The fact you care about my happiness puts you leagues ahead of men like Kendela, who only think of their own desires. Remember when I told Yasso I prefer compassionate men?"

The apothecary nodded.

"The truth is, there was only one man on my mind from even before those words were spoken, and he's standing right here."

The moonlight hit Maple's eyes at the perfect angle in that moment, giving the violet orbs an ethereal shine that left Kai breathless. Reaching up to brush a stray hair away, he felt her wings wrap around his back, sheathing him in their warm embrace.

Without thinking, he leaned down towards her, his eyes locked on Maple's thin lips, which twitched into a smile as she closed her own eyes and moved to meet him. He could feel her breath on his face as they came closer together.

Just a moment longer—

"Well, what do we have here?" a saucy voice rang out from above.

As if struck by lightning, the pair shot apart, their eyes swinging upwards to find Orelia staring down from the observation deck, a wide grin splitting her face in two. Maple puffed her cheeks out and stomped a talon on the deck, demanding to know why the priestess was interrupting.

"My apologies," said Orelia with a bow, "but you two look so sweet together! I couldn't help but tease."

Huffing, Maple leaned against Kai while pouting at the priestess, allowing his arm to wrap protectively around her shoulder. "You really know how to ruin the mood. You did that on purpose, didn't you?"

Deciding to stay out from between the two, Kai slipped his hand behind Maple's neck and, gently pressing the fingertips into the muscle, began to knead. The merchant let out a small gasp, her eyes swiveling to meet his. Kai said nothing, but let his smirk do the talking as he deepened the pressure. Maple emitted a throaty keen, growing louder when Kai's hand moved up and massaged her scalp, the fingers threading through her hair.

"Kai," she groaned, drawing out the sound of his name, "that feels *really* good."

Laughing from her vantage point, Orelia muttered for Kai to slow his ministrations. "Take it easy, Gravebane, before you put the poor girl into a coma. Or at the very least, get your tails up here and do it to me too."

Despite not wanting to stop, Kai suppressed his blush and gave Maple's scalp a few more scratches before sliding his hand down to the small of her back. She whined a little, pressing her back into his chest while wrapping herself in her wings. "Please promise you'll do that again," she begged.

Kai snickered and, fighting the thrum in his heart, leaned close to Maple's ear as his arms encircled her waist. "Of course," he murmured. "I'm just glad you enjoyed it." Looking back up, he stammered a little seeing Orelia copying the same tilted grin he was used to seeing on the merchant in his arms.

"What in the winds is going on?" a sharp voice snapped. Rolling his eyes, Kai glanced up and saw Lucretia staring in unbridled shock. "Maple, *what* are you wearing?"

Resting her hands on her hips, Maple snapped back, "It happens to be a traditional garb for my tribe. My mother sent me money to get it specially tailored while we were in Whistlevale."

"Does your mother know about this?" the scholar asked, gesturing to the pair's closeness.

"She knows from my letters I'm interested in someone, but that's it. I'm not sure yet how I'll bring up the truth."

Mimicking Kai's eye roll, Lucretia reminded her she needed to figure it out before the truth was outed on its own. Kai frowned and heard Maple sniffle in his arms. Thanking Lucretia for her insight, the apothecary took Maple by the hand and led her up the stairs. They passed by the two women, though Kai noticed Orelia shooting an agitated look at Lucretia as he led the merchant to the cabins.

Once they reached her door, a wave of sadness came over him. He didn't want the night to end, but he knew there would be other chances.

Taking her hand, he brushed his lips against the fingers and flashed a calming smile. "Well, the ending could've gone better, but I still enjoyed myself."

"I did too," Maple replied, her cheeks flushed. "I'm really happy you accepted my request. I don't know where this courtship will lead, but I think it's going well."

Grabbing Kai by the mane, Maple pulled him down close enough for her to plant a soft kiss on his cheek. The apothecary's face burned crimson at the contact. Maple pulled away, her own cheeks turning an even deeper shade of red than before.

"You mentioned earlier I was the one who approached you about a dance, and I'll admit I was terrified about asking. But I realized something." Seeing Kai's curious look, she continued. "I thought of what could happen if I allowed those shadows of fear to control me, and it made me think of seeing you in someone else's arms. Seeing that felt like a knife in my heart, so I swore to cast my line and see where the river took us."

As he stood there, watching Maple talk, a stray thought passed Kai's mind. He cupped her cheek, caressing it with his thumb. "We'll talk more later. For now, just know I've never been so happy in my life. Having you at my side is the best thing to happen to me."

She quirked an eyebrow at him, poking a finger into his chest. "Would you say it's better than becoming an Exarch? Or earning your apothecary crest?"

Tilting his head with a smug smile, Kai whispered in her ear, "Not even close." Pulling a small parchment from his pocket, he scribbled a short note, folded it, and pressed it into her hands. "Think about it."

Without another word, Kai bowed his head and returned to his own cabin, leaving Maple to stare at the folded parchment in her hand. He wondered if he was overstepping again, but Maple's words sparked something in him.

He liked to think she wasn't the only one who could be brave when it counted.

Maple watched from her window as Kai walked away. Once he turned the corner, she threw herself on the bed with a delighted squeal. Reaching up, she brushed a finger over her lips, thinking about the peck she gave him. It may not have been the kiss she was hoping for, but they'd have another chance.

Assuming she could convince the others to quit butting their beaks into the mix.

A soft knock at the door drew her back, opening it to reveal Orelia staring at her with a smug grin. Lucretia stood behind the priestess, arms crossed under her chest with a grumpy expression and small knot growing on her forehead.

"I'm still kinda brassed off at you two," Maple mumbled, casting a frown at the younger women. "I swear to Ausrina, he was going to kiss me!"

"Perhaps it is a little soon for you both to be making such advances," Lucretia commented, though the scholar stepped back when Maple turned on her with flared nostrils and a look promising swift judgment.

"Don't you even start," the merchant hissed. "You already knew I would be making my move. Why would you say something like that?"

Lucretia groaned and leaned against the deck wall, cupping her face in her hands. "I truly do not know what came over me. I believe I panicked, much the same as you did before. For years, we have heard from the church how horrible things happen to those who intermingle between the tribes. I reacted out of pure instinct, and I apologize."

Releasing a groan of her own, Maple fell back on her bed. She couldn't fault Lucretia's reaction. The church, while not officially in charge of either Livoria or Galstein, was a persistent presence that made avoiding it, and its precepts, nearly impossible.

"Apology accepted," Maple replied to Lucretia's visible relief. "However, I'd appreciate it if you hold back any comments on our courtship for now. I want to ease him into this. You brought up a good point about his self-worth, and I saw part of it tonight. I want to make sure he knows I have no intention of leaving him. Kai is the strongest person I know, but he still needs reassurance at this stage."

Offering another apology, Lucretia excused herself and rushed back to her office for the night, leaving Maple and Orelia staring at each other with hesitant grins.

"Were you serious," asked Maple, "about wanting to pursue Kai?"

The priestess nodded. "Without a doubt. Still, I believe I shall stand aside for now, since you're my friend and he expressed interest in you first. As far as I know, only the nobility engage in multiple marriages, even though I've heard it said Livoria permits them for everyone."

Maple shivered and pressed a hand against her chest. The knowledge that Orelia also harbored a level of affection for Kai was nerve-wracking, but there was relief that she promised to not interfere, despite her teasing interruption earlier. The merchant questioned her ability to compete with her younger friend in the event they both actively pursued him.

"Thank you. You have no idea how much I appreciate being given a chance to make this work."

"That's fair," said Orelia. "Just try to take things at a pace comfortable for you both while enjoying the moment. You do make a lovely couple if you ask me, no matter how much I wish it was me in your stead." The redhead's eyes gained a cold hardness for a moment. "Just remember: if you do anything to hurt him, not only will you answer to me, but I'll put my own glove back in the ring and pursue his heart with everything I have. A man like Kai is a generational treasure."

Stroking her fingers through her feathers, Maple agreed with Orelia's assessment. Giving the younger woman a cheeky grin, she asked why Orelia never pursued Teos with the same vigor.

"Teos is sweet when he wants to be, but let's be realistic. He's more than twice my age and I think of him more like a favored uncle. Now try to get some sleep. We've still got a fair amount of time left on this journey."

Maple agreed and waved Orelia off as she left for her own cabin. Hearing the priestess' footsteps fade away, she pulled the note Kai gave her before he left and opened it. Her eyes widened seeing the words scribbled there in a hurry.

I can live without those jobs.

The merchant's breath hitched in her throat as she read the sentence again and again. Thinking of Kai's dedication to his apothecary work, she pressed the note against her heart and felt a gentle warmth as she considered the gravity of his words.

She prepared to perch herself on the headboard once more, but a rogue thought stopped her. Gazing at the bed, she nestled herself under the blankets instead. It took a few moments for her wings to get comfortable, but she soon felt herself drifting to sleep.

I think I could get used to sleeping like this, especially with Kai by my side, Maple thought as her vision faded to black.

Two days after his dance with Maple, Kai was roused from bed by Montagru. The deckhand informed him Teos was requesting his presence in the pilot house at once. Donning his robe, Kai rushed out to see what the fuss was.

While ascending the stairs, he noticed the rest of the party and crew standing along the edge of the deck staring at something along the river. Following their gaze, he spotted a town up ahead, partially concealed by morning fog. His eyes pinched together, sweeping over the entire river before continuing his march towards the pilot house.

"What's happening, Teos?" Kai asked as he strode up to the wheel. Sidling next to his friend, he noticed the Soltauri's furrowed eyebrows and set jaw. His hands clenched the spokes of the wheel strong enough for Kai to hear the wood cracking under his grip. Something was wrong.

"Morgan and the deckhands have been trying to flag down the port we're coming up on, but there's no response. And we haven't seen much movement from the town itself, though it's possible the fog is responsible."

Nodding, Kai stroked his mane while considering their options. His tails were tingling again; not a good sign. Heading over to the map nailed to the wall, Kai studied it for a few moments. "It seems we're approaching a town called Glimmerdale," he announced. "Do you know much of it? Even though I'm from the area, Da and I never had much reason to come here."

"Only the basics," Teos replied. "From what I know, it's your standard fishing town. A bit over three thousand people, give or take. Not many bandit raids thanks to its relative proximity to Havenfall, but you already knew that."

"Thanks. I'll go see if I notice anything. Have the engine crew take us to half speed so we don't overshoot before deciding on a course of action."

Teos burst into his bray-like laughter. "Well I'll be damned! That was going to be my honest suggestion. Maybe we'll make a sailor out of you yet!"

The apothecary sent his helmsman a smug grin. "Perhaps. Then again, I learned from the best."

"Damn right you did."

Clapping Teos on the back, Kai made his way down to the main deck and joined the others. He passed the cabin girls, Kerta and Annika, on the way and tapped Morgan on the shoulder.

"Teos briefed me on the situation. Any ideas why the port isn't responding?"

"Who knows, 'pothy? My first thought was they can't see us through this soup. Wouldn't be the first time I've seen the like. But I even struck a torch and tried signaling with that. Nothing."

"Damn," Kai muttered, scratching at the itch in his mane. The fog was beginning to condense on his fur. "Maple, think you can get on top of the pilot house and take a peek? You've got the best eyes here."

"Not a problem," she assented, clambering up with impressive agility. It took little time for her to perch atop the pilot house, peering towards the town.

"See anything, lass?" Morgan shouted.

"I see some people," Maple answered, "but they aren't moving very fast. It's almost like they're in a trance."

"Check the port," Teos ordered, emerging from the bridge. "There should be a tall pole with flags on it."

A few moments passed before Maple responded she could see flags fluttering over the port. "There's three of them," she explained.

Kai pulled the spyglass from his satchel and turned it towards where Maple was pointing. He quickly spotted the flags in question. One was a black cross on a white background. The second displayed a red circle within a blue square. The last one showed three vertical stripes in black, yellow, and blue. Kai described the flags to Teos, stunned when the smuggler exploded into a string of obvious curses in his native Soltish.

"Bloody Nulyma!" he finally called out in Centric, striking the wall with his fist. "Kai, we need to make a decision quick."

"What do those flags symbolize, Teos? I'm guessing it's something bad."

"It's a safe wager, I'd say. The first one is a signal for immediate assistance. The second one warns of contamination. The last is a warning to stay clear."

Worried whispers broke out among the crew. Even Dekel and his firemen ascended from the boiler deck to see what was going on.

"There ain't much we can do for this town," Dekel declared. The aged engineer drew on a weathered wood pipe, emitting small puffs of smoke. "Those signals on their own are bad enough. I ain't ever seen all three at the same time. That's a bad omen. I'd say Cacovis owns the place now." The rest of the crew trembled in fear, though the party regarded the Aerivolk with skepticism. Cacovis was considered the harbinger of death by the Windbringer church, but Kai's group knew more than most high-ranking priests.

They did have the woman's journal, after all.

"Kai," Maple stressed, "There's someone on the pier, trying to flag us down."

Dekel looked up at the merchant and berated her. "Don't be stupid, girl! We're better off moving on and forgetting we ever saw this place."

Scowling, Kai turned on the engineer with a frosty stare. "Mind your tongue, Dekel." Glancing up, he asked Maple to describe the person on the pier.

Taking another look, she answered that it was a young Vesikoi man, wearing a dirty white tunic and tattered black trousers. She stared at Kai with tears glistening on the edge of her eyes, asking what they could do.

Snapping his spyglass closed, Kai ordered Teos and the boiler crew back to their posts. "Take us in, Teos. I'm going to see what this is all about."

"Have you lost your damned kettle, boy?" Dekel bellowed, jabbing a gnarled finger into the Norzen's mane. "You're gonna get us all killed!"

Taking a deep breath, Kai pinned Dekel with a glare. "Did I say the crew were going ashore?" The engineer shook his head. "Good, you *can* pay attention. I'll investigate myself. Whatever is happening, it must be reported to Lady Fusette."

The party broke into hysterics, warning Kai against leaving the ship on his own. "What if this is like the *Fallbrook*?" Maple asked, dropping to the main deck in one leap before grabbing Kai by the elbow. "You are not going out there alone. I forbid it!"

"She's right, 'pothy," Morgan piped up from the back. "We're going with ya, and that's the end of it." The others, even Lucretia, shouted their agreement.

He met their gazes and smiled. "Thanks, everyone. Dekel, you're in charge while we're out there. Keep the boat docked and don't let anyone onboard under any circumstances. I don't care if they're a bloody noble. Unless they're with us, nobody comes on. Am I clear?" Dekel nodded and swore the crew would protect the *Senberg* at all costs, so long as they didn't have to leave the ship.

Teos broke into a run, lumbering back to the wheel while Dekel shouted for the firemen to return to the boiler and work the fire.

The ship slowly turned its bow towards Glimmerdale. Kai instructed the party to grab cloth strips and tie them around their mouths to prevent potential contamination.

"Until we know what we're dealing with, assume anyone and anything could be dangerous," he reminded them.

Soon enough, the *Senberg* was in place to dock at the pier. With the deckhands too frightened to tie the mooring ropes in place, Teos and Morgan handled the job themselves. Once the gangway was set, the rest of the party disembarked and watched the Vesikoi approach them at a sedate pace.

"W-who are you?" the man asked. Kai noted the stranger's skin looked paler and drier than a normal Vesikoi. Judging from the smell, it also seemed as though he hadn't bathed in quite some time.

A quick look at Teos' sour face and wrinkled nose confirmed this. The Soltauri's nose was much more sensitive than his own.

"Rest easy," said Kai. "I'm an apothecary from Havenfall. My friends and I were traveling downriver when we noticed the port wasn't responding to our signals. What's your name?"

"Celio, sir. Is the lady with you a priestess?" Kai glanced back at Orelia before nodding, drawing a look of relief from the timid man. "Oh, praise the winds! The Saints are smiling upon us at last. Maybe you can stop the malevolent spirit besieging our town, dear Sister."

The entire party quirked their eyebrows. An evil spirit? "What do you mean, Celio? Why do you feel the town is afflicted by a spirit?" Orelia asked while introducing herself to him. Kai allowed her to lead the questioning, seeing as their single witness seemed more comfortable with her.

"So many people have fallen ill in the past moon, Sister. At first it was only in certain areas of town, but then it began spreading all over. Before we knew it, almost everyone in Glimmerdale was afflicted. The town apothecary was among the first to die from the illness. Since then, everything has gotten worse. It all happened so quickly, what else could it be but an evil spirit?"

Orelia paced back and forth while Kai mulled over Celio's words. "Do you know what kind of symptoms the afflicted are showing?" he asked the Vesikoi. "Anything you can remember would be helpful."

"Well, almost everyone has been vomiting from what I've seen. Nobody can hold down their food before it comes spilling back out." The women flinched back in disgust. "Some of the elderly seized up from stomach pains and couldn't move. I've also seen folks who said they felt as though their heads were on fire."

Kai's tails coiled around each other, tensing until he felt Maple's comforting hand stroke the fur. The symptoms sounded like a poisoning similar to what they encountered in Grantide, but what he couldn't figure out was how it spread.

"Celio, do you remember the areas where the illness first took hold?"

"Aye, sir. There were three parts of town where it started. I can take you there if you like, but don't be surprised by what you see. Glimmerdale is a dark place, now." Offering his sentiments, Kai and the party followed Celio into the fog.

There was something sinister going on in this town, and he would figure out what was going on, one way or another.

Chapter XIII

Compared to the shimmering lights of the festival in Grantide, Glimmerdale seemed entombed in a shroud of darkness contrary to its very name. The fog was thinning in the emerging sun, and yet an aura of despair remained, thick and heavy.

As the party followed Celio through the deserted streets, Kai took notes of his observations. The streets were unkempt and littered with debris, and none of the torches meant to light the pathways at night and early morning were lit. The few people they encountered looked weary and broken, as if they had lost the will to go on. So far, the only children they had seen were a pair of Aerivolk girls who looked to be sisters, sitting on the street corner wrapped in a ratty blanket, a small cup in the smaller one's hands. Their red feathers looked withered and droopy, reminding Kai of Locke.

He briefly wondered where the traveler was before a clatter broke the silence like a cannon shot. His eyes settled on the girls, who looked up at Teos in astonished wonder. Peering into the cup, he noticed the smuggler had dropped a gold mark inside. It was the only coin. Reaching into his pouch, Kai added a gold of his own to the girls' vessel, leading the rest of the party to join in. Removing his pack, Kai dug around and brought out a small bundle of sweet rolls he saved from yesterday's dinner. He handed the bread to the now crying girls, ruffling their hair. Thanking the group, they took their prizes and scampered away with happy smiles.

The fact that such a small act of kindness could cause such unrestrained joy was disheartening to Kai, who swore to piece this newest puzzle together.

Celio stared in awe but continued leading the party to the center of town. Entering the main plaza, he swept an arm over the area. "This is where it all started," he explained, "but I don't know what you expect to find here. Many are too sick to leave their homes."

In the exact center of the plaza, Kai noticed a well. "Does the town get its water from there?" he asked.

"Aye. There are several wells scattered throughout town."

"You don't get water from the river?"

"No, sir. The wells are fed from an underground spring outside of town. The spring water is much cleaner and purer than anything from the river. Plus, many townsfolk believe it disrespectful to drink the river water, calling it an affront to the water Origin."

Stroking his mane, Kai asked Celio if any strangers had arrived in Glimmerdale before the people began falling ill. He answered that, other than the occasional traveler passing through, no one new had moved into town for an extended period of time. Going down a list of possibilities, Kai learned there were no recent festivals, no new foods or wares brought in, and no changes in the river or surrounding forests. As far as Celio was aware, life was seemingly normal when the illness came from nowhere.

"Well, I'm not seeing anything suspicious here so far. Show us the rest, please."

Dejected, Celio led the party further on, towards the east side of town. Everywhere they went, the same scenes played out as the ill stayed holed up in their homes while those who could still move ambled through town begging for food.

"I am curious, Celio," said Lucretia as they turned onto the market road, their next destination, "many of these people appear sickly and weak. However, you are quite fit of health by comparison. Why is that?"

"I don't rightly know, ma'am," he replied. "Most of us living down by the river port weren't affected as much, but we still have trouble finding enough to eat. Maybe it's cause we fishermen are a hardy bunch. Ever since the distress flags went up, though, no ships will dock to deliver fresh food."

As Lucretia talked with Celio, Kai noted another well in the middle of a circular area where several other streets branched off in different directions. A twinge of curiosity crossed Kai's mind.

"Celio." The man turned towards him with curious eyes. "You said there were three sections of town where the illness began spreading first, correct?" He nodded. "Do you happen to remember if there was a well in the third area?"

"Actually, sir, there is. What does that have to do with anything, though?"

Gesturing for the party to follow, Kai approached the well. The bucket was wet and seemed recently used. There was nobody around to see them, unless they were watching from the multitude of windows in the surrounding buildings. He tipped the bucket over and waited. Everyone watched with bated breath as they waited, jumping when an ominous splash echoed from the bottom. Grasping the rope, Kai began hoisting the bucket with smooth, repetitive motions.

"Kai, what are you doing?" Ione asked. "If you're thirsty, you do have a canteen."

The apothecary chuffed. "I want to check something." Soon, the bucket emerged from the shadows, filled to the brim with water. Kai lifted it over and set the bucket down, using a ladle hanging from the well wall to draw a scoop. The water itself was opaque, something Kai found concerning. He brought the water to his nose and sniffed. There was an odd, sour smell coming from the liquid.

"Teos, mind taking a sniff and telling me what you think? There's something in the spring water."

The Soltauri copied Kai's action and flinched away from the ladle, wiping his nose. "I don't know what it is, but water ain't supposed to smell like that. Something about the scent is familiar, though."

"I thought so, too. Regardless, I think it's safe to say we found the source of the illness; the spring supplying the town's drinking water is contaminated."

Celio stumbled backwards, falling onto his rear with a grunt. "But everyone in town drinks from these wells! How is it possible for those living around the Vesikoi district to not be as ill?"

Kai asked if there was anything they did with the water before drinking it, also suggesting the greater distance could have diluted the contamination before reaching their district's well. The greater question niggling at the apothecary's mind was how nobody noticed the unusual change in the water.

"The only thing I can think of is that we Vesikoi usually boil and strain our water before drinking it. It's an odd practice, but our people have done it for generations." A quick glance to Orelia confirmed the man's explanation, as she admitted to learning a similar tradition from her mother.

Kai chuckled. "It's actually quite smart, and very well may have saved your lives. Boiling water is an effective way of cleansing it of certain illnesses and straining can remove things like rocks and metal which can make you sick. It's not a guaranteed method of making water pure, but it helps."

"Is there a way to fix this?" Celio asked.

"I need to investigate the spring itself and find out what's causing the contamination. Then we can figure out how to reverse it."

A soft but familiar voice resounded from behind. "How is it I always find you in these situations, my friend?"

Kai's eyes widened, spinning to see a pair of recognizable white wings. "Locke! What are you doing all the way out here?" The rest of the party jumped back in shock on seeing the migrant.

"I *was* trying to keep ahead of the Liberators while I still can. Sadly, I think my time and my luck are running short there," Locke said, bursting into a horrible cough. Since their last encounter, the man looked even more ragged and exhausted than before. His cheeks were sunken, and several of his feathers seemed to have fallen out.

"By the winds, man, what happened to you?" Kai asked. Ione took Locke by the arm and sat him down against the well. The others gathered around, some offering the Aerivolk their canteens, though he waved them off.

"I'm afraid my affliction is worsening. I've been cursed with illness since I was a boy, but it appears the stress of constant running in this war has caught up to me. Curse this broken body! I doubt I'll last much longer, but I feel like there's more I can do. Kai, I know what I said before when we last saw each other, so I feel I have no right to ask for your assistance. However, I find myself begging: Can you craft me a tonic to at least stave off my illness? If you can, I have new information about the Liberation Army you might find useful." The man's voice cracked the longer he talked, each sentence punctuated by a coughing fit.

"Of course. What types of symptoms have you been exhibiting?" Setting his satchel on the ground, Kai began laying his tools out.

"The worst symptoms would be the constant fatigue and weakness in my body. It's gotten more difficult to walk. Every step feels as though my feet are made of lead. My hands are also rather twitchy and always tremble as though I'm cold. However, my body sweats easily when walking. I'd suppose the last is that my heart beats so fast it feels ready to burst from my chest, like a mole rising from the dirt."

Kai bobbed his head to Locke's words as he grabbed several vials, muttering to himself. "Let's add some citrial balm, with some ginseng to boost his energy. Then a couple leaves of bugleweed, but not enough to overpower the rest." The party watched on in fascination as Kai focused on his work. With a grin, Kai pulled a vial from his robe pocket and retrieved a single red bud before adding it to the mixture. The concoction billowed a copious amount of smoke while glowing bright red.

"What was the last herb you added?" Locke asked. "It seems to be affecting the rest of your mixture."

"I was lucky enough to find this at an apothecary's market in Whistlevale. It's called emberona, also known as the—"

"The Spark of Life," the traveler whispered. "That must've cost you a fortune!"

Maple leaned over Kai's shoulder, asking what they were talking about. "Emberona is a *very* potent healing herb. It's said to only grow in a few places throughout all of Nixtral, and Galstein is the only known place to find it in Alezon. The blooms are ludicrously expensive, but thankfully the buds aren't as pricey. In fact, the color of my apothecary robes is meant to be a match for the same bright hue of a fully bloomed emberona flower. They empower any concoction they're mixed into. A potion that takes a full cup to take effect will only require a quarter or fifth the amount to achieve the same effect under the influence of an emberona bud. Less if the bloom is used."

Muttering under her breath, Lucretia grumbled at the idea of spending so much on a flower bud. Kai retorted that he rarely got a chance to work with emberona, so he admitted to using some of his own savings to acquire the three buds he found. "Okay, I think it's ready," he declared. Handing the cup to Locke, the concoction was now emitting reddish-yellow smoke and gave off a powerful smell that tingled Kai's nose.

"Are you sure about this?" Locke wondered aloud, eyeing the smoldering cup with hesitation.

"At worst, you'll experience a burning aftertaste not unlike what you'd find in strong liquor. But it should alleviate a lot of the major symptoms you're describing."

Shrugging his shoulders, the Aerivolk threw back the entire concoction in one gulp, slamming the cup down on the cobblestones. "Oh, merciful Galen!" he gasped. "You weren't wrong about the aftertaste. It feels like I just drank a stein of whiskey."

"Give it a little while to work its way through your body, but with any luck, the concoction should help, though I can't guarantee for how long."

"It won't heal me fully?" Locke's feathers appeared to droop even more.

"Sadly, no. I know little about your ailment, and I can't think of anything in modern medical tomes which matches the symptoms you're experiencing, At least, not all at once. It's almost as if there's pieces of various illnesses attacking your body at the same time."

"Well, I suppose it was too much to hope for. Regardless, I thank you for at least trying to give me a little more time. In fact, I'm already starting to feel less tired. Perhaps it's an effect of the emberona."

Indeed, Locke's sickly pallor was alleviating, and his skin took on a healthier tone. He stood without difficulty for the first time since Kai met him and grasped the apothecary's hand in an iron grip. With multiple platitudes of appreciation, Locke spun in place, giving a cheerful whoop.

"I can't believe this! Is this how healthy people feel every day? By the winds, what have I been missing?"

"It is good to see you enjoying your new vitality," Lucretia spoke, "but you mentioned having information about the Liberation Army. Knowing you still flee from them and have come all this way suggests they have begun marching west. Are they making their move towards Whistlevale at last?"

"For you lot, it might be worse. I had hoped the Liberators *would* head towards the capital, as I came this direction over a moon ago gambling on it. Sadly, it appears I lost that wager. They turned *south*west rather than north. I'd say we're a few days march ahead of them, judging by how slow it is to move thousands of soldiers. It would take them at least another seven or eight days to reach their destination, if my theory is correct."

Orelia frowned, tapping her chin with the rounded head of her staff. "Southwest? But that path would take them *away* from Whistlevale. The only notable towns in this direction are Everstill near the Voidlands border or..." Everyone shared a horrified look as the implication became clear.

"Havenfall," Kai snarled, his teeth grinding together. If Locke's suspicions were sound, then Havenfall was the only significant town within an eight days march of the Liberators' position.

Locke confirmed the path he last saw the rebels taking would put them on a direct collision with the Hunter village. The party broke into a furor, many of them suggesting they return to the *Senberg* at once and make haste.

Mulling the idea over in his head, Kai was conflicted. His first instinct was to turn and get home as soon as possible to give them time to prepare.

He was also worried about the safety of his family, his sister Serafina in particular. Thus far, his instincts had served him well. However, something was holding him back from making the order.

His eyes turned to Celio, who watched them with wide, terror-filled eyes. He saw the two Aerivolk girls they met earlier in his mind. Seeing their eyes sparkle at the kindness they received tugged at his heart. Without aid, they risked the possibility of living in these conditions for much longer. And considering what the contaminated water did to Glimmerdale's inhabitants, the girls and many of those already sick wouldn't last long enough for an apothecary to be sent from Whistlevale.

It was true he had choices available, but they were not equal, regardless of what others told him. His oath was the foundation upon which he'd built his life. To abandon it now would be forsaking his pride and honor as an apothecary, something he considered far more important than his duty to the Hunters.

Turning to his bickering friends, he silenced them with a single, powerful word.

"No!"

They all faced him in shock, their eyes unblinking. Ione shook her head before replying, "What do you mean, 'no?' Kai, we need to warn Havenfall! If the Libbies really are heading there, they could kill everyone."

"We still have time before they arrive. Believe me, I want to go warn them right away. However, we have other options available."

Morgan emitted a gruff chuckle, drawing all eyes to him. "You're gonna warn them using the ship's carrier hawks, aren't you?" he predicted. Kai responded with a single nod.

"I forgot we have carrier hawks," Ione groaned to everyone's amusement. "So we need to head to the ship to warn them first?"

This time, Kai shook his head. "No need. We're still about four days out from Havenfall by boat. A carrier hawk can cover the same distance in less than a day. Celio, if I write a note to our crew, can you send it to our ship with one of the hawks in town?" The fisherman nodded. "Good.

That will allow us to focus on the crisis here. We'll worry about Havenfall afterwards."

"I am surprised," Lucretia muttered. "I would think, given how much love you have expressed for the village, your first thought would be to run to its rescue."

Rubbing behind his head, Kai grinned. "To be honest, that was my gut instinct at first. Still, the Hunters are not incompetent. They can fend for themselves. My priority now is saving this town and everyone in it that I can."

Locke was the next to speak up. "Are you sure you want to take the time to worry about this town's troubles? What if something happens because you hesitated to act?" The traveler's eyes were full of confusion, sweeping over the party as his fingers curled into hooks.

"I'm willing to take the risk. The people here have done nothing wrong to deserve what's happened to them. As an apothecary, it's my duty to ensure their health and well-being."

"Perhaps, but you've seen the Liberators in action since the beginning," Locke retorted. "At times, they seem more monsters than men. You say you were raised there; are you not concerned for your family?"

Kai cast a hardened stare at the Aerivolk. "I've faced some of the most monstrous creatures to set foot on Livorian soil, but I've learned something from my experiences. There is no greater monster than a lack of compassion towards those in need."

His eyes softened when Maple hooked an arm around his elbow, her face split into a wide smile. "That's our Kai, always looking out for others. You already know I'll follow wherever you lead us."

Orelia stepped forward and swore to help as well, tears prickling at the edges of her eyes. The rest of the party followed suit, standing around Kai in a protective circle. Locke gazed at the group before shrugging his shoulders with a dismissive air. "I see you're determined to follow your convictions. You truly are the most unusual Norzen I've ever met. Pray Cacovis doesn't come for you too soon. I suppose with my body feeling better, I should look to leaving while I still can." Bowing his head, the Aerivolk bid them farewell and thanked Kai for his assistance before wandering away.

"I don't think I'll ever understand that guy," Morgan quipped. "Plus, he said before he gets around thanks to others helping him out. I just realized we've never met any of the folks who have supposedly helped him. Makes you wonder."

Lucretia scoffed. "I think you might be overthinking things, Morgan. I will admit something about him seems odd, but it may be my bias speaking against his nonchalant way of life. My best guess is he separates from his supporters upon arriving at his next destination. Given the issues here, he may have found himself stuck without anyone to help him travel further." Facing Kai, she asked if they were ready to search for the spring. The sooner they solved this latest mystery, the faster they could move on.

"As long as everyone is prepared and ready to go," Kai answered. He asked Celio if he knew the spring's location.

"Aye, it's underneath the old manor outside of town. I'll take you to the edge of town and show you the path, but you're on your own afterwards."

"You won't join us?" Teos asked, his eyebrow tilted.

"Sir, you couldn't pay anyone here a thousand golds to set foot in those ruins," the fisherman said. "They say the spirits of the noble family who once lived there still haunt the grounds and will curse any trespassers. No to mention the possibility of any animals or other dangerous beasts may have turned it into their den."

"I'll take my chances," Kai muttered. "The worst that should be in this area are daggertooth lions, and those are small potatoes compared to other beasts we've dealt with. Nulyma, I'd rather face a pride of daggertooths over another bulwark deer!"

Celio gulped and led the party down the southern road. Like many cities along the Great Ardei, Glimmerdale sat on the south end of a fork in the river. This left the town surrounded by water on three sides, the only exit in the southeast, leading into a forest of pine trees.

After a fair amount of walking, Celio pointed to a wide-open gate leading out of town. "Take the main road about a thousand yards," he explained.

"You'll see a path break off to the right and lead into the woods. Follow it maybe another three or four hundred yards. That's where the old manor is. There's a staircase somewhere inside leading underground that takes you down to the cavern where the spring is. Good luck, and may the winds guide you to safety." Celio brought his palms together in the Windbringer greeting and bowed.

"Many thanks, Celio. We'll figure out what's causing this and remove it so the spring can cleanse itself," said Kai. Pulling some parchment from his satchel, Kai scribbled a quick note and handed it to the fisherman. "Make sure this gets sent to our ship, the Senberg," he instructed. "It's addressed to our engineer, Dekel, telling him to send a warning letter to Havenfall."

"I have a silly question," Ione piped up, "but is that gate always open?"

Taking another look at the gate, Celio scratched his head. "Now that you mention it, that *is* strange. Most of the town guard have fallen ill too, so I suppose they forgot to close the gate before abandoning their post to stay home."

Frowning, Kai wondered if it really was an act of forgetfulness or if somebody ventured into the woods and left it open. Drawing his mace, he ordered Celio to go home and led the party through the gate.

They would find the source of this infection. Glimmerdale depended on it.

Chapter XIV

Fusette stared at her most recent letter from Kai, her lips forming a thin line. She and the Lord Chamberlain were making use of her study to work on documents to present to Admiral Basner once he arrived. The carrier hawk bearing Kai's report sat on the corner of her ornate oak desk, awaiting a reply. "Saredi," she said.

The Vesikoi noble looked up from the documents on his own desk in the opposite corner, peering at the duchess over the tops of his spectacles. "Yes, Your Grace?"

"Make a note that the next time Gravebane sets foot in the capital, we're holding a celebration in his honor. Also, remind me to wring his neck."

A rare smirk settled on Saredi's face. "I know that look, milady. What has the bloody fool done now to put you in such a tiff?"

"How he accomplishes so much despite nearly getting himself killed is a talent I will never comprehend," Fusette answered. "First, he uncovers a plot by a corrupt apothecary in Grantide to poison *dozens* of children with illegal medicine. One of the children afflicted was the only daughter of a member of Gravebane's own party."

Saredi blanched, the pale skin of his face turning even more sallow. "By the winds," he gasped. Like any good Windbringer, he knew the consequences of endangering children. "Were any of the young ones lost?"

"No, thank the Saints. Gravebane counteracted the poison's effects before any could succumb. I'm glad I slipped several herbs from Galstein into his satchel. I've no doubt he used some in his concoction, which would enhance the effects significantly. Sir Hanblum was sweet enough to procure the herbs before our return from Runegard."

"This is most fortunate, Your Grace. However, the fact you wish to throttle Gravebane suggests he also did something stupid. What happened?"

Fusette leaned back in her chair and rubbed her temples, groaning aloud. "It appears Lord Kendela is proving himself a menace. I learned from a guard he accosted Lady Maple during a Parliamentary recess, before Gravebane's party left. Now the stupid fool seems intent on following them. How he has kept tabs on them, I don't know, but it came to a head in Grantide."

Leaning forward, Saredi steepled his fingers and rested his chin on them. He wore a look of genuine interest. It almost made Fusette burst into giggles. She never imagined the older man to be one to indulge in political gossip. "Do tell, milady. This story is getting more interesting by the moment."

"Kendela not only attempted to undermine Gravebane's protective measures, but he also threatened to have Parliament force Lady Maple into a marriage contract."

The Lord Chamberlain's eyes bulged. "I can't imagine Gravebane taking such a threat too well. Also, would Kendela even have the authority?"

Now it was Fusette's turn to smirk. In her eight years on the throne, she gained a thorough understanding of how Parliament liked to work in the shadows. They may have succeeded in taking large swaths of her authority away since her ascension, but some things remained absolute. "I wouldn't put it above him to try and bribe enough nobles to force the matter through, not that it would do any good with Lady Maple considered my direct subordinate. An attempt to force her into anything would be met with severe consequences. Gravebane warned he would declare Blood Feud against Kendela if he threatened a member of his party again."

A loud bang echoed through the study; Saredi had jumped to his feet and slammed both hands on the desk. "Blood Feud?! Has the man lost his kettle? I'll admit Kendela is a boorish pain in the gills, but that sounds excessive."

"Saredi, I know you've never been one to put much stock in romance, but have you seen the way Gravebane looks at Lady Maple? Or the way Lady Maple and Sister Orelia look at *him*, for that matter?" Saredi's eyes widened even further. Fusette continued, "I know Gravebane is a tad...slow, so to speak, when it comes to romance, but he's so obvious about it at times I'm amazed the ladies in question haven't figured it out yet. Actually, never mind; they can be as dense as he is. As it stands, though, I would not be surprised to see one or both of those girls formally attached to Gravebane before the war's end."

"You would allow him to form a triad, knowing both partners are from different tribes? I know poly marriages are growing more common among the nobility, but I doubt Jovanni and the Quorum of Bishops would permit what you're suggesting."

"They won't get much of a choice in the matter, though I don't foresee Father Jovanni opposing it. You know how he is regarding faumen rights. I never put much stock in the church's nonsense about the tribes intermingling, and Madam Dineri's last report, among other things I've discovered, provides solid evidence supporting my opinion. Financially, Kai makes more than enough off his moonly wages as an Exarch to support such a family, to say nothing of his mission bonuses or the income from his apothecary business. So long as he files the appropriate paperwork within a moon of the ceremonies, I see no reason to forbid it."

"I pray you know what you're doing, Your Grace. Going back to Kendela, what makes you believe Gravebane would choose Blood Feud over his other options?"

Fusette giggled, casting a confident smirk at her advisor. "Regardless of his placid temperament, you've never seen Gravebane in a full fury. I've read the reports his party sent, detailing everything that's happened since Mistport. I have no doubt Kai would turn Parliament into a second Voidlands if he believed any of his friends were threatened. He has admitted in private he refuses to let them suffer the same fate as his former squad."

It took everything Fusette had to not laugh at the overwhelmed look on Saredi's face as he slumped into his chair. Saredi was notorious among the palace staff for his lack of ardor for the fairer sex. Fusette asked at least once a moon why he never married, but the Vesikoi always evaded the question. "I'm hesitant to ask what else might have happened in this mess," he grumbled.

"Funny you say that. Turns out the apothecary who poisoned the children somehow procured an adult bulwark deer to guard the herb Gravebane needed."

Now Saredi was digging his fingers into his temple, emitting a groan of frustration. "I won't even guess how that was accomplished. How in Nixtral did Gravebane get around a Great Beast?"

"Read this and you'll understand," she replied, handing a separate parchment to Saredi. "It's a report from Sir Teos. He was part of the group who faced the creature."

The pair sat in silence as Saredi studied the parchment. Fusette saw his face going through a multitude of expressions, though she did her best to ignore him, lest she break out into hysterics and receive another boring lecture on decorum. Instead, she fiddled with a quill she recently received from Belomas, made from a crescent eagle feather, another of the Great Beasts.

Thump!

The duchess' concentration broke, erupting into laughter at seeing Saredi's forehead strike the top of his desk repeatedly. "I assume you read everything?" she asked, holding back her mirth long enough to ask the question.

"*How*? How in the winds does he do it? Nobody has felled two of the Great Beasts in single combat since Dolmaru the Quillblade!"

"Perhaps we should avoid sending Gravebane on any missions into Rodekan or Galstein," Fusette quipped. Given the apothecary's penchant for trouble, she had no doubt he would somehow find his way into a situation involving a pack of bramble foxes or a tempest otter.

"By the Saints, no. With his luck, the man would add at least one more to his tally, if not all six. Parliament would lose the plot! At least now I know why you want to wring his neck."

Deciding to take it easy on her friend, Fusette changed the conversation to their search for the weapon used to frame Ambroz. To their irritation, no credible leads had been found. None of the constable chiefs admitted to seeing the musket, leaving them with little to go on.

"What of the Liberation Army?" Saredi asked. "Do we have any word on their whereabouts?"

Fusette's hand clenched into a fist. Her anger at the Liberators grew with every report she received on their attacks. She still thought of the day her scouts reported on Thorncrest's destruction. The reports were given in gruesome detail, putting images in her mind she could scarcely believe. There were days she would order Saredi to handle affairs in the throne room just so she could run back to her chambers for a good cry.

The Liberation Army was doing its damnedest to destroy everything her family had fought to build and protect for three hundred years. All for the sake of some stupid notion that humans were superior because faumen looked different. For the love of Luopari, even the Rodekan Empire had outgrown such backwards thinking, and they were the most prominent slave traders in all Nixtral for much of their history!

"I haven't heard much since Waveweaver's last report," Fusette confessed, using the Exarch Brand of her top admiral, Larimanz. A Wasini of considerable combat skill, Larimanz was the longest-serving Exarch who earned his Brand near the end of her grandfather, Duke Gunnar's, rule. "From what he saw, it appears the Libbies have broken into two forces. The smaller appears to be marching towards the Videring Forest. I can only imagine they're planning something with Duskmarsh. The larger force is heading for Havenfall."

As much as it pained her to admit it, she would likely have to travel to Duskmarsh at some point and handle the situation there herself. She needed to address the issue of captured Norzen, but with everything else hitting her from all sides, she didn't have the time. For now, she would send a carrier hawk to Osko, the city's headman, and warn him of the encroaching threat.

Her tails tingled as she imagined the Liberators marching on the Norzen city. She felt no sympathy for the terrorists, as they would quickly regret not bringing their full force against Duskmarsh. People could say what they wanted about the Norzen, but they thrived in the swamps' shadows and any attempt to conquer them would be met with swift and brutal retribution.

"Oh sweet merciful Galen," Saredi groaned, "this will put Gravebane on a direct path to face them again. What can we do?"

"I trust Duskmarsh to handle itself in a fight," Fusette answered. "Now that you mention it, I must provide Waveweaver with direction. I'll pen an order to engage the main army before they reach Havenfall. With any luck, Hanblum has news of when our friends from Galstein are expected to arrive."

A knock at the door startled the pair from their conversation. Answering it, Fusette was stunned to see Hanblum himself standing there, a sheaf of parchment clutched in his arms. "Well I'll be, just the man we were talking about."

"All good things, I hope, Your Grace?"

Fusette tittered. "Of course, Sir Hanblum. We were just wondering aloud if you heard any news from Admiral Basner."

Seeing the Aerivolk envoy's look of relief sent a spark of amusement through the duchess' heart. The man was well-mannered, intelligent, and a joy to talk with. During the brief respites where he wasn't penning letters back home, she found herself sharing stories with him about their experiences. Fusette particularly enjoyed hearing Hanblum gush about his wife and son back in Rosenholm. It gave her hope that, someday, she could have a family of her own. Then again, she was only 26, though her birthday wasn't until the end of Regemond, another three moons away; there was still time to worry about the future after the war ended.

"He should be here very soon, Your Grace. Within another day or two, if my guess is correct."

"Excellent! The man knows how to make good time. Saredi, please ensure the staff are ready to welcome the admiral. We want to make a good impression." The Lord Chamberlain nodded and jotted a note down, promising to arrange a proper welcoming ceremony before the night was done. Fusette appreciated Saredi's diligence and ability to juggle his many responsibilities. She didn't know where she would be at without his steady guidance.

"Begging your pardon, Your Grace," Hanblum said, drawing her gaze back to him, "but have you received any response to your inquiry to President Harmod?"

Hearing the Corlatian leader's name made Fusette sigh in resignation. "I did, in fact, receive a response. As you might expect, Gideon was rather put out we would insinuate he broke the Fulano Pact. I consider it a victory he didn't make an outright declaration of war. Mind you, we never made a straightforward accusation, but I did submit the evidence we have collected thus far."

"Did he accuse you of falsifying it?" Saredi asked, his voice firm and unyielding.

"No. If anything, he seemed unnerved by the evidence. He admitted the muskets were the most pressing matter, as he was aware of several forge masters working on developing such weapons."

"Is he planning to do anything about it?" Saredi pressed further.

"He has to," Hanblum answered. "To ignore the implications would be too risky. If Her Grace wanted, she could call a summit of the Five Realms Council and present her evidence there. Such an event would bring questions Harmod's way I'm sure he doesn't have answers for."

"What do you mean?"

"The fact that he's unnerved makes me think he isn't aware of what's going on. This would imply there's a rogue faction in Corlati breaching the Fulano Pact right under his nose. Such a revelation would make Harmod a laughingstock, to say nothing of the danger it would bring Corlati's way."

Fusette grinned. "And with how much Gideon loves his reputation..."

An equally smug grin settled over Hanblum's face. "He'll want to do whatever it takes to weasel out the true culprit, if only to throw them in front of the Council's ire. Any formal inquiry finding Corlati guilty of breaking the Fulano Pact would force the other realms to act."

"Indeed," Saredi spoke. "We may have our hands full with the Liberation Army now, but it wouldn't stop Chief Velibor or Emperor Kabuji from declaring war. Supposing we defeat the Liberators in due time, Corlati would face battle on all sides. I don't care how advanced their military is, not even *they* could survive that."

Leaning back into her chair, Fusette felt several layers of stress peel away at the news. She knew she would have to reply to Harmod and offer her verbal support in his search for the one instigating all this. Still, something Hanblum said tugged at her mind.

A summit, huh? Perhaps it's finally time I use the full breadth of my authority.

Chapter XV

Despite it being the middle of the day, a heavy cloud cover gave the forest a silvery blue hue as the party trekked along the path. As Celio said, a thousand yards outside Glimmerdale, a separate trail broke off from the main road leading into the woods. A thin layer of fog hung in the air; not enough to hamper visibility, but it left an eerie ambience that sent chills down Kai's spine.

The fog was something Kai grew used to while growing up, but he never enjoyed it. Springtime was the worst, with most of southern Livoria being covered in the stuff for half the day. Pulling a small strip of cloth from his satchel, he brushed away the dew spreading over his mane. The only saving grace was that the fog wasn't as thick as he had seen in Mistport, a fact he was grateful for. He didn't relish the thought of navigating these trees in a mire of soupy mist.

He felt Maple shiver next to him and took her hand in his, giving it a small squeeze. His gaze flickered to meet hers, seeing a relieved smile cross her face. His eyes swept over the party, sensing an aura of hesitation as they marched at a slow pace.

"You think we'll find anything in these ruins?" Morgan asked. The sellsword's eyes darted about, one hand resting on his falchion and ready to draw at a moment's notice.

"I pray we don't," Ione answered from her place in the middle of the group. She clutched her sheathed dagger with both hands and nearly tripped over an ivy bush crawling across the forest floor. It was only Lucretia grabbing the tavern maid by the arm that kept her from falling face-first into the dirt.

The scholar helped Ione steady herself. "I find myself agreeing with you," said Lucretia. "Nevertheless, we must remain diligent. There is no telling what dangers could be lurking here."

Stepping over a log, Kai's ears twitched, swiveling in search of any unusual sounds. There was the occasional chirp of a bird from far away, and a soft skittering from bugs or lizards darting through the grass. Other than that, he heard very little, though he couldn't shake the feeling they were being watched. There was a prickling tingle in his mane that had nothing to do with the mist, and that unnerved him.

He almost jumped when he felt something against his tails, only to sigh in relief when he saw Maple's hand. Kai allowed the appendages to coil around her arm. The touch of her skin against his fur was soothing and left him brimming with confidence. Her whisper of gratitude brought a smile to his lips. He gave her hand another squeeze.

"We're clear back here," Teos called out from the party's rear. He and Orelia were making sure they weren't being followed. Both had their weapons drawn and ready.

An ominous shadow grew among the wisps of fog. Kai's hand moved to his mace but stopped short of drawing it when he realized the shadow wasn't moving. "I think we found it," he announced, drawing everyone's attention to the front.

Sure enough, the fog lifted as they approached, revealing the remains of a massive stone house. It was easy to see the dilapidated ruin as a noble's manor; its size alone was evidence enough. What was left of the iron fence surrounding the grounds was tilted over, held up only by the rusted posts keeping it nailed into the ground. Spread out over an area at least a hundred yards wide, the grounds were reclaimed by nature and overrun with weeds, thickets, and sparse bundles of wildflowers. Several large pits dotted the grounds as well, though what purpose they served, Kai wasn't sure.

Walking past the ruined gate, its pickets bent outward as though something *forced* its way through, the party gazed up at the manor's remains.

The building itself had a majestic air despite its decrepit state. The smell of rotting wood was prevalent, forcing everyone to cover their noses. Huge chunks of the stone exterior were broken off, leaving numerous holes scattered along the outer walls. A gust of wind passed over the group, producing an odd whistle as they approached.

"This place looks as though it hasn't been used in years," said Orelia as she planted herself at Kai's side, her body visibly trembling. The front door was missing, allowing everyone to stroll in unimpeded.

The interior looked worse than the exterior. Bits and pieces of abandoned furniture were strewn over the main hall. Multiple large gashes were torn into the walls and floor, suggesting some sort of beast had been inside at some point. Whether it remained or not, Kai didn't know. He strode up to one wall and inspected the damage.

"These look like daggertooth claw marks," said Kai, peering through the slits to the room on the other side; the kitchen from the looks of it. "If I didn't know better, I'd say there was a small pride here, and they were fighting over something."

"Who says they were not fighting *against* something?" Lucretia asked. "Something bigger or stronger than them."

Kai frowned. The thought crossed his mind, but there were few creatures capable of defeating a pride of daggertooths, none of which he desired to face himself.

"Celio said the spring was down an underground path," Orelia reminded them. "Should we split up and try to find the opening?"

Images of Mistport flashed through Kai's mind. His squad leader, Calvino, had split them up while searching for Grimghast. The man paid for his decision with his life. Tears prickled the edge of Kai's eyes. Blinking them away, he took a deep breath.

"Absolutely not," he ordered. A soft creak broke through the silence. The apothecary's head swiveled, casting a searching glance around the main hall. "We stay within eyesight for now. I don't want any unnecessary risks. We do this as a team and make sure everyone stays safe, understood?"

Turning to face the party, he was relieved to see everyone nodding. "You make a good point," Lucretia said. "We do not know how stable this building is. With all the decay, the floor could very well collapse beneath our feet. Kai is right; we should stick together and watch each other's backs." Sharing a look, everyone agreed to stay close.

Teos suggested checking each door on the ground floor in a circular path. They started to the right of the stairway leading to the second floor, opening a small door to find a tiny storage closet. The party entered the kitchen, seeing only a few doors.

They split into two groups, each taking one side of the kitchen. Kai was surprised to see Lucretia join him, Orelia, and Morgan in checking the rear half. The scholar sent him a confident smirk; one he couldn't help but return. They may not be close friends yet, but she was making strides to reach out. It filled him with hope.

"Nothing over here!" Teos shouted from the other side of the kitchen. Opening each door, the quartet found nothing and prepared to move on. Kai was surprised to hear Lucretia call him over to the far corner.

He and Orelia came over to see what she found. Lucretia was staring hard at the wall, waving her arm in front of it with a look of intense concentration. Kai asked her what she was doing.

"It feels like a breeze is coming from this wall but I am unsure as to how."

Raising his own arm, Kai waved it in front of the same wall. Sure enough, there was a soft rush of air against his skin.

"I think we may have found what we're looking for," he muttered. "This could be a hidden entrance like the one Saredi showed us in Runegard."

"But why would wind be blowing from it now? Seems like the door wasn't shut all the way," Morgan piped up from the rear.

"Think about how old this place is, Morgan," Lucretia replied. "It is possible the entrance has eroded to the point it no longer fully seals."

"That makes sense. I appreciate ya laying it out for me."

A slight tint of red bloomed over Lucretia's cheeks as she coughed into her hand. "Think nothing of it."

The rest of the party ambled over, Maple asking if they found the entrance. Kai gave Teos a grin. "Think you can pry it open?" he asked. As a Soltauri, and thus the party member with the most physical strength, Kai knew Teos was their best option for forcing their way in.

The smuggler shot back a grin of his own. "With pleasure. Get back, everyone." Using his arm to determine the wind's origin, Teos slammed his halberd into a small crevice in the wall. Little force was needed for him to break the entrance open; the wooden frame was so thoroughly rotted it crumbled to pieces, kicking up a cloud of dust and mold.

Using an arm to cover his nose, Kai peered into the passage and noticed it opened up further ahead as it descended.

"This is it," he announced. "The spring should be at the bottom of this path. Grab any planks or old torches left over. We'll need light down there."

Everyone spread out and grabbed hold of the longest, sturdiest pieces of wood they could hold. Teos took an old tunic and wrapped it over his shoulder like a shawl, telling everyone to set the boards inside.

Lighting one up with a sparkstone, Kai led the party into the passage, which contained a thin layer of mist within as well. As expected, the scent of mold worsened the further they went, and thick clumps of algae appeared along the walls. Soon it covered the floor as well. The firelight revealed the craggy stone walls to have a deep reddish hue. Running the edge of her dagger over the stone, Ione snorted at seeing the blade leave a visible scratch.

"These walls in here look to be predominately red calcite," she said. "It's not a very durable stone, so be careful not to hit the walls too hard; crack a wall in the wrong place could it could bring the whole passage down on top of us."

A muffled grunt sounded from Morgan when he slipped on a moss-covered stone, falling hard on his knee. His falchion sent up sparks as it dug into the edge of the path. A small chunk of stone broke off and tumbled into the abyss below. Kai turned and flashed an unamused look towards the other man as the others peered over the edge in obvious apprehension. Nobody dared move, the only sound coming from the broken slab of calcite bouncing off the cliff face in its descent.

Morgan hissed in pain but waved off Ione's offer of assistance. "I'll be fine, lass," he said. "Just hit my knee rougher than expected."

"What's up ahead?" asked Orelia, pointing past Kai's shoulder to a glimmer of light growing brighter the closer they approached. As they descended, the passage widened into a true cavern. The stone walls were slick with condensation, and a musky smell permeated the air with the intensity of a fish market receiving fresh catch.

Kai frowned, his eyebrows narrowing. "I'm not sure. There shouldn't be any light down here." The apothecary was also concerned by the lack of staleness in the air. It was possible the rotted entrance allowed some air to circulate, but not to this extent.

"Think there's someone else here?" asked Teos.

Kai was hesitant to answer. There was no telling what awaited them at the spring. Ione took quick, repeating breaths behind him as her grip on her dagger tightened. "I don't know, Teos," he finally replied. "If there *is* someone hiding out down here, it might help explain what's going on. Stay alert."

Without a word, everyone nodded and followed Kai deeper into the path. The only sound echoing in the cave was the skittering of loose rocks as the party eased forward. The walkway led to a small entrance through which the light seemed to be coming. Holding the torch up, Kai saw the path's edge continued its drop off into a black emptiness. A shiver ran through his mind as remembered the events that day on the *Fallbrook*. Maple and he saw a void much like this in the wrecked pirate vessel's hull. He could still see the terror in her eyes when she almost plummeted into the hull's abyss.

Shaking off the unease, he leaned forward and passed through the new entrance, unsure of what they would find. The light continued growing brighter, setting Kai's nerves on edge.

They were stunned to reach the end of the path and enter a massive cavern overflowing with natural light. Glancing up, Kai saw light shining through multiple slanted holes in the ceiling. After gathering his bearings, he realized something.

"I think those are the same pit holes we spotted on the grounds," said Kai.

Everyone's heads craned up. Ione sighed in visible relief. "I believe you're right," she replied. "Oh, thank Luopari. I was worried we might have bandits or something hiding out in here. At least we know the light is natural."

Orelia emitted a soft gasp that drew Kai's attention to her. Saying nothing, she raised a finger and pointed out into the cavern, her other hand grasping his elbow in a tight grip. The apothecary couldn't stop from gaping at the sight.

The spring was much larger than he anticipated. The surface alone stretched out at least three dozen yards in diameter, and there was no telling how deep it ran to the source feeding it. The spring flowed out through an open passage maybe two yards wide at the opposite end of the cavern. Dilating his eyes, he ignored the sting from the flaming torch in his hand and inspected the passage, seeing it wind its way towards what he assumed was Glimmerdale. He was grateful to see plenty of space for them to walk in the underground room; trying to navigate the area on the same type of narrow path they encountered at the passage entrance would've been difficult.

A tall plateau stood in the opposite corner, its ledge scant yards below one of the ceiling openings. The cliff was sloped at a steep angle; difficult to climb, though not impossible. Throughout the cave, the same algae from earlier was joined by sporadic clumps of weeds and clover sprouting from the many cracks in the rocky floor and walls.

Extinguishing their torch, Kai approached the edge of the spring with some hesitation. He peered into the water and saw the same cloudy appearance from the well back in Glimmerdale. His eyebrows furrowed, he leaned closer and took a hesitant sniff. The sour scent was the same as what they found in town, but more potent.

"Well, the good news is we definitely found where the contamination is coming from," Kai grumbled. "The bad news is I have no clue how to fix it. It's like something fouled the water over a significant time. I can see mud, debris, and other leavings inside, but there's any number of things that could've left them. I can only pray the taint hasn't reached the deeper groundwater."

"There's truly no way to cleanse the spring?" Orelia asked, falling to her knees. The others watched with expressions of melancholy.

Kai swore and slammed a fist into the ground. "If there is, I've never heard of it. Boiling the entire spring could work to an extent, but there's no way we can heat all the water to such a high temperature at once. Not only that, there's no guarantee the heat would reach all the way through to cleanse the water already in Glimmerdale."

Taking a knee next to Kai, Lucretia examined the spring as well, gazing at the murky water with an intense expression. "It feels like we are missing something." She pointed out bits of debris floating on the surface. "What is all this? I cannot tell without pulling it from the water, and I refuse to put my hand in this muck."

Maple sidled alongside them and squinted at the material Lucretia pointed out. "If I didn't know any better," she muttered, "I'd say it looks like bits and pieces of fur, bone, and meat. And that's not even mentioning the amount of dirt and whatever else is in there."

"Perhaps someone was using it as a hiding place and discarded the remains of hunted animals into the spring?" Ione suggested.

"That's the most likely explanation. It's entirely possible they were also using the spring as a privy as well." The entire party flinched in disgust. "They would have to have been hiding here for quite some time to cause such severe contamination. At least a moon. If most of the residents in Glimmerdale view this place the same way Celio does, it would be the perfect hideaway."

Tapping one foot, Morgan ground a fist into his beard. "This might be a wild arrow shot in the dark, but I just thought of something." Everyone's eyes swung to the sellsword, who stared at Kai with a confused expression.

"What about the crazy glowing concoction the Grand Duchess gave you before we left the capital? Didn't she say it was a purification mixture of some kind?"

Kai blinked. The only sound heard in the cavern was the gusts of wind from above blowing through the holes in the ceiling, producing a thrum not unlike that of a horn. The apothecary stared at Morgan in clear befuddlement before striking his temple with the heel of his palm. "Bloody Nulyma, I can't believe I forgot about that," he grumbled.

He reached into his satchel and pulled the bottle he received from Fusette, removing the leather wrap he encased it in. To the party's amazement, the concoction retained its ghostly glow, shining like seawater in the moonlight. Kai removed the cork, allowing a puff of smoke to rise from the open bottle.

A soft hum came from Maple. "Uh, Kai, is it supposed to smell like that?" she asked. Taking a hesitant sniff, he flinched back on instinct. The concoction gave off an unexpected pungent odor. The rest of the part backed away, covering their noses.

"What the hoarfrost is in that stuff?" Morgan coughed, gagging as he turned away to dry heave. The others were in similar positions, though to Kai's relief, none of them actually vomited. Teos looked to be a near thing, however.

"I don't know," Kai admitted, "but Fusette said it came from Galstein, which means whatever it's meant to do, it'll do it *well*." Frowning, Kai poured the contents into the spring, unsure of how the concoction was supposed to work. His best guess was, as a purifier, it needed to be mixed into the water to work.

His eyes bulged when the glow from the potion began to spread throughout the spring. The party watched with fascination as plumes of steam rose up from the water, the spring bubbling and frothing in a rolling boil.

"By the winds," Lucretia whispered.

Holding his hand above the water, Morgan drew it back with a hiss the moment the steam touched his skin. "Merciful Cadell, it's hot! What did we just do? You said Fusette got this from Galstein, right, 'pothy?"

With a nod, Kai reminded them that Fusette received the concoction from Hanblum, the Galstan envoy, as a gift from the queen. Everyone turned to Orelia when she emitted a stunned gasp.

"I've always been taught that herbs and concoctions from Galstein were among the most potent in Nixtral, but I never could've imagined something like this," the priestess said. The steam was now rising in waves and Kai could feel the intense heat from his place near the edge. The sound of a rock skittering above them prickled his ears, prompting his eyes to flicker towards the ceiling openings, but he saw nothing.

"How are Galstan medicines so powerful? Nothing Kai has ever made could create such a reaction," wondered Lucretia. She had a piece of parchment in her hands and scribbled notes as she observed the bubbling spring.

"No one truly knows," Orelia answered. "It's been said parts of Galstein lie at a nexus of the Origin ley lines flowing throughout Nixtral. Less than a dozen of these nexus points are said to exist around the world, with numerous rumors among our scholars of one located somewhere on the Belomas coast. It's possible those ley lines are responsible for the potency of our medicinal herbs. After all, the energy produced by that junction is said to be responsible for the Garden of Levot."

"Do you have any proof?" asked Teos. "And last I heard, the Garden of Levot was a myth."

"I've been lucky enough to sit in on meetings between my father and the Holy Matriarch, along with my brothers. To hear Her Majesty speak of it, the Garden is not only real, but was a factor in saving the realm during a medicine shortage back in AR 941. Since then, the Garden is considered sacred ground and few outside the royal family are allowed to set foot there. I've heard the story so many times, the year is committed to memory."

"AR 941?" Lucretia muttered. "But that was only a little over eighty years ago, right?"

"86, to be exact," Orelia corrected. "Queen Isolde's grandmother, Lotte, was the reigning queen during the incident."

"I don't mean to interrupt," Maple cut in, drawing everyone's attention, "but I think whatever the potion is doing is almost finished. The steam is dissipating."

Turning his gaze to the spring, Kai saw she was right. As fast as it had formed, the steam faded from sight while the glow diminished to nothing, and the bubbling slowed to a stop. What remained left the party in stunned silence.

Where the spring water was cloudy and littered with debris before, now it was as clear as glass. Kai peered over the edge and saw the bottom of the spring at least a hundred yards beneath the surface. Kneeling, Kai took a tentative sniff. There was no scent. Whatever contamination had caused the sour smell from before was gone. Teos confirmed as much when he took a sniff of his own and swore he'd never smelled water so clean.

"I'm not sure what that concoction was," the smuggler admitted as he stood, "but it worked far better than we could've hoped for. The spring has been cleansed."

"Remind me to send Her Majesty an appropriate gift once we return to the capital. As much as I don't like admitting it, I'm not sure I could've fixed this without that concoction," said Kai.

He shivered when Maple slipped next to him and wrapped her wings around his arm. "Saredi owes you an apology as well," she said. "After all, he tried to convince us and Fusette it should've stayed in Whistlevale. I'm certain thousands of people are going to be saved because of this."

A loud, cackling laugh echoed through the cavern. Kai's ears turned sideways. It was coming from behind. He spun to see a short, cloaked figure coming through the entrance. Kai couldn't see their eyes, but the unhinged smile beneath his hood was enough of a warning. The newcomer wasn't friendly.

"I must say, that was impressive," the figure spoke. His voice was smooth as velvet and carried an accent Kai was unfamiliar with. A foreigner, perhaps? The back of their cloak shifted, as if something were moving beneath it. "After my comrade spent so much time and trouble trying to wipe out this backwater town, you fools come in and ruin the fun like it's nothing. If it weren't so infuriating, I'd recommend you for a medal!"

The party drew their weapons. "Who are you?" Lucretia demanded, pointing her rapier at the man's face.

Morgan's eyebrows pinched together as he watched the figure with a puzzled expression. "What the piss...?" he mumbled.

The man erupted into another peal of laughter, not fazed at all by the variety of weapons pointed in his direction. "This is quite amusing. See, I followed you lot in here after I spotted you wandering through the woods. I know quite a bit about you fools, too. After all, you've been getting in the way of our comrades' plans for some time now. And yet, I've never been given the opportunity to deal with you myself. I suppose that changes today."

Giving his mace a test swing, Kai chuffed. "Guess that means you're with the Liberators. Why am I not surprised to find you bastards behind this?"

"I'd be embarrassed to admit being a member of those half-witted morons. They can't even conquer a city properly. No, I think Duarte put it best." Lucretia gasped at the mention of the Soltauri monk's name. "They're nothing but convenient allies too stupid to see the big picture. They probably think they're using us instead of the other way around, seeing as how we're just 'filthy faumen' to them."

The man grabbed his hood and flipped it back, revealing a roguish face with almond-shaped ice blue eyes and pale skin. He was clearly a faumen, but Kai found himself entranced by the man's triangular ears, longer and thinner than his own with tufts of white fur lining the inside. Undoing his cloak's clasp, he tore the garment from his body, tossing it aside.

His body was stocky and heavily muscled. Wearing a sleeveless tunic of pure white, his arms were powerfully built and covered with a thick pelt of grey fur. A red metal breastplate with black trim covered his upper chest. His loose-fitting trousers were the same shade of white, tucked into a pair of boots extending to mid-calf and tied at the waist with a grey sash.

The most surprising thing Kai noticed was his tail—A long, bushy appendage twirling at random. While mostly covered in grey fur, the last hand or so of the tip was white. To the apothecary, it looked like a large fox's tail.

Morgan emitted a choking gasp, drawing everyone's attention. "No bloody way," he gasped. "You...how are you alive?"

The man gazed at Morgan in confusion until a flash of recognition shone in his eyes. He gave another high-pitched bout of laughter. "Well I'll be damned. I could be asking you the same question, Morgan!"

"Morgan," Orelia hissed, turning a fierce glare at the sweating sellsword. "Who is this man and how in the winds do you know him? For that matter, what even *is he*?"

"In my defense, lass," Morgan replied, "I thought Grimghast swallowed him up along with the rest of my company. That's Obram, commander of my old band, the Scarlet Spears. As for what he is, I'll confess I've no clue. The previous commander brought him over from somewhere up north before retiring, and he took over the group only a few moons before the war. He never talked about himself much. Never took his cloak off either, now that I think of it. This is as much a surprise to me as the rest of ya."

"It's rather hard being forced to stand out," Obram explained. "After all, I'm probably the first of my people to set foot on this backwater continent since the days of the Great Rebirth. However, I suppose I can at least enlighten you before you die. I do love telling a good story, after all, and I'd rather sit here gloating at you instead of chasing after that dipwit, Agosti." Teos growled at the mention of the Liberator officer. "As for what I am, I hail from a faumen tribe native to the northern continent of Feswili: the Risbado."

Kai allowed his eyes to dart across the cavern, looking for a way out. As long as Obram kept talking, he had time to figure out a plan. They outnumbered him, for certain, but the apothecary figured he wouldn't expose himself without a plan.

"My people have always taken issue with the damnable Norzen," Obram continued, his eyes locking onto Kai with a hardened scowl. "Our tribes are alike in a lot of ways. Hated. Hunted for the atrocities of others. But back home, our peoples have been at war for hundreds of years."

"Why?" Ione asked. "What could possibly be so important for your tribes would be fighting for so long?"

To their surprise, Obram didn't outright dismiss the question. Instead, Ione's inquiry had him leaning against the wall pondering the idea. "To be honest, I don't think anyone remembers," he admitted. "But...I suppose when you've been fighting for so long, the reasons don't really matter after a while. It's all we've ever known."

"Then why join up with the Libbies?" Morgan asked. "You already know how they feel about faumen."

"My employer, the man who hired us for that transport job to Mistport, has his own plans for those pebblewits. In all honesty, you boys were never meant to get involved the way you did with that beast. It was an unfortunate accident. The creature had a different target that day but went on a rampage after developing a taste for the flesh of men."

To many, Obram's solemn gaze would look authentic. But Kai sensed something deeper in the Risbado's eyes. Something darker. Then, there was his revelation about Grimghast...

It seemed Morgan picked up on it as well because he snarled at the other sellsword, brandishing his falchion. "A different target," he murmured, his pupils shrinking to pinpoints. "Are you telling me that damned beast was *meant* to be in Mistport? How would you even know that?"

Everyone blanched at the accusation. Ione looked ready to faint. Kai felt the unmistakable shroud of a Frenzy Haze falling over him. A quick glance at the others showed them in various states of shock.

"Of course it was meant to be there, you idiot," said Obram. "That monster and his handler have been a part of the boss' plans from the outset. In fact..." the man gave the party a smug grin as everyone almost jumped at a new sound within the cavern.

A familiar growl from the bowels of their nightmares.

Her body trembling, Orelia shot the others an uneasy smile. "Please tell me that was your stomach, Morgan." Her voice cracked with each word, her tone pleading for any semblance of hope.

"It wasn't my stomach, lass, and you know it."

A second growl shattered the quiet of the cave. Kai muttered a curse under his breath and dilated his pupils. The sudden brightness from the light shining through the ceiling burned his eyes, but he forced himself to bear it. His ears swiveled outward, hoping to detect any clue of Grimghast's whereabouts.

"Kai!" shouted Maple. "The plateau!"

Everyone's heads spun up towards the cliff at the end of the cavern. To Kai's horror, the air rippled wildly above the plateau. A single red dot hovered in the air, meeting the apothecary's eyes. In a scene the party was more familiar with than they wished for, the air melted away to reveal Grimghast towering over them.

The sound of a drawn blade pulled Kai's attention just enough to watch Obram reveal a broadsword with an unusually short blade from behind his back.

"Sorry, Morgan, old boy," Obram chuckled, "but I'm afraid this is the end for you. You and this pack of fools won't be leaving here alive."

"We have bested this thing before," Lucretia declared with a twirl of her rapier. "Adding you to the mix will not change the outcome."

"I like the confidence. Now let's see you back it up."

"Morgan," Kai commanded. His eyes shone bright, and his muscles tensed in anticipation. "You, Ione and Lucretia will handle taking him down." He pointed at the smirking Obram. "The rest of us will deal with Grimghast."

The sellsword nodded, turning to face his former commander with the two women standing beside him.

"Remember our tactics," Kai reminded the others. "We can do this." Despite saying it with conviction, Kai wished he believed the words as much as he sounded like he did. With Obram on one side and Grimghast on the other, this would not be easy.

They would need the Saints' own luck to leave this battle unscathed.

Chapter XVI

Images flared in Kai's mind as he met Grimghast's single beady red eye. A scarred dent was all that remained of the one he destroyed back in the forests during their trek to Runegard. Staring into the crimson abyss reminded him of the terror in his squad mates eyes before they died. The sight of his squad leader, Calvino, lying in a bloody heap before being torn apart was an image that would stay with him for the rest of his life. Knowing now that Grimghast was planted in Mistport on purpose stoked the rage building in his chest. However, the knowledge brought just as many questions as it did answers.

How are they able to control the damn thing? Kai wondered. *It's clear this monster is more intelligent than any normal animal, maybe even on par with the Great Beasts, so perhaps they were able to train it. Obram did mention a handler, which means it* isn't *him. We would've encountered him before now, if that were the case. But if he's not the handler, who is, and where are they hiding?*

Any further thoughts were stalled when a gust of wind echoed through the cavern, resulting in a loud whistle. Grimghast roared, causing Kai to flinch back, his ears flattening against his head. The beast leapt from the plateau towards Kai's group, scattering them.

Kai rolled into a crouch and heard Grimghast shriek in pain. Spinning around, he saw Teos' halberd rammed into its shoulder, just beneath the bony plates nailed into its body. A wide swipe of its paw sent the smuggler flying backwards, hitting the cliff with a crash.

A whistle from behind caught Kai's attention. Turning his head, he saw Maple barreling towards him with her wings spread. A spark of realization shot through the apothecary, and he positioned himself in a kneeling crouch in front of Maple. The click of her talons rang in his ears, growing louder with each step. He felt her talon press into his back within moments. With a sharp trill, the merchant launched herself into a glide off Kai's back. Her jump carried her above Grimghast's head, allowing to tuck herself into a dive. The beast was too busy snapping at Teos and Orelia to notice her attack.

Seeing Maple pick up speed, Kai burst forward refusing to let her attack alone. He also had an idea of what she was planning.

Maple crashed into Grimghast's back, her claws digging into its emaciated flesh. It reared up with a shriek, flailing around to throw the Aerivolk off. Kai grinned, ducking under its thrashing limbs and throwing a double-handed swing into Grimghast's gut. The mace's flanges bit into the skin just beneath its rib armor, causing it to collapse on all fours in pain. With a cry of triumph, Maple threw herself off the beast's back, slashing her talons across the exposed skin in the process.

Even with the multitude of new wounds, Grimghast glared defiantly and roared a challenge. Kai and Teos nodded to each other and charged forward, baiting Grimghast into lunging at them before sidestepping out of the way. Orelia gripped her staff and stepped in, swinging in a wide arc right into the beast's snout. Grimghast ambled away before bellowing at the priestess, shrieking in pain once more when an arrow from Maple dug into its neck.

Chancing a glance back at Morgan's group while Teos and Orelia rallied around him, Kai hoped they were having better luck with Obram. Holding his mace in a defensive stance, he awaited the beast's next move.

Morgan growled as his sword was parried once again by Obram. Lucretia and Ione weren't having much luck against the Risbado sellsword either. Ione was able to use her pan as an effective shield to deflect the man's jabs, but she couldn't land even a glancing blow with her dagger.

Obram was too skilled and wielded his blade with a deftness that proved why he was a sellsword commander.

Lucretia was performing better, but not by much. Her lithe frame and speed with the rapier allowed her to land several hits on Obram. The main problem lay in his ability to shrug her blows off with ease. Morgan swore one of the scholar's thrusts dug deep into his left thigh, and yet Obram moved as if the wound wasn't there.

It was maddening, though Morgan couldn't be surprised too much. He'd heard rumors the former commander had a reputation for being a brick wall in battle, and he was witnessing the proof first-hand.

Morgan saw Obram spin around another clumsy attack by Ione and swing his blade at the woman's prone back. With a snarl, the Wasini mixblood charged, using the tip of his falchion to parry the attack and drive it into the stone floor. He took advantage of Obram's momentary confusion to land a solid jab to his face, sending him stumbling.

"Damnation," Obram hissed as he backed away. He prodded his broken nose with a wince before using his fingers to pop it back in place with an audible crunch. Ione and Lucretia both winced. "I gotta admit, I forgot how fucking tough you are, Morgan. That was a hell of a punch."

"Well, there's plenty more ready for ya," Morgan retorted. "Did our time in the Spears mean nothing to you? Are you really gonna brush off what happened as a damned accident?"

"Oh please. We're sellswords, you blithering moron. We always get betrayed in the end, one way or another. I just got out of the way of that monster's rampage before it hit you boys because I already knew it was there. I wasn't about to get caught up in the mess it was bound to leave behind."

Taking deep, heavy breaths, Morgan felt pure rage bubbling within his chest. "Well it may not have meant much to you, but those men were my friends. My brothers of the blade. And we looked out for each other, like you're supposed to do."

"Your loyalty is commendable, if naively stupid. You have to be willing to do what it takes to survive in this world, even if it means stepping over yesterday's comrades."

Morgan chuckled, causing Lucretia and Ione to look at him with worry in their eyes. "Guess that makes you a piss-poor excuse of a man, Obram. My loyalty is my honor, and I'd rather die than give it up."

"That can be arranged. Is that why you're wasting time with these pathetic sods?"

Putting himself between the other sellsword and his friends, Morgan slammed a fist against his chest. "These people have taught me the true meaning of family and loyalty. We have our differences, but what family doesn't? We still watch out for each other, anyway, regardless of those differences. That's why I fight beside them. Makes me wish I were born a Livorian or Galstan, rather than a mangy Corlatian."

Morgan was surprised when Ione sidled beside him and thwacked him over the head. "You'd best hush up right now, Morgan. It doesn't matter a wit that you're Corlatian. You're still our friend."

"Ione is right," Lucretia added. "You have your flaws, but you have still proven to be a loyal ally. We may not be the best of friends, but you are still a comrade."

Wiping his fist across his lip, Morgan smirked at the two. "Thanks, lass. What do ya say we put this mongrel down?" He was stunned to silence when a new but familiar voice joined the fray.

"How do you lot always get yourselves in these messes?" Locke quipped as he sprinted into the cavern. Morgan gaped at the changes in the Aerivolk traveler.

Where his white feathers looked withered and droopy before, now they were firm with a lustrous shine. His body had visibly filled out, the ratty tunic he wore exposing the wiry muscles common among his tribe. His triangular face was fuller, its hard lines giving him a chiseled, roguish appearance. Two piercing lilac eyes hovered over the group, bright and alert. Overall, he looked fitter and healthier than Morgan ever remembered.

Locke carried a straight-edged knife with a short hilt, spinning it like a baton.

"Locke?" asked Ione, staring at the man in shock. "What in the winds happened to you?"

"I must say Kai's tonic worked better than I hoped for. I feel like a new man! Following you here was quite easy now that my ability to move isn't hampered."

Obram stared at Locke with a curious expression, his gaze shifting to where Kai and the others were fighting off Grimghast. "Interesting. So the boy's an apothecary? A skilled one, too, from the looks of it. We may have to change our tactics."

"Don't worry about us," Morgan called out. "Go give Kai and the others a hand, if you're feeling up to it!"

"Certainly," Locke replied. "I'll take care of things." The traveler took off sprinting towards the others. Spreading his wings, he leapt into a full glide, soaring into the fight.

Turning back to Obram, Morgan rattled his blade against a nearby stone. Ione held her pan in front of her and Lucretia slid into a stance.

To their shock, Obram began cackling. With his head leaned back, staring at the ceiling with his mouth wide open in maniacal laughter, he looked insane.

"You-you idiots still think you're going to leave here alive?" he asked.

Scowling, Lucretia scoffed at the question. "You may be holding us off for now, but you still have not dealt any significant damage to us either. You will tire at some point."

"Perhaps, but I'm not the one you ought to be worried about. Your precious leader is going to be the first one to go if we have anything to say about it."

Ione blanched. "'We'? What are you going to do to Kai?"

"I ain't going to do a damn thing. Like I said, *I'm* not the one you should be watching out for."

Sharing a worried glance, the trio turned while keeping an eye on the Risbado sellsword. Morgan paled, seeing what was about to happen.

"Aw spit. Look out, 'pothy!"

Kai ducked under another swipe from Grimghast and threw an awkward swing at its exposed leg. The blow glanced off the bony plate protecting its thigh and only served to knock Kai off balance. He caught himself in time to avoid a snap from the beast's fangs. Frustration festered in his chest with each ineffective attack. He wasn't sure how long they could keep this up. They had to drive Grimghast off before it wore them down enough to get a lucky bite in.

On the other side of the beast, Teos and Orelia took turns weaving in close enough to land a hit on the legs or lower body before backing out of striking range. From her perch on a crag halfway up the cliff, Maple launched arrows at it with impressive accuracy. The small missiles only served to irritate the beast, though, as it tore each arrow out with ruthless efficiency.

His eyes landed on Maple, who matched his gaze with a small smile that sent a tremble through his back. His face shifted to confusion when he saw her glance at something behind him. His confusion transformed into worry when he saw her eyes bulge. Dropping her bow and ignoring the audible crack as it snapped in two on the rocky floor, she kicked off the cliff wall into a dive towards him.

Kai's ears snapped back when he heard Morgan's shout.

"Aw spit...look out, 'pothy!"

Spinning around, he saw a flash of white before Maple slammed into him. The impact sent him sprawling to the floor, dazed. His world froze when he heard it.

Maple's scream of pain.

Everything else dulled to a buzz as Kai wrenched himself up and scrambled to Maple's side. She lay curled on the ground, trying to cradle her back. A long slash stretched diagonally from the left shoulder down to the small of her back. Her torn vest was stained crimson with blood oozing from the cut.

Kai's gaze swung up to see, to his astonishment, Locke. The migrant stood there, a bloody knife in one hand, one of Maple's pinion feathers in the other, and a deranged expression of amusement on his face. He stared at Kai with a maniacal grin, his blade dripping with the merchant's blood.

"L-Locke?" Kai whispered. "What have you done? Why would—?"

The man gave a grim chuckle, his eyes burning bright. "Your stupid bitch is the only one to blame. That was meant for you, after all. I suppose getting rid of her is just as good, though. By the winds, it feels great to cut loose after all this time."

"What in Nulyma are you talking about? Why would you attack us?!" Kai shouted.

"Why do you think, you half-witted buffoon? Obram, Duarte, and I work for the same master. Most know him as Razarr, a renowned forge master. I suppose I should also tell you my full name: Hemlocke Desmort. I needed to keep an eye on my little pet, who you've already harmed enough since this damnable war started. She does have such a voracious appetite, as you've seen."

Kai's face turned white. It felt as though an iron ball was lodged in his throat. "Wait...then Grimghast is...?"

"Oh, is that what you've been calling Nulla? Come to think of it, the legends of Grimghast *do* line up with her appearance."

A tremble in his arms caused Kai to look down. Maple stared at him with half-lidded eyes, a soft smile on her lips. "You're okay..." she murmured.

"Maple," said Kai. Tears pricked at the edges of his eyes. He noticed her breaths coming in short, shallow gasps. "Why would you do that?"

"I couldn't let him do it. I had to save you," she replied. Even in pain, Kai could see the unrestrained emotion shimmering in her eyes.

"I love you."

The words were softer than silk, his ears barely picking them up. Kai's heart thrummed at the declaration, a soft rumble echoing from his chest. He pulled Maple close and buried his face in her hair, unable to hold back his tears. In the back of his mind, he sensed a nearby presence as Orelia kneeled next to him and wrapped her own arms around Maple.

A loud trilling cackle came from behind as Hemlocke threw his head back in glee. Further back, the apothecary heard Obram joining in with a piercing giggle, like a hyena.

"This is so sweet. I think I'm going to vomit," Hemlocke taunted. "She sounds so much better when she screams. I may not have buried my poisoned blade in your back like I planned," Kai's face paled further, "but at least I still took something precious from you. Especially since you already somehow cleaned this spring of Nulla's leavings. Your little concoction just ruined my whole plan to kill everyone in that pathetic eyesore of a town."

Eyes narrowing, Kai demanded to know why the migrant wanted to wipe out Glimmerdale.

"Do I really need a reason?" Hemlocke chuckled, his smile growing wider and more deranged. "There's nothing I love more than seeing people suffer. For humors' sake, I suppose I can blame my parents. Growing up, my father hated the fact my illness left me unable to work the fields, so he beat me rather frequently while mother watched and did nothing. Pain was a near constant companion. Eventually, I got tired of feeling a damned belt across my back, so I gutted the both of them before fleeing into the night. Let me tell you, the thrill of killing them was like a drug! Seeing the despair in one's eyes when they realize their end is coming and lose all hope is so tantalizingly delicious! Why do you think I spent so much time hiding in this cavern? It was easy to contaminate the spring over this past moon, having Nulla bathe and relieve herself in the water, littering it with all the filth she's accumulated. Watching the townsfolk fall ill in the process while they thought it was caused by an evil spirit was poetic. At the very least, I can still enjoy letting you watch my pet's venom kill the vulture from the inside."

Kai's gaze shifted to Grimghast, which stood alongside Hemlocke now. The beast rubbed its head against the traveler's shoulder, panting like a dog.

"You bastard!" Orelia shouted as she stormed to her feet. Teos held her back from charging at Hemlocke, though he glared at the Aerivolk with fury plain on his face.

"Don't worry your pretty little head, priestess. You'll be joining her very soon. Then again, I suppose you'll go a bit quicker than your friend." Turning to Grimghast, he scratched the beast under the chin, cooing in its ear. "Nulla, dear, it's time. Devour them. *All* of them, except for the Aerivolk and the Norzen. I want to hear those glorious screams from their throats as they watch their friends die."

He pulled a short reed whistle from his tunic and blew several sharp notes on it. The sound provoked a growl from Grimghast, which turned to face the party as Morgan's group rejoined the others.

What little hold Kai had on his emotions shattered. Hemlocke's gloating brought the dam crashing down, flooding his mind with rage. The cloud of the Frenzy Haze snapped into place. However, instead of fighting it as before, Kai allowed his mind to bask in the emotions, feeding it the anger and disgust he felt thinking about Hemlocke and how the man played him for a fool.

Because of my stupidity, Kai thought to himself, *Maple could very well die from trying to save me. I treated that bastard as a comrade. A friend, even. And all this time, he's been the one controlling that monster and trying to kill us.*

The wall separating his mind from his body seemed thinner than his first experiences with the Haze, though Kai suspected it was because of his decision to not fight it. He turned towards Grimghast with a purposeful step. Power surged through his muscles, each limb hardening from the tension.

Morgan took an uneasy step forward. "What the hoarfrost are you doing, 'pothy?" the sellsword asked. "Get back here! We have to fight them together."

"How precious," Obram jeered. "Are you trying to avenge your chicken wench?"

Kai growled, not saying anything as he approached at a steady pace.

With a scoff, Hemlocke waved his hand as Grimghast advanced on the apothecary with hunger blazing in its gaze. "You're nothing but a weak, gullible fool. What could you possibly do? Nulla, knock him aside and finish the others." He blew a string of notes on his flute, sending Grimghast into a galloping run.

Rather than answer, Kai spread his arms wide and released a deafening roar at the approaching beast. Grimghast skidded to a stop, its eye wide with surprise. It wasn't prepared for Kai to drop his mace and spring forward.

The Norzen reared back his arm and threw a devastating uppercut into Grimghast's chin. The impact rang throughout the cavern, as did the beast's shriek of pain. Hemlocke and Obram stood transfixed when Kai's punch took Grimghast off its feet and pitched it across the stone floor for several yards before slamming into the cliff face.

"No sodding way," Hemlocke whispered.

The party gaped. "I think Kai might be a bit pissed," Teos quipped.

Lucretia kept her eyes on Hemlocke and Obram, holding her rapier at the ready. "That is putting it mildly. We must pull him out of the Haze before he loses his mind."

"But how?" Ione asked, kneeling next to Maple and cradling the injured woman in her arms. "I don't think we've ever seen him this furious."

Casting worried glances towards the fight, the others couldn't refute Ione's comment. Grimghast stumbled to its feet and rushed forward, only to be stopped cold when Kai caught its paw mid-swipe and spun in place, throwing the monster over his shoulder and smashing it onto its back.

"We have to bring him back," said Morgan. The sellsword's gaze flicked down to Maple, who laid in Ione's arms moaning in pain. Her body remained curled inwards, the slightest movement eliciting another cry of agony. "He's the only one who can save Maple from whatever that bastard did to her."

Orelia nodded, clutching her staff in a white-knuckled grip.

"What the damnation is this?" Obram hissed, both hands tightened into fists as he watched Kai put Grimghast on the ground again and again.

"I'm not sure," Hemlocke confessed. His eyes were wide, and his lips curled back in a snarl. "I'm afraid we must make a tactical retreat and retrieve the fool the boss sent you here for. Nulla is the strongest weapon we have, and that bastard is manhandling her despite being over three times his size. I've never known a Norzen to have such a powerful Frenzy Haze, and I've seen my share of them."

Emitting a low huff, Obram nodded his assent and Hemlocke blew two shrill blasts on the whistle. Grimghast turned with a curious look. Kai took advantage of the beast's lapse in focus to land a savage left hook on its cheek. The strike knocked it backwards with a gargled cry. Staggering to its feet, Kai saw Grimghast's mouth hanging limp on one side; the punch had broken its jaw.

Grimghast returned to Hemlocke and allowed the Aerivolk and Obram to mount its back. Sending one last fierce look towards Kai, Hemlocke ordered it to scramble up the cliff and leap into the hole just above the plateau.

In the back of his mind, Kai screamed for his body to stop. The festering rage in his chest, however, still yearned for vengeance. Roaring in frustration, his body marched towards the cliff, intent on chasing Locke down.

He found his path blocked when Orelia ran past and put herself between him and the cliff. "That's enough, Kai!" she exclaimed.

Yes, she's right, the fight is done. Now give me back my body! Kai shouted in his own mind. The wall thickened, blocking his mind's ability to control his body. *Damn it to Nulyma, I let myself lose control. I have to stop this before Orelia gets hurt.*

The priestess tackled Kai's body but was tossed aside as he brushed her off. She refused to back down and kept pulling and shoving against him, trying to halt his advancement.

"Listen to me, you dumbass! They aren't important right now. Get your head back where it belongs and come help us."

Unable to speak, Kai's mind screamed for his body to stop and turn back, though it refused to listen. *What am I going to do?* He wondered. *If I don't get my body back, Maple really* will *die!*

A loud crack echoed through the cavern, leaving the party speechless.

Kai's body stopped, a bright red hand-shaped mark on his cheek from Orelia slapping him. "Stop this nonsense and get your furry ass back there," she murmured, each word dripping in barely restrained anger. "I know you, Kai, and I refuse to believe you'd let someone you care for die over something like revenge. We need you! I need you! *Maple* needs you!"

The younger woman's words broke through the wall like a battering ram, stopping the apothecary in his tracks. The uneven sensation Kai associated with the Frenzy Haze hit him full force, sending him to his knees as he regained control. Orelia reached down and helped him back to his feet.

"Thanks," Kai groaned. An unnatural prickling sensation shot through his limbs, ending in the tips of his fingers. He looked away from Orelia as she hauled him up by his mane. "I'm sorry I lost control again."

"I'm not the one you should be apologizing to. We'll discuss this more after you save Maple."

Nodding, Kai stumbled back towards the party. He took his satchel from Morgan's outstretched hand and knelt next to Maple, turning her on her stomach and inspecting the jagged cut. Inhaling deep, Kai cracked his knuckles and took several slow, controlled breaths, preparing himself to do whatever it took to heal the damage Hemlocke caused.

He would *not* lose her.

Chapter XVII

The cavern was silent except for Maple's labored breathing. The others watched as Kai removed several tools and herbs before ordering Morgan to grab the wine from his pack.

Using his harvesting sickle, Kai tore the cut in Maple's vest open wider to better inspect the wound. As expected, a light sheen of Grimghast's venomous lavender saliva was mixed with the blood, likely coated onto Hemlocke's knife beforehand. He used a strip of cloth to wipe away the blood. He tossed the dirty rag away and applied a new one, telling Orelia and Lucretia to apply pressure on opposite ends.

He paused for a moment when an odd sensation drifted across his hand. Raising it to his face, he peered at the appendage in confusion. Kai stared at Maple's wound and held his hand above it again. This time he was certain; it felt as if a gentle breeze were coming from the bloody cut.

What in the winds?

Morgan's heavy footsteps thundered in the cavern as he handed the wine to Kai. He brushed aside his thoughts of the strange manifestation and uncorked the bottle, pouring a dram into a stone bowl. Setting the wine aside, he opened a small vial with a liquid that emitted a powerful odor.

The scent caused Teos to reel back, waving his hand in front of his face. "What in the winds is that?' he asked. "Smells like a pot of vinegar gone bad."

"You know how I give you all a dram of warm mulberry wine to take the sting out of getting stitches?" Everyone nodded. "Well this is muwavi, which is mulberry wine mixed with other herbs to increase the potency. I wouldn't recommend taking a full glass straight, though, unless you feel like passing out for five days. This serving alone will knock you out for half a day. Help me sit her up. She needs to drink so she can sleep."

Kneeling next to Kai, Teos cupped a hand behind Maple's head and turned her over. She gave a soft moan and flashed Kai a weak smile when he held the vial to her lips. "Hey," she whispered, "I can't move my arms."

Giving her a nod, Kai asked her to sip the muwavi. "It'll dull the pain while I patch you up and figure out what that bastard did to you," he explained. "I promise, I won't let you die. I refuse to. I can't lose you, Maple."

"You won't...because I know you."

Leaning her head forward, she sipped at the wine, her lips puckering at the strong taste. Teos held her firm and helped ensure she finished it.

Kai set the vial down, asking Ione to lay out a blanket. Before long, they had Maple laying on her belly and the party could hear her gentle snores.

The apothecary applied iodine to his stitching needles. Setting them on a clean cloth, Kai pulled several thick leaves from a pouch in his satchel and tore them into chunks before chewing them in his mouth. While doing that, he brushed wine over the wound.

Her nose scrunched up, Lucretia watched his work with a mixture of curiosity and unease. "Kai, what are you doing? What is that leaf for?"

Spitting the masticated leaf into his mortar, Kai added several other powdered herbs to it, mixing them together. "It's from the parpusa plant. It's a common enough shrub to find in Livoria. What makes it special is the leaves are highly absorbent, making it useful for cleaning fresh wounds. I'm going to apply the paste to her wound to draw out the poison along with anything else Hemlocke laced his knife with."

"Won't it get in the way of stitching the wound closed?" Morgan asked.

"For now, I'm only going to stitch the far ends of the cut, so the parpusa has time to work before I close it completely. I'll finish up once we're back on the *Senberg*. While I'm working, we need to prepare a tonic to counteract the poison and inhibit its effects. Orelia, I'd like you to help me with this step if possible."

"Of course."

Gesturing for Morgan to come over, Orelia allowed him to continue putting pressure on the wound with Lucretia. Kai pointed out several vials and instructed Orelia on how to mix them.

At the same time, he threaded his needle and began stitching the ends of Maple's injury closed. He began near the top, with Morgan adjusting his hands to allow easy access. Tiny beads of sweat slid down the side of Kai's face. To his relief, Ione sat next to him with a spare cloth to wipe it away before it could reach his mane.

"Thank you," he muttered. Kai moved on to the lower end of the wound, continuing to stitch with Lucretia's assistance. "Orelia, take the mixture you have now and add the last two vials on the end of the line. Those are burdock and thistletwill, which have strong purging properties. Once you mix those in, add this and grind it all together." Reaching into his robe pocket, Kai procured a small red bud; emberona. He reached out to hand the bud over.

"Isn't that the same herb you put into Locke's concoction to make it more potent?" Lucretia inquired.

Kai's hand froze before he could drop the unassuming bud into Orelia's hand. Thinking of the tonic he provided the traveler stung Kai's pride. All his life, he tried his best to help any who asked for it. To him, helping people felt natural and was the reason he chose to do what he did. His apothecary's oath was the bedrock of his work, and the idea of someone taking advantage of his beliefs in such a way to hurt someone Kai loved made his blood boil.

His anger dissipated once he felt the chill of Orelia's fingers on his hand. Shaking the thought from his head, Kai settled for a thin frown and handed the emberona over, instructing her to grind it into the concoction before mixing it with wine and coaxing Maple to drink it. Because she was sleeping, they would need to massage her throat to make her swallow.

The priestess went to work, pummeling the mixture into a multicolored powder. Adding it to the empty cup, Orelia poured the wine over it and stirred at a feverish pace. Soon, the wine emitted the same smoky odor as the concoction Kai gave to Hemlocke.

Once more, Teos propped Maple up and helped Orelia administer the concoction. The process took longer due to a need to open Maple's mouth and tip the mixture in. Still, things went smoother than he expected. Casting his eyes upward, Kai stayed alert in case Hemlocke and Obram decided to return.

"And we're done!" exclaimed Orelia as Maple swallowed the last of the medicine.

Nodding, Kai took a larger bundle of cloth from the satchel and tore it into long strips. With Lucretia still pressing down on the open part of Maple's wound, Kai and Morgan worked together to wrap the strips around her body.

The apothecary suppressed a blush when he realized they needed to push Maple's vest up to finish bandaging the wound. It didn't help when Lucretia, noticing his discomfort, planted herself at Maple's front with a glare and held the vest in place just under the merchant's breasts, scowling at him until the wrapping was secure.

"This should hold until we get her back to the *Senberg*," declared Kai. When Ione asked how long it would take for her to fully heal, Kai admitted he didn't know. "There's no telling what Hemlocke's knife was coated in besides Grimghast's venom. The only one I know for sure is a paralytic; Maple said she couldn't move her arms."

After putting his tools away, Kai asked Morgan to help hoist her onto his back. When the sellsword offered to carry her himself, Kai shook his head.

"I need to do this myself. It's my fault she got hurt, so it's only right I take her back."

"Okay, 'pothy, but if you need a break, either me or Teos can take turns."

Kai thanked Morgan for the offer before using a rope to secure Maple to his back. Hooking his hands under her knees, he allowed Teos to lead the way out of the cavern. The others formed a protective circle around him, their weapons drawn and ready for the slightest hint of a threat.

Upon arriving back in Glimmerdale, the party was approached by Celio. The Vesikoi fisherman ran up with an expression of pure glee on his face.

"Oh praise the winds!" he shouted. "I don't know what you did out there, but it worked. Every well in town is now full of pure, clean water again. Even better, those who have been drinking from the wells in the past hour are getting better with shocking speed. It's a miracle!"

Giving the man a half-hearted grin, Kai continued forward as Orelia took Celio aside and explained everything to him. While he was happy to hear that the townsfolk were recovering, his main concern was getting Maple back to the *Senberg* and beginning work on an antivenom. While the concoction Orelia crafted in the cavern would slow the poison's effects and purge the weakest of the toxins, he needed to figure out how to remove Grimghast's venom and the paralytic from Maple's body before they killed her.

Now I wish I had kept that monster's saliva, Kai thought. *It would have been a perfect binder.*

His course determined, Kai trudged towards the port. Lucretia took the lead, map in hand, while the party offered simplistic greetings to the townsfolk they passed. Many tried to rush forward to shake their hands, only to be gently rebuffed by Teos and Morgan as Ione and Orelia explained the rush they were in.

Kai fought hard to control his blush when he felt Maple's face pressed against his shoulder. He felt a slight shift as her cheek nuzzled his unconsciously, causing his blush to intensify. He peeked up and noticed Lucretia putting all her focus on the map in her hands. Without thinking, Kai allowed himself to nuzzle Maple's cheek in return. He thought he heard a soft trill from her throat but dismissed it as another snore. A short cough shifted his gaze to Orelia, who looked at him with a light pink tinge on her face.

Before he realized it, Kai spotted the *Senberg*'s flag fluttering in the breeze over the buildings at the port's entrance. Sighing in relief, he noticed the crowd was dispersed except for a few stragglers who continued to hound the party with gratitude.

It wouldn't be long now before Maple was safe in bed.

"Gravebane!" a familiar, unwanted voice shouted from the docks. Kai groaned aloud when he saw Kendela marching towards them, his guards trailing behind. A second glance at the port had him notice the margrave's gaudy river cruiser docked in the farthest pier.

Does this bastard really have nothing better to do? Kai thought. *What will it take to get him to leave us alone?!*

"With all due respect, Kendela, I don't have the time or patience to answer your questions right now, so get out of the way" Kai replied. He ignored the noble's belligerent threats and ambled to the ramp leading onto the *Senberg*.

What he wasn't expecting was for Kendela to grab him by the shoulder and spin him around. He saw the flash of silver from a knife and the ropes holding Maple in place went slack as she was torn from his arms. His head twisted to see a pair of guards hauling her away. Kai's vision turned scarlet in an instant. Another three men leapt on top of him, grinding his face into the wooden planks of the port. The party shot forward and ordered the guards to let Maple go. Their weapons were trained on the men, who held Maple in front like a shield.

"Absolutely not," Kendela retorted. His lips were curled into a smug grin as he twirled one of his many bracelets. "My fiancée has been injured due to your incompetence, so I'm taking her with me. What's more, there's not a damn thing you or the Grand Duchess can—"

Anything else he wanted to say was drowned out by Kai's furious bellow. The apothecary shot up, throwing Kendela's guards off. All three were left sprawling backwards when Kai grabbed one by the leg and swung him into another, knocking both unconscious. The last one was sent airborne when Kai slammed a boot into his chest.

In a flash, he was on top of the guards holding Maple and broke the closest one's jaw with a backhand to the face. The man's hold on Maple wasn't enough to keep him from flying fifteen yards over the edge of the port and disappearing into the river. The second guard was too stunned by the attack to move when Kai grabbed him by the throat. Orelia and Teos rushed to catch Maple before she could hit the ground.

Holding her pan at the ready, Ione put herself in front of Kai as he turned to face Kendela, eyes blazing with fury. When Kai refused to look at her, his gaze locked on the noble, she stepped forward and swung the iron utensil into his knee with a clang.

The blow had the intended effect of shocking Kai out of his Haze, his eyes returning to their typical grey. Groaning, he dropped the guard to nurse his knee and cast a surprised look at the tavern maid. She smirked and brandished her pan at him.

"I know he's a wretched man," said Ione, "but I'm pretty sure you can't kill him, no matter how much he deserves it."

"How dare you?!" Kendela roared. He charged towards the two before skidding to a stop, the tip of Lucretia's rapier pressed against his throat.

"How dare we?" the scholar hissed. "You just attempted to kidnap our friend, so be grateful I have not already put a hole in your neck. Maybe you should think about what will happen if we were to inform Her Grace of this attack."

"I am taking her with me! You clearly have no idea what you're doing, so she'd be safest in my manor where she belongs. I know everything you lot have been up to since you left Whistlevale. I told you, I *always* get I want!"

Resting his palm against Kendela's chest, Kai shoved the noble backwards. The wealthy Aerivolk fell on his rump in an undignified heap. "You know nothing of what we've been through," Kai snapped. He advanced on Kendela, who scrambled back with fear in his eyes. His mace slipped into one hand, its flanges shining in the sunlight. "Maple is still in danger from what happened in those woods, so I'm warning you one last time to stay out of our way. Forget the epidemic in Grantide; if anything happens to her because of your interference, I won't bother with Blood Feud. I'll kill you where you stand and let the dice fall where they may with Fusette and Saredi."

"You wouldn't dare."

"Try me." Kai's voice was laced with such venom the party took an involuntary step back.

Without another word, Kai left the stammering merchant and stalked back towards the *Senberg.* His mace hung limp in a slack grip, its flanges scraping against the wooden planks. The others surrounded him and together they ascended the gangway.

Behind Kendela, the people of Glimmerdale watched the scene, their mouths hanging open in shock. It was likely the first time any of them had ever seen someone stand up to the margrave. The *Senberg's* crew stood aside as the party boarded the ship. Kai took Maple from Teos and ordered the smuggler to get the ship back on the river. As he stood in front of Maple's cabin, he saw Kendela rushing to the edge of the pier, waving a fist at the ship.

"Just you wait, Gravebane; you'll regret putting your filthy peltneck hands on me. I'll have you on the executioner's block for this!"

Rather than listen to the Kendela's rambling, Kai marched into the cabin and placed Maple in bed. A tremor rumbled through the ship as the engine roared to life. A slight shift told him Teos was at the wheel, pulling the *Senberg* from the dock.

He felt bad about leaving Glimmerdale behind without seeing the effects of their work, but Maple's health was his priority. He would send a letter to Fusette thanking her for the potion, as well as explaining everything that happened.

Once he checked her bandages, he swore to call a meeting of the entire crew.

Standing in the dining hall, surrounded by his friends and crew, Kai inspected everyone with an intense gaze. The light of the room's lanterns gave a brighter shine than usual, set against the backdrop of the evening sunset. They all stared back, many with confusion evident in their eyes. It wasn't a surprise to the apothecary; he hadn't warned anyone of the meeting beforehand.

"What's the deal, 'pothy?" asked Morgan. "It's not like you to call a meeting like some sort of officer."

"Something Kendela said has been bugging me since we left Glimmerdale. He claimed he knew everything we've done since leaving the capital."

"The man is a blowhard," Lucretia piped up from the back of the room, her arms crossed under her chest. "He seems the type to say things to unsettle his enemies."

A deep chuckle came from the fire crew, where Dekel leaned against the wall chewing on a wooden pipe. "The lass got it in one," he added. "Kendela's a rich bastard who hates admitting he's lost. The idea of not getting what he wants has to be driving the pitiful sod mad, so he'll say whatever he thinks will let him win."

"Normally, I'd agree with you. From my own experience with him, though, Kendela isn't one to hold onto something like a hound with a bone. If he thinks something is too difficult to obtain, he'll lose interest fast. The fact that, even now, he's *still* trying to force Maple into marriage, means the normal rules don't apply."

"Kai might be onto something," said Ione. "That man reminds me of several brutish men I've encountered over the years. They expect everything to be handed to them. Then they'll pitch a fit if they don't get it, claiming they weren't very interested anyway. Given his continued advances, we have to assume Kendela's aspirations towards Maple are serious."

"But if that's true, how does he know everything we've been up to?" asked Kerta. Kai was surprised to hear the younger cabin girl speak up, as up to now she and Annika preferred keeping to themselves on the cabin deck.

A scoff from Morgan brought everyone's eyes to the mixblood. "There's only one way he would get that level of knowledge: He's got an informant on the ship."

Orelia's breath hitched. "You mean someone in this room is working for that vile man? But why? He tried to kidnap Maple!" Everyone scanned the room, eyes resting on each person in turn as if trying to decide if they were working with the pompous noble.

"We do not have many options to protect her from him right now," said Lucretia. "As a young woman of marrying age, I can see him bribing Parliament to grant him a marriage contract, despite knowing they do not have the proper authority to do so."

Teos raised his hand. "Wouldn't Lady Fusette be able to overturn that? All of us, Maple included, do officially work under her as royal officers. I wouldn't imagine she'd be happy with Kendela trying such a ploy."

"She would not," answered Lucretia. "However, Parliament can go over her head if they get a large enough vote, something Kendela seems able to take advantage of. It also wouldn't stop them from procuring a corrupt magistrate to officiate the wedding to give it legitimacy. Parliament likes to squabble about a lot of things, but I have noticed one thing they are united in is whittling away at Her Grace's authority and ability to block their power-grabbing. As for Maple, the only ways to truly offer her protection would be to send her across the border to Galstein for asylum or have her get married. Kendela certainly could not do anything if she were wed to another."

With a light titter, Ione's lips shifted into a smug smirk. "That's a viable option. We could always marry her off to Kai before Kendela can blink."

Most of the party burst into laughter at the suggestion, though Kai's face was doing its best impression of a strawberry and Lucretia's lips were pursed. "Should you even be discussing such an option?" asked the scholar. "After all, if someone here *is* working for Kendela, they might report our discussion to him. Or the church."

"We'll simply have to put the ship's carrier hawks on lockdown when they're onboard," said Kai. Though his face was still red, he surveyed the room with a hardened stare. He hated the idea of having someone on board working for a vulture like Kendela, but Morgan had a point. It was the most likely way he knew of their actions. "As it is, I'll be using one tonight to send my report to Fusette. Make sure your notes are on the board outside my cabin before midnight." He stretched before heading to the door.

"What do we do about the spy?" Annika asked. The older cabin maid was gazing around the room with a cautious glance.

Kai stopped, his hand gripping the doorknob hard enough to leave an imprint of his fingers. "For now, we do nothing. We have no solid leads. Regardless, I'd like everyone to stay vigilant and keep an eye out for anything suspicious. Even if Kendela knows what we're up to, we still have the upper hand. He can't cause direct interference with our mission. Not even he would be able to escape the consequences of such a serious charge. Kendela may not be a Libbie sympathizer, but he'd be treated as one if he blocked us from reaching Havenfall and delivering Fusette's edict."

"Where are ya going, 'pothy?"

"I want to check Maple's bandages before finishing my report. We need to reach Havenfall as soon as possible. It's obvious Hemlocke used his prior knowledge of the Liberation Army's movements as collateral to wring the emberona tonic out of me. Obram said he and Grimghast have been part of their master's plans from the outset, so the bastard has likely been spying on us for the enemy ever since I met him in Mistport. Morgan, I want you and Teos to handle all sailing responsibilities for now."

"And what are you going to be doing?" asked Teos. Kai's hand clenched into a tight fist as he glanced out the window at the rising moons barely peeking above the horizon.

"I'm going to craft an antivenom to save Maple if it's the last thing I do. I don't care if the work drains every drop of my own blood. I *will* save her."

Chapter XVIII

After reading Gravebane's most recent report, Fusette couldn't determine which primal emotion was fueling the quivering in her body. Was it fear over the most recent incident to befall the Exarch and his party, resulting in serious injury to a woman the man held clear feelings for? Or was it fury from Lord Kendela's most recent assault and attempted kidnapping of the same woman?

The fur of her mane was smothered underneath her robes, but she still felt the prickling beneath her skin as each hair stood on end. The pounding in her heart muddled her thoughts. As she considered each incident separate from the other, she decided on fury being the dominant emotion, as she trusted Gravebane enough to heal Maple's injuries, no matter what those monsters did to her.

Kendela, on the other hand, was proving to be an unnecessary thorn in her side even when he was nowhere near the capital! A thorn which would have to be plucked from the looks of it.

Standing alone in her study, she took several deep, calming breaths. Any moment, Saredi would return to inform her of Admiral Basner's arrival. It wouldn't do to give the man a bad impression. If they were lucky, the addition of the Holy Navy would keep the momentum of the war in their favor. The last thing they needed was the Liberation Army pulling any other new weapons out of nowhere. The stonehood bombs and muskets were enough of a problem.

A knock on the study door jolted Fusette from her thoughts. "Your Grace," said Saredi as he strolled in with his typical dignified air. "Sir

Hanblum has returned with Admiral Basner and a small retinue of sailors. They will meet us in the grand hall."

"Of course, Saredi. I must confess I'm looking forward to this meeting."

"You received another report from Gravebane, I assume? I pray the man hasn't gone and done something else foolish."

"Worse, I'm afraid. I'll explain as we walk."

Allowing the Lord Chamberlain to lead the way, Fusette gave him a brief summary of the incident in Glimmerdale, including Kai's report on the effects of the purification concoction she gave him. She wasn't surprised by her friend's grim expression when she explained the attack on Maple.

"Saredi, we really must send Her Majesty a gift. If Gravebane's report is accurate, it's probable the concoction she gave us was the only way Glimmerdale's spring could be purified, considering the extent of the damage."

"Indeed. I'm man enough to admit when I'm wrong, Your Grace, and it appears I was mistaken regarding you gifting that potion to Gravebane. He certainly made good use of it."

"No doubt. I trust his judgment as much as I do yours, my friend. *That* was why I gave him the potion. I'm praying his next report will provide good news of Lady Maple's recovery." Saredi only nodded his agreement as they stepped into the grand hall.

Fusette let her eyes roam over the collection of baubles scattered throughout the hall. The largest room in the palace outside the main ballroom, the grand hall was filled with various ornaments gifted to Fusette's family over the years. Along the wall hung elegant tapestries depicting stories of the Wind Saints and multiple stone pedestals were topped with intricately painted porcelain ceramics. It was a room filled with years of history, and memories of her father's lessons on the history behind each object rose to the forefront of Fusette's mind.

The door to the palace opened to reveal Hanblum leading a group of men from varied tribes wearing the immaculate white uniforms of the Galstan Holy Navy. Fusette didn't need to see the crystal stars adorning the epaulets of the bronze-skinned human standing beside Hanblum to know he was Admiral Ottoten Basner. Of the six men accompanying the Aerivolk envoy, Ottoten was the oldest, with a luxuriant pepper-and-salt mustache and beard adorning his face; yet he marched with a stately grace the duchess found familiar.

Of course it would be familiar, Fusette realized after pondering the thought for a moment. *He carries himself with the same confidence Sister Orelia does.* Taking a deeper look, she saw just how much Orelia took after her human parent. The same teardrop face. The same piercing blue eyes carrying a hint of steel within their depths.

Stepping forward and bowing at the waist, Fusette extended her hand. "Greetings, Admiral Basner. We are honored and pleased to see you. I only wish your arrival were under better circumstances."

"The pleasure is mine, Lady Fusette," Ottoten answered. His resonant voice matched well with his controlled manner of speaking. "I must say, the last time I saw you, you were just a wee sprout bustling about your father's knees. It seems so strange to be back after so long to see you a woman grown." Despite the heaviness in his voice, Fusette found it rather calming.

"I'll admit my memories of those years aren't as sharp as I wish. I understand you and my father were good friends?"

"Aye. Vonlo was one of the finest men I ever knew, and honestly a better father than I could hope to be. Even though he was so busy with his duties, I'll always remember the way his eyes lit up like the sun when you ran into the room. He thought the world of you, Your Grace. Queen Isolde's mother, Greta, was rather cross with Vonlo many times when he missed or was late to meetings because he was tending to you. Remind me to share some stories after this horrible business is over with. Your father and I got up to some madness in our youth."

Fusette fought back the tears threatening to spill from her eyes. The older man's words brought memories of her father to the fore which Fusette thought long buried. Memories of his boisterous laugh and how he would spin her in his arms on the Parliament floor, to the visible discomfort of the nobles. "I would love that. Thank you, Admiral. If you'd follow me, we can continue in my study. Also, I'd say you're a fine father if your daughter is any indication."

One of the admiral's bushy eyebrows rose as the group began walking. "Really? I wasn't aware you and Orelia were acquainted. I haven't seen nor heard from the girl since she scarpered off three years ago to join the clergy."

"I'm fortunate enough to call Sister Orelia a dear friend." Fusette didn't miss the slight wince Ottoten gave when she mentioned Orelia's title. "I first met her in Runegard in the company of one of my Exarch Knights."

His lips shifted into a thin line. "I hope she wasn't in trouble. Last I heard Orelia was supposed to be working in Stahl Granz Temple. Then again, she's always been a rebellious one; a trait I'm afraid she gets from her mother."

"Oh, don't misunderstand. Orelia was caught up in the battle at Faith Hollow and ended up leaving as part of my Exarch's party when the temple was torched by its own bishop." Fusette explained the circumstances as she knew them surrounding the siege and Orelia's participation in it.

Stunned, Ottoten swayed in place as a pair of his men steadied him. "You're telling me my little girl is neck-deep in this war?" The man's face was tinged red as he paced back and forth over the marble floor. "Damnation, she's not properly trained to fight! I always knew it would've been better for her to join the Navy like her brothers. At least then she'd be able to protect herself."

"With all due respect, Admiral, perhaps you're being too harsh."

Locking eyes with the duchess, Ottoten asked what she meant.

"Sister Orelia is by no means defenseless. When I brought them back to Whistlevale following the incident in Runegard, your daughter was one of the first to demand training with my personal guards. She took to the training like a fish to water, as it were. Since then, she's grown into a formidable woman, and I pity anyone foolish enough to incite her wrath. That staff of hers hurts like Nulyma, to hear my guard captain tell it."

The admiral couldn't hold back his chuckle. "I sense there's more to this than what you're saying." He bowed his head when Fusette opened the door to her study and invited the Galstans to enter.

"The Exarch she's been traveling with. He's a member of my Hunter Corps who lost his original squad when the beast Hanblum briefed you on attacked Mistport. Since then, he's grown rather protective of your daughter and the rest of their group."

His eyes twitched before turning back to Fusette. "Is that so? Will I need to sharpen my spear before I meet him?"

As much as Fusette wanted to laugh at the admiral's scowling expression, she knew Saredi would lecture her ear off if she did so. "Ottoten, first of all, I shall be rather ruffled if you stab one of my most competent knights. Second, I can personally guarantee he would never do anything to hurt Orelia or anyone else in their group. The man would rather saw off his own hand with a rusty blade before harming anyone he cares about."

Ottoten's eyes furrowed, his lips set in a grim line. "Do I know this particular Exarch?"

"I'd be astonished if you knew him personally, though you may have heard of him. Gravebane."

Ottoten stroked his beard. "The Brand sounds familiar. Hanblum?" he inquired, giving a sideways glance to the envoy.

"He's the Exarchs' most recent addition, Admiral. According to my notes from talking with Her Grace, he earned his Brand for killing a rampaging nettleboar single-handed when he was seventeen. The beast was threatening Havenfall during their annual Trial of Ascension, an event in which he was one of the participants."

It took all Fusette's will to bite back her laughter at seeing the fish-slapped look on Ottoten's face. "He took down a nettleboar on his own so young? I'm going to assume this Gravebane is either a Wasini or Soltauri; I'll admit no human could pull a trick like that, regardless of training."

Fusette allowed a confident smirk to split her face in two. "Norzen, actually. And despite his accomplishments, he'll be the first to tell you he prefers his work as an apothecary over being a Hunter."

"I...I need to sit down," said the admiral, his tanned face paling considerably. Fusette and Saredi led the group back to her study. As they approached the door, the duchess heard a familiar voice from the other side of the hall.

"Lady Fusette!" Tuvi called out, racing towards the duchess and throwing herself into Fusette's legs. The young Norzen was carrying a long bundle wrapped in a blanket which stung when it smacked Fusette against her knee. Tuvi squeaked upon seeing Ottoten and his men, hiding behind Fusette and regarding them with a hesitant stare. "I'm sorry," the girl said, shifting her gaze to the floor. "I didn't know you had company."

"That's perfectly alright, Tuvi. You didn't mean any harm."

"Who's this?" asked Ottoten. He cast a curious look at Fusette as his eyes shifted between them. She wondered what he was thinking until she remembered Ottoten was likely aware she herself was Norzen, considering his friendship with her father.

"This is Tuvi, one of the orphans your daughter cared for during her service at Stahl Granz," Fusette replied, taking the girl's bundle before leading her by the hand to the back of the study. "She suffered quite a harrowing ordeal with the Liberation Army and lost her hand, so I've taken her in until the end of the war." Tuvi took the package back and planted herself into the small chair next to Fusette's desk.

When the duchess introduced Ottoten to Tuvi and told her of his relation to Orelia, the girl gazed at him with sparkles in her eyes.

Hanblum chuckled and ribbed Ottoten with his elbow. "She reminds me of your daughter when she was that age," said the envoy. "Lots of spunk and a mind of her own."

The admiral burst into laughter. "Impressive. I will confess, as a father, I'm unhappy about Orelia being so involved, but as a sailor, I'm still proud she can hold her own."

"Lady Fusette—" Tuvi started, only for Saredi to hold a finger to her lips.

“Not now, Miss Tuvi,” the Vesikoi noble interrupted. “The adults have important business to discuss.”

“But—“

“I said *not now*. We shall talk later.”

The adults laughed when Tuvi crossed her arms and huffed, leaning back against her chair with an indignant expression.

Doing her best to stifle her giggles, Fusette turned to Ottoten and asked about his plans for the war. Saredi laid out a map and everyone gathered around it. The sailors accompanying Ottoten stayed silent, standing at attention while their commander discussed potential ways to counter the Liberation Army’s new weapons.

A hint of movement caught the duchess’ eye as she noticed a Norzen maid approaching Tuvi, kneeling to offer the girl a blank canvas, an easel, and paint. She took the items with a smile and allowed the maid to set up them up on top of a cloth.

A loud thumping sound prickled Fusette’s ears beneath her shawl. Her gaze shifted past Ottoten to the door. She met Saredi’s eyes, who responded with a shrug and raised eyebrow. The thumps grew louder and more numerous with each moment, sending a tremor of worry through Fusette’s spine. She signaled the guards at the door, thankful for Gravebane teaching her the Hunter Corps’ basic hand signs. It was an idea the young monarch thought ingenious, and she wondered how her father never knew of them. Or if he did, why he never made use of them himself.

Soon, someone began pounding on the study door, surprising Ottoten and his men. The guards, swords already drawn, demanded identification.

“It’s Lord Remigo, you blithering idiots! I know Her Grace is in there. We need to have a discussion.”

Frowning, Fusette saw Ottoten rest a hand on the hilt of his sword. She emitted a soft sigh and told the guards to open the door but remain vigilant. Given her company, she doubted Remigo would be angry or stupid enough to get too belligerent.

The doors swung open and a tall, lanky man barged in, surrounded by attendants. A human around Ottoten’s age, Remigo wore the garish indigo robes of a high-ranking Parliament lord, a Count to be exact, which looked too large for his thin frame. His almond eyes were an iridescent brown, and his square jaw was set in a grim scowl.

Remigo served as Fusette's duly elected Prime Minister and the leader of Parliament. On a normal day, she and the man shared a tense, if civil, relationship. However, she knew he had a habit of being even more serious than Saredi, if such a thing were possible, and pandering to the wealthier lords of Parliament more than he should.

"In case you haven't noticed, Remigo, I am discussing important matters relating to the war with our friends from Galstein. What in the winds could be so important you needed to barge in here?"

Tucking a hand into his robes, Remigo pulled a small scroll from inside and waggled it in Fusette's face. The action drew a fierce scowl from Ottoten. "I received a missive from Lord Kendela this morning. Your Grace, Gravebane has gone too far! He threatened the life of a titled lord and has prevented Kendela from providing care to his fiancée. Such disgusting acts cannot be allowed to continue. As Prime Minister, I demand you revoke his Brand and he be arrested for his crimes! I will be calling a special session at the earliest convenience to issue Lord Kendela a marriage contract so he can get his fiancée away from that man."

Rather than let herself get drawn into the minister's anger, Fusette held her hands in her lap and cast a blank stare at him. "Remigo," she began, "I was under the impression you were an intelligent man, considering your former work in the Citadel. I sincerely hope you've performed some form of investigation to reach this decision. If not, I must say I'm both disappointed and furious you would attempt to undermine one of my Exarchs in such a blatant manner."

"Kendela was right about that Norzen," Remigo countered. "Branding him was the worst mistake you've ever made, Your Grace. I'm sorry to say your little experiment was a failure. It's best we remove any authority he has before he causes more harm."

Nostrils flared, Fusette marched forward and jabbed a finger into Remigo's crooked nose. "Gravebane and his party are the only reason Saredi and I weren't murdered by Liberator allies in Runegard. Are you suggesting it would've been better if we were killed?"

Remigo's face paled as he stumbled back. "O-of course not, Your Grace! How could you even think that?"

"You certainly insinuated it. Don't overestimate your authority and influence, Remigo. It's true Parliament has some level of veto power. However, I am *still* the reigning monarch of this realm and the Exarch Knights remain under my sole purview. In addition, Parliament has no authority to issue marriage contracts. Only ordained clerics of the church and magistrates have that power, so any contract you issue would be void and unenforceable regardless. Lastly, Kendela has given you false information."

"What do you mean?"

"The woman Kendela claims to be his fiancée is not only a member of Gravebane's party but has publicly denied his claim on at least two occasions. I have written reports of this from multiple witnesses I'd be happy to share with you."

"But why would—?"

Fusette rolled her eyes. "It's obvious Kendela is too used to getting what he wants. He's manipulating you and Parliament into doing his bidding, something I will never allow."

"You are aware he's wealthy enough to bribe the majority he needs to override any decision you make, right?" asked Remigo.

"His wealth won't do him a lick of good when I strip his title for deliberate interference in a royal officer's mission and indirect support of an enemy faction." The minister gulped and took a step back from the fuming Fusette. To many nobles, the thought of losing their wealth and titles was anathema. "Assuming he survives, of course, considering the woman Kendela's so desperate for is Gravebane's best friend."

Ottoten put himself between the two and gave Fusette a warning glance. "Do you believe this man would kill a noble and risk execution over something like this?"

"Gravebane takes his protection duties serious enough that he crafted the plan which wiped out half of the Liberators' six-thousand-man army at Faith Hollow." The admiral blanched and Remigo stumbled against the wall, his pallid face making him look like a specter. "If he thought anyone in his party was threatened, Gravebane would reduce Kendela's manor to splinters and dust. You underestimate him at your own foolish risk."

"Are you suggesting we just ignore these blatant threats, then?" asked Remigo.

"I'm suggesting you keep your nose out of Kendela's business before you get hurt. He decided to infuriate one of the most dangerous men in Alezon on his own. It's not Parliament's duty to protect him from his own stupidity."

"Then what do I tell him? He's most certainly expecting a response."

"Inform Kendela that I have forbidden anyone from intervening in the dispute between himself and Gravebane on either side. I'll draft an official edict stating as such before the end of the day. Any nobles found guilty of breaking this decree will be censured and could be stripped of their land and titles pending investigation."

Saredi stood and addressed Fusette. "Your Grace, aren't you worried about accusations of favoritism towards Gravebane?"

"How am I showing favoritism? I'm doing nothing to directly order or aid him. I'm only making a legal decree to prevent outside parties from intervening on either side's behalf. Just as no one may assist Kendela, the same is true for Gravebane."

Ottoten and his men all erupted into braying laughter. "You truly are brilliant, Your Grace," the admiral praised. "This is how disputes *should* be handled. If these two have a problem, they'll need to hammer it out themselves."

"You've never met Gravebane before, have you, Admiral?" inquired Remigo. He chuckled when Ottoten shook his head. "The man is a vicious brute, even for a Norzen."

"That's a lie!" Tuvi shouted, leaping from her chair and sending her bundle clattering across the floor. "You take that back; Mr. Kai is nicer than you'll ever be!"

A gasp sounded from the maid, prompting Fusette to turn and face the other woman. Her eyes were staring at the ground, wide and fearful. Looking down, Fusette was shocked to see the blanket unfurled enough from the bundle to expose the long metal barrel of a musket. The bright red stock looked exactly as Gravebane had mentioned in his reports.

"Tuvi," whispered Fusette, pointing at the weapon, "where did you find that?"

The girl looked at the floor, emitting a sniffle. "That's what I've been trying to tell you. I found it under the wardrobe in my room while looking for the doll you gave me. It looked dangerous, so I wrapped it up and brought it to show you. I don't know who put it there."

"What in the winds...?" Ottoten muttered, picking the weapon up and inspecting it with a critical eye. "Is this one of those muskets Hanblum mentioned?"

"It is," Fusette confirmed. She cast a fierce glare at the musket, "and if my guess is correct, that very weapon was used to murder Gerhardt Falber."

The musket fell to the floor with a clang, Ottoten too stunned to maintain his grip. "Is this true?" he asked.

"I'd be willing to wager my treasury on it. A proper questioning with Ambroz revealed a musket was the most likely weapon used and was abandoned to pin the blame on Ambroz himself, who happened to be in the wrong place at the wrong time."

Fists clenched, Remigo stormed towards Tuvi and reached for the girl, only to be blocked when the maid wrapped the girl in her arms. "Hand the child over, girl," he hissed. "She brought a deadly weapon into this room. Who knows if she was planning to use it on Her Grace?"

A loud crack echoed through the room and Remigo was thrown back, striking the bookshelf with a crimson imprint of the duchess' hand on his cheek.

"How dare you!" screamed Fusette. Her grey eyes were rimmed with crimson and her lips peeled back in a vicious snarl. "Tuvi is one of the sweetest, most gentle children I've ever met. You even heard her; she brought it here to show us because she rightfully believed it was dangerous. We were just too busy to pay attention. You need to leave, Remigo. Now! We will be discussing this further tonight; of that you can be certain. At the moment, I have more pressing matters to deal with than your desire to pander to Kendela's enormous ego."

Rubbing his sore cheek, Remigo scowled at Fusette and rose to full height, as if ready to burst into a rant. Anything he wished to say died on his lips when the sharp point of Saredi's sword pressed against his gut.

"I dare you to try," warned the Lord Chamberlain. Remigo took the hint and straightened his robes before bustling out of the study with his head down.

Turning back to Ottoten, Fusette bowed low and apologized. "I hope you can forgive us for allowing such hideous manners from one of my ministers."

The Galstans all burst into laughter once more. "If you ask me, Your Grace," said one of the men, a youthful-faced Vesikoi ensign, "this is the best entertainment we've seen in a solstice."

Ottoten cuffed the young man behind the ear. "Mind yourself, Elkrud" he reprimanded. "I will say, though, that was an impressive slap. You truly *are* your father's daughter, though if it had been Vonlo, he would've kicked that cur right in the baubles."

With a groan, Fusette hid her face in her hands, knowing her cheeks were burning bright red as the sailors showered her in congratulations.

"Perhaps we should table the strategy meeting for after dinner," she murmured. "I need to handle this musket situation before something else happens. Saredi, please ensure these gentlemen have a place to rest until then and draft the edict regarding the Kendela situation. The sooner we get this out of the way and the Admiral back to his fleet, the sooner we can take the fight to the Liberation Army. Lastly, I'd like you to arrange for Ambroz to be moved to the medical wing. That man will not spend another night in the gaol."

"Certainly, Your Grace. Was there anything else you required of me?"

"Yes. I need you to fetch Lady Bidelga after you've done everything else. It's time I called for a summit of the Five Realms Council. Gideon Harmod has much to explain, and I will have my answers, or *he'll* be the next one I slap."

Chapter XIX

The idea of food not being able to lift his spirits was a thought Kai never imagined possible. In the past, the idea of a warm meal shared with friends never failed to perk him up, no matter how low he may have felt.

Now, however, the food Ione worked so hard on tasted bland and stale no matter what herbs he added to it. Kai stared at the seared beef rib on his plate, drizzled with brown gravy and steamed vegetables on a bed of rice, and wondered how everything could have gone wrong so fast. He knew the others were eyeing him out of concern, as he poked at the food. Still, he held back the storm of emotions bubbling in his chest, if only to put them at ease. The worst part was he already knew the reason for his slump.

The apothecary's eyes shifted to the empty chair to his right, where Maple usually sat. It felt unnatural to not see her there, cheering everyone up with her boundless energy and never-ending smile. His thoughts drifted to Glimmerdale, and he agonized over how different the battle could have gone if he were more careful.

"You alright, Kai?" Ione asked. His head lifted just enough to meet her gaze and his breath caught at the worry he saw buried in her features. Both eyebrows were pinched together, and the corners of her lips sagged.

Shaking his head, Kai told her not to worry. He set his utensils on the table and stood. Ignoring the stares from the crew and his friends, Kai shuffled out of the dining hall and slumped upstairs to the cabin deck. The brisk night air bit into his exposed skin as the wind washed over him. While he had told the others there wasn't much they could do about Kendela's spy, he still found himself going over each of the crew members in his mind.

As much as he hated thinking it, Kerta and Annika were the most likely suspects, given the fact that they worked in the palace and thus would have been easily accessible to Kendela. Even working as maids under Fusette, it was easy to see the brash noble offering either girl a substantial monetary reward for agreeing to help him. Kai stopped at Maple's cabin and reached for the door, though his hand stopped short of gripping the knob.

The sound of shuffling footsteps alerted him to Orelia easing up beside him, a small sack in her clutches. Her hand reached out and brushed against his arm, filling him with a brief spark of hope before his darkening thoughts squashed it.

How can I even face her after what happened? Kai thought, his hand quivering as it hovered over the doorknob. *What I told Orelia before was true; she deserves someone better. They both do. Someone who won't get them hurt due to their own—*

"Are you two gonna stand there all night or are ya gonna come in?" Maple's voice called out, shocking him from his thoughts. Blushing, he opened the door and stepped inside to see the merchant giving them a weak smile. Orelia set her package by the door as she followed him in.

"How'd you know we were there?"

She emitted a soft chuckle. "First off, I saw your tails through the window." Kai flinched, wishing he had better control over the appendages. "Second, I know you. It was easy to guess you'd come check on me. Orelia was a bit of a surprise, though I suppose she shouldn't be at this point."

Pulling up a chair, Kai sat next to Maple and set up his tools and herbs on the side table. Soon, he handed her a cup of tea with a new herbal mixture to try inhibiting the poison. His hand twitched when she rested her hand on his with a gentle squeeze. Orelia sat nearby, watching the exchange with a solemn expression.

"How are you feeling?" he asked.

"Better than before. I can move my arms and fingers, but my hips still feel locked, and I'm certain a newborn chick could kick my tail feathers. Orelia said you stitched me back together after we got back."

By sheer force of will, Kai bit back the tears threatening to spill from his eyes. "Whatever Hemlocke laced his knife with was a mix of Grimghast's venom, some sort of paralytic, and who knows what else. I used parpusa to drain the thickest concentrations of poison, but there's still enough in your blood to weaken you substantially. I have one last emberona bud, but I don't want to use it until I've developed a potent enough herbal mix to purge all the poison. If I had a full bloom, I could've already healed this. A blooms' effects are over ten times stronger than a bud."

"I'm sure you'll have me back up in no time," Maple whispered. "I believe in you."

Unable to hold back, Kai's body tensed, and his tears fell freely. "How can you say that, Maple? It's *my* fault you were hurt. If I hadn't made that tonic for Hemlocke, none of this would've happened."

"You don't know that for certain."

"I made him stronger. His body was failing him, and I healed his affliction enough for him to attack us. It was my decision that caused this."

"And I don't blame you." Kai's eyes, shimmering with fresh tears, gazed at Maple in stunned silence. The merchant propped herself up and leaned against the wall, flashing him her tilted smile. "That bastard played us like fiddles and used your compassion against us," she continued. "The only person to blame is Hemlocke, not you. I don't doubt he'll get what he deserves one day. But don't think for a moment anyone here holds you responsible for his decisions." Orelia nodded her agreement, wrapping her arms around Kai and promising she didn't blame him in the slightest.

"But—"

Both women turned towards him with steely gazes. "Don't you put yourself down, Kai Travaldi!" Maple exclaimed. "This is the kind of man you are. You help people, no matter what. It's the gentleness in your heart that made me fall in love with you. That made *both of us* fall for you." Kai winced, trying to pull his hand away. Maple refused to let go, tightening her grip and rubbing a finger over his knuckles.

The apothecary's breathing quickened, the entirety of Maple's words reaching his brain and sending a jolt through his body. "Wait, what are you saying?" he asked. "You *both* love me? Then, when you..." He left the rest unsaid as he met the priestess' eyes, knowing Orelia would understand. Sure enough, her blush deepened and she gave him a hesitant nod that had him slumping against his chair. The memories of her affections replayed in a constant loop within his mind.

Even in the dim light of the room's lantern, Kai could see Maple's gleaming smile. She tapped his nose with a single, dainty finger. "Of course we do, ya dipwit. Ever since we met, you've been our steady rock, guiding us through every problem we've faced together. You think I asked you to dance with me for laughs? And Orelia has said she feels much the same way. You made a hell of an impression at Faith Hollow."

"Maple, what are you doing?" Orelia questioned, her eyes growing wide. "I told you I was stepping back so you two could focus on each other."

Grabbing hold of the younger woman by the arm, Maple dragged her onto the bed with a big grin. "True, but I refuse to let you just give up. He may even find me unbearable to think about living with and choose you instead. Don't think I haven't noticed the longing in your eyes ever since we last discussed this. Besides, what's to stop Kai from taking you as a mistress? He's an Exarch with tons of good favor with Her Grace, so I doubt anyone would dare say anything." The moment Maple brought up mistresses, Kai's face took on a familiar cherry tint as he cupped his face in his hands with a loud groan.

That was nothing, however, to the crimson shade of Orelia's dimpled cheeks. "First of all, I doubt Kai could ever find you unbearable. Second, have you lost your kettle?" she hissed. "My father would lose the plot if he heard I allowed myself to be taken as a Norzen's mistress! He gets enough criticism back home for my mother being his youngest mistress."

"Wait, your mother is a mistress? One of multiple?" Kai asked, his eyes bulging. "Your father must be a noble or pretty well-off to take more than one."

"You're not wrong. He's Fleet Admiral of the Holy Navy."

Kai's complexion took a complete reversal, switching from deep red to a sickly white. "Your father is Ottoten Basner, one of Galstein's greatest war heroes? Bloody Nulyma, I'm doomed."

A soft giggle came from Maple. "I doubt Orelia would let her old man kill you. She's too sweet on you, even if she's really bad at hiding it. For that matter, you're not as sneaky as you think at hiding your own thoughts about our lovely priestess. I've seen the way you look at her sometimes."

The burning in Kai's face was growing unbearable, though there was no way he could deny Maple's statement. If this got any more out of hand, he wouldn't be surprised if he suffered a relapse of Grantide and passed out where he stood. Rising to his feet, he hurried to the table at the opposite side of the room, where a jug of water sat. Kai splashed some over his face and faced the two women as he walked back with a healthier tone to his skin.

The moment he reached the bed, though, the dam of emotions welling in his chest broke. Kai collapsed to his knees next to the bed and wept, allowing Maple and Orelia to envelop him in a tender hug while threading their hands through his fur. He felt four sets of fingers brushing his cheeks, wiping the tears away. The three held each other, the only other sound coming from the wind outside.

He asked, "Am I even allowed to love both of you like this?"

"Of course you are," Orelia murmured, burying her face in Kai's hair. "Remember our discussion on how love is never simple? Believe me, I've learned the truth of that statement several times over. But don't *ever* think you're not allowed to love."

"Orelia's right," Maple added, "and don't even consider trying to push us away in some misguided attempt to protect us. Then you'll have both of us taking turns smacking you around. We're allowed to love you just as much as you can love us."

The playful threat sent Kai into a burst of chuckles, though his mind continued to race in an attempt to comprehend what was happening. "What if I can't choose? I'm no noble...not even a baron. I doubt I could meet the financial requirements for a poly marriage. Worse still, I couldn't imagine breaking either of your hearts. The mere thought makes my skin feel like ice." Sure enough, his hands were clammy to the touch and a chill settled over him colder than the northern tundra of Feswili.

"We're not forcing you to choose anyone right now," said Orelia, "but this wouldn't be fair if you weren't aware of everything going on."

"Then what do we do?"

Maple nuzzled her cheek against Kai's and cupped his chin, forcing him to meet her eyes. "It's simple. While it's true you're officially courting me, I have no problems with allowing you to see how things progress with Orelia. In fact, I'd prefer it so you see what we both have to offer in a relationship. Dance with her, show her your affections. Be the same charming fool you've always been. We'll figure things out, one way or another."

Fingers twitching, Kai allowed himself to reach over and take Orelia's hand, squeezing it and rubbing his finger along her knuckles. At the same time, Maple grabbed his other hand and brought it up to her lips, planting a gentle kiss on the fingertips. Kai gulped audibly and cast his eyes downward.

"What did I ever do to deserve either of you? You ladies are like priceless jewels, and I'm not just talking about how beautiful you both are."

A soft chirp came from Maple. Pulling back, Kai saw her eyes glistening. Orelia was staring at him with a bright smile that seemed counter to the tears flowing down her own face. "Did I say something wrong?" he wondered aloud, his face paling.

"Not at all," Orelia soothed, her smile stretching from ear to ear. "I suppose we ought to reward you for being such a sweetheart." Kai watched the two women share a mischievous grin before they each leaned in and pressed their lips against his cheeks. A powerful wave of heat washed over Kai; he wouldn't have been surprised if steam was spewing from his ears.

"What in the winds is going on here?" a sharp voice came from the door.

The trio sprung apart, with Maple casting a hardened glare at Lucretia. The scholar stood in the doorway with her lips settled in a thin scowl.

"You truly have the worst timing," Maple snapped, allowing Orelia to prop her pillow up and ease her against the wall.

"I do enjoy watching you squirm," Lucretia retorted. "That doesn't answer my question, though. Orelia, don't tell me you're involved with *this* as well." The priestess rolled her eyes and rebuked the young noble, reminding her what the three of them did in private was hardly her concern.

"I appreciate your insight on most things, Lucretia, but must you always do this?" asked Kai. Despite the gruffness in his voice, the apothecary's face was burning red. Lucretia brushed the question aside and told Kai she and the others needed to speak with him.

Maple emitted a trilling laugh and told him to go see what the party needed. "It's not like I'm going anywhere. Besides, Orelia and I have a bit more to talk about."

Kai followed Lucretia up to the pilot house, though the Norzen refused to meet the scholar's piercing stare.

"So Maple was not enough?" she asked, though her voice remained steady and firm. "Now you are casting aspirations on Orelia as well?"

"Hey, that was more shocking to me than I'm sure it was to you."

"And here I thought you were supposed to be smart."

"Oi!" Despite his umbrage, Kai couldn't stop his face from sinking at the harsh words. "Forgive me for being a novice at romance. I can't even imagine being worthy of either one of them, much less both."

Lucretia smirked, emitting an amused huff. "At least you recognize that. Were you anyone else, I would be inclined to tell you to stay away from them. But...for some inexplicable reason, those two have chosen to give you their affections. What's more, I am certain any attempt to keep them from you would result in swift and painful retribution, and I have no desire to anger either one of them. Whatever you do, promise me you will not break their hearts. Things are bad enough with Kendela's advances. I know that, as an Exarch, you retain a special class of noble title, but I pray you three aren't biting off more than you can chew."

Raising his eyes to meet Lucretia's, Kai gave her a firm nod. "Of course. That's one promise I intend to take to my grave." He knew fulfilling that promise would be difficult, but there had to be a way to—

In that moment, a stray thought burst to the fore of Kai's mind. Lucretia's comments on Kendela and his Exarch status reminded him of the Aerivolk noble's comments made before they left Whistlevale. That one stray thought took hold and Kai's mind began calculating. Plotting. It was a risky plan, certain to set him against the leading council of the Windbringer church, but if he worded things right, he was confident it could work. He just needed to verify some information with Fusette.

His eyes spotted Lucretia walking with a stoic purpose in her steps, both eyes locked on the path in front of them. They passed Montagru and Yasso along the way, the two Soltauri heading down towards the main deck. Kai's ears twitched when he heard Yasso grumbling to his uncle about Morgan not giving them as much time to relax as they wished. Kai fought back the snigger that wanted to escape his lips. While he could empathize with the young deckhand, the fact remained the two were hired to work. So that's what they'd be doing.

"There you are," Teos commented as the pair strolled into the pilot house and closed the door behind them. "How's Maple?"

Sending Lucretia a pleading glance to not say anything about what she saw, Kai replied, "She says she feels better, but the paralytic is still locking her hips and the poison is sapping her strength. Orelia's with her right now, probably enjoying some lady's talk right now. I think Hemlocke didn't have as much venom on the blade as he thought, otherwise her condition would be worse. We were lucky."

"I'd say we're lucky enough to have you here taking care of her, 'pothy," Morgan spoke up from the far wall. Both his arms were crossed over his chest, the muscles taut.

Releasing an audible sigh, Lucretia tapped a finger on the edge of her spectacles. "As much as it pains me to agree with him, Morgan is right. You are the only apothecary skilled enough to handle this situation. Your knowledge of Grimghast is so comparatively vast no other apothecary in Alezon can match it. You truly are the best suited to cleansing Maple of that monster's venom."

Kai's face erupted into another blush. "I appreciate the confidence. I'll do my best to find some way of purging it from her body. I feel like I'm getting close, but it I'm still missing a vital piece."

"Perhaps you're overthinking things," suggested Ione. "I know for a fact you've been blaming yourself for her injury." He gaped at the tavern maid in shock. "Oh don't act so surprised. We know you well enough to guess you'd be berating yourself over it."

"You don't understand though," Kai stuttered. "I—"

Ione cut him off with a poke to the chest. "We understand you think you're responsible because of the tonic you made for Hemlocke. However, you shouldn't allow that to shatter your confidence."

"That's not the problem."

"Then what is?" asked Teos. "We can't help much if you won't let us know the trouble."

Cradling his head in his hands, Kai threw his back against the wall. "I could've survived it!" he shouted, turning and slamming a fist into the wall with a bang.

Silence reigned in the pilot house. The others stared at Kai with befuddled expressions. "What do you mean?" Ione asked.

"The poison," Kai muttered, "from what I've found studying the small amount I separated from Maple's blood, Hemlocke used Grimghast's venomous saliva as a base. If Maple hadn't jumped in front of the knife, if it had struck me, his intended target...we wouldn't be in this situation because I could've withstood the attack."

Lucretia scoffed, eyeing Kai with an intense glower. “Preposterous. You yourself told us to avoid Grimghast’s poison by any means necessary. Are you saying you should not follow your own advice?”

“Remember when I told you my stomach cramps were because I was testing new medicines on myself?” Everyone nodded. “The truth is the medicine I was testing was made using Grimghast’s venom.”

The party erupted into a furor. Lucretia spat out the tea she was sipping, drenching Morgan who looked frozen in place. Teos dropped to his knees in a slump. Ione brandished her pan and advanced on Kai with divine fury in her eyes.

“Why?” she hissed. “What in the winds could’ve possessed you to willingly take anything made from that creature’s venom without more research?”

“It’s not the first time I’ve done it,” the Norzen grumbled. He yelped in pain when Ione’s pan struck him in the shoulder.

“How long?” The steel in the woman’s voice promised judgment if Kai’s answer wasn’t to her liking.

“Are you asking how long I’ve been imbibing Grimghast’s venom in particular or all poisons in general?” Somehow Ione’s tanned skin turned pale enough that Kai wondered if she would pass out in front of him.

He really hoped not; he had enough to worry about.

“Please tell me that doesn’t mean what I think it does.” Her eyes pinched together, and she stared at him with palpable desperation.

“How do you think I became so knowledgeable about poisons in the first place?” Kai replied. “It all started during my apprenticeship. In order to know how to treat them, I figured the best way to learn was to endure the effects of each poison myself. Never even bothered telling Master Gerardo about it. I would mix small quantities into my tea, just enough to induce symptoms. Over time, I had to increase the dosages to generate the same effects as my body’s resistance grew.”

Ione leaned against the wheel, shedding fresh tears. “And you’ve been doing this to yourself for years?” she asked. Kai nodded, unsure of how to respond.

Morgan raised his hand, his eyes shifting to the door. "Do Maple and Orelia know?"

"I think they suspect it was more than just untested medicine, but we haven't discussed it. However, I swear I haven't taken any since the night Agosti attacked. I threw it in the river."

Lucretia's eyebrow raised. "I am surprised. I would have thought you would continue anyways. You can be rather stubborn when it comes to your job."

Kai sent the scholar a fierce stare, his fur standing on end. "I made a promise," was all the answer he gave, causing Lucretia's expression to shift to one of respect.

"So where do we go from here?" Teos inquired.

"We continue as normal. If we're lucky, Kendela's spy won't find anything to use against us. Just to be safe, I think we better keep an eye on Maple in shifts. The carrier hawk should return before lunch with Fusette's reply, as well. For now, we hold our cards close and get to Havenfall as soon as possible. The enemy is still five or six days away by foot, if Hemlocke's information was accurate."

"Sounds like a plan. I do have one question, though."

"Hmm?" Kai glanced at the grinning smuggler with unease.

"What will your family think of your courtship?" The others burst into snickers as Kai's face turned an unhealthy shade of white, both tails hanging limp.

Bloody Nulyma, he thought. *I completely forgot to send them a hawk! Guess I'll be sending two letters tonight.*

"Everything alright?" asked Orelia as she took the seat Kai occupied mere minutes ago.

Maple gave the priestess a nervous smile. "To be honest, I'm not sure," she replied. "I did want to ask your opinion on something, though. You reckon we should get on Kai's rump about drinking Grimghast's venom?"

Orelia's eyes widened. "You knew?!"

"Of course I did. I shouldn't be surprised you figured it out as well. We have other problems, though. I think I may have bollixed everything when I made him promise to stop using the venom."

Tilting her head in confusion, Orelia asked what Maple meant.

"I know Kai well enough to know he disposed of all the venom he had left over. He wouldn't want to leave himself open to temptation, and we saw him chuck the vial into the river." Beckoning the younger woman closer, Maple grinned before leaning in to whisper in her ear, "Just like how you and I both know he'll probably be standing outside that door the moment the others finish interrogating him."

The two women giggled as Orelia removed a slender bottle from the pack; a fragrant white wine. "Do you think it was the right thing, telling him about my interest?" Orelia wondered. Taking a quick swig straight from the bottle, her entire face flushed and a high-pitched hiccup escaped her lips. She offered the other woman the bottle with a wry smile.

"I know it was. It's like you said; he needs to know the stakes. This is just as much about him as us," Maple explained. Taking the wine, she threw back a short draw before returning it. "Hopefully we can finish this chat before he comes back. The truth is, I'm worried." Orelia tilted her head in befuddlement. "I can feel Grimghast's venom draining my strength. Kai's tonics help ease the pain and give me a boost, but it feels as though my body is growing weaker faster than the tonics can relieve it."

The merchant's fingers twitched as Orelia took her hand and squeezed it while holding up the bottle. Violet met blue as the two women stared at each other. Maple was confident her friend knew what she was hinting at. Grinning, the two women each took another drink that brought a renewed crimson tinge to their cheeks.

"If you think I'm prepared to read you your last rites already, you've lost your kettle. Besides, I don't think I'm permitted to read them while drunk. Kai will find a way to heal you. I know he will!"

Maple scoffed. Apparently she *didn't* quite get it. "I'm not saying I'm on my deathbed quite yet, damn it, but I'd rather we be prepared for the worst possible outcome."

"Wait...what are you saying, Maple? You can't be serious." Orelia's lips parted, her tanned cheeks paling to a dusky sienna.

Fighting back the urge to sigh in relief, Maple cast her signature tilted smile. "You and I both know Kai's going to work himself to the bone to try and get this filth out of me. That protective determination is one of his sweeter qualities. Still, there's always a chance he may not be able to find the missing piece he needs. I-if that happens, and I don't make it out of this—"

The room wobbled as Orelia grasped Maple by the shoulders and shook her vigorously. "You quit that line of thought right this moment," the priestess demanded. "Damn it, woman, you will live!"

"We don't know that," hissed Maple. Gripping Orelia's wrists, she pulled the other woman into a tight embrace. "I want you to promise me something. If I don't make it, then take your chance and pursue him. Kai, for all his virtues, is a bit dense. Even knowing how you feel, he'll be hesitant. Regardless, he needs someone to show him he deserves love and care, and I couldn't imagine anyone I'd rather have in my place than you."

The salty scent of tears filled Maple's nose as Orelia sobbed into her shoulder. "I don't know if I could take the chance like this. It wouldn't feel right. I love Kai to death, but I can see his eyes always searching you out first whenever we're all together. You have his heart in a way I never could. And let's be honest, I doubt I'll ever find a man who could treat me the same way Kai would. Listen. You'll get better, then you'll marry him one day and have lots of cute little mixblood babies. I've made peace with the fact that you'll be his wife and I'll likely die a spinster."

Maple frowned and flicked her friend on the nose, drawing a startled yelp from her. "You might be surprised to know he notices you a lot more than you think he does. My eyes don't lie. Besides, you're counting yourself out too early. Are you certain enough about this to place a wager on it?"

Rapping her staff on the floor, Orelia met Maple's glare with one of her own. "Sounds good to me. What are the stakes?"

A cocky smirk stretched across the merchant's lips. With the other woman drunk, she decided on a whim that maybe shaking things up could work out to both of their benefit. Besides, she doubted Kai would complain when he learned about it.

Assuming the shock didn't kill him first...

Maple would admit she saw Orelia as a romantic rival to an extent, but they were still friends first and foremost, and she wanted her friend to be happy. "Stakes are based on whether Kai cures me or I succumb to this damn poison. If I die, I want your solemn oath you'll pursue Kai in my stead and make him happy."

"Very well. And if he saves you?"

If Maple's smirk were any wider, her face would've looked to be split in two. She held out her hand towards Orelia. "If I live, I'll do everything I can to give him the life he deserves. However, as a favor to you for being open with me about your thoughts and feelings, then you can still have him. We'll share."

Orelia slapped her palm against Maple's and grasped it in a firm handshake. "Deal!"

After several moments, the priestess' eyes grew wider than saucers as the words visibly pierced through the drunken fog. "Wait...what?"

"You heard me. We'll share him. Unlike Galstein, Livorians are permitted to take multiple spouses so long as they can prove a sufficient income to care for all of them plus any children produced within the union. It's why Kendela keeps pursuing me even though he already has three wives. Considering his Exarch status, I'm dead certain Kai makes more than enough to provide a stable life for us, even if he doesn't realize it yet. I love the man with all my heart, but budgeting is *not* one of his strong points."

Her gaze shifting back and forth, Orelia sent Maple a nervous smile. "Are you absolutely sure you'd be comfortable sharing him with me?"

Maple nodded. "Even if I live, Orelia, I don't want to see you miserable for the rest of your life. You're the only one I'd even *consider* doing this with. Besides, you have to admit it'd be fun swapping off on riding his 'holy spear' every night." The merchant broke into a cackle at the searing blush on Orelia's face when she mentioned Kai's 'holy spear.' "Besides, you already shook on it, so you're stuck anyway. I wouldn't have offered if I wasn't positive it would work out. Now get some sleep. You look like you hit the bottle a little too hard."

Stumbling backwards, Orelia slumped against the wall next to the door and stared at Maple in an open-mouthed gape. Her hand reached up and fumbled with the lace choker adorning her neck, the large spherical ruby at its center symbolizing her bond to the Windbringer church. A wave of fresh tears slid down her bronzed cheeks, though her lips curved upwards in a hesitant smile.

"I wonder..." she whispered. The priestess' head tilted downward, her chin resting on her upper chest as she drifted off to sleep.

Chapter XX

Fusette grumbled as she waited on her throne. Saredi had been sent to handle the arrangements in allowing Admiral Basner's fleet to recuperate in the fields outside of Whistlevale. The Galstans would need to rest from their long march before they were ready to fight alongside her own forces. With any luck, the task would take up the rest of the Lord Chamberlain's day and keep both men out of the palace long enough for her to accomplish her task. If either one of them had an inkling as to her intentions today, there was no doubt she would be forced to endure a lecture for the ages.

Never mind the fact she was a grown woman; she'd learned fast that age was no shield against men like Saredi and Ottoten. If anything, all her adulthood did was *lengthen* their tirades on etiquette and what a noble lady was supposed to spend her time doing.

The letter she received last night, still clutched in her fingers, was sure to raise a rumpus, no matter how it played out. The cloth-like texture of the parchment soothed her for some reason. She found herself running her fingers along the thick material, her eyes roaming once more over the words written in obsidian ink.

I suppose I shouldn't be too surprised to receive this request from Gravebane, she thought, *but he's moving more quickly and decisively than I expected.*

Her lips quirked up into a content smile. As much as she detested the war, Fusette was glad to see it pushing her cousin to reach the potential she always knew lay within, even before learning of their distant relation through Cacovis. In six years as a Knight, Kai had been content to follow orders and keep his head down, likely to avoid unwelcome attention from the other Exarchs or Parliament. Unlike his peers, he was uncomfortable with pulling rank, despite his status giving him the same level of authority as a Margrave in non-administrative matters. With the attack on Mistport and the subsequent loss of his squad, Kai was forced to take command in a way he had little formal training for.

From what Fusette had seen, the Hunters rarely trained anyone for leadership the way the Navy did, which explained why the vast majority of Exarchs were sailors.

It was clear Kai was new to being in charge. From the early reports she'd read, he could be reckless and unsure in issuing commands outside of crises, preferring to rely on his instincts. Still, he was quick to realize how much his new party leaned on him and rose to the occasion. Even if he never realized it, Fusette was proud of his growth into a capable leader, one Livoria could depend on for protection.

A gentle rapping on the throne room door jarred the young monarch from her thoughts. "Come in," she said. Her heart swelled at seeing the doors swing open to reveal Archbishop Jovanni. The old priest's weathered skin carried a broad smile, and he moved with a surety the duchess wished to have at his age, should she live so long.

"Pleasant morning, Your Grace," Jovanni greeted. "What has you in such a tiff you needed to see me so early?"

"Read this," Fusette answered, holding out Kai's letter. "I have received a most unusual request from Sir Gravebane, and it's obvious the contents fall under your purview."

Accepting the letter with a flourish, the bishop donned a pair of circular spectacles and held it at arm's length. Silence reigned as Jovanni muttered nonsensical words under his breath. Fusette could hear him well enough, even with her ears hidden beneath a shawl, but she couldn't make heads or tails of what he was saying. It was as if the aged priest were speaking a language outside of anything she knew of.

"I must confess," said Jovanni as he removed the spectacles and used his vestment to wipe them clean, "this is going to stir up quite a bit of noise for sure. I can see why you opted to bring this to my attention rather than the Quorum of Bishops. They would excommunicate him on the spot. How confident are you in Gravebane's intentions to go through with this? Also, does he meet the financial requirements?"

"Are rivers wet?"

The two shared a silent moment, content to stare at each other until Jovanni burst into wheezing laughter, bent at the waist. "I suppose I only have myself to blame for that answer," he choked out. "The church has maintained for years that relationships between the tribes are forbidden due to an assumed inability to produce viable offspring. I must assume Gravebane is aware of this, or does he have evidence to the contrary? His missive strongly suggests the church's official doctrine is flawed."

"Actually, Archbishop," Fusette replied, "all the evidence we need is right here in the palace. As for Gravebane's finances, he requested I deposit any wages he earned from his Exarch duties into a separate vault here in the capital's bank. Keep in mind, Exarchs earn about a hundred golds a moon as a base, plus any mission bonuses accrued due to exceptional performance. That amounts to at least ten platinum marks each moon." The duchess couldn't hold back her smirk as Jovanni's eyes bulged at the amount. Platinum marks, equal to ten golds each, were rarely used outside of prominent transactions among the nobility and government. "To my knowledge, he hasn't touched the vault in the six years since his Branding."

Returning to the throne, she retrieved a small pile of parchment and handed it over. At the very top was what she considered the most importance document: Ambroz's medical report, detailing his unusual mixblood heritage and overall general health. Right beneath it was a scribbled note with a rough estimate of Kai's financial capability.

Once again, Jovanni set his spectacles in place and read. With each successive page, his eyes grew wider and his hands trembled enough the duchess could see the parchment fluttering in his ironclad grip. "Is this all true?" he asked.

Fusette only nodded.

"By the holy winds." A guard stepped forward with a small chair, allowing the stunned Archbishop to sit without collapsing on the floor as he looked ready to do. "I suppose Gravebane doesn't have much to worry about. As for Ambroz's heritage, why has this never been brought to the attention of the church?"

"Who's to say the church didn't already know it?" the monarch answered with a shrug. "It's clear some within these walls knew the truth of his lineage. However, seeing you so shocked by this yourself makes it obvious nobody saw fit to inform others within the church hierarchy. My best guess is they either assumed you already knew the truth, or they brought Ambroz's situation to the Quorum's attention and it went no further."

From where she stood, Fusette wondered if she might have to send for a Royal Apothecary. Jovanni's complexion was growing paler and she could hear the short, heaving gasps he took with every breath. Just as she prepared to wave for a guard, the priest gestured that he was fine and gave her a tender smile which reminded her of the warmth he projected in his sermons.

Jovanni was considered an odd choice upon his selection as Archbishop, given his background as a bard and his dedication to Vadako the Maiden. However, he was far and away the most popular bishop among the realm's extensive faumen population, due primarily to his kind manner and willingness to treat everyone he encountered as equals, no matter their tribe, age, or means.

It was an attitude that Fusette felt made the Archbishop uniquely suited to handling Kai's circumstances.

"If this information is all true, then I will need to speak with Gravebane directly, along with anyone else involved. I was surprised to see Sister Basner's name mentioned in his letter."

"Orelia is the one I'm most concerned about," Fusette admitted. "I can only imagine the fuss the Quorum will raise should she agree to take part in the proceedings."

"Indeed. There is still time for us to form a proper plan before their return. That being said, I am willing to support this, so long as Gravebane and his entourage are willing to meet with me to discuss the particulars. There will likely need to be concessions from both sides, but I have faith it will work out."

"That's all I needed to hear. Thank you, Jovanni, and I mean it with every fiber of my heart."

"Nonsense, child. I swore to your father I'd look after you before that wretched plague took him from us. I know he'd be proud of you, though if I know Vonlo, he'd tell you to firm up and take charge like only an Ardei can."

"I intend to," Fusette said, her grey eyes flashing with determination. "I have decided to summon the Five Realms Council. With luck, Gravebane and his party will return well before the other leaders arrive. This realm must change if we are to survive the turmoil facing us, and if I have to make use of every authority granted to me by the Livorian Codex to invoke those changes, so be it."

Jovanni broke out into hysterics. "There it is! I knew you had the same fire your father and grandfather were famous for. If I may, I do have one request."

"Hmm?"

"When you send your reply, tell Gravebane I'm looking forward to the chaos his decision will set loose. This church has needed upheaval in the worst way for over a hundred years. It's my greatest hope that, with you and him leading the charge, we may finally forge a path for our realms that brings a measure of peace and equality for all."

Chapter XXI

After three more days of tense travel, Kai was both relieved and nervous to see Havenfall's tiny port as the *Senberg* approached. This would be his first trip home since last summer, almost an entire year.

Tears pricked at his eyes when thoughts of his squad assaulted his mind. He already knew the letters were delivered to their families, but now he would see everyone in the village for the first time since the war began. He didn't know what he could possibly say to anyone.

Marko and he grew up together, even if their relationship was strained before being assigned the same squad. The thought of seeing his older sisters after what happened sent a chill of dread up his spine. Faust was single and his family lived on the opposite side of the village, so perhaps he could avoid any awkwardness there. The real trouble would be if he saw Calvino's wife, Isadel.

Shaking his head, Kai let his legs carry him to Maple's cabin. Teos informed him Orelia was still in bed, sleeping off a minor hangover, so Maple would be alone at the moment. He hoped seeing the peppy woman would lift his spirits. Sure enough, the merchant greeted him with a soft smile that soothed his building unease.

"Good morning," she murmured. "The mixture you gave me last night helped a lot with the cramps in my hip. I hope it means you're getting close. I was not meant to live in a bed!"

Kai chuckled and wrapped an arm around Maple's waist, pulling her close. "I think I'm almost there," he replied. His gaze fell to the floor with both shoulders sagging. "The venom is still the block I can't get around, though. I threw away the samples I had before and without the saliva, making an antivenom will be hard."

"I believe in you, even though I'm confident you were drinking the stuff." His eyes bulged, turning to face Maple with unbridled horror. She laughed. "I already told you, love: You're easy to predict. I'll admit Orelia and I are a little upset you didn't explain exactly what you were doing, but I know it was because you didn't want us to worry."

The Norzen's face sunk. Thoughts of both women looking at him in disgust from that night jumped back into his mind. His body inched away, pulling his arm back until Maple held him still.

She pressed Kai's head into her neck and rubbed his mane while emitting soft cooing trills in one ear. "You're not going anywhere, Sir Gravebane, and neither are we," she whispered, drawing out his Brand in an alluring tone. "Just because we're upset doesn't mean we hate you. Neither of us could ever hate you." Instead of responding with words, Kai let his arms encircle Maple and draw her into a tight embrace.

"Thank you," he mumbled.

The pair drew apart when Morgan's booming voice carried across the cabin deck. "Oi, 'pothy! Teos says we're about to dock. You probably wanna get Maple ready."

Rolling his eyes, Kai's face burned red when Maple leaned over and nuzzled her nose against his cheek. He knelt in front of the bed and let Maple hook her arms around his neck. Rising to his feet, Kai used a cloth band to secure her to his back. There was a gentle pressure where her talons gripped his thighs.

"Ready?" he asked.

"As ready as I can be," Maple answered. "I'm nervous about meeting your family, though. You've mentioned them so much, and now I'll see them face-to-face." The merchant's eyes shifted down with a forlorn expression. "What if they don't like me?"

"Are you serious?" asked Kai. "They'll love you. Orelia too, even though she and I aren't really official at the moment. I should warn you, though;

don't be surprised if my sister starts peppering you with questions. Serafina can be a chatterbox and isn't afraid to speak her mind."

She giggled. "I think I'll be fine." Heaving a sigh, she suggested they head out. Nodding, Kai reached up to massage Maple's scalp a little, smiling when she rested her chin on his shoulder.

Straightening his back, he stepped into the morning sunlight and felt a wave of nostalgia hit him when he saw a sizable group waving from the dock. The familiar scents of home assaulted his nose, from the tika moss growing in beds along the riverbank to the piles of homemade food covering a group of makeshift tables at the end of the port.

Orelia strode up from behind and rested her arms on the deck wall with a tired groan. Her eyes looked baggy and she stared at Kai with a pitiable frown. Chuckling, Kai removed a vial from the fur of his robes and dropped it into her waiting palm, informing her it was a hangover tonic.

"If there weren't so many people watching out there, I'd kiss you right now," the priestess grumbled as she downed the vial's contents in a single gulp. Kai hoped he wasn't blushing too hard, though it became a moot point when Orelia leaned over and rested her head in his mane. His gaze swept over the rest of the party, only to spot Teos and Morgan both standing with smug grins on their faces.

"Don't even start," Kai warned.

"Wouldn't dream of it, Sir Gravebane," Teos retorted, his smirk growing wider. "Just remember what I said before."

A tremor wracked his body as he spotted his family at the crowd's front. As they got closer, he realized the crowd was smaller than he expected. The blush in his cheeks intensified when he spotted the smallest figure whistling at him while holding a thumb up; his sister, Serafina. The group parted as a portly older man wearing a silk suit of bright scarlet and black breeches advanced to the front.

"Who's that?" Ione asked, gesturing to the lavishly dressed man.

"Barraco, the village headman. He's a bit of an odd one, but he's crafty as a fox and well liked among the villagers. Also, don't be too surprised when he starts talking; he's got a voice like a warhorn."

Morgan rumbled up beside Kai and barked orders to Montagru and Yasso. The deckhands flew into action as Yasso hurtled onto the dock and spun in place, catching the gangway sliding towards his head. Kai was impressed at the speed with which they got the mooring ropes tied down and the ramp locked into place. Montagru cast a cocky grin at the apothecary and gave him a thumbs up.

"Well, this is it," Kai muttered as the rest of the party gathered at the top of the ramp. "We finally arrived."

Lucretia, holding Cacovis' journal tucked against her side, flashed him a rare smile. "How does it feel being home after so long?"

"I'm not really sure. Part of me is really happy, but at the same time I'm terrified."

"Unsurprising, considering everything you've been through since the war started," said Orelia from Lucretia's other side. "You'll be fine."

Taking a deep breath, Kai let himself take in the peacefulness of the scene. The sights, sounds, and smells. He clicked his tongue and led the party down the ramp, which caused the crowd to erupt into cheers. Maple's chin dug a little deeper into his neck and he whispered for her to relax.

The apothecary swung both his tails around as best he could, wrapping them around the young girl throwing herself at his waist. "Easy, Sis! I'm carrying a patient." She buried her face in Kai's mane, her voice muffled until the Norzen rolled his eyes and told her to step back. She did so, giving the party space to spread out and for Kai to get a good look at his family for the first time in a long while.

Serafina, at sixteen, was still a year away from completing her own Trial of Ascension to become a full Hunter. She was tall for her age at just under two yards in height. Her brown hair was tied up in a tight bun while wearing a flowing green dirndl styled similarly to Ione's with a black corset and stars embroidered into the skirt.

His eyes shifted to his mother, Verona, standing just behind Serafina. Her dirndl was white with a blue corset. The two looked so similar, and Verona so youthful, that the two were often mistaken by outsiders as sisters rather than mother and daughter. Indeed, Serafina inherited her mother's brown eyes, nose, hair, and slender frame.

A loud guffaw burst from the third member of the group. Kai's father, Gaspard, was a short and stocky middle-aged man with a thin mustache, dressed in scruffy work clothes and a dirty baker's apron. A thick cane rested in his left hand.

To this day, Kai still didn't know the details of the mission near the Corlatian border that left Gaspard crippled. All he knew was a nettleboar had crushed his father's left leg and left his entire squad dead. After being forced to retire, Gaspard received a hefty payout from Fusette's father, Duke Vonlo.

He edged forward and clapped a broad hand on Kai's shoulder. "It's about bloody time you saw fit to drag your carcass back home, son!" Gaspard exclaimed. "By the winds, I was beginning to wonder if you would ever come back."

"I know you read my hawk posts, Da. Things have been complicated, to put it simply. I explained at least that much." Kai's gaze flitted amongst the crowd, but he couldn't see any of the families of his squad mates.

"Aye, but your father and I still worry," Verona spoke up. "When we heard what happened..." Her voice trailed off, and the family lowered their heads in a moment of silence.

Shaking his head, Kai adjusted his stance when he felt Maple shifting behind him. The slow, short movements helped take his mind of the memories threatening to spring forth. "I know, Ma. Listen, it's been a long few days and I'd like to get my friends and crew settled in before Barraco starts up with his speeches. We can discuss the more serious stuff later. Where's Commander Petro, by the way? He's the main reason we're here, after all."

"According to Barraco, he's out scouting the area. After we received your hawk about the Libbies, we evacuated most of the regular civilians to the woods north of town. Your father reminded Petro you'd be here early, but you know him. The man is married to his job."

"Enough about the serious things," said Gaspard. "Why don't we meet your new friends?"

Gesturing to each one in turn, Kai introduced the party to his parents. The group clasped their hands and gave a Windbringer greeting, though Morgan's attempt was still a bit awkward, his hands held too low.

Gaspard laughed at the sellsword's choppy movements and told him to keep practicing. "I can tell you ain't from around these parts. You'll get it eventually. It takes repetition to get the motion just right. Finyt, the fact you're even trying says a lot, if ya ask me." Morgan rubbed the back of his head and thanked the other man for his kind words.

Kai fought a sudden urge to flee when Verona turned to him, gazing at Maple with a mischievous leer in her gaze. "And who is this lovely young lady using you as a perch, son?"

Knowing he couldn't avoid it any longer, the apothecary cast a sweeping glance at the crew to see if any of them were listening in. Given their spy problem, he was hesitant to speak too freely. However, he spotted them preoccupied with the wave of locals surrounding them on all sides, while the rest of the party had sidled to the edge of the crowd and was busy shaking as many hands as possible.

He leaned in and whispered in his mother's ear. "This is Maple, Ma. I know it may sound strange, but the truth is...well, I've been officially courting her."

Kai flinched when Verona emitted a shrill squeal of glee and wrapped her arms around the two. "Oh Kai, that's wonderful news! I *do* hope you plan on bringing her home for dinner tonight." The older woman eyed him with a look promising he wouldn't like the consequences if he declined.

Deciding to err on the side of self-preservation, Kai nodded. "Of course, Ma. I trust there are enough rooms at the inn to get everyone settled." A shiver ran down his spine when he felt Maple's breath tickle his neck as she giggled.

"Excellent," Verona exclaimed. "And of course we'll make sure your crew are all provided the best rooms. She, on the other hand," Kai gulped when his mother lifted a finger towards Maple, "shall be staying with us. Your friends can stay in the guest shacks on the grounds."

"Ma'am, are you sure that's appropriate? I wouldn't want to get you in trouble," Maple asked, her voice hitching and cheeks burning red.

"Nonsense, sweetheart, it's no trouble at all. Besides, it's obvious you're still recovering, so having you stay with us will make it easier for Kai to keep an eye on you. Finyt knows his dispensary is a bit far from the house and the cots there are too hard on a recovering woman's back."

Turning back, Kai noticed Orelia leading the rest of the party in mingling with the crowd, though she stayed along the edge to avoid getting dragged in. The priestess looked back at him with a nervous smile. Barraco was somewhere in the throng, his booming voice carrying over everyone else as he tried prompting the Hunters to stay back.

After making sure the crew was still occupied, he gave his mother a sideways glance. "You're taking this surprisingly well. You know how the church treats relationships like ours."

"And yet you're still trying to make it work," Verona replied with a firm voice. Kai had to admit it was a good point. "I will confess the circumstances make me worry, but I'm your mother, so it's my job. Besides, you never were the most attentive during church. I swear the only reason you even went when you were a sprout was because your father and I made you go. Either way, we'll discuss this more during dinner."

Fighting back an audible gulp, Kai didn't have to turn his head to know Maple was giving him a smug look. "Sounds good, Ma. It's good to be home."

"It's good to have you back, son. We give thanks to the Saints every time we get a letter but having you here in the flesh is so much more appealing. Now let's go save your friends before the villagers swallow them alive."

CHAPTER XXII

Rescuing his party from a crowd of rowdy Hunters proved a greater struggle than Kai expected. He knew the village would be excited to see him come home, but to his surprise, they seemed more interested in his friends. Every attempt he made to move in their direction resulted in having to step back to avoid being knocked over. Looking at everyone, he could see them growing weary with all the handshakes and greetings. Even Orelia appeared exhausted, the edges of her eyes visibly sagging. Her gaze met his and she gave him a pleading look.

Flattening his ears, Kai blew a shrill whistle which brought the uproar to a sudden stop. Every pair of eyes swung to face him, sending a tremor of hesitance through him.

He cleared his throat before shouting, "Listen up, everyone! I know you're all excited about this, and I'm sure you know the main reason why I've returned." The villagers erupted into cheers. Kai heard several in the group shouted they were ready to fight. "Yes, yes, I understand how you feel. However, we cannot begin official preparations until I meet with Commander Petro, so please be patient. Now then, we've had a long journey and would like to take some time to rest and recuperate."

More than half the crowd emitted disappointed groans at that news. Stepping to the front, Gaspard hollered for everyone to quiet down. "Settle it, you lot," he shouted. "You heard the man. Besides, this gives us a chance to show Kai's friends some real Havenfall hospitality!"

More cheers erupted, though Kai grew nervous at the declaration. If there was one thing Hunters were known for outside their normal duties, it was a penchant for raucous celebration.

"I agree," bellowed Barraco. The man's sudden appearance startled Kai, who stepped away from the stout headman. "I suggest you all head home and prepare. Today will be for rest and spending time with family. On the morrow, we celebrate!"

The cheers reached a crescendo that forced Kai to flinch away, both ears flat against his skull. A calloused hand gripped his arm, and he opened his eyes enough to see Gaspard giving him an apologetic look. "Sorry about them," he muttered. "Guess you've been gone so long, they forgot how sensitive you are to noise. Even knowing the Libbies are on their way, they can't bring themselves to worry about it with the civilians all gone. Barraco can herd them away. For now, let's get your crew settled before they get dragged into whatever preparations the old snaggletooth is brewing up."

Kai breathed a sigh of relief and waved the others over as the crowd dispersed back towards the village. They all stumbled over, looking tired despite the earliness of the day.

His eyes sought out Orelia, who gave him an exhausted smile and leaned against him while pinching the bridge of her nose. "I'm glad you stopped that when you did," she muttered. "Otherwise I might've been tempted to smack someone. My head is pounding." Kai whispered a contrite apology before reaching up and digging his fingers into her vermillion hair. His ministrations produced a contented moan from the priestess.

"This is what you dealt with every day growing up?" Morgan asked. "No wonder you're so damn durable and patient all the time."

"I agree," Lucretia added, her spectacles askew and hair unnaturally disheveled. "Though with all the men I hear clamoring for ale, it amazes me you are such a lightweight in the meadhouse."

"Don't you bring that up," Kai pleaded. His hand inched away from Orelia, only for her to grab it and return it to her head, imploring him to keep scratching.

"Now I'm really curious what you lot have gotten up to since you met my boy," said Gaspard, shoving a gentle elbow into Kai's ribs. Lucretia promised to share some stories with the older man later to the apothecary's dismay.

The rest of the crew joined them, looking uneasy at the attention they received. Yasso grumbled about being manhandled by a dozen different people, men and women.

"I should've warned you all the Hunters can be a bit much if you're not used to them," Kai apologized, offering a repentant bow. "My mistake."

The crew brushed it off, with Dekel telling Kai they should've expected it, knowing what they did about the mission. Verona took the lead from there, urging the group to follow as she led them into the village proper.

Kai fought to hold back his amusement at seeing the party gaze about in wonder. After being called a country bumpkin due to his reaction to large cities, it was amusing to see the boot on the other foot for once. Unlike other towns they'd visited, Havenfall was unique in that it had no protective wall; a fact the party was quick to notice.

"Mr. Travaldi," asked Ione as they entered the village's main road, "is there a reason why Havenfall doesn't have any noticeable defenses? Aren't you worried about wild beasts coming into town?"

"Why would we worry about that?" Serafina answered for her father. "We're Hunters. If anything, the beasts would be the ones building a wall to keep *us* out."

Teos lifted his hat and scratched behind his ear, a befuddled look on his face. "I...can't really argue that point."

A deep chortle came from both parents. "We'll be the first to admit," Gaspard said, "as a group, Hunters are madder than a pack of hatters. Makes me wonder where we went wrong raising Kai, considering how normal he is by comparison."

A soft breeze brushed against Kai's cheek. His gaze shifted to see Maple's own cheeks puffed out with a sour expression in her eyes and nostrils flared. He noticed a similar look in Orelia's visage as she stood next to him and grasped his wrist in a show of support.

"If you ask me," Maple asserted, "I think you raised a fine man."

"Oh, I like her already," quipped Verona, waggling her eyebrows at the blushing merchant. "If nothing else, we taught the boy good taste in women."

The group settled into a comfortable silence as Kai's family led them further. Without a wall to constrict them, the town sprawled with sizable homes built from thick logs. The slanted roofs, while having visible wooden frames, were covered with bundles of hay and straw held in place by a chunky brown mortar. Unlike the cramped residential districts of larger cities, there were wide open spaces between each house. This gave the village a grander sense of size, making it look much larger compared to its relatively small population.

The sizes of the houses varied as well, with some being small enough to be called shacks while others were expansive buildings the size of small manors. However, each looked clean and well-maintained. Rather than the iron or wood fences common elsewhere, the Hunters surrounded their homes with stone walls a yard tall and a sizable opening directly in front of the main entrances.

As they walked, the party was greeted with friendly waves by everyone they passed. Kai felt a surge of fondness well up in his chest seeing the villagers. Groups of children, likely the families of Hunters remaining in the village, ran through the open areas, chasing each other and rolling amongst the wildflowers growing all around.

"This place," Maple murmured, "it's so beautiful and peaceful."

"Well thank you, Maple," Gaspard replied. "We like to think we've got a good thing going here. I will say it's not as lovely as a small ocean port like Featherbrook out east, but it has its own charm. Havenfall's been around for over two hundred years, and our mission hasn't changed much since then: Protect the duchy from anyone who would threaten it, no matter who they may be. It's why so many are eager to pick up their blades and fight. If it weren't for those damned duffers in Parliament, we'd already be in the thick of it."

"I never understood the reason behind that," Orelia piped up. "We know the Hunters are considered combat support for the Navy; the battalion commander at Faith Hollow tried conscripting Kai before getting put in his place. But why would Parliament make it so difficult to muster the entire Corps for something so important as a war threatening Livoria's very existence?"

The older man gave a nervous chuckle. "To tell you the truth, we're a lot more than just combat support. Too many morons in the Navy get up on their wide wiroch, thinking they're better than us because they get all the credit when things go right. The Hunters are who the Duchess calls in when, if you'll pardon my crass language, shit rolls downhill."

Ione gripped her skirt, both eyes darting about. "Why?" she asked. "I thought the Hunter Corps' duty was to handle problems relating to rampant beasts. It's how Lucretia and I met Kai back in Mistport, after all."

It was Lucretia that spoke up, her eyes focused on Cacovis' journal held open in her hand as she read. "Their mission as nature wardens is what most folks associate with the Corps, despite being only a sliver of their true purpose. It is not common knowledge, but the Hunters' unique skills make them suited to combat and intelligence missions the Royal Navy is considered too upfront and brutish for. In short, they serve as Livoria's unofficial spies and assassins."

Everyone's eyes darted to Kai, who replied with an uneasy smile. "She's not wrong. We're not really allowed to discuss that part of our duties, though I'm not surprised Lucretia knows of it. I've never liked the idea of being an assassin, though. Too much subterfuge for my tastes."

"I consider that a great blessing," the scholar added. "When I first learned you were both an apothecary and Hunter back in Mistport, it was one of the main reasons I was so wary of you. Given your skills and knowledge, you could rank among the deadliest assassins in all Nixtral. Getting to know you since then was perhaps the first time I was ever thankful to be wrong."

"See what I mean?" Gaspard said, shaking his head. "We muddled up his training if he gets shaky on killing people. He's been that way since he was a sprout. Never had a problem putting down beasts, but a person was a whole other barrel of fish."

"I don't think killing *people* is the problem," Orelia replied. Kai's family turned to face the priestess with looks of confusion. "The Libbies marched on Faith Hollow with a force of six thousand men. Kai was responsible for the plan that left half their army dead, just because he wished to save as many innocent lives as possible."

Kai's parents looked at him with wide eyes. "I'm an apothecary, Da, not an assassin," he said. "My job is to save people, even from those who would murder and pillage for their own sick pleasure. I'm not cut out for the secrets and scheming that go with those duties. There's also too much political involvement in those missions. I'm sorry if you're disappointed in me for my decision, but it's how I've chosen to live."

A sense of shame welled up in Kai's gut. He cast his eyes downward and suppressed the desire to run. The pressure around his neck tightened and he raised his head to see the girls flashing him bright smiles.

He was so focused on their beaming grins, he was startled when he felt Gaspard clap a hand on his shoulder. "I shouldn't be surprised. You've always been the first one to offer help to others, even when they may not deserve it." Kai flinched, reminded of Hemlocke. "Still, I'm not disappointed at all. If anything, I couldn't be prouder. Only a real man can stand for their convictions like that."

Tears threatened to well up at the edges of Kai's eyes, but he blinked them back, giving his father a short bow. "Thanks, Da. That...means more to me than you realize."

"We're here," Verona interrupted. The party gasped at the sight.

Gaspard's investment of his retirement payout proved well spent, as the Travaldi house was one of the larger buildings in the village, though still only two-thirds the size of the manor outside Glimmerdale. The garden was full of numerous multi-colored flowers, and a wall of boxwood bushes surrounded the outer edge of the house itself.

A dozen smaller buildings were scattered throughout the expansive grounds, with Serafina pointing them out and explaining their purpose as temporary quarters for family guests. Verona smiled and confessed the main party would be making use of them while the rest of the crew would be staying at the town inn at the bottom of the hill.

Yasso let out a groan, only to be cuffed behind the head by his uncle. "Don't be a beggar," Montagru scolded. "We should consider ourselves lucky our hosts are willing to give us accommodations in the first place. They could've made us sleep on the ship."

"I get it, Uncle," the younger Soltauri whined, "but coming uphill on the way back sounds exhausting."

"You're still a young buck. You ain't got no reason to complain." The rest of the group shared a chuckle at Yasso's annoyed expression.

Gaspard raised his cane and pointed at a large, widespread building downhill. "There's the inn. Just tell the innkeeper you're with Kai and he'll arrange everything."

Beckoning Dekel over, Kai handed the engineer a hefty bag that clinked when it changed hands. "Give this to the innkeeper as well. It should more than cover everyone's room and board for the time we're here, plus a nice tip. It's probably a good thing Her Grace is the one paying for our expenses. We'd go broke otherwise."

The older Aerivolk broke out into a heaving laugh. "You're not wrong, lad. Thanks for the marks. I'll make sure it gets into the right hands. Come on, you lot! There's a stein of ale down there with my name on it and she's calling for me something fierce." Tipping his cap, Dekel led the crew down the winding cobblestone path towards the inn, singing a shanty the entire time.

Waves of relief hit Kai's mind all at once. A part of him worried what Kendela's spy would get up to, but he was soothed by the knowledge that, thus far, none of the crew had been harmed. He would have more time to consider the problem tonight, after making sure everyone was fed and watered.

"Well, folks," Gaspard announced as he trudged up to the front door. "welcome to our home. It ain't much, but it's warm and cozy at least. Now let's set your packs aside before we talk shop. Verona, sweetheart, you wanna get started on dinner early tonight? We got a full house, after all."

"Stuff that," Serafina snapped, "I haven't had Kai's cooking for almost a year. I want him to make dinner!"

"Serafina!" Verona scolded. "Your brother is probably exhausted. Let the poor man rest."

Stepping forward, Kai gave his mother a comforting pat on the arm. "It's fine, Ma. It's the least I can do. What do you say, Ione? Wanna give me a hand?"

The tavern maid rolled up her sleeves and pulled her trusty pan from its place in her sash. "Not even an army could keep me out. Go set Maple somewhere comfortable while I fire up the stove."

The variety of delectable aromas wafting from the kitchen after several hours could make a stone drool, if Kai were honest with himself. Stepping back and reviewing the veritable feast he and Ione prepared, he silently hoped it would be enough to feed everyone. His main concerns were his father and Morgan, both of whom had stomachs deeper than bottomless pits.

"You think we made enough?" he asked the tavern maid, who was moving a large pot of rabbit stew from the stove to the center table. They brought two smaller tables from outside and set one on each side of the central one, stretching over the entire length of the dining room. The pair had sent for a bevy of supplies from the *Senberg* to avoid putting too much pressure on Kai's family.

Aside from the stew, several large bowls of varied vegetables such as steamed corn, carrots, caramelized onions, and a large salad were scattered along the tables. At the center were three plates covered in different types of meat; a roasted giant mallard stuffed with leeks and potatoes, six slabs of beef ribs covered in braised mushroom sauce, and two massive nobletusk bison flank roasts in almond-nutmeg sauce. Numerous other side dishes and bottles of drink rounded out the repast.

"Oh I'm sure we have plenty," she sighed. "Besides, if Morgan starts getting out of line, I can deal with him. I just hope everyone likes the food."

"Only one way to find out." Poking his head into the parlor, he shouted for everyone to come in for dinner. Turning back to Ione, he asked if she would be able to get them all situated while he went to get Maple.

"If I can handle a meadhouse of bawdy men, I can handle this lot. Go get your lady."

"Hold on a second, young man," Verona said, gripping the apothecary by the shoulder. "I need to speak with you first. Come."

Though unsure of what his mother wanted, Kai followed the older woman to the base of the stairs with a raised eyebrow. She turned on him and held out her hand, a small cloth-wrapped bundle laying in the center of her palm.

"You really know how to make a statement, son. Maple seems like a sweetheart, and I can tell your intentions just by looking at you, no matter how concerned I may be. I will admit I'm also curious about your relations with that priestess, Orelia; she seems as attached to you as Maple. Either way, it's time I gave you this."

She pressed the object into his hands, watching as he peeled back the layers of cloth to reveal a pendant; a blue glass sphere encircled within an intricately looping gold casing, attached to a simple silver chain. His eyes rose to her neck, wide as saucers.

Verona drew Kai into a tight embrace. "My mother presented this to your father when it became clear he intended to ask for my hand in marriage. I haven't removed it since our handfasting." Kai's cheeks burned crimson at the obvious implication. "This pendant has been passed down in my family for generations, given to the eldest child when they find their intended."

"Shouldn't you give this to Serafina then, Ma?" asked Kai. "She's the only one with your blood. She deserves it more than I do."

"We've been through this. I may not have given birth to you, Kai Travaldi, but you're still my son. Even a blind man can see how much you adore those young ladies. I've noticed you like to keep them both in your sight.

Just be aware of the fight you're picking if you decide to go through with this. Take it. I've been waiting for this day for many years."

With a blush, Kai nodded and tucked the pendant into his robe pocket as he hurried upstairs, his friends and family ambling into the kitchen. Reaching the second floor, he turned left and approached the door at the far end of the hall where he left Maple. While originally a playroom for Serafina when she was young, his father converted it into an extra bedroom after Kai's Trial for the rare occasions when Verona's parents visited from Everstill.

Taking a deep breath, Kai opened the door and called for Maple. Confusion wracked his mind when he saw the bed empty. The linens were still there, perfectly made. The room looked as if it hadn't been touched.

"Strange," Kai mumbled to himself, "I know I left her here before we started cooking. Where could she—"

"Kai," he heard her voice ring out, muffled by distance. "I'm over here!"

Spinning in place, Kai's eyebrows pinched together while staring down the hall. It was obvious someone moved her without telling him, but who? And where would they—

The apothecary's face paled, his eye twitching. *They wouldn't,* he thought. Following the sound, he stopped at a door just to the left of the stairwell.

His room.

Stepping inside, Kai's cheeks flushed in embarrassment seeing the woman he loved laying in his bed, a small tome in her hands. Her head turned just enough for her gaze to match his. A bright smile stretched over her face, though her cheeks were just as red as Kai's.

"Sorry about this. Your parents moved me in here, saying it would be more comfortable, though I don't know why. The other room was cozy enough."

"I think they're trying to send a message; this is *my* room."

Kai didn't think Maple's face could get any redder, yet it did. "Then that means...I'm lying in—"

"Aye."

She cradled her face in her hands, blushing profusely and stammering an apology. "I swear I didn't know," Maple begged. "I can't believe I just let them pick me up and put me in here. By the winds, this is so embarrassing!"

Despite his blush, Kai chortled and took the merchant in his arms, cradling her against his chest. "Hush now. It's not your fault. Come, let's get you some food."

"You're not angry?"

"Why would I be angry over something so simple? If anything, I'm happy."

Maple gasped. "Why?"

"My parents have always made it a point to tease me. They said it was their duty to embarrass me whenever life gave them the opportunity. It may seem strange but, in its own odd way, the teasing was their way of saying they loved and accepted me."

"What does that have to do with our current situation?"

"Simple. If they're including you, it means they think of you as part of the family."

The voices from downstairs grew louder and Kai heard Morgan bellowing for him to come eat. Rolling his eyes, Kai audibly pondered if the sellsword's brain was in his stomach. The quip elicited a giggle from Maple, who leaned into his chest and closed her eyes as he descended the stairs.

"There they are," brayed Teos as the pair entered the dining room. "Sit down and eat, you two. Kai, I swear you and Ione really outclassed yourselves this time. The food is delicious!"

Orelia and Ione set up a long bench lined with cushions for Kai to lay Maple on. Thanking Teos for his compliment, Kai hauled a sack of grain over and used it to prop her torso up as Lucretia offered the injured woman a plate.

"Thank you everyone," said Maple. With slow, methodical movements, she took a bite of the roast bison and gave a squeal of joy. "Teos is right, this is so good! The meat just melts in my mouth." Ignoring her injury, she attacked the plate with gusto. It was only when she hissed and arched her back, provoking a warning from Kai to not tear her stitches, that she returned to a more sedate pace.

"How did you like the gift we left in your room, Kai?" asked Verona.

How she was able to ask the question with a straight face, Kai couldn't guess. He and Maple shared a shy glance before clearing his throat. "It was a surprise, to say the least, Ma. I sure wasn't expecting it."

"What did you get?" pressed Ione.

Despite his best efforts, Kai couldn't contain the crimson tinge spreading across his face. "All I can safely say is it was a *personal* gift. And not one I would expect to receive from my parents, of all people."

Serafina stifled a giggle, prompting Kai to cast a flat stare in her direction. Of course, his sister would be privy to the situation. The more he thought about it, the more he wondered if Serafina was the one to devise the idea in the first place.

The other women shared a confused look before shrugging and returning to their meals. Morgan met Kai's gaze and waggled an eyebrow at the apothecary, who refused to let himself be baited.

"I must say," started Gaspard, "I never could've imagined my son would find such good friends. I remember he got along well enough with his squad, but I can tell he really lets his guard down with you all." The retired Hunter tore a rib from the closest rack and took a sizable chunk with one bite.

Verona added, "My husband is right. We truly must thank you all for looking after Kai. I don't know if we could ever repay your kindness."

"It's not a problem at all, Mrs. Travaldi," Orelia answered for the group. "Kai has been nothing but an amazing friend to us all, even if some took a little longer to warm up to him." The priestess' eyes flickered to Lucretia for a split moment before returning to meet Verona's.

"Oh I've no doubt about that," Verona retorted. "Kai can be a handful, though I reckon you know how he is by now." The older woman wiggled her eyebrows at Orelia, who gave a nervous chuckle before returning her attention to her plate.

"The real question," Gaspard muttered as he sent Kai a smug grin, "is when can Verona and I expect to see some grandkids?"

Kai spun around just in time to spray his mead onto the floor rather than across the table into Lucretia's face. Slamming a fist into his chest, he felt Orelia on his left side, rubbing his back as he coughed up the remnants of his drink. "Da!" he exclaimed. "Ain't it a bit early to be thinking about that?"

"Hey, we're not getting any younger, boy! I think it's pretty obvious our grandchildren will be running around with either feathers or red hair...or both," Gaspard retorted, his eyes switching between Maple and Orelia while they stared at each other with stunned expressions.

To Kai's irritation, Morgan howled with laughter on his other side. "You haven't even been back a day and your folks already have you pegged, 'pothy!" the sellsword brayed.

The apothecary eyed the enormous drumstick in his friend's hand. "Morgan, I hope you realize you're in perfect position for me to gag you with that mallard leg."

Morgan gave the piece of meat an appraising gaze. "At least I'd die happy."

"Kai Travaldi," Verona snapped. "You know better than to fool around with food at my table!"

"Then can I do it?" asked Lucretia to everyone's shock. The scholar returned their open-mouthed stares with a single raised eyebrow. "What...?"

"It's always the quiet ones," Teos muttered as he returned his attention to the food.

Swiveling his ears, Kai turned them towards Maple, who found herself being barraged with questions by a wide-eyed Serafina. Tuning out the rest of the surrounding conversations, he listened in on what the two were discussing.

"Is my brother really courting you?" she whispered to the Aerivolk.

Maple gave the girl a tender smile. "He is, and I couldn't be happier. I will say, though, I was the one to ask him to dance."

The younger girl's eyes locked on her brother for a moment. "I'm not surprised. Kai is one of the smartest people I know, but he's always been a court fool when it comes to romance."

"I don't know," Maple uttered, meeting Kai's eyes and giving him a crooked grin. "You wouldn't think it at first glance, but your brother is quite the natural charmer. And I reckon I'm not the only one who thinks so."

"Now *that's* a surprise," Serafina replied with a snort. "Not sure what you and Orelia see in my brother. I'm sure you've seen he can be a bit dim. Let me tell you about the first time I remember hearing Kai try to talk to a girl outside the family."

His blush returning full force, Kai flattened his ears and diverted his attention elsewhere. He was confident he knew what story Serafina was going to share, and he had no desire to revisit the disastrous memory. Instead, he focused on Morgan, who was engrossed in offering compliments to his parents.

"You folks have an exquisite home," said Morgan with a noticeable slur in his voice. Kai's eyebrows rose at the description and noted the half-empty wine bottle in the sellsword's hand. "This whole village is impressive. You never see anything like this back in southern Corlati. How long did it take to build this place? I can't imagine these logs were light."

Flipping a page in the journal nestled in her hands, Lucretia shot Morgan a coy smirk. "Morgan, I do not know what is more impressive: That you know the meaning of the word 'exquisite,' or that you somehow used your entire vocabulary in a single conversation."

"Ouch! You wound me, woman."

"Not nearly enough, from the look of it."

"Sometimes I forget your tongue is as sharp as your sword, maybe sharper."

"I shall take it as a compliment."

Soon, the room settled into a relaxing ambience, with everyone laughing and sharing stories as they ate. Kai kept an eye on Maple, ensuring she didn't overexert herself. To his immense relief, Gaspard and Morgan both restrained themselves from devouring more than their fair share, though that might have been helped along by Verona and Lucretia keeping a steady flow of wine going their way. By the time everyone had eaten their fill, both men were passed out drunk on the floor. Teos heaved the mixblood sellsword over his shoulder and offered to take him to his quarters.

Kai moved to do the same for Gaspard until his mother thumped him over the head with a wooden spoon. "You leave him where he is. Maybe the hangover he gets in the morn will teach him some restraint."

"Da wouldn't know how to slow down his drinking even if every sip gave him a half chance of dying."

"Well, a woman can hope, can't she? You take care of those lovely young ladies of yours and leave your father to Serafina and I."

A sharp tug on his tail sent a spike of pain through Kai's back. Looking back, he saw Serafina giving him a blank stare that unsettled him.

"Come to my room after you get Maple settled. We need to have a talk, big brother."

Chapter XXIII

As the party prepared to head to their shacks to rest, they had mostly recovered from the events of their arrival.

Barraco stopped by after their massive dinner and invited the party to a small celebration the village would be hosting in their honor. When Kai mentioned the possibility of the Liberation Army heading in their direction, the headman waved him off, insisting that things would be fine with the majority of the village already evacuated. Barraco insisted the Hunters were already prepared for the approaching enemy and would not allow themselves to be intimidated.

"You know we won't take this threat lying down," the heavyset man told Kai. "Even if they outnumber us, we'll give as good as we get. We always do."

He also warned Kai that Commander Petro had claimed exhaustion upon his return, and thus wouldn't be able to meet with the Exarch in an official capacity until tomorrow. Despite worrying about the headman's relaxed assessment of the situation facing them, Kai wrote two copies of a note and handed one to Barraco, reminding them to speak with the commander before the celebration.

When Barraco left, Gaspard warned the group the older man's definition of 'small' was a bit skewed and the celebration would likely be much larger than expected.

After a long day of sharing stories with his family, Kai peered out the window to see the moon cresting over the treetops. His friends were now settled in the shacks scattered throughout the garden, though his mother marched him into returning Maple to his room. The couple blushed when

Verona offered a not-so-subtle warning of what would happen if she found the Aerivolk back in the guest room at any point.

Once Maple was tucked into bed, Kai soothed her, saying he would be back as soon as he was done talking to Serafina. She nodded and pulled him into a warm hug.

Giving her nose a playful tap, he stepped back into the hallway and strolled past the stairs. The walls of the upstairs hall were covered in various trophies of his father's days as a Hunter. Kai's body shivered as his eyes swept over the grisly items. He never understood the reasoning behind the Hunters' obsession with collecting parts from the beasts they defeated. It seemed morbid and wholly disrespectful to the slain creatures.

To this day, the Norzen only had two such trophies, both of which rested at the bottom of his satchel rather than hung up for display: the fang he broke from Grimghast during their battle in the forests, and the nettleboar tusk that pierced his arm the day of his Trial. Unlike other Hunters, who displayed their trophies as proof of their skill and the variety of their prey, Kai kept his as physical reminders to never let pride or complacency blind him. Each time he saw them, he remembered how lucky he was to have survived and gave thanks to the Wind Saints for protecting not just him, but his friends as well.

At the end of the hall, he stopped in front the final door on the left side of the wall. His sister's room. Raising one hand, he gave three solid knocks.

"Come in," he heard from within. Kai reached for the knob and stepped inside. He scanned the area on instinct. Serafina's room was filled with a mix of flower wreaths and varied Hunter implements. A long dagger was buried in the corner of the desk near the far wall, where Serafina sat, while several handmade traps were piled up in the nearby corner.

The girl herself was focused on a sheet of parchment covered in scribbles. Leaning over her shoulder, Kai recognized the rough drawing after pondering a few moments. "Isn't this the leghold trap Da designed back when he was active?" he asked.

"Aye," Serafina replied. "I'm trying to see what adjustments I can make to improve the effectiveness."

"So what did you need to talk about? I assume you didn't call me in here to go over Da's old blueprints."

"How serious are you?"

"Eh?" Kai blinked, briefly stunned before leveling a hardened stare at his sister. "What in the winds are you blathering about?"

"I'm talking about that girl. Maple. How serious are you about her? For that matter, what's going on between you and the priestess? She looks at you the same way Maple does."

His breath caught in his throat. Of all the things he was expecting Serafina to ask about, he wasn't expecting this to be first on the list. "If I'm being honest, I'm very serious. As for Orelia, things are more complicated, though no less serious. I care very deeply for both of them."

"You know what the church would say about this, right? I know you didn't pay much attention during sermons and have no self-preservation to speak of, but not even *you* could be that reckless. Wouldn't this get you in a lot of trouble?"

"Are you trying to talk me out of it?"

Serafina's eyes locked on his with steel in her gaze. "Don't avoid the question."

"Yes, it could cause trouble. I know excommunication would be the likely result."

"Then why take such a huge risk? Ma and Da seem to like them and are trying to brush it off as no big deal, but I can tell they're worried. Seeing you excommed would break them both, Ma especially. You'd all be branded sinners of the highest order. Literally, as in red-hot irons across your chests! I doubt anyone would bother helping you outside of us, assuming you aren't actively run out of town. Damn it, Kai, you were supposed to be the smart one between us! You already face enough problems."

"I know!" exclaimed Kai. "Listen. Orelia once told me something: Love never truly makes sense until you're willing to grab it with both hands and never let go. I've thought about it ever since. The more I mull the words over in my brain, the more I understand."

"What do you mean?"

"Love isn't something you can control. When it hits, you only have two options. First, you push it aside and go through life wondering what could have been. Or, you grab the chance with everything you have and try to make it work, no matter what challenges await."

"I think you're facing a lot more than just some challenges. They both seem nice, but are they really worth the potential danger that comes with loving either one? Or both."

Kai didn't hesitate. "Absolutely. I have no desire to hurt either of them, but I'll need a little help to bring about a best-case scenario. I'm already dealing with Kendela trying to force Maple into a marriage contract."

"Oh, Tapimor's hairy ass, *Kendela's* after one of them? You really are in love if you're willing to fight that feathered windbag for someone. You've always avoided him."

"It's true. I love them both equally. Maple is the sweetest, gentlest, most amazing woman I've ever known. When she smiles, it feels like all my worries disappear. She has the cutest laugh, and she tries to see the good in everything. Despite being the smallest in our group, she's braver than a daggertooth and has a heart of gold.

"And Orelia...she's fiercely independent in a way you can't help but admire. She's not afraid to stand up for what she believes in. Where Maple is the sweetheart, Orelia is the firm, steady one who's learned to never give up no matter how dark things seem. Even then, she's still kind and warm, always willing to help those in need.

"That's why I've sworn to figure out how to purge that poison and get Maple back on her feet. I've already reached out to the capital about my options."

Silence covered the room. The adoptive siblings said nothing, staring at each other as Serafina contemplated what she heard. "Impressive," she finally said. "I can't believe I'm saying this, but you've convinced me, brother."

"I wasn't aware I was supposed to be convincing you of my intentions."

"You know me; I always have to give you sass and question every dumb decision you make. Still, I'm happy for you. I really hope you can make it work, but you'll always have us if things ever fly south."

"Thanks, sis."

"Don't mention it. And I'm serious; if you say anything about this to my friends, I'll strangle you with your own tails. But what will you do about Orelia if you ask Maple for her hand?"

"Like I said, I don't want to hurt either of them. I have an idea in the works, but I can't implement it on my own. I'm just glad that—"

A sharp creak cut through the air like a flintlock. Kai spun to face the door, his hand flying to his waist on instinct. He muttered a low curse when his fingers grasped empty air. His mace was back in his room.

"Ma?" he called out. "Da?" Nobody answered his call, sending a tremor of concern through his body.

"Kai," said Serafina from the window. She waved him over and pointed outside. There, at the garden's edge holding hands while watching the moonrise, were their parents.

The siblings shared an uneasy glance. "You don't think someone would be dumb enough to try robbing a house in Havenfall of all places, do you?" Serafina asked.

"Can't be Maple," Kai replied. "Her hips are still stiff, so I doubt she's walking around, and the others are all out on the grounds." His ears prickled at hearing a click down the hall. A series of muffled thumps followed soon after. Then he heard something that caused his vision to turn a hazy crimson.

The sound of Maple's wings flapping alongside a muffled trill, as if someone were covering her mouth.

With a snarl, Kai wrenched the door open and stalked down the hall. Serafina plucked the dagger from her desk and followed. Kai's heart thundered in his chest as he approached his room while cracking his knuckles. The closer he got to the door, the louder the sounds of struggle became. Reaching for the doorknob, he found the door barred shut. The sounds quieted down, though Kai's ears weren't fooled. He heard the soft rustle of cloth as Maple kept struggling against whoever was inside with her.

"Brother..."

"Stand back," Kai muttered, reeling back his arm. Emitting a roar, he swung his fist at the door with all his strength. His arm muscles bulged with power, blasting the door off its hinges in a thunderous crash. Dust and wood chips flew everywhere, blocking the siblings' view. A boom resonated and Kai saw the outline of the crossbar hitting the floor. His ears twitched, hearing confused shouts from everyone outside. Without waiting for his vision to clear, Kai charged inside. He felt the sharp edge of a blade graze his shoulder but brushed the sting aside and lunged forward.

A sharp exhale came from above as his shoulder slammed into a body. The attacker was pitched back by the impact, colliding with the window and shattering the glass. The weapon, a simple spear, clattered to the floor and Kai struck his foot out, kicking it aside.

"K-Kai!" exclaimed Maple from the floor, her voice stuttering. The apothecary dropped to his knees and took her into his arms. She clutched at his robes, sobbing. Kai ran his fingers through her hair, whispering softly that she was okay.

The dust cleared and Kai's gaze swung towards the window, where he heard the intruder groaning as they stumbled amongst the broken glass. Something about the voice sounded familiar, and Kai's heart sank when he got a clear view of the shabby work tunic and short, stubby horns jutting from the attacker's head.

It was Yasso.

"You..." Kai whispered. Eyes hardening, he shifted Maple behind him where Serafina took the merchant and leaned her against the wall. "Yasso, you better have a damned good explanation for this."

"Sorry boss," the deckhand grumbled. After clambering to his feet, his eyes locked onto Maple, lips curling into a sly grin, "but I can't afford to botch this job up, so you ain't getting in my way."

"I suppose this means you're the one feeding Kendela information."

"Of course. You'd be surprised at how many people ignore the deck crew on a boat, and the job gave me unfettered access to the whole damned ship. It was easy to keep an eye on everyone while you were scurrying about."

"Why?" Kai asked. "Kendela is one of the worst nobles you could swear fealty to. The man's a lowlife, no matter how he likes to portray himself."

"You think I don't know that?!" Yasso snapped, pawing the wooden floor with his hooves. He threaded his fingers through his hair, one hand gripping his ear while chewing on his upper lip. "The bastard has me by the baubles, though. Me, my uncle, and my parents are all field hands on his farms outside Grantide. He's got my folks locked up in his manor, and if I don't do this, he threatened to sell my Pa to the Corlati slavers and Ma to the brothels. Uncle Monta's too simple in the head and believes Kendela wouldn't lie to us, no matter how much we've told him otherwise. He still thinks we took this job as a reprieve from the farm."

Releasing a heavy sigh, Kai cast a solemn look at the Soltauri. He understood Yasso's reasoning and was willing to admit he would be tempted to follow a similar path in the same situation. However, he refused to back down. His ears twitched as the sounds of his friends clamoring outside grew louder. He heard the front door burst open, sending a thrum through Kai's skull.

"You know, if you had come clean earlier, I might have been able to help you. Lady Fusette would never tolerate your situation going on under her nose."

Yasso scoffed. "I already learned you can't trust nobles. Why should the damn Duchess be any different? Besides, you talk as if you're not willing to help anymore."

Eye twitching, Kai shot a glance at Maple before a deep rumble echoed from his chest. "You made someone I love cry. For that, I'm going to make *you* cry."

Before he could rush the deckhand, the rest of the party barreled into the room, followed by his parents. The women huddled around Serafina and Maple in a protective circle. Teos and Morgan slid to stop next to Kai, their eyes widening upon seeing Yasso.

"Bloody hoarfrost," the sellsword hissed. "*He's* the spy?"

"Aye," Kai nodded. "He was trying to take Maple, probably out through the window. My guess is Kendela is somewhere outside the village waiting for a drop-off, except I don't think Yasso expected Serafina and me to still be in the house."

"Get out of my way, you old bastards," Yasso warned. He hunched over with his horns pointed at Kai's heart.

Rolling his shoulders, Kai readied himself to meet the deckhand's charge head-on until Morgan threw an arm in front of him. "Hold it, 'pothy. This one's mine."

"You sure?"

The older man nodded; his lips were set in a grim, stony line. "He was my subordinate. I failed to realize what he was, so responsibility for that falls on me."

Both men were surprised when Yasso broke into peals of laughter. "You really think you can take me, you old chimera? I'm going to crush your ribs in."

"Yer welcome to try, ya cocksure pebblewit," Morgan growled, his accent thickening from rage.

A sense of unease settled in Kai's stomach. He knew Morgan was tough. Still, Yasso was the same height as Duarte and carried a solid mass of muscle beneath his wiry frame, despite not having the monk's more impressive bulk.

Stamping a hoof into the floor, Yasso splintered the wood and lunged forward with a bellow. Kai heard Lucretia shout a warning before sliding into a stance. Morgan may have wanted to handle the traitor himself, but he refused to be caught unaware.

He couldn't hold back a wince when Morgan stepped into Yasso's charge and pushed off the floor with the force of a cannon, headbutting the Soltauri in the temple. A sharp crack reverberated through the room.

Kai felt his bones shake seeing Yasso stopped cold, swaying in place with the dazed expression of a drunkard.

Popping his knuckles, Morgan gave the stunned deckhand a smirk. "One of the nice things about being quarter-Wasini: my scales and bones are a lot thicker than your hide. If you thought that hurt, kid, you're really not gonna like this." He marched forward and thrust a quick jab into Yasso's gut. The blow bent the deckhand in half, leaving him exposed as Morgan wound up and threw a heavy hook into the side of his head which left him unconscious on the floor.

Morgan chuffed, muttering some choice curses about wanting more of a challenge, before lifting Yasso by the tunic with both hands and hurling him through the shattered window. A loud thump rang out and Kai peered down, seeing his unmoving body sprawled out in the garden.

He raised his eyebrow at Morgan. "I suppose I should thank you for avoiding the flowers. Ma loves those things."

"What will we do with him?" asked Ione. The tavern maid's sudden question startled Kai. He looked back and saw her massaging Maple's back. "I don't suppose you have constables who can put him in the gaol?"

"Miss Ione, we're Hunters. By our very nature, we *are* the constables," Verona quipped. "I'm more impressed he thought he could get away without being seen."

Adjusting her spectacles, Lucretia's eyes swept over the room. "The bigger question is what to do about Kendela," she added.

"The lass is right," said Morgan. "He'll be expecting this fool bring him his prize. What happens if he turns up looking for Maple?"

"Since Yasso admitted to doing this on Kendela's orders, it means the good lord is on borrowed time," Kai retorted.

"The man has half of Parliament in his waistcoat pocket," Gaspard warned. He slapped a hand into Kai's shoulder, though the Norzen didn't budge. "Even if he's a pissant of the highest order, he's still the Margrave of this province. You can't be thinking of killing him. Those snooty nobles would have you hung before you can blink."

"I've given that blowhard multiple warnings about threatening my party. He just committed a *second* attempted kidnapping, even if by proxy, of someone under my protection. The next time he shows his face will be the last."

Pain flared up Kai's leg when Orelia snuck beside him and jabbed the end of her staff onto his foot. "I believe we have other things to worry about. Need I remind you the Liberators will be here in two or three days, if not sooner, and we still haven't spoken with the Corps Commander. For now, let's make sure Yasso is secured and try to rest."

Her gaze met Kai's and her face softened. "I know how you feel, but if I've learned anything, it's that we can't react based solely on anger. I almost got Tuvi killed acting like a reckless fool. I won't let you make the same mistake. Kendela will face justice, but we must bide our time."

"Thanks Orelia."

"Don't thank me yet," she said with a coy grin, "We have something to discuss tomorrow, and it you might find it off-putting."

Chapter XXIV

Razarr held back a chuckle as the small caravan he led trekked through the forest. A troop of wiroch-mounted guards formed a protective circle around the caravan, many with their free hands resting on the hilts of their swords. Mirabell rode alongside him, her eyes downcast and unfocused as her wiroch trudged along.

At the center of the group was a single wagon, pulled by a team of ten wirochs, laden with a small mountain of material hidden beneath a leather tarp.

"Master," Mirabell said, her eyes flickering up to Razarr, "are you sure this plan of yours will work?"

The forge master's eyes rested on the maid, his lips curving into a grim smile. "Mirabell, my dear, is that doubt I hear?"

Flinching back, Mirabell shook her head. "No! Of course not, Master. It's just..." The woman's voice dropped to a low drawl, "We are preparing to face the Hunter Corps. They earned their reputation for a reason."

"Indeed they have Mirabell. And no doubt they are already aware of our forces converging on them with a relaxed air. It would not surprise me to see them confident in their ability to hold off Doulterre's army, and in any other situation, I'd be inclined to agree with them. However, if there's one thing I've learned in my years, it's that pride is only useful if channeled properly. Left to run rampant, it is the quickest way to ensure one's downfall."

A trilling chuckle came from behind the pair. Razarr turned to see Hemlocke riding a shivering blue wiroch with his head down and body quaking in amusement. Grimghast ambled along beside the migrant, a brace crafted from bone mounted to its broken jaw. The rest of the caravan kept their distance from the beast, eyeing it with obvious trepidation.

"Rather unusual way of looking at it, boss," the Aerivolk commented, raising his eyes to match Razarr's gaze. The migrant's lilac orbs gleamed in the early afternoon sun peaking through the trees overhead. "Here in Livoria, pride is usually seen as a vice. Then again, I suppose most people associate it with Cacovis, so the skepticism is understandable."

"I don't wanna hear that damn peltneck woman's name for a good long while, if you don't mind," Agosti snapped from the back of the group, his mount strutting beside the rear wheel of the wagon with Obram riding next to him. His eyes burned in anger with lips curled back in a snarl as he glowered at Hemlocke's back. The officer's hands were covered in several deep scratches, while his face was marred with multiple bruises.

Agosti flinched when Hemlocke spun and regarded him with a malicious sneer. "You're a little *low* in the pecking order to be mouthing off. Do I need to remind you of your place?" the Aerivolk questioned while licking his lips, both pupils shrinking to pinpricks. It gave Hemlocke a manic look as he eyed the other man like fresh meat.

"Enough, Hemlocke," Razarr ordered, drawing a small knife and waving it at the Aerivolk. "You'd do well to remember something yourself. Who pulled you out of the Everstill alleys all those years ago?"

"...You did, Boss."

"And who allowed you to keep your dangerous pet after you found it in that abandoned circus, when anyone else would've had it shot dead the moment they saw it?"

"You did, Boss." Even as he said it, a low rumbling growl could be heard from Hemlocke's chest.

"Exactly. If it weren't for me, you'd have died in the shadows, completely forgotten, with the rest of those worthless vagrants I found you wasting away with." Eyes half-lidded, Hemlocke offered a demure apology while leading Grimghast further back, behind Obram and Agosti.

Razarr shook his head in frustration and continued staring forward before bringing up his spyglass. In the distance, their destination stood tall, visible even through the mass of trees surrounding them: a massive rock formation towering over the forest like an obelisk. One side was slanted at a steep angle, with Razarr noting a winding path zig-zagging its way up the cliff face to the top.

"That's our destination, isn't it?" Obram asked, using a hand to shield his eyes from the sun's rays peeking through the canopy.

The forge master nodded. "Aye, Tapimor's Crest. I much doubt the Hunter's will be expecting us to launch our attack from there. Doulterre and Duarte should already be waiting at the plateau's summit with their men."

A nervous chuckle came from the Risbado. "Uh, how are they gonna fit the whole army up there...?" he asked. "It don't look big enough to hold all of them."

"Obram, could you at least *try* to appear as intelligent as you are sneaky?" Razarr groaned. "Doulterre won't be taking the entire army with him, given the limited space. At most, he should be able to comfortably fit around two hundred soldiers on the plateau while still having room to maneuver. The rest of the army is being hidden north of here, hidden in the forest under Bishop Adalbard's watch. In fact..." The forge master turned to Hemlocke. "Perhaps you'd best send your pet up there as an extra layer of defense, in case the Royalists come sniffing too close."

Raising an eyebrow, Hemlocke reached out and scratched Grimghast underneath its scruffy muzzle. "I was hoping you'd say that, Boss. I was concerned about sending her against an entire village of known beast killers in her condition," he admitted.

"I am many things, Hemlocke, but a fool is not one of them. We will be fine without your beast's assistance. There is only one path leading to the plateau, so we can easily deal with any enemy troops attempting to engage us. Besides, it requires rest for its jaw to heal after your...incident in Glimmerdale."

Hemlocke gave a silent nod and whispered something into Grimghast's ear, though Razarr frowned when he realized he couldn't hear what the diminutive faumen was saying. Pulling out his reed whistle, Hemlocke blew a few notes. Shaking its head with a gruff snort, Grimghast emitted a low growl before breaking away from the group, wandering away in its lumbering gait.

"How are you able to make it do what you want like that?" Mirabell asked, her head tilting in clear curiosity.

"It wasn't easy, believe me. Took me years to train her to recognize the different notes and what each one meant," Hemlocke admitted with a proud smile on his face. " Got more than a few bites in the process but it *did* teach me to handle her venom. Completely worth it, though, as the whistle is easier for Nulla to hear and communicates my orders better than worded commands ever will."

Nodding, the maid returned her gaze to the road ahead while Razarr eyed the two with amusement. His servants were an odd bunch, for certain, but they knew how to get results.

Their lives depended on it, after all.

Sitting at the top of a stone pile in the middle of the woods, Adalbard bit back a groan of frustration as he listened to the Liberator soldiers around him complaining about anything and everything they could imagine. The majority of their army, an impressive eight thousand, was scattered among the vast hill-covered forests northeast of Havenfall. The men were grouped into smaller companies, much easier to hide within the hills' numerous mines than if they all stayed together.

"Why do we have to stay behind while the others get to beat on the Royalists?" one of them asked. " I've been spoiling for another good fight since Thorncrest!"

"Then *you* go fight them," another snapped back, his eyes darting about full of apprehension. "I never wanted to be here in the first place. I just want to go back home to Galemore." The man's words provoked a bevy of jeers and taunts from several others, calling him a coward.

"Enough!" Adalbard stood and bellowed, his raspy voice causing the surrounding soldiers to snap to attention. The bishop's eyes roamed over the scattered Liberators with a discerning gaze. Content with the newfound silence, Adalbard nodded and sat back down. "Save your frustration for the Royalists. There's always a chance they may stumble across us before the others return. We can't let our guard down for even a moment."

Grumbling amongst themselves, the soldiers settled into an uncomfortable chatter as Adalbard returned to sweeping his eyes over the area. He had no idea why Doulterre put him in charge of this particular group when there were plenty of officers who could take command. Still, he supposed he should be grateful the Liberator general appreciated his glib tongue and knack for rousing the troops with his sermons. At least, the ones who volunteered to fight...

He knew there were many conscripts in the army who were pressed into service on pain of death. That knowledge unnerved Adalbard in a way he felt uncomfortable expressing, mostly out of his own sense of self-preservation. What would happen if the conscripts decided enough was enough and defected back to the Royalists? Having a significant portion of their forces turn on them mid-battle was not an experience he wished to have!

A soldier approached the bishop at a light jog, a black carrier hawk on his shoulder which incited a pained groan from Adalbard. He'd seen that hawk visit Doulterre enough times to know who it belonged to.

"Your Excellency," said the soldier as he offered a contrite bow, handing Adalbard an envelope sealed with wax, "this carrier hawk arrived at the campsite with a letter addressed to you. Will you be penning a reply?"

Before Adalbard could answer the man, the hawk ruffled its feathers and bolted from the soldier's shoulder as if shot from a cannon. The two watched the bird disappear into the trees with stumped expressions.

The bishop shrugged. "I suppose our benefactor does not require a reply. Perhaps this is simply an update as to what's going on. General

Doulterre did say Master Razarr would be overseeing this battle himself, after all." Breaking the wax seal, Adalbard removed the parchment from its envelope and read at a tepid pace. The letter was rather verbose and hinted at an extra layer of security arriving to protect the main army, once the priest managed to peel away the layers of eloquence Razarr seemed fond of in his written correspondence.

What in blazes does he mean by extra *security?* Adalbard wondered. Despite being scattered into separate groups, the Liberators still outnumbered most of the Royalist fleets. He doubted they had much need for security when they could simply overwhelm their foe through sheer numbers if they got the drop on them.

A loud, rhythmic thumping sound gave the bishop pause, his eyes swiveling in search of the new sound. He noted several soldiers also glancing about in confusion, something that filled him with relief. He wasn't much fond of being accused of hearing noises not really there.

After a few moments, he heard a shocked gasp from nearby. Glancing up, he spotted one young soldier, a sergeant judging by the striped cloth wrapped around his arm, paling to an alabaster sheen and looking at something above and behind him. A heavy chill filled Adalbard's bones as he slowly turned and gazed up at what frightened the boy.

He quickly wished he'd remained ignorant.

A great hulking beast stood on a small plateau overlooking their company, bear-like in appearance but emaciated with thinning grey hair and littered with scars. It only appeared to have one eye, a beady red dot examining Adalbard and the soldiers with a calm, almost dismissive air. Nobody dared to move—or even breathe—as it prowled along its perch, emitting a raspy huff which reminded the bishop of someone who smoked a pipe for most of their life. Adalbard, for one, felt as though his heart was pounding against his ribs with such force that it was ready to erupt from his chest. His body quaked in terror, praying the monster was in no mood to think of them as dinner, though he wasn't about to do anything to draw its attention and test the thought.

Luckily for the Liberators, the beast seemed content to curl up in a shape vaguely resembling a furry boulder, its eye sweeping over them once more before it drifted off to a peaceful slumber.

Eyes twitching towards the letter in his hand, Adalbard considered whether surrendering to the Royalists might be the better option, if Razarr believed this was suitable security for their forces. There was no doubt handing himself in would leave him hanging from the gallows by the end of the moon, but having his neck broken by a rope was preferable to being devoured by whatever *that* thing was.

Eyeing the creature one last time, Adalbard turned to his men and ordered them to do their best to ignore the newcomer at all costs before ambling back towards his tent. When asked by a stuttering soldier where he was going, the bishop leveled a deadened gaze at him.

"Quite frankly, young man, I need to get drunk. I'm praying the fog of alcohol will keep me from having nightmares about our new guest...or dull my senses enough that it won't hurt should it decide I look like a snack."

Gazing about the woods in a confused daze, Admiral Larimanz fought back an urge to release a roar of frustration. The last thing the men and women under his command needed was to see him lose composure, especially with so much at stake. Of course, it didn't change the fact he wanted to let out a good old fashioned bellow.

Breathe, Waveweaver, Larimanz told himself. *There must be a logical explanation for this. It's impossible for eight thousand enemy soldiers to just up and vanish so suddenly...so where in bloody Nulyma are they?!*

Up till now, tracking the Liberation Army had been a straightforward task. Eight thousand troops should have been easy to follow; a crowd that size doesn't wander about without leaving glaring reminders of their presence. Yet somehow, most traces of their movement had vanished like a wisp of smoke over the past two days, ever since the trail led them to the banks of the Great Ardei. Given the evidence, the group they were now following looked to number two hundred instead of a horde forty times that amount.

"Admiral," an Aerivolk lieutenant spoke up from beside him. The young woman's eyes roamed over the forest, an agitated expression covering her features. "I must apologize for my team's failure; we still haven't found hide nor hair of the enemy. It's as if they vanished off the face of Nixtral."

"Nonsense, Lieutenant Thorne. It's hardly your fault the enemy is proving more slippery than a water serpent," soothed Larimanz. "I'll confess, though, this is proving to be a most irritable problem. I can't think of any possible explanation for how they disappeared so completely."

The lieutenant grumbled under her breath, uttering some choice words which had Larimanz biting back a snort of amusement. The sounds of the forest echoed around them, leaving a sense of calm in the aging Exarch as he and his companion scrutinized every tree with an intense gaze.

"I suppose it would be too much to hope they all drowned trying to cross the Great Ardei," the young Aerivolk snapped while ruffling her feathers. "At least it would be a plausible reason for the enemy to have up and vanished like this!"

Blinking, Larimanz slithered to the edge of the tree line, staring out at the river. His scales and armor glimmered in the morning sun. "Well I'll be damned," he murmured.

"What's wrong, Admiral?" the lieutenant asked.

The grizzled Wasini chuckled and jerked a thumb towards the flowing waters of the Great Ardei. "I think you may have figured out where our errant prey went, Lieutenant. They didn't cross the river...they *followed* it."

The woman's eyes widened, her own eyes turning towards the river and trailing along its southward path. "Sweet Finyt," she whispered, "they covered their tracks using the river. Who knows where they could be by now?"

"Oh, it's no secret where they went, Lieutenant," said Larimanz, his thick tail coiling beneath him like a chair. "There's only one target in striking distance around here, though I'm surprised the enemy is crazy enough to attack it."

"Wait, you can't mean—?"

The admiral nodded. "If my guess is correct, the Liberators are trying to take the Hunter Corps out of the war before Her Grace can muster them for battle. The enemy is marching on Havenfall. I suppose we should consider ourselves lucky, though. We'll have the support of another Exarch in case the battle goes ass over kettle."

The lieutenant regarded Larimanz with a confused glance. "Another Exarch? Sir, I wasn't aware there were any other Knights in this region. The next closest ones I know of should be Lady Burnsong and Sir Swiftlock, both marching with the Third Eastern to defend the Galstein border near Featherbrook. I heard most of the rest are all defending their hometowns throughout the realm."

"I suppose this works out for us, then. Havenfall happens to be Gravebane's hometown. He's the official emissary Her Grace sent to rally the Hunters. Appropriate, considering he's a Hunter as well."

"Gravebane?" the woman asked, her nose crinkling. "The Norzen? I apologize if this seems disrespectful, Admiral, but can we rely on him? I heard he's rather young."

"I won't deny that. Being 23, he's far and away the youngest Exarch, but don't let his age fool you; he and his party have the most active combat experience of all of us in this war. If there's anyone who can give us the edge in this battle, it'll be Gravebane. Alert the other officers, Lieutenant. We need to find those Libbie bastards fast!"

Chapter XXV

Considering the events since their arrival, Kai hoped in going to bed early he'd be able to get some extra sleep. With his room damaged, he was forced to stay in the guest room, though he found it more unusual than irksome.

Sunlight peeked through the window, causing him to groan and try to turn his body away from the annoying shine. This proved ineffective, however, as a sizable weight on his chest kept him in place. Or rather, *two* sizable weights.

What is this, he asked himself. *There's something on my—oh, right...*

Stifling a groan as he stretched, his gaze inched down to see Maple and Orelia curled against him, his arms encircling their waists. The merchant's wing was draped over his chest while the priestess' fingers were threading through his mane. They were all fully clothed, though Kai's cheeks burned scarlet when he shifted, and Maple's reaction was to emit a lilting trill and bury her face in his neck. Their position reminded him of the early morning they spent together outside Runegard, though their relationship hadn't been so official back then.

He considered his options in removing himself, few as they were, when he noticed an eye fluttering open. Releasing a wide-mouthed yawn, Maple rubbed her eyes and gave him a half-lidded stare. After a few moments, she seemed to realize the position they were in and she squeaked, her cheeks matching his.

The abrupt sound startled Orelia from her slumber as well, her face turning pink when she found herself buried in Kai's embrace. The apothecary fought to suppress his body's natural reaction when he felt both women pressing themselves against his sides, their lips now curving into cheeky grins.

"Good morning," Kai whispered.

"Good morning," Maple trilled back. Pushing on his chest, Maple turned onto her back and sent him a sideways glance. "We didn't do anything improper, did we?"

Kai shook his head. "Not at all. Just sleeping. I was going to kip on the floor, but the two of you grabbed hold of me when you fell asleep and refused to let go. Needless to say, Ma caught us and basically ordered me to stay put. So, here we are. I hope you're not upset."

"Of course not. Truth be told, this was probably the best I've slept in years," Maple confessed.

"I must agree. I don't believe I've ever slept so soundly before," Orelia added. "Nor have I ever felt so safe at night."

"Well, I do live to serve. So long as you ladies are happy, that's what matters."

Maple broke into a musical laugh. Kai's smile widened, his heart soaring at hearing her. She flicked him on the nose and flashed him a warm smile, though he saw a slight wince when her body moved. "I swear, you're still the same charming fool I met several moons ago. But I wouldn't have you any other way."

Encircling her arms around Kai's neck, Orelia pulled him close. "Neither would I," she said. His chest rumbled with contentment when the priestess nuzzled his cheek and placed a soft kiss on his twitching ear.

"I'm just happy you're willing to have me at all."

"We're not letting go of you that easily, Kai. My hips may not work yet, but once they do, we're having another dance, and this time I'm not letting Madam Prim-and-Proper Dineri get in our way."

"I look forward to it," Kai murmured, blowing softly on her ear.

The act intensified Maple's blush, her body shivering. "That felt much more pleasant than I expected. Do it again."

His lips curled into a smirk. "Perhaps later. Orelia wanted to speak to me about something important. She hasn't given me the slightest clue as to what, though," he added, casting a raised eyebrow at the blushing priestess. " Besides, I need to check my dispensary to see if anything there can help your injury."

With a haughty pout, Maple keened and slapped his mane. "I'll hold you to it. You two go have a chat while I ask Serafina to bring up some breakfast. Not sure I trust Morgan enough to carry me downstairs with how drunk he got last night. I'm sure you'll fix this soon. The pain's been spreading to my legs, though, so I'd appreciate it if you helped me sit up before you go."

After setting her back against the wall with a pillow, Kai rolled from the bed and pulled his boots on. He gave Maple a tin of cream to dull the pain, said his goodbyes, and left the house with Orelia on his arm, waving to his parents as he passed through the parlor.

As they left the grounds, Kai and Orelia discussed the aftermath of Yasso's attempted kidnapping.

"Teos went to have a talk with the crew last night about what happened. It didn't go well, from what he told me. He said poor Montagru looked like a kicked wiroch chick. Apparently he suspected Yasso of being the spy but didn't want to believe him capable of it. Did you get enough sleep?"

Despite the innocence of the question, Kai saw the mischief in the priestess' eyes. "Yes, I slept quite well, thank you. Now—"

"That's all?" asked Orelia, breaking out into a titter. "No witty comment about how you had two eager young ladies in your arms the entire night? How scandalous!"

Scoffing, Kai refused to rise to the bait. "You know I would never do anything to hurt either of you. You're both precious to me."

"Oh, I know," she teased. "You're much too honorable to take advantage of anyone. It's one of the things I love most about you." Kai wondered if his face would permanently turn the color of Orelia's hair with how much blushing he'd done on this trip. "More important, have you made any progress with Maple's condition?"

Kai shook his head and admitted he still hadn't figured out how to neutralize the venom.

"Travaldi!" a loud voice rang out. The pair turned and saw a tall, muscular man striding towards them. Broad shouldered with a diamond-shaped head, the newcomer moved with a confident stride, his deep brown eyes locked on the apothecary.

"Commander Petro!" exclaimed Kai, stepping forward and clasping the man's hand in a powerful handshake. "It's good to see you. Barraco told us you wore yourself out on the hunt yesterday."

"Bah, that old bastard is up to his tricks again. He told me you were too exhausted from your trip to meet."

Kai groaned, pinching his eyebrows. "Why does this not surprise me? He probably did it to get away with planning his celebration without interruption."

"Sounds like Barraco, alright. Anyway, who is this young lady with you? It's been a while since we've seen a sister of the winds pass through here."

Holding her hand out, Orelia introduced herself.

"It's a pleasure, Sister," said Petro. "Where are you two off to so early?"

"I needed to check the dispensary stock and Orelia is accompanying me as we have other matters to discuss."

"Oh, well don't let me keep you."

"Hold on," Kai muttered. He reached into his satchel and removed a bound scroll. Fusette's edict. Straightening his posture, Kai bowed to Petro and handed him the scroll.

"Commander Petro Renzolos, in accordance with the wishes of Her Royal Grace, the Grand Duchess Fusette Ardei, the Hunter Corps is being ordered to muster its full force to face the encroaching Liberation Army. I, the Exarch Gravebane, present this royal decree stating Her Grace's command on her behalf."

His lips set in a small grin, Petro nodded and accepted the scroll. He removed the cord binding it and made a show of unfurling it and reading its contents. Humming to himself as he read, he closed it once more and returned Kai's bow.

"Exarch Gravebane, I gladly accept this edict. I shall call the Corps' leadership together and we will prepare to depart as soon as possible. I'm aware of the enemy's approach, so Barraco will have to wait to get his celebration. It'll be better if we can have the entire village enjoy the festivities, anyway."

The two men shared a smirk and shook hands once more before Petro walked past, strolling down the main street. Then, the commander did something to make Orelia stop and blink. "Is he *skipping*?" she asked.

Kai bit down hard on his lip to stifle his laughter, not trusting himself to do anything but nod. The pair continued walking with Kai leading the way. Orelia brought their conversation back to Maple, asking what he planned to do about her injury.

"At this point, all I can do is test different herbal mixtures and hope to hold the poison at bay until I can acquire more saliva from Grimghast." Several Hunters loading boxes onto carriages waved to the two as they passed, though no one got in their way. "If I knew this would happen, I never would've thrown the vial I had away. But I needed to, otherwise I would've been tempted to keep taking it."

"Is it really so important to have the actual venom?"

"It's crucial," Kai answered. "There are herbs capable of reversing the effects of poisons, but there's two major problems. First, those types of herbs are heavily regulated by the apothecary's guild *and* rare, only growing in certain regions. Second, the herbs need at least some vestige of the original venom to bind and react with."

They stopped at a small building with a hand carved wooden sign that said 'Dispensary' in large block letters. A small garden overflowing with multicolored flowers and various herbs sat prominently to the left of the entrance. At the far edge of the garden, a small wooden box sat, covered in small honeybees. Kai took a small key from his robe pocket and unlocked the door, bringing Orelia inside.

An open floor with several tables in the middle greeted them. The walls were lined with shelves covered in small bottles and pouches of various herbs. Kai was proud of his dispensary. Thanks to his travels, he had access to materials otherwise too expensive to import from other regions of Livoria. Gazing at the shelves' labels, he mentally tallied which herbs he wanted for his next test mixture.

"So not only are we short on the venom, but we also don't have an herb capable of reversing it in the first place."

"I never said that. I just said they were rare and regulated. Sadly, the guilds are often controlled by those imbeciles in Parliament. Fusette has done me several favors in the past as a reward for Exarch missions. One of the best, though, was getting me this." Kai crossed the main floor and used a second key to unlock a small closet in the corner, behind the counter. Reaching for the top shelf, he removed a small box roughly the length of his hand on its longest side. He set the box down on the table and opened it.

Orelia joined him at the table and raised an eyebrow at the small nut he set on the table. Similar in size and shape to a typical acorn, it was topped with an orange cap covered in thin thorns and twisted in a whirling pattern. The strangest thing about its appearance was the deep blue coloration of the main shell, contrasting starkly with its bright cap.

"What is it?" Orelia asked, staring at it with an inquisitive gaze.

"This, Orelia, is the nut of a whorled everoak."

The priestess' eyes widened. "Impossible. I heard they were almost completely wiped out by overharvesting."

"You're not wrong. Every part of the tree has exceptional healing properties on par with emberona. Many were harvested during a storm of assassinations that swept through Alezon back in the late second century AR. Galstein was still a fledgling realm in those days if I remember right. There's only a few scattered groves left in the continent, most in the Belomas Highlands."

"How did Fusette get one?"

"It's rather amusing, really. One of the rare trees outside the Highlands is in a secret garden beneath the Royal Palace. Only Fusette and a few trusted individuals are allowed to set foot there. Whorled everoaks produce maybe half a dozen acorns each year, so I was lucky to get this one. The Royal Apothecaries keep the rest, though who knows what they do with them. I've been keeping it safe for an emergency."

With a sly smile, Orelia asked if Maple's situation counted as an emergency. Kai said nothing, only nodding as he jotted notes down on a scrap of parchment. Without warning, he was stunned by the young priestess spinning him around and pressing him against the table, nearly pushing him on top of it.

"Uh...Orelia?"

She gave him a provocative smirk, licking her lips while leaning into his arms. "I don't think you realize how attractive you look whenever you explain things with that intense focus."

"T-thank you," Kai breathed. He wasn't sure what brought this on, though he could feel the effects of Orelia's smoldering gaze well enough below his waist. "Listen, I know Maple wanted us to see how things progress together, but if you keep this up, I might lose control."

"That's a tempting idea, though I think Maple would be cross with me if I took your first kiss, or your first anything for that matter. I know we can't take things too far, but I was hoping we could share a dance while we're alone."

Releasing a sigh of relief, Kai returned her smile and reached up to take her hand in his own, steepling their fingers together. "That, I most certainly can do. I'd be honored."

Pulling her into his arms, Kai led Orelia in the same basic waltz he danced with Maple. Staring into her soft blue orbs, he felt a wave of joy welling up from the depths of his spirit. Orelia's skin felt cold and slick compared to Maple's, though it was hard to ignore the warmth in her smile. Kai almost stilled when she leaned closer and pressed her nose into his chest.

"Thank you," she hummed.

"For what?" Kai asked, glancing down in befuddlement.

"For being you. Every day, I've felt nothing but gratitude that you still indulge my feelings, even though Maple has proven she has so much more to offer."

With a shake of his head, Kai spun Orelia in a twirl before drawing her back and running his fingers through her hair. "Don't think that way. You have plenty to offer and any man would be lucky to have your love. If anything, I should be grateful even one of you is willing to give me the time of day. You're just as beautiful and amazing as Maple is, and I'd gladly declare it in front of the whole world."

Orelia's blush intensified, though she didn't pull away and her smile widened to expose her ivory teeth. "How are you so sweet to me? At this point, I wonder if biting you would make you bleed syrup rather than blood."

Unable to hold back a chuckle, Kai tapped her on the nose. "Please don't actually test that theory. I promise I don't taste delicious."

Before he could continue their dance, he froze when Orelia pushed up on her toes and ran her tongue along the corner of his mouth. It was a simple, intimate act, but the tremors running through Kai's body in the moment left him gasping for air.

"You seem delicious enough to me," Orelia whispered. She tilted her head and blew in Kai's ear, deepening the jolt of every nerve from his head to his toes firing.

I swear to Tapimor, these girls are going to turn me feral, he thought. Letting his face slip into a grin, he slid his finger over the edge of Orelia's ear. She shivered in his arms, taking the initiative to move his hand down to her waist and resting it on top of her gills. Each breath she took caused the slits to rumble beneath his fingertips, a sensation he'd never experienced before. Looking down, he could see the dusky grey skin surrounding her gills, a sharp contrast to the bronze tan covering the rest of her body. Kai heard her emit a soft giggle before hooking a finger around the vestment's edge. She shifted the fabric just enough for him to confirm with a glimpse that her belly below the chest was the same stone-like shade.

Kai twisted his head around, heart pounding as his face reached shades of red he didn't think existed. Orelia's laughter, warm and hearty compared to Maple's musical titters, eased the frantic thoughts flying through his mind to an extent. It wasn't until she cupped his cheek in her palm that his chest stopped feeling as though a beast were trying to burst out.

"It's okay, sweetheart," she soothed. "I promise you did nothing wrong. All I wanted was to tease you a little. Did I take it too far?"

Not trusting his voice, Kai simply shook his head. Thoughts of Orelia's exposed skin produced a throaty rumble in his chest. Without thinking, he licked his lips and met her nervous gaze. "Perhaps we should slow down," he replied after taking some long, deep breaths. "Otherwise, I may do something we'll both regret."

There was a slight pressure as Orelia molded herself against his body, interlocking her fingers with his as she nuzzled his mane. "I would never regret doing anything with you. But you're right; we should ease up. I doubt I'd bother stopping you if we took things further."

The two stood there a few moments longer, content to simply hold each other and bask in the warmth of their embrace. Once his breathing returned to a steady pace, Kai separated himself from Orelia and placed a tender kiss on her forehead. He thanked her for giving him a chance to enjoy her company alone before he returned to the shelves, plucking vials as he went and jotting notes on his parchment.

Walking to the opposite wall, Orelia inspected each of the labels while muttering to herself.

"It's a shame you don't have any of the saliva. Right now, I'd guess the only venom we have now is whatever your blood absorbed from drinking so much."

Kai's quill stopped. Orelia's words hit him with the force of a bison stampede, stalling his thoughts. "What did you just say?" he asked.

"Hmm? I said the only venom we have now is from what you drank and absorbed into your blood. I'm guessing you imbibed a lot, since you said your body would have been resistant enough to survive Locke's knife."

She's right, he thought. *I know my body developed a high resistance because, by the time we left Whistlevale, it was requiring at least ten drops to induce the same level of symptoms as a single one when I started. But that would mean...*

"*Taen*! Tapimor's hairy ass, that's it!"

"Wait, what's it?" asked Orelia, turning back to face him in confusion.

Brushing the acorn aside, Kai ripped open a nearby drawer and removed a small chopping knife from within. Setting the knife down next to a small cauldron of spring water that he set to boil, he picked up the parchment and bustled about the dispensary, rifling through bottles until finding the ones he wanted. His ears picked up Orelia's questioning tone as she asked what he was doing, but he was so focused on the task at hand he found himself too nervous to reply.

His hands became a whirlwind of motion; dried herbs were measured and added to the cauldron, while fresh ones were chopped and ground into powder first. Kai removed the final emberona bud from his satchel and set it next to the acorn. Soon, the cauldron hit a rolling boil as a powerful earthy scent permeated the dispensary. All the while Orelia looked on, eyes wide in curiosity.

"Right, the main body is steeping well. Please let this work," muttered Kai as he took the knife in hand. Clasping his hands together, the knife clutched between them, he began to pray. "Oh Tapimor, keeper of the wilds and guardian of those who heal, hear my plea. May this medicine, made under your compassionate eye, revitalize those who imbibe it."

His eyes flickered to Orelia, who stood beside him in the same position, joining him in prayer. Their eyes met and she offered him a comforting smile that filled Kai's chest with warmth. Somewhere in his heart, he knew there was a chance for it to work.

No, it will *work!*

Gritting his teeth, Kai stretched his right hand out, holding it over the cauldron with the knife in his left. Before the priestess could blink, the blade flew across his arm. Orelia's face paled when she saw lines of blood spurting from the wound. A splash of crimson coated the everoak acorn and emberona bud while Kai's lifeblood streamed into the cauldron.

"Kai!" shouted Orelia. The younger woman's sapphire eyes were bulbous, her skin taking a sickly pallor. "Have you lost your damned kettle?! What are you doing?"

"The venom," hissed Kai. "You helped me realize it; Grimghast's venom runs through my blood, so I can use it as a binder to complete the antivenom."

Orelia tore a strip of cloth from her vestment and pressed it hard against the wound. "How confident are you something this crazy will even work?"

"Considering no apothecary has ever created a concoction using a blood binder, more than half, but less than certain. I have to try, though. If I don't, the venom in Maple's body will only grow stronger until it kills her. You heard her this morning. It's already spreading to her legs. Once it builds up enough in her heart or brain, it'll be too late."

"You are without a doubt the craziest man I've ever met, Kai Travaldi. But if this madness of yours truly heals her, I swear on Lord Galen's name I'll let you marry her and officiate your handfasting myself."

Kai's cheeks flushed red. He gave Orelia a baffled look, though it was easy to see the shadow of melancholy surrounding her. "Wait, would you even be allowed to—?"

"Oh please, one would think you already know I'm not a traditional woman of the cloth. Besides, anyone can see how happy you two are together. I'd be honored to perform such a momentous rite for my dearest friends, even if it means I'll never have you myself."

Overcome with emotion, Kai couldn't stop a stray tear from escaping, though he bumped his hip against hers with a confident smirk. "Never say 'never,' milady."

The bubbling cauldron reached a crescendo, drawing the friends' eyes back to the boiling concoction. With Orelia's help, Kai wrapped his wounded arm and removed the cauldron from the fire. The mixture settled and emitted an aromatic steam.

"Now what?" asked Orelia, inspecting the cauldron from different angles.

"Next, I crush the everoak acorn and emberona and add them to the cauldron. This would be so much easier, though, if I had a bloom instead of a—what in the winds?!" A flash of emerald light erupted from the table, blinding them both. The two were forced to raise their arms up until it receded. Kai heard Orelia gasp when they saw the source of the light, and he had to hold back one of his own at seeing what happened.

The acorn and bud both glowed. Covered in Kai's blood, both expanded rapidly, like wool soaked in water, causing the pair to stagger back. The acorn's blue shell split open as a network of roots grew from its bottom. To Kai's shock, the emberona bud began to open.

"What is going on?" Orelia whispered. She grabbed Kai by the arm with a powerful grip. Were the cloth of his robes any thinner, her nails would likely draw more blood from him.

"I-I don't know." The glow from the two seeds ebbed away, leaving an everoak sprout and fully bloomed emberona flower in their place.

"Please tell me you can still use those, Kai."

"If those are what I think, my confidence in this concoction is now damn near certain." With shaking hands, he took the emberona and inspected it. Inhaling the aroma from the hand-sized flower, Kai's lips transformed into a wide grin. "I don't know how, but these just became several times more potent than before." Questions upon questions raced through his mind, but all that mattered in that moment was that their chances of saving Maple were soaring.

Kai brought both items closer and used the flat edge of the knife to crush the everoak. Then he diced the emberona petals after plucking the pistils. Adding the new ingredients to the concoction, he stirred it evenly. As with the tonic he gave to Locke, the cauldron belched a thick smoke with a heavy odor. The concoction itself turned a murky burgundy and tiny white sparks shot from the surface.

Taking several empty vials from the shelf behind him, Kai spooned the simmering potion into each one before corking them shut. With care, he wrapped the bottles in wool and nestled them into his satchel.

He swung the pack over one shoulder and hurried towards the house with Orelia nipping at his heels. They received several more greetings along the way, including several men asking the Norzen why he was in such a hurry. Kai brushed the questions off, stating he had important business.

At their brisk pace, it didn't take long for them to spot the Travaldi house at the top of the hill. His heart pounding, Kai fought the temptation to break out into a full sprint. As much as he wished to, he refused to risk damaging his precious cargo. He doubted he'd get another chance like this, thus he needed to be careful.

"Oi, Kai, where in the winds have you been?" Gaspard shouted. The older man stumbled across the garden, his cane wobbling. The rest of the party heard the commotion, emerging from the shacks in near unison.

"No time to explain, Da, but Orelia and I were at the dispensary. Now watch out! I have to get this to Maple."

The others shared a look and followed behind. Serafina and Verona appeared from around the corner, both wearing confused expressions.

"What in Tapimor's name is going on?" asked Verona.

The party admitted they didn't know, and Lucretia leveled a firm stare at the priestess. "What happened, Orelia? It has only been one day; surely he did not already have a breakthrough?"

Without breaking stride, Orelia returned Lucretia's stony stare with one of her own. "I'm still trying to make sense of everything myself. We will have to discuss things at length. Things have occurred which neither Kai nor myself can fully understand." Ione pulled alongside Orelia and asked what she meant. Teos and Morgan, meanwhile, brought up the rear of the group.

Before Orelia could explain, Kai bolted up the stairs two at a time, pivoting towards the guest room and readying his satchel. Pushing the door open, he smiled seeing Maple reading a small tome, though she still had a pinched look of pain at the corners of her mouth.

Her eyes darted to him, and a small laugh escaped her lips. "You're back much sooner than I expected. Did you and Orelia have a good talk?"

"It was enlightening, to say the least, and we did get to share a dance before everything went sideways," Kai answered. Going around the bed to the work desk, he set his satchel down and removed one of the wool-wrapped bottles. "How are you feeling?"

"My legs are starting to tingle something fierce, and my back is stinging more than usual, but otherwise I'm fine." Maple's breath hitched when she saw the steaming potion. "What's that?" she asked. "I've never seen any of your concoctions look like that before."

"I'd like to know that myself," said Gaspard. The rest of the group was pushing their way inside, and everyone besides Orelia regarded the bottle with unease. "I ain't ever seen a medicine this color before. And I'm pretty sure they don't spark. What did you even make it with?"

Kai's gaze flickered to Orelia, and the two gave each other a silent nod. He was worried how everyone would react, but they deserved to know the truth.

"If my hypothesis is right, it should destroy any traces of Hemlocke's poison still in Maple's body. The base is a mix of spring water and some of the most powerful purgatives in my dispensary. I..." he gulped, knowing he had to admit *everything*. "I used my own blood as the binding agent."

"You did what?!" Verona shouted. "Did you hit your head last night, boy? You can't possibly be thinking of giving that to Maple; mixing blood between the tribes is forbidden for a reason. You could kill her!" The rest of the room broke into a tumult. Kai did his best to sooth the group, explaining that the emberona would have purified his blood of any taint that made it dangerous for Maple's body.

A sense of dread swept through Kai's body as his mother continued berating him. He noticed Lucretia giving him an odd look. "Actually, it may not be as dangerous as you believe," she said.

As one, every head in the room spun to face the scholar. It was Serafina who asked the question on everyone's mind.

"What are you talking about?"

Lucretia reached into her coat and pulled out a slender tome. Cacovis' journal. Kai's breath quickened. Was she planning to reveal the truth of the tome? Thinking about it, he hadn't heard much since her last update on the translation.

"This is a travel log we discovered in Runegard, written during the Desolation Wars," she explained. "I cannot disclose who the writer was due to royal decree, but they were well versed in the cultures of every faumen tribe. Lady Fusette ordered me to translate it hoping we could understand more about those events, given the lack of official records. In addition to their thoughts on the war itself, the writer shared many stories and myths passed down by the tribes dating back to the Great Rebirth."

"Fascinating," said Gaspard, "but it doesn't exactly tell us about Kai's mad idea."

"All in due time, Mr. Travaldi. Some of these legends speak of what life was like before the Rebirth. As a scholar, I can verify that many legends have at least some basis in fact. Some of my colleagues at the Citadel specialize in this very area of study. According to the old stories in this journal, the faumen were once human themselves, before the Rebirth."

"Wait," said Ione, shaking her head in disbelief, "they were originally *human*?"

"That seems to be the case. Official records state the faumen were already bestial in appearance before the Rebirth, but this journal suggests otherwise. When you consider what we know today, it makes logical sense. Think about it; faumen are capable of producing children with humans with absolutely no adverse effects. The argument becomes stronger when you realize the children of these relationships are themselves capable of producing viable, healthy offspring. For Galen's sake, we have two perfect examples in this room!"

The party's eyes bulged, their gazes spinning towards Morgan and Maple; one a quarter-faumen and the other a quarter-human.

"She's got a point," the sellsword said. "Hoarfrost, I don't think anyone ever thought of the significance of humans and faumen being able to interbreed. We just knew it worked and didn't ask any deeper questions as to why."

"What about two faumen of different tribes?" pressed Gaspard. His eyes shifted between Kai and Maple. "Would they even be able to have children?"

"It's possible," Kai answered. The attention swung back to him, and Maple's cheeks flushed as she stared. It was obvious what she was thinking about. "I know for a fact two faumen of different tribes can interbreed."

"According to church doctrine, that's preposterous," retorted Verona. "It's why relationships like yours are considered such a severe taboo; the church has decreed any relationship which can't produce children is forbidden. The only reason we approve of yours is because it's obvious how happy you are."

"I met someone in Whistlevale who was the result of a dalliance between the tribes." The room exploded into a clamor, everyone wanting to know more. "I won't reveal their identity, but they were born to an Aerivolk mother and Vesikoi father. The person in question was also a full-grown adult, so inter-tribal relations are capable of producing children; they're just exceptionally rare, likely due to the stigma attached."

The group's reactions to this information were mixed. Verona looked ready to faint, while Gaspard and Serafina stood frozen in shock. The party, with the exception of Maple, huddled together with pensive looks.

Maple's eyes locked on his and her blush intensified. Having an idea of what she was thinking of Kai's cheeks turned a bright shade of pink as well.

"So then, if there's no issue with inter-tribal couples producing children, why would the church go to the trouble of forbidding them?" asked Serafina.

Lucretia let out an indignant huff. "I have learned much from this journal, though for personal reasons it pains me to admit it. It appears large portions of our history have been fragmented, warped, and otherwise hidden to promote certain ideologies. Who knows what the Windbringer leaders of the church's beginnings hoped to accomplish? The Corlatians like to promote the idea that the faumen are stained. Cursed. However, the journal also suggests the faumen carried a blessing others were envious of."

Kai's interest was piqued. "What kind of blessing?"

"I would need to visit Belomas to confirm anything with certainty—it is, after all, the traditional homeland of the faumen—but the legends say the tribes had a connection to nature which defied logic and reason. Before the Rebirth, they hint at the faumen being capable of harnessing elemental magics derived from Origin itself."

A twitch of his fingers sent a spike of pain through Kai's arm. His thoughts flew to the events in the dispensary. "Does the journal say anything about how the connection worked? Did each tribe have a specific element, or were they intermixed?"

The scholar blinked, adjusting her spectacles and regarding Kai with an impressed expression. "That is a rather astute question, Kai. As a matter of fact, the stories say there was intermixing, though each tribe had a predilection towards certain elements. As you can probably guess, many Vesikoi were noted for the ability to manipulate water. The Aerivolk, on the other hand, were masters of shifting the winds to their favor."

"What about the Norzen? What was their specialty?"

Lucretia gave a rare laugh. "I suppose I should not be surprised at your interest. Given your background, you know less of your tribe's history than you should." She flipped to a page in the middle of the tome, pointing to a specific passage. "It says here the Norzen were considered guardians of the forests, and thus able to manipulate plants and wood."

"Plants..." Kai murmured.

"Lucretia," said Orelia, "this might be an odd question, but are the faumen still able to harness those abilities?"

"As far as we know, they cannot. Whatever happened during the Great Rebirth destroyed their connection to Nixtral."

"I don't think the connection was destroyed," suggested Kai, "but it *was* altered in some way, possibly even clogged or contained like a beaver's dam."

Were the situation not so serious, Kai would've laughed at the way Lucretia balked at him. "How would you know anything about it? Pardon my candor, but you only just learned about this. It does make for an interesting theory, but without evidence that is all it is."

Taking a deep breath, Kai explained the events at the dispensary. Orelia supported him, testifying to the truth. The explanation left Lucretia overwhelmed; she slumped into an empty chair, staring at the journal with an empty gaze.

"You somehow tapped into your innate Origin magic. There has not been a public record of faumen doing this since before the Rebirth! How did *you*, of all people, manage it?"

"If I knew the answer, I'd tell you. My best guess is it has something to do with blood. The emberona and everoak didn't transform until they were soaked in it."

"It is a solid hypothesis. Perhaps later, we can experiment to ascertain the truth."

A loud bang from the bed brought everyone's attention back to Maple, who gave Lucretia a fierce glare, her fist slammed against the wall. "If you think I'm letting you drain my intended's blood for some mad experiment, you'd best rethink the idea." Orelia snapped her agreement, hooking her arm around Kai's elbow and holding him tight while glowering at the scholar.

"Damn," Morgan said, "I almost forgot how much of a spitfire these two could be."

Releasing a short chuckle, Kai promised no such experiments would be occurring until protections were made. He agreed he wasn't keen on the idea, though he confessed to a morbid curiosity of how the connection worked. Maple grimaced but nodded and made Kai promise not to do anything before they discussed it as a group.

Removing the cork from the bottle in his hand, Kai handed it to Maple. She took a hesitant sniff and wrinkled her nose.

"Smells like the ashes of an old fire pit. Well, here we go," she murmured before closing her eyes, leaning back, and draining the entire bottle at once. After swallowing, Maple smacked her lips a few times but was otherwise silent. Everyone looked at her with nervous anticipation.

Suddenly, her face broke out into a tilted smile. "Huh, that wasn't too bad. It tastes a lot better than it smells, that's for sure."

"How do you feel?" Kai asked. Kneeling next to the bed, he took Maple's hand and gave it a gentle squeeze.

Her smile grew wider as she reached out and ruffled his hair. "We'll find out soon enough, love. If it works as effectively on the tonic you gave Hemlocke, then—oh!"

Kai ignored the laughter that rang out when he leapt up at Maple's surprised gasp. "What happened? Does it hurt?"

She shook her head. "No, but I feel a tingle; a really pleasant kind of tingle, at that." Maple's body visibly shivered as she sat straight and pressed her hands against her lower back. Kai offered to massage the area if it was painful, but she brushed him off. Her smile grew wider. "I think it's working!" she exclaimed. "The pain…it's going away so fast. This is—oh no."

In a matter of moments, Maple's face turned ashen, and her feathers drooped. "I think I need a bedpan," she grumbled.

The party blanched, stepping back when Kai yanked a bucket from beneath the bed. Maple wasted no time in retching into the vessel, emitting sounds that churned Kai's stomach in knots. He suppressed the queasiness in his gut and remained in place, rubbing circles on Maple's back as she emptied her stomach.

Kai wasn't surprised when everyone but Orelia bolted from the room, Teos at the front. He felt a pang of sympathy for the smuggler; the scent of the bucket's contents was overpowering even to him, so he could only imagine the effect it had on Teos' nose.

Eventually she finished, allowing Kai to remove the bucket with a promise that he would dispose of the contents elsewhere. Returning to Maple's side, he noticed her skin already shifting back to its normal healthy tone. Kai offered her a canteen and she tore it from his hands, guzzling the water with gusto. He bit back a chuckle, shifting his gaze sideways when she pouted at him.

"You ass," she griped, "you knew that would happen, didn't you?"

"I suspected," Kai confessed, "but the effect was stronger than I anticipated." Maple smacked him in the shoulder. "Easy, woman, you'll bruise me!"

"Kai, if you ever make me hurl like that again, you'll be sleeping in a barrel."

"That sounds uncomfortable."

"Exactly." Casting a smug grin at him, Maple drew him into a hug. "I'm proud of you, love. I knew you could do it."

"You should be thanking Orelia. She's the one who gave me the idea."

A sharp sting erupted in Kai's skull when the Orelia smacked him behind the head. "All I did was make a comment on one of your questionable decisions. You're the one who decided to slice your own arm open like a lunatic. Though I will admit, if Maple puts you out in a barrel, you're more than welcome to share my bed."

The merchant rolled her eyes as Kai choked on his canteen, easing herself back into bed and pulling the blanket up. "We'll talk about your decision making skills later. I'm feeling worn out. I think I'll get some more rest; that noxious brew of yours hit me harder than a wiroch stampede."

"Sure, honey. You worry about getting your strength back. The Liberators will be here soon enough, possibly even tomorrow, but with a bit of luck we'll be gone before they can make a nuisance of themselves."

"What about the village? We can't leave them, can we?"

"Da says he and Commander Petro already had a plan in place before we arrived and evacuated most of the villagers. The Hunters are tough, but they'd be run down trying to face the Libbies *and* defend the town at the same time." Giving Maple his warmest smile, Kai patted her hand and told her to whistle if she needed anything. He blew out the lantern on the desk and went downstairs with Orelia to rally the party to help with the preparations.

The Liberation Army was in for a shock if they were expecting Havenfall to be an easy target.

Chapter XXVI

It's been far too long since I last saw this place, Vizent reflected as he stared at Havenfall from afar. Scattered along the flattened stone behind him, the small company of men he brought on this mission rested in scattered groups preparing their lunch. His scouts reported a royal envoy ship arriving in Havenfall days ago which had yet to leave. He grimaced at the thought, knowing there was only one reason why a royal emissary would be in the Hunter village.

From their vantage point atop Tapimor's Crest, they could see everything with startling clarity. A mountainous plateau towering over the trees across the river on Havenfall's eastern side, the Crest offered the best point for the Liberators to launch their attack. The village sat between two branches of the Great Ardei river, with the forests to the south being the only land route for escape. It was Vizent's hope they would be wiped out before they realized what happened and could mount a response.

"They know we're coming, don't they?" Duarte huffed, strolling alongside the general. Obram sidled to Vizent's other side, accompanied by the scruffy Aerivolk with white feathers who'd shown up with him. The general shifted, thinking about the day Razarr arrived with Agosti and the rest of his crew in tow.

"Aye, I'd wager a moon's rations on it, assuming I have any left after Obram's last visit to my tent," Vizent replied. The sellsword said nothing, only giving the general a cheeky smirk. "What confuses me is why the envoy ship hasn't left. I thought the Grand Duchess' representative would deliver their missive and leave at the first opportunity."

"Who knows? Perhaps they were asked to wait until the battle is over."

The Aerivolk emitted a strange trill, as if he were cackling. "I doubt it's anything as foolish as that. Their envoy is the Norzen who's been giving you grief. I'd wager on them staying put because they're trying to save their injured friend."

Duarte raised an eyebrow. "Really? Kaigo is the one they sent? Perhaps I'll get a chance to pay him back for what he did to me in Runegard. Also, how do you know they're treating an injured comrade, Hemlocke?"

So Hemlocke is his name, Vizent thought, committing the name to memory. Something about the shorter man disturbed Vizent. Despite being the shortest of the four, the general sensed something dangerous about him. His stone-like countenance, the mad gleam in his eye; Hemlocke carried himself like a viper waiting for the chance to strike. Then there was the fact Agosti refused to meet the Aerivolk's gaze, as if he feared the other man. That any faumen could put such a look on the abrasive officer was cause for concern.

"I know because I'm the one who tore that chicken wench's back open," the Aerivolk answered. "They can try all they like; the toxin I created has no cure. Any attempts to hinder or purge it will simply feed into it. I've never seen anyone last more than six days after empoisoning. She'll be dead before morning."

Obram broke into braying laughter. "I was wondering why you looked so cocky after we left. A normal injury like that would be stitched up in no time!"

"I *hope* they stitched it up. Doing that would trap the poison in her body and make it easier to infect her blood stream. I wish I could hear her screams as the poison enters its final stage."

Duarte gazed down at the small village and snorted. "I would advise against getting too confident. Kaigo is not an opponent to be underestimated. The moment you think you've got him, he'll make you pay. My wounds are proof enough of that."

"The bastard was sent into a Frenzy Haze when I cut his girl open," Hemlocke retorted. "I wouldn't be surprised if he were going mad with grief not being able to heal her. No, he'll be easy pickings once we make our move."

"Make our move?" Vizent asked. His eyes swung to a small mountain of metal and wooden blocks covered by a deerskin tarp sitting in the middle of their camp. "If what your master told me about this new weapon is correct, we may not have to move from this spot."

Obram brushed the comment aside, his own gaze lingering on the pile. "Oh, we'll have to move *somewhere*, I wager. The few Hunters who survive our assault will try escaping to the south. Such a pity our friends will be waiting to cut them down like swine." A light chuckle escaped the Risbado's lips, growing into a full belly laugh as he and Hemlocke left and made their way back towards the camp. A passing soldier was accosted by the pair; Vizent watched as Obram shoved him aside while Hemlocke snatched his helmet only to beat the man unconscious with it.

Vizent huffed and did his best to bite his tongue. Obram had become unbearably brazen in recent days, and Hemlocke provided his own problems in stoking the sellsword's more detestable habits. Not that he had many desirable ones to begin with.

"Duarte, I truly don't know how you put up with them," the general muttered. The heaviness in his eyelids only grew with each day he was forced to tolerate Razarr's minions. Of the lot, only the monk held any degree of discipline or honor, which was more than Vizent could say of any other faumen he knew.

"I wonder the same thing every day if we're being blunt. Were he not an important piece in my master's plans, I'm certain Obram and I would have already beaten each other bloody, even if Master would punish us both for the foolishness. I'll admit he's skilled enough I'm not sure I could defeat him in a duel."

"What do you think of this contraption we've been brought? It seems simple enough, but I question its usefulness in live combat. Something this large is bound to be unwieldy."

"I suppose we'll find out soon enough. Master designed it, however, so it should be of impeccable quality."

Nodding his agreement, but keeping his true thoughts private, Vizent thanked the monk for listening before trudging back to camp. When Duarte inquired as to his intentions, the general responded with a shaky smile.

"I need to brief my officers, so they don't lose their heads during the battle. Afterwards, I have some...personal business to handle. Tell Agosti to have the men start putting this behemoth together. We'll need it."

Until Maple's injury, Kai would have said the most terrifying thing he ever experienced was facing Grimghast for the first time. The beast unnerved him in a way no other opponent did and seeing it's hideous visage appear from thin air never failed to send a frosty chill through his body. Not even the nettleboar he faced in his Trial instilled the fear Grimghast did. When compared to the possibility of losing Maple, however, Kai realized there were more horrific things than facing his own mortality.

If Grimghast brought a chill to his body, Maple's poisoning was what he imagined Nulyma to be. An endless void where all his senses felt deadened, and the fear of his mistake left a stabbing pain through his entire soul. Only his determination to find an antidote kept him from losing himself completely in the grief.

While they still had to wait for his concoction to finish working, Maple was making swift improvements. Her skin tone was back to normal. The pain in her back and legs was waning fast, and the best sign of her recovery was regaining the ability to move her hips. In Kai's mind, the massive anchors weighing on his heart were finally cut loose, and he could now put his focus on dealing with the imminent problem of the Liberation Army.

He doubted Hemlocke would be entangled with the main army, given he was an Aerivolk, but if he was...Kai swore to be ready for him.

"Oi, get your head out of the clouds, Kai!" Teos barked, jostling the apothecary from his thoughts. Shaking the cobwebs from his mind, Kai apologized while scanning the group. They were meeting in Petro's command building at the edge of town to discuss the upcoming fight. The party was huddled on one side while Petro, Gaspard, and Verona stood on the other, surrounded by the five Hunter company commanders.

The Hunters knew a battle was inevitable. Word from Admiral Larimanz warned them the Liberators were approaching fast, possibly already within sight of the village.

Kai read the missive from his fellow Exarch and breathed a sigh of relief, knowing the Marine Cavalry Fleet was nearby to provide support. They would need every hand they could get. The reports from Waveweaver suggested the Liberators had replenished their numbers since Faith Hollow and now numbered more than eight thousand. Despite their lack of discipline, the Libbies still had numbers on their side and the Hunters, while skilled, contained twelve hundred battle-ready fighters at most and couldn't face that kind of horde alone. While they would put a serious dent in the enemy force, they would likely be wiped out in a frontal assault.

Combined with the five thousand members of the Marine Cavalry, however, they at least stood a fighting chance.

"If we're lucky," Petro said as he examined the large map covering the table, "Larimanz and his fleet won't be too far behind the Libbies. This will allow us to focus on defending the village while waiting for reinforcements. The traps we have scattered in the surrounding area will help tremendously."

Ione raised her hand. "Do we know where the Libbies will come from? The last thing we need is to run into the enemy while escaping."

Petro frowned, sticking pins into several spots around Havenfall. "If Larimanz's information is accurate, they'll come from the northeast, skirting around Tapimor's Crest. I don't know how experienced their commander is, but I can see them trying to pin us by crossing the river south of the Crest and attacking from both south and east."

"Commander Petro!" shouted a young Hunter as they barreled into the room. His eyes were wide as saucers, and he looked as though he sprinted from one end of the village to the other. "You're not gonna believe this, sir, but there's a Wasini here to speak with you. He says he's from the den out on Tapimor's Crest and that it's urgent."

"Wait, he came all the way here from the Crest?" asked Petro. "Didn't we knock the eastern bridge out already to keep the Libbies from crossing?"

A guttural voice came from outside. "I'm more than capable of crossing the shallows of the eastern fork. I may be old, Petro, but I'm not dead."

Kai and the party watched as an elderly Wasini with a tanned, weathered face slithered into the small building. The Hunter who announced his arrival gave a heaving gasp and scrambled out of the faumen's way. His scales were a dusty blue up top and beige on the bottom, and he wore a battered breastplate covered in dents and rust.

"It's been a while, Cairn," Petro replied. "What's this urgent business you have with us? It must be serious for you to travel all this way."

The Wasini's citrine eyes narrowed, coiling his tail beneath him. "As our long-time comrades, I felt it was best to inform you that a portion of the Liberation Army is camped atop the Crest and watching your every move."

"Bloody Nulyma! Wait, you said they're *on top* of the Crest? Why in Tapimor's hairy ass are they all the way up there?" The party shared a look of confusion.

"I know not, but they appear to be building a strange contraption on the plateau. Whatever it might be, I doubt it bodes well for you."

"No, I can't imagine it does. Thank you for warning us, Cairn. I truly appreciate it. I've been wondering how far away those bastards were, and now we know." Petro barked an order to the young Hunter, telling him to warn Barraco and have him give the evacuation signal. He then ordered the company commanders to follow and lead the Hunter's retreat while he finished up.

Kai sensed he was being watched and saw Cairn staring at him as the five commanders barreled out the door at full speed..

"Did you need something, sir?" he asked.

"No, young one, but I must ask. You are the one they call Gravebane, correct?"

The apothecary blinked. "Uh, that's correct, sir."

Cairn's face slipped into a relieved smile. "I thought so. My son's told me some stories about you."

Now Kai was well and fully confused. "Wait, do I know your son?"

"I would hope you know my boy, Larimanz." A short gasp escaped Ione. The party hadn't encountered the admiral since their trek to Runegard, though Kai knew it was because he was spending most of his time chasing the Liberators all across the realm. "The scallywag warned me he was coming to put the fear of Nulyma in those damned Libbies. He also asked me to watch your back every step of the way. We may not be much with only fifty warriors on hand, but the Wasini of Tapimor's Crest will gladly fight at your side in this battle."

Standing tall, Kai bowed to the old Wasini. "Thank you, Cairn. Your son and I aren't as well-acquainted as we should, but I like to think of him as a friend, considering he saved our tails while we were traveling to Runegard."

"Bah, don't mention it. In times like these, we all need to look out for each other. Hate only begets more hate. The Liberators are proof enough of that."

Nodding to Cairn, Kai's ears twitched when the loud blast of a horn resounded throughout the village. The din outside grew to deafening heights as the village became a flurry of movement. Scores of people ran about, loading up wiroch-drawn carriages with supplies and sending them on their way. Some of the Hunters gave short blasts on their horns, pointing and directing the river of bodies towards the western side of the village.

Turning to his family, Kai gave a short nod. "We'd best get a move on. There's no guarantee we'll have enough time to clear the village before the enemy arrives. Ma, can you and Serafina grab our crew from the inn and have them fire up the *Senberg*? I reckon you can use it to get some of the supplies out much faster than by foot."

Verona grinned. "Certainly. We'll pick up Maple on the way and make sure she's safe. You kids watch yourselves and come back in one piece, ya hear?"

"Maple's gonna be brassed off if you have her put on the ship. You know that, right?" Teos warned.

Kai nodded, knowing even with her health improving, Maple still wasn't in fighting condition. "I'm aware she'll be upset, but I don't want her risking herself so soon after recovering."

"Ain't that my decision to make, love?" Kai and the others spun in shock, seeing Maple stagger in, using the wall to steady herself.

"Maple!" Kai rushed forward and pulled the merchant close, allowing her to wrap an arm around his shoulder and lean against him. "What are you doing here? You should be resting."

"Pish," she grumbled, "I'm well enough to walk, so I'm going with you."

Lucretia stepped forward and took Maple by the arm, helping Kai set her down in a nearby chair. "It is obvious you can barely stand. Do you *want* to re-injure yourself?"

"No, but I can feel my strength returning little by little. I'll be fine, I swear."

Pinching the bridge of his nose, Kai chuffed as he squeezed the Aerivolk's hand. "Maple, I can't risk you getting hurt again. I already almost lost you once!"

"We're in the middle of a war, Kai; the risk will always be there. Besides, wouldn't I be safest with the party, where I know you'll all be there to watch my back?"

"But—"

"Love, please, I understand how you feel. Truly. But I'm asking you to respect my decision. I already swore not to let you face this alone, even if Orelia and the others are with you. That hasn't changed a lick since my injury. Even if I can't fight at the same level, at least let me be an extra pair of eyes."

It took all of Kai's willpower to not break down at the wide-eyed, pleading look on Maple's face. She leaned in close and drew him into a hug. Even wrapped in the warm embrace of her feathers, a shadow of fear towered over Kai like a menacing obelisk. In his mind, Kai could hear Hemlocke's throaty cackle, accompanied by the image of Maple lying on a stone floor, covered in blood. His breathing quickened, and he felt drops of sweat crawling down his face. The pounding of his heart created a tightness in his chest that had him clutching his mane in terror.

A sharp pinch in his cheeks yanked him from the abyss. His vision came back into sharp focus, filled with Maple's violet eyes. Her face was so close, their noses were pressed against each other, and he could feel her breath on his lips.

"I'm right here, Kai," she whispered. He briefly thought of glancing at the others, but Maple's nails digging into his cheeks discouraged the idea. "I'm not going anywhere. Neither is Orelia. We promised. We'll get through this together, understand? I know you're scared, love. I'm scared too. By the winds, I'm terrified. But we're going to keep going. You know why? Because Orelia and I are willing to fight for you. For *us*. Hemlocke may have won our last battle, but he won't win the war. We'll beat him together."

Gazing into Maple's eyes, her words cut through the darkness hovering at the edge of his mind. He reached up and clutched her hand tight, letting a smile stretch across his lips.

"You're right. I'm sorry I tried to force you to stay away."

"Fear is a terrifying thing and brings out the worst in people. Look at the Liberators. I think they hate faumen because they fear what we're capable of. Fear gives birth to anger, which gives birth to misery, and only misery could bring so much death."

"She's right," said Orelia. "The best thing we can do now is work together and make sure we get out of this alive. I'm ready to follow you into Nulyma itself, and I'm certain everyone here feels the same. Let's get—"

A slow clapping from behind drew everyone's attention to the door, where a tall figure in a cloak stood leaning against the door frame. Their lower face was concealed by a cloth wrap, but their piercing eyes sent a tremor of nervousness through Kai.

The figure, a man judging by their stocky body and deep voice, began to chuckle. "Such a shame," he said. "Not a single shot has been fired yet and the mighty Hunter Corps is already fleeing into the woods. What a disgrace."

Gaspard struggled to his feet and pointed his cane at the man's heart. "I think you're hardly one to judge. Besides, what makes you think we're fleeing?"

"Da," warned Kai, "be careful. We don't know who this is or what they're after."

"Perhaps you'd best listen to the boy," the stranger added. "He seems to have a good head on his shoulders, even if he is a damned Norzen."

"Who in bloody Nulyma are you?" Orelia demanded, brandishing her staff. The rest of the party, sans Maple, drew their weapons and stood defiant, ready to battle. To their surprise, the stranger broke out into a full belly laugh.

"I must say, you lot are braver than I would've imagined. Then again, I suppose you've earned such bravery in spades on the battlefield." His gaze shifted, locking onto Kai who returned the man's stony glare. "You, especially, have been proving to be a royal pain in the ass."

That proves it, Kai thought. *Whoever he is, he's with the Liberators.* Something about the man seemed familiar to Kai, but he couldn't recall where he'd seen him before. "You're rather brave yourself to come alone, considering our sides are preparing for war."

"I like to think I can handle myself. Besides, I didn't come to fight. I came to parlay with Commander Petro as a representative of the Liberation Army."

Petro stepped forward and crossed his arms over his chest, leveling a hardened scowl at the stranger. "What makes you think I'll negotiate with you Libbie bastards? Besides, what's to stop us from taking you hostage and forcing your troops to back off?"

"The men have standing orders to destroy this village if I don't return within a set time. If we're being honest, I'd like to avoid that. The way I see it, you don't have much choice. We outnumber you more than five-to-one. Despite your formidable skills, we have weapons capable of ruining you. However, I'm willing to spare you, so long as you meet two conditions."

The Hunter commander's glare turned icy, his muscles tightening beneath his vest. "And if we refuse?"

"Then we burn Havenfall to cinders and hunt the rest of your village down, slaughtering them to the last man, woman, and child."

"You wretch," Teos growled. The smuggler's hoof pawed the ground, his lips curling back into a snarl. "People like you are a disgrace, defiling everything the Wind Saints fought for."

"Galen and Tapimor were the only true Saints," the man said. "Their blood was untainted. Pure. Faumen have been nothing but a stain on this world since even before the Rebirth."

"You know nothing of the true history," Lucretia retorted.

"So you say, but the Hunters are currently protecting these disgusting creatures, which must be addressed. If you want Havenfall to be spared, Commander, first the Hunter Corps must swear fealty to the Liberation Army and join our ranks."

Petro scoffed. "And your second condition?"

The man's gaze swept over the room before he pointed a stubby finger at Kai. "Hand over the Norzen and his party. They've interfered with our crusade too many times and will face execution. Now think hard, Petro. Are you willing to sacrifice your village for the sake of seven heretics?"

Every eye watched as Petro met the other man's stare. Neither moved or blinked. Kai wondered why the older Hunter was hesitating to answer the Liberator's demands. "You really are a fool," Petro finally replied. "You can take your demands and stuff them up your ass! Kai may be a Norzen, but he's still a Hunter, and Hunters are family. Not that I'd expect vermin like you to understand."

An aura of trepidation settled over the group as the Liberator burst into another laugh. "I understand more than you think, Petro."

"You understand nothing. How dare you threaten my family," Gaspard hissed. Stumbling forward, he raised his cane and swung it at the man's head. The attack stopped short when the Liberator snatched the cane mid-swing. His eyes settled on Gaspard and a grim chuckle escaped him.

"Really now, Gaspard, I never knew you to be so rude."

The retired Hunter choked back a gasp. "How do you know my name?"

From his vantage point, Kai saw his father quivering. Seeing Gaspard exhibiting so much fear was unnerving to the apothecary.

In all my years, he thought, *I don't remember seeing Da afraid of anything*. His fingers curled around his mace, ready to attack.

"I know a lot about you, Gaspard. It's funny you and Petro talk about family regarding that filthy peltneck, when we used to say the same about each other."

Petro scoffed. "What do you mean? Why would we think of *you* as family?"

"Did you pebblewits forget what I always used to tell you? Friends are the family you choose," the man said. He tossed his cloak aside and lowered the wrap from his mouth, revealing a chiseled face with hawkish blue eyes and a neatly trimmed beard. A set of gleaming brass stars rested on his uniform epaulets.

Memories from Faith Hollow assaulted Kai's mind. His eyes widened when he recognized the man's armor. *He's the one I saw outside the city wall before the battle started!*

Gaspard's face grew pallid, his eyes bulging as he stared at the man. "It can't be..." he muttered. "You're supposed to be dead. They never found a body!"

"Bloody Nulyma," Petro gasped. "Is it really him, Gaspard?"

"Aye, it's him alright. I'd recognize that ugly face anywhere."

The stranger released a booming cackle. "Ugly?! Who are you calling ugly? You're hardly one to talk, old friend."

"Da," Kai said, inching closer to the retired Hunter, "who in the winds is this?"

"His name is Vizent Doulterre," answered Gaspard. "One of my old squad mates and the man I used to call my best friend. And judging by those stars, it seems he's the enemy commander."

Chapter XXVII

Nobody moved. Not a soul spoke as everyone's eyes shifted between Gaspard and Vizent. The two men stared at each other, neither turning away. Kai felt a throbbing in his skull as he tried to make sense of it all. A quick glance at Maple and Orelia suggested they was having similar thoughts.

"How in the name of Finyt are you still alive, Vizent?" asked Gaspard. "They never found your body after the nettleboar mission. We've all thought you were dead for 25 years! I think, given our history, I deserve an explanation for how you ended up a damned Liberator."

"I suppose you do," Vizent replied. "To start, I'm sure you remember seeing the beast knock me into the river during our fight. Hit my bloody head on the rocks when I fell in. I reckon I was unconscious for a while; it was well past moonrise when I awoke. The river had carried me well within Livorian territory when a passing merchant caravan fished me out."

Kai peered out the window, where the Hunters continued bustling about in the rush to evacuate. They were so focused on their tasks, no one seemed to realize a Liberator had strolled into the village without warning.

He's stalling, the apothecary realized, glancing between Vizent and Gaspard. *Though whether it's because he lied about not wanting to have his men attack the village or because he has backup following behind, I'm not sure. Still, this gives the others time to clear the area.*

"Then why not come back to Havenfall? Why would you just disappear? At the very least, you could've let us know you were still alive."

"I was ashamed, alright!" the Liberator general snapped. "After all the work we put into tracking that nettleboar back to the border, I was nothing but a dead-weight. If I hadn't been so damned cocky, maybe Bucca and Pomani would still be alive."

"You don't know that!"

"It doesn't change the fact the mission failed because of me. I couldn't face the village afterwards, especially when I heard about your leg. I refused to go back. Instead, I sent a hawk to Parliament resigning my crest and asked to join the Navy. Figured I would be better off with their more rigid structure. It took what was left of my savings, but I greased the nobles' palms enough to make it work. I even torched my old crest to forget everything from my past." He tugged the warped piece of metal from his pocket and held it up. Kai could see the faint remnants of the Hunters' seal on one side.

Gaspard scoffed, easing himself against the wall and casting a pitying look at Vizent. "So you ran like a coward and hid in plain sight because you knew no one would think to look for you among all those bluecoats."

"Yes, I admit it. I was a coward. I was afraid of what would happen if I returned to Havenfall. For what it's worth, old friend, I'm sorry about your leg."

"Not good enough, Vizent. What in bloody Nulyma happened to you? By the winds, you never had a problem with faumen before. The running away I might be able to forgive in time, but this Liberation Army business is beyond the pale."

His eyes locking on Kai with unrestrained rage, Vizent jabbed a finger towards the apothecary. "So is the brat. I'm more outraged you would take a Norzen in and raise it as your own. Even before the nettleboar mission, I never trusted them. Those damnable cats are a plague and must be destroyed!"

"Shut yer trap," shouted Gaspard. "You don't know my boy, and not all Norzen are as bad as they've been made out to be."

"I'll never forgive them," whispered Vizent. His fists were clenched tight, and Kai caught the scent of blood coming from the Liberator officer, his nails biting deep into his palms. "Those monsters took her from me."

"What are you talking about?"

"They killed my wife!" Vizent screamed, his eyes wide with rage. Kai noticed Lucretia wince at the fury in the man's words. "I met a nice girl while overseeing the Shineford regiment after I made admiral. Her name was Alira. Not even sure how I convinced her I was worth her time, but we eventually got married and were even expecting a child. Then, one night, a massive Norzen thieving band attacked the town. My wife and some of the other women tried escaping while we fought them off, but they had a group hidden away. They found her group and cut them down as they fled. I swore to wipe those beasts out the day they took my Alira from me. When Falber was gunned down and the Conclave put out the call for men to join the revolution, I was among the first to answer and given the rank of general due to my experience."

Rapping his cane on the ground, Gaspard stood back up and sent Vizent a stony glare. "Then there's nothing left to discuss. I understand your pain, but you won't lay a finger on that boy. He may not be of my blood, but he's still my son."

"Da, you're in no condition to fight," Kai warned.

Vizent chuckled. "You really are a fool, Gaspard, if you think you can take me in your condition. Besides, even if you somehow killed me, my allies will make you suffer."

"And what allies would those be?" asked Lucretia. The scholar stood in a defensive stance; her rapier poised to strike.

"Why the Corlatians, of course. Our benefactor may be a fool for keeping faumen minions, but the man makes quality weapons and promised soldiers to our cause."

"So the Federation really *is* to blame for all this? What could they gain from starting a war?" Morgan pressed.

"Does it really matter? All I know for sure is Razarr's likely selling the others to the slave houses for a hefty profit while he hoards the Norzen. Personally, I'd prefer if he killed the damn beasts, but I can appreciate how he got some use out of them."

Ione trembled, clutching her dagger in a shaky grip. "What do you mean?"

"Turns out he opted to use the Norzen as slave labor. Thanks to those demon cats, we have a weapon capable of wiping you Royalist bastards out once and for all."

Teos slid into a stance, his knees bent and ready to charge as he addressed the general. "Now you're making even less sense. What kind of weapon could possibly give you so much power?"

"Looking at the components, I'd wager it's a massive cannon. A siege engine unlike anything Nixtral has ever seen. Razarr calls it the Shatterstar."

Kai's gaze shifted to Orelia, who looked out the window with a spyglass towards Tapimor's Crest. He grew worried when the priestess' face sunk. "He's right," she said. "The Liberators are building something on the Crest. By the winds, I can see it from here."

Sidling next to Orelia and taking the spyglass, Kai looked towards the Crest and felt his heart collapse into his stomach like a lead ball. Vizent was right about one thing: Kai doubted anyone had ever seen such a weapon. Taking the distance between the Crest and Havenfall into account and comparing it to the nearby soldiers, it was at least three times taller than a man.

"If they manage to properly aim that thing, the village will be destroyed in a few blasts," said Kai.

"Now you see how futile it is to resist. I'll give you one last chance to surrender, Petro. If not, your precious village will be laid to waste."

"You're not the man I once knew, Vizent," Gaspard hissed. "You've become nothing more than the beasts we swore to cull all those years ago at our Trial."

Petro nodded and drew his sword, pointing it at the general's heart. "Gaspard is right. We will never surrender to the likes of you. You may outnumber us. You may have that monstrous cannon. You may even have the backing of the Federation. But the Hunters of Havenfall still have their pride, and we'll face you to the last."

"What a shame," Vizent said, shaking his head. "It seems you lot are just as stubborn now as they were back then. I suggest you prepare yourselves, as none of you will live to see the next sunrise."

With surprising agility, Gaspard threw himself over the table and thrust the end of his cane into Vizent's gut. The general bent at the waist, gasping for air. Gaspard pulled his cane back and struck fast, smashing the handle into his former friend's cheek. The blow pitched Vizent backwards into another table, bringing it down with a loud crash.

Petro twirled his sword in one hand and put himself between the party and Vizent. "You all get out of here. Gaspard and I can handle this."

"Are you sure you two will be fine?" asked Maple. She stumbled to Kai and leaned against him, sighing in relief when the apothecary pulled her onto his back.

"Don't worry about us," Gaspard answered. He spun his cane like a baton, a confident grin on his face. "Petro's no slouch on the battlefield, and while my leg isn't in top form, I can still swing a mean stick."

Choking down gulps of air, Vizent staggered to his feet. With a growl, he charged the two men. Kai took a step towards the fight, only for Orelia to give him a sharp poke in the thigh with her staff. He gave her an agitated frown but backed down when Maple's talons dug into his legs. Turning away, they hustled out the door.

"You'll regret that," Vizent snapped. He swung his sword and batted the retired Hunter's cane away. He took advantage of the opening to throw a punch into Gaspard's cheek. Kai shouted when he saw his father collapse to the floor, but the Liberator's next attack was knocked aside by Petro.

The commander returned the favor in landing a solid punch to Vizent's kidney, then a jab to the nose with the sword's pommel. "You won't win so easily."

"Not bad, Petro. You would've made a brilliant ally if not for your foolishness."

The two men darted around the room with the grace of dancers. Their blades rattled with each blow, sending sparks through the air. Kai gave the fight a final glance before darting into the open air. The party huddled together the next building over and shared uneasy looks.

The evacuating Hunters were ignoring them in their dash to reach the bridge across the western river fork. That suited Kai just fine, as it gave them time to strategize without interruptions.

"We need to make sure everyone gets out safe," said Orelia. "If they fire that cannon, the villagers won't stand a chance."

"What about the Marine Cavalry?" asked Morgan. "Aren't they supposed to be close by?"

Kai shook his head. "They'll be expecting the enemy on the ground. Those bastards outplayed us this time by sneaking the Libbies onto the plateau. The only way up Tapimor's Crest for most folks is a narrow path leading up the southern cliffs. There's no way Larimanz can get his army up there without taking heavy losses."

"Then what do we do?" Ione asked. "Wait for them to start launching cannonballs the size of wirochs at us?"

"The Liberation Army may have the high ground," Cairn said, startling the party as he rounded the corner. "but they've also trapped themselves. We can drive them back down the cliff if they aren't expecting us. There's also only the one cannon. They still have to take time and reload between shots."

"I reckon that's our best option then," said Maple. "You should head back to the Crest and get your people ready. We have to stop them from firing the cannon." Cairn bowed at the waist and slithered away at a speed which belied his advanced age.

A deafening crash rang out, drawing their attention back to headquarters. Kai gasped when he saw Gaspard fly through the door and hit the ground hard. Petro came barreling out and raced to the other man's side.

"I'm fine," Gaspard wheezed as the commander helped him to his feet. A deep chuckle came from the rising dust and Vizent stalked towards them, his sword hanging limp at his side.

"You two are putting up a surprising effort. I'm impressed."

"We ain't done yet," Petro replied. Turning towards the party, he barked out for them to stay back before charging the Liberator again.

Teos shouted a warning when Vizent reeled back and, with a flick of his wrist, *threw* his sword at the advancing Hunter. Petro blanched and dove to the side, letting the spinning blade pass him. He scrambled back to his feet, only for a cry of pain to stop him cold.

Eyes wide, Kai stood frozen as the sword continued flying until striking Gaspard, cutting into his shoulder near the neck. The older man fell to the ground clutching the wound, unable to slow the flow of blood.

"Da!" Kai roared, moving to run towards his father. A shout from Petro stopped him from going any further.

"Don't worry about us! Protect the villagers," Petro ordered. Kai understood why the Hunter commander was telling them to leave, but a quivering sensation in his tails told him they needed to stay nearby. For what, he wasn't sure, but he knew his instincts were right more often than not.

Turning back to his opponent, Petro launched himself at Vizent and swung his blade in an arc, intending to decapitate the general. The attack struck only air, though, when Vizent ducked forward and threw a punch into Petro's ribs.

The blow did little else but anger the Hunter. With a scoff, Petro grabbed Vizent by his cropped hair with his free hand and slammed the pommel of his sword into the other man's skull. Vizent collapsed to the ground with a groan, his head swaying as he attempted to lift it from the dirt, only to drop back down as he fell unconscious. Petro left the general where he lay and rushed back to Gaspard, tearing the sleeve from his tunic and using it to bind the wound.

Kai had to restrain the urge to rush in and tend to his father's injury. Instead, he focused on keeping an eye out for any other enemies, warning the party to search for any other Liberators that may have followed Vizent. The apothecary expanded his pupils and swiveled his ears, ignoring the familiar pressure. His body twitched at a glimmer in the air just behind Petro.

"Petro, behind you!" he bellowed.

The sudden warning saved Petro's life. He ducked down just in time to evade a curved sword slicing through the air where his head was scant moments ago. The blade sang when it bounced off a broken wall. Its wielder, a tall man in steel armor and a hooded cloak, leapt backwards to dodge Petro's retaliatory stab.

What's with these crackpots and wearing hoods in the spring sun, Kai wondered to himself.

A puff of air on his neck sent a tremor through him as Maple whispered for him to kneel so she could get down. He asked if she felt well enough to stand on her own and she nodded. Kai was pleased to see her stand tall once she got off his back, with only a slight bend in her knees. He refused to take his eyes fully off the newest attacker.

The newcomer appeared to be a few years older than Teos, though he moved with an astonishing grace. His grizzled face was sun beaten with a trimmed beard. A faint red mark wrapped around his neck and his eyes were hidden behind a pair of dark spectacles. The man's oval face and heavy jawline gave him a roguish appearance, and his broad chest was thick with muscle.

"If you're who I think you are, boy, I've lost count of how often you've impeded my plans," the man stated, his face turning to stare at Kai with a grim expression. "The most frustrating thing, however, is just how long you've proven a menace. Ever since you were an infant, in fact!"

Kai recoiled, his eyes widening. "Who are you, and what are you talking about?!"

"Oh?" The man gave an amused chuckle. "How awkward. It was my belief Duarte informed you of your parents' miserable fate at my hand when you were an infant."

Kai's blood ran cold at the man's words.

Memories of his fight with the Soltauri monk in Runegard burst to the forefront of Kai's mind. Learning of Fusette's true heritage. Hearing Duarte describe his master's quest to hunt down the last descendants of Cacovis' eldest son, Erklaus. How his birth parents were tracked down and chased from their home, only to be murdered after setting him adrift on the Great Ardei River. He fell to one knee as the implications of the man's comment grew clear.

"So you're the one who killed Kai's parents?" asked Ione, rushing to help Kai to his feet. "Who in bloody Nulyma do you think you are?! What kind of man tries to slaughter an innocent *baby*?"

The stranger exploded into a raucous, braying laugh. "The brat's family is cursed, wench. The Cacovis line has needed culling for three hundred years, and today I finally take one step closer to fulfilling my family's oath. As for who I am, I'm no man. No, my dear, I am more than that. Much, much more." Reaching up, the man pulled his hood back and removed his spectacles, tossing them to the ground.

Kai choked on his own spit while Maple's face turned an unhealthy grey. Ione and Orelia stumbled back, falling against Morgan and Teos who both stood rigid. Lucretia dropped to her knees, her eyes dilating.

"This can't be happening. Not again," the scholar murmured.

The man's steely grey eyes matched Kai's own. A pair of silver cat-like ears twitched atop his head and a pair of thick, bushy tails fluttered behind him.

"My associates know me as Razarr, master of the Corlatian forge company known as Ferden Ironworks. My true name, however, is Hakan of the noble Norzen tribe."

Chapter XXVIII

Unable to speak, Kai's body quaked. Why did he feel so *terrified*? For years, he wondered what happened to his true parents, and why they left him to be found by Gaspard and Verona all those years ago. Worse, ever since Runegard, few of those questions were answered and the rest seemed to multiply. He often thought of what he would say to the man who killed them if they ever met, but Kai admitted he never expected that day to come.

And yet now, through some strange twist of fate, he stood facing the one responsible for how his life turned out. What made the situation more surreal was finding out his parents' murderer was a fellow Norzen.

They were cut down by a member of their own tribe.

"Kai," Maple whispered. His body twitched when she slid her hand into his, giving it a reassuring squeeze. "Remember, love, you're not alone. And you never will be again. Not if we have anything to say about it."

Orelia slid into place on his other side and took his other hand. "She's right," the priestess whispered. "We'll stand beside you no matter what. This changes nothing."

"What's the matter, *boy*?" Hakan sneered. "Cat got your tongue?"

A pale scarlet fog emerged at the edge of Kai's vision. Blinking away the haze, he bit his tongue. He wouldn't lose control again. The sensation of his partners' fingers stroking his hands soothed him. As long as they were by his side, he had a reason to be strong.

It was then, in a moment of clarity, he realized something.

"It's funny," Kai started. "I've often considered what I wanted to say if we ever met, but nothing I could think of felt truly right. There's no doubt

I despise you with every fiber of my soul. You're nothing but a murderer with some odd grudge against my family. The oddest thing, though, is I feel I should thank you."

Everyone stared at the apothecary in shock. "Thank him?" Lucretia gasped. "Kai, what in the winds is wrong with you?"

"I won't even pretend to assume why you chose Blood Feud against Cacovis' family. My only guess is you hate her for causing the Desolation and leaving the Norzen to shoulder the blame for her choice. But your senseless enmity did result in some positive things."

Raising an eyebrow, Hakan chortled with his arms crossed over his broad chest. "Is that so? And just what good things did I cause by killing your parents?"

Memories of the two women next to him and everything they'd shared on their journey flickered before his eyes. Their smiles and laughter gave him the courage to face his parents' killer with a firm stare. "What does it matter? It doesn't change the fact we can't co-exist. It's obvious you intend to try and kill me, so I'll just have to do my best to stop you."

Without another word, Kai ran his own finger over Maple and Orelia's palms and cast a quick, tender smile at them.

"Stay out of this, Kai," Petro said. The commander put himself between the two Norzen, holding his sword at the ready. "We'll hold this bastard off. You need to get the winds out of here."

"The boy won't be going anywhere except his grave. I won't be stopped by some pathetic human. Not when this moment has been three hundred years in the making."

"Why are you so determined to wipe out Cacovis' family?" Orelia asked. "What possible purpose would it serve to kill them when the woman has already been dead for so long? How can you possibly be so angry over the Desolation?"

Hakan regarded the young Vesikoi with a stony gaze. His hands tightened into fists and Kai could see his muscles spasm with anticipation. "If it hadn't been for that bitch, the Norzen never would have had to suffer so much humiliation. We would be in our proper place if only Grandfather had survived to achieve his ultimate goal."

"Wait, 'Grandfather'? What in hoarfrost are you talking about?" Morgan demanded.

The forge master chuckled. "I suppose there's a reason Obram and I get along so well. I do love a good gloat, after all, and it's not as if you'll live long enough to cause me further problems. Perhaps I should at least tell you why you fools are about to die. What do you know of the warlord Berelmir?"

"Wait, wasn't that the name of the bastard the Wind Saints defeated in the Desolation Wars?" Teos inquired, his eyes turning towards Lucretia.

"Berelmir," she muttered with a nod. "The warlord who conquered most of northeastern Alezon before meeting his end at Cacovis' hands in the Desolation. He was also the Shadow's younger brother." The party flinched, not liking the reminder of the fallen Saint's relation to the warlord.

"Indeed," Hakan confirmed. The older Norzen's lips curled back in a sneer, "and just as his sister hid her children from his allies, Berelmir also had an adult son left behind who fled following the Desolation. He ended up settling in western Livoria, his hatred for his aunt passing through the generations to this day." Kai and others cast worried glances at each other, not liking the man's implication. "As you might have guessed, Berelmir is my many times great-grandfather, and our family's mission since the founding of Livoria has been to wipe the Cacovis line out and achieve Berelmir's great vision!"

"*Taen!*" Kai exclaimed. He felt a sudden gratefulness for the Norzen vagrant who taught him every swear imaginable in their tribe's native tongue. "Son of a *saento heverte dritering* fluff nugget!" Of all the bloody possibilities, he had to be related, however distant, to the same bastard trying to kill him!

"Were this situation not so serious, Kai, I would wash your mouth out with a soap cake," Lucretia deadpanned. "Not even Morgan has ever said anything *that* obscene."

Drawing his falchion, Morgan scratched at the scales on his neck with a groan. “I don’t know if I should be impressed or concerned. Nevermind, I probably don’t want to know the exact translation. There is one thing I don’t understand; how in hoarfrost did a bastard like you end up in Corlati?”

“The same way so many other faumen did: slavery. I was taken from my parents by a pack of slavers raiding our village. It was a terrifying experience for a ten-year-old child. In truth, I was among the lucky ones. It wasn’t long after I arrived that I was bought by a wealthy forge master to serve as his personal attendant, a role I served in until taking control of his business after he died in my twentieth year.”

The party refused to relax their guard as Hakan spoke. His voice had a deep timbre despite the hoarseness of age. In the back of his mind, Kai couldn’t help but admit the man had a talent for eloquent speaking. He wondered if it was a skill he picked up from his former master.

“Why take over, though?” asked Orelia. “Why would you stay instead of fleeing back to Livoria and starting over?” Kai said nothing, knowing that keeping him talking was their best hope at figuring out a way to take him down.

Heaving a labored sigh, Hakan leaned his head back and stared at the clouds floating above, a melancholy shadow lurking in his eyes. “I’ll confess revenge was a heavy motivator. With the master’s holdings under my control, it included all of his slaves. Needless to say, I was soon in the market for new servants after I flayed and butchered them for the pain they caused during my tenure as an attendant.”

Kai’s grip on his mace tightened. It disturbed him that Hakan could speak of torture and murder in such a nonchalant way. This man was so intimate with death, he spoke of others’ lives with a detached resentment, as if they were little more than bugs.

“My newfound wealth did provide me with a way to accomplish my ultimate vision, though. Ever since I was a boy, I never forgot my parents’ lessons instilled in me regarding our duty to take our vengeance on the heirs of Cacovis. With the wealth of a forge master behind me, I now had a means to travel Livoria and seek out the Shadow's descendants. As well as pay for enough brutish sellswords like that mixblood chimera over there to make sure the job was done right."

"And you eventually ended up in Duskmarsh," Kai said, "Duarte told us you posed as a historian to track down the last of Erklaus' family. Did you already know about the royal family's connection to Cacovis by that point?"

"Oh, that's been an open secret amongst the Norzen of eastern Alezon for years, not that they let anyone else know it," Hakan answered. His eyes shifted to Vizent's unconscious form with a malicious sneer. "The trouble has always been getting close enough to the Grand Duchess to finish the job. Which is why I went to the trouble of having Hemlocke kill Galstein's trade minister and pin the blame on a faumen to arrange this war. The Liberators were meant to handle the most difficult part of my mission: Flushing you and the duchess into the open. Of course, they need to stop proving their incompetence at every turn."

"Are you telling me," Kai whispered, his voice cracking, "this entire war is because of *you*? All the senseless death and destruction, it was just so you could kill Fusette and me?!" The apothecary fought to control the rage festering in his chest. His mind was flooded with images of all those who perished. His squad. Dannel and the orphans from Stahl Granz. Viscount Savo. All their lives, snuffed out for the sake of a centuries-old grudge.

Hakan smirked and lifted a finger, pointing it at Kai's heart. "In a sense, you are both also partly to blame. Or at least your parents are, in your case. If you hadn't been set adrift on the river the day I killed your parents, I wouldn't have needed to waste so much energy and money finding you. It's why I intend to kill you before you have a chance to sire more offspring and make my mission so much more difficult."

"That's the biggest load of balderdash I've ever heard!" Orelia screeched. "Don't you dare try to pin this on Kai or Fusette. These people died because you're a petty, miserable man who refuses to let go of the past!"

"Silence, fish bitch, unless you want me to tear your limbs off and roast them for dinner."

The ground quaked as Kai slammed a boot into the dirt, cracking it apart. The others stepped back, watching him with worry etched on their faces. His mace raised, the younger Norzen cast a frigid glare at Hakan. "That winged rat Hemlocke is already on borrowed time, Hakan. You lay one finger on her or anyone I care about, I'll rip your heart out with my bare hands and crush it under my boot."

"You think I'm afraid of some pathetic whelp? You're nothing but a boy with a penchant for luck. You don't stand a chance against us."

A glint of silver flashed behind Hakan, the forge master's eyes narrowing as he spun in place. He snatched the sword aimed at his neck with a gauntleted hand, stopping it cold. Gaspard's chest heaved as he matched Hakan's stony gaze, his injured arm swaying in the wind at his side. His good arm shook as he tried pulling the sword back, but the Norzen's grip was unyielding.

"You stay away from my boy, you bastard," Gaspard warned. Hakan sneered and slammed a boot into the injured Hunter's knee, sending him to the ground.

"I'm going to enjoy wiping this village off the map. And once the Liberators and my pawns deal with the Grand Duchess, they won't last long before the world at large orchestrates their destruction. And by that time, I'll be in the shadows with my true army, ready to make my move."

"What, killing us wasn't enough," spat Kai. "What else are you planning?"

"Nothing too special, simply uniting the Norzen of Alezon under my banner and bringing the entire continent to heel as it always should've been."

A clatter rang out as Lucretia dropped her rapier. "You intend to conquer the entire continent? How could you possibly hope to accomplish such a feat with only the Norzen at your side?"

"The gears are already turning to draw the other realms into this war, exactly as I hoped. While they're busy dealing with the Liberation Army, my men will slink in like a mist to conquer each capital city and assume control of the realms. Soon, the Norzen will finally be able take their place as the ultimate rulers of Alezon!"

"What possible reason would you have for conquering Alezon?" asked Ione. Her hands were clasped together in prayer as her face reddened and fresh tears threatened to escape. "Why does it always have to be about strength and control, when we can work towards living in peace?"

Hakan burst into laughter at the tavern maid's words. "You're a naïve fool if you believe peace is possible. Even before the Rebirth, we Norzen have been outcasts and subjected to the hatred of others. According to the notes and stories passed down in my family, Berelmir's whole reason for conquering the provinces was to create a land where the Norzen could live in peace without anyone's interference. However, your precious Wind Saints refused to allow it."

"Perhaps if he put less effort into killing people and more into building goodwill, he might've been able to accomplish his goal," Orelia said.

The forge master scoffed. "Since the people of Alezon refuse to allow us a land of our own, then we'll simply take everything by force. Perhaps an eternity in bondage will do the rest of you wretches some good."

A loud roar sounded from behind Hakan as Petro charged. He launched a quick thrust with his sword but hit nothing as Hakan ducked underneath the attack, throwing a heavy uppercut into the Hunter commander's ribs. Petro gasped and staggered back. He only avoided having his head removed by Hakan's blade when he tripped over the prone Gaspard, stumbling onto his backside.

"This ends now," Hakan muttered. Standing over the prostrate men he raised his sword, intending on skewering them both. Petro and Gaspard flinched as the forge master thrust down with a triumphant roar.

Clang!

A soft breeze ruffled Gaspard's thinning hair, and the rattle of a fallen weapon rang moments later. The downed Hunter opened his eyes. He blanched, seeing Kai standing over them instead with his mace at the ready.

He followed Kai's line of sight to find Hakan glaring at the younger Norzen with barely restrained rage. A thin cut on the forge master's cheek trickled blood, and his sword lay just behind him on the ground.

"Back off," declared Kai. The rest of the party strode up and stood beside him, each bearing their weapons. "I'm not afraid of you, and I'm not afraid to kill you to protect those precious to me."

"Brave words coming from a whelp with so many blades behind him," Hakan snarked.

"Unlike you, I have friends and allies I can trust with my life. All you have are lackeys, pawns, and slaves who serve you out of fear or deception."

"That may be true, boy, but a body is still a body, regardless of why it serves. And you're a fool if you think I came here alone."

Eyes furrowing, Kai swiveled his ears to the sides while his friends glanced around with nervous hesitation. Moments later, a whistling noise came from behind them. A gasp to his left brought his gaze to Ione, who lunged forward and raised her pan behind the apothecary's head. A sharp ping stabbed Kai's ears as he turned around.

He was stunned to see a small weapon ricochet off the pan and pierce the ground. It had a leaf-wrought blade the length of his hand on the end, attached to a short handle with a ring on the pommel.

"That's a kunai," Lucretia breathed. "It's a knife-like weapon common among assassins from the realms of Feswili. Lightweight and easy to throw. Also easy to hide."

The faint sound of footsteps brought Kai's attention to the young black-haired woman in tight-fitting clothes as dark as her hair approaching. The newcomer knelt to pick the strange blade up and held it in a reverse grip. A second one rested in her opposite hand.

"I'm impressed you blocked that," Hakan said, an amused smirk lining his face. "Few are able to hear Mirabell coming. Now, let's see if you can handle us both. You may outnumber us, but as they say: quality trumps quantity."

Chapter XXIX

It was rare for such a sense of urgency to settle over the village of Havenfall. The Hunters prided themselves on their mellow disposition as a whole and ability to adapt to most any situation. Their home built on this with its openness and convergence with the surrounding forests. In the shadow of the Liberation Army's imminent attack, however, the Hunters were scrambling to put themselves out of range of the massive cannon taking shape atop Tapimor's Crest. It was clear they were both unused to dealing with such a weapon and hesitant to risk seeing what exactly the siege engine was capable of up close. To Kai, seeing the villagers fleeing for the river like frightened squirrels was unnatural, and it stoked a bubbling anger within him.

The tension in the air surrounding Kai's party was thick enough to cut with a dagger. With Hakan on one side and his servant Mirabell on the other, the party eyed both enemies warily. Other than her silent approach and unusual weapons, they knew nothing of the lithe woman's ability.

"I must confess," said Mirabell, scanning the group with visible curiosity. "I never would've expected anyone to deflect one of my kunai." Her gaze locked on Ione, who met the maid's cold eyes with nervousness. "How did the weakest of these mongrels manage to block my attack?"

Resting a hand on Ione's shoulder, Kai gave the tavern maid a reassuring squeeze. He frowned at the emptiness in Mirabell's gaze. Where most people he met had some type of glimmer behind their eyes, no matter how weak, this woman was different. Hers were glazed over and dull; it reminded him of a painting he once saw with nothing but a listless sky of grey and black. "If you believe Ione to be weak, then I'm amazed you can throw those blades so well with how blind you are."

"She is pathetic," Mirabell groused. "I can see her body trembling with fear. Such a weakling has no business on a battlefield."

"Do not mistake her fear for weakness," Kai retorted. "Even the most hardened warriors are afraid of something; what matters is continuing on through one's fear. Don't assume you know us. Ione may not have official training, but she's certainly braver and has better instincts than many sailors I've seen in battle."

The woman gave a cocky smirk, spinning her blades like batons. "We shall see, then. I think Master will enjoy watching me skin your tails for a new belt." Despite the expressiveness of her face, Mirabell's eyes remained listless. Kai peered back at Hakan, frowning at the tickled grin on his lips.

The sound of rustling fabric brought Kai's attention back to Ione, who stood in front of him with a defiant glare. Her pan was raised in front like a shield with her dagger clutched in the other hand, tucked close to her side.

"With the Saints as my witness, I won't let you hurt my friend," Ione challenged.

"Very well. Let's test your resolve."

Without another word, Mirabell launched herself at the group. Ione braced herself and, to Kai's pleasant surprise, parried the maid's attack, knocking her off-balance. The party scattered into two groups, with Orelia and Morgan choosing to assist Ione while the others joined Kai in bearing down on Hakan.

"You have quicker reflexes than I thought," Mirabell said as she lunged towards Ione again. Her attack failed to connect, brushed aside by Morgan's falchion, though Ione stumbled back from the sudden assault, falling on her rear. The sellsword sent an upwards slash towards the other woman, only to miss when she sidestepped. Mirabell's dodge, however, brought her within Orelia's sights and the priestess exploited the opening with a heavy strike to her ribs.

Ione rose to her feet and stepped into Mirabell's range while she was still stunned, using the pan to block a kunai aimed at her lung. She thrust her dagger forward and felt satisfaction at the tug and audible rip she felt and heard. Mirabell's eyes widened, leaping back and aiming a swipe at the body approaching from her other side.

Morgan emitted a gasp of pain when the kunai collided with his neck. Only his scales kept his throat from being slit open. Grabbing the woman's wrist, he pushed the weapon away and tried to sweep her legs from under her.

The trio were shocked to see her leap over Morgan's leg, grasping his shoulders and using him as a pivot to flip herself over his head. She pushed off his back and put some distance between them. Dusting her pants off, Mirabell regarded the trio with a befuddled expression.

"How odd. Perhaps I underestimated your tenacity."

With a wry smirk, Ione couldn't help but let out a soft giggle. "I'd wager we learned that from Kai. He may be young, but our leader's never been one to give up even when the odds are stacked against us."

"Ione's right," Morgan added, flashing the tavern maid his signature cocky grin. "Kai helped us believe in ourselves and refused to let us give up hope. Not even that bastard Hemlocke could break him. Yer good; damned good, to be honest. But we ain't going down so easy."

Something flashed in Mirabell's eyes, though Ione wasn't sure what it could be. For a moment, there was a *spark* in her gaze which flickered away as quickly as it appeared.

"Now I remember," she mumbled. "Locke mentioned dealing with one of your number. I thought he said something about the Aerivolk girl, yet I see her standing and ready to fight, though she's still weak. Locke won't be happy about this."

"Maple's condition will be the least of his worries if Kai ever catches him," Orelia warned. The two sides stared each other down.

Adjusting the grip on her kunai, Mirabell surged forward and leapt towards Morgan, who stood between Ione and Orelia. Her feet crashed against his breastplate, sending him to the ground as she stood on his chest. Her right hand rose and blocked the staff flying towards her ribs again. Shoving the priestess away, Mirabell spun in place with a high kick aimed at Ione's head.

The tavern maid tried to dodge but couldn't fully avoid getting grazed in the cheek by Mirabell's shoe. Backing up again, Ione threw a wild, blind swing. She felt the pan hit something with a loud thwack, followed by a shrill yelp from the assassin she wasn't expecting.

Catching her balance before she could fall over, Ione looked at Orelia to see her friend struggling not to laugh. Morgan lay on the ground staring at her in unabashed glee. Her eyes swung to see Mirabell scowling, hands clutching her rear in obvious pain.

"You...you hit my ass, you damned tavern wench!"

"You're trying to kill us, so you don't get to complain!" Ione shouted back, fighting back the laughter threatening to burst from her own chest. "Maybe it's time *somebody* beat your ass!"

"I get that enough back home, thank you very much," Mirabell grumbled.

Ione crinkled her nose but didn't respond. Instead, she grabbed Morgan by the crook of his arm and helped him up. Orelia sidled next to them and raised her staff. The three faced Mirabell shoulder to shoulder, watching the assassin ready herself once more before charging.

On the other side of the building, Hakan threw Vizent's unconscious body aside and parried a strike from Teos' halberd. Kai came in from the other side and aimed his mace at the forge master's back. To his shock, Hakan's tails wrapped around his wrists and stopped him cold.

"You'll need a few decades more experience before you can hit me with a blow like that, boy."

Kai grunted when Hakan threw his leg back and struck him in the sternum. His back struck the ground hard, knocking the wind from his lungs. A sharp twang sounded from Maple's new bow, and the blur of a whistling arrow flew towards Hakan. He proved ready for the attack, though, throwing Teos back and ducking beneath the arrow.

Another whistle pricked Kai's ears, and he was stunned to see Hakan's pained hiss moments later when a second arrow lodged in his upper thigh.

"How...?" Hakan asked, his eyes landing on Maple who responded with only a wry smirk. Kai saw him rip the arrow out with a growl, ignoring the stream of blood spurting from his wound. Hakan stalked towards Maple, dodging Lucretia's rapier mid-step and tossing the scholar aside with a backhanded swing of his arm. Raising her weapon was the only thing that kept Lucretia from being slashed by the blades on Hakan's gauntlet. Teos stopped her from hitting the dirt and swung his halberd in a wide arc, deflecting Hakan's sword.

Scoffing, the forge master continued advancing on Maple, who nocked an arrow and let fly. Hakan tilted his head and let the missile fly past harmlessly. Maple cursed and reached for her quiver, shrieking when Hakan rushed forward. She bent her knees, ready to glide away, but Hakan was in front of her before she could blink.

A thunderous roar boomed from behind Hakan. In an instant, Kai collided with the older Norzen, knocking him aside and sending them both to the ground in a heap. Maple gasped, clutching her heart as she watched Kai and Hakan rain punches on each other. The apothecary landed some solid blows, but Hakan gave as good as he got. A flash of silver from the gauntlet on the forge master's arm was followed by spraying blood.

"*Taen*!" Kai swore, retreating with a deep cut at the edge of his left eye.

"Kai!" Maple cried out, moving towards him. Her eyes widened when she saw Hakan's sword flying again, this time towards Lucretia's neck, as the approaching scholar was closer. Time stood still, her eyes only seeing the silver glint of the blade racing to end her friend's life.

Teos' halberd met the sword with a clang. Hooking the opposing weapon between the blade and shaft, the smuggler wrenched the sword from Hakan's grasp. The loss of weight in his hand put Hakan off-balance, leaving him vulnerable.

Pushing off her back foot, Lucretia pierced his right side with her rapier, provoking an agitated growl from Hakan. He threw an open palm at Lucretia's face with his left hand, only to be stopped halfway when Kai landed a hammer swing to the forge master's elbow. The blow prevented his strike from digging too deep into Lucretia's face, causing her to only be pushed backwards.

Hakan released a pained bellow, shoving the two aside before backing up to the broken wall. "You little pests are proving more irritating than I imagined," he growled.

"Master!" Mirabell called out while rounding the corner behind Hakan. "I think it's best we withdraw to Tapimor's Crest."

Hakan shot a furious glare at the assassin, who winced at the harsh look. "As much as I hate to admit it," he hissed, "you may have a point. Dealing with these fools will be simple soon enough."

"You're not going anywhere," said Morgan, brandishing his falchion at the two.

Emitting a dark chuckle, Hakan reached for something hidden in his trouser pocket. He lifted a small pouch and extracted a small, glimmering crystal from inside.

Frowning, Kai wondered what the forge master was planning when he felt a sudden pressure on his arm. He looked down to see Maple holding his forearm in a tight grip and staring at Hakan with unbridled fear.

"Maple, what's wrong?" he asked.

"That crystal," Maple whispered. "It looks like the one we found in the mines right after I first joined you. The one that blew a giant hole in the ground."

Kai's face paled and he locked his gaze on Hakan's hand. He mumbled a curse when he realized that Maple was right. *Where in bloody Nulyma did he get that?* His eyes bulged when Hakan raised the crystal above his head, his intentions clear.

"*Taen*! Duck for cover!"

The party scattered as Hakan flung the crystal into the ground as hard as he could. While not as powerful as the explosion in the mine, the small crystal still created a deafening boom the moment it struck the dirt.

Dust and smoke flew everywhere, obscuring the area. Kai leaned against a cracked wall, Maple in his arms with her face buried in his neck and her wings held above them like a shield. He wrapped an arm over her head to protect her from flying debris.

After the ringing from the explosion died down, the noise settled into an uneasy silence. The dust dissipated before long to reveal Hakan and Mirabell both gone. Vanished like wisps in the wind. His gaze swung to the building, and a curse flew from his lips at seeing Vizent's body missing as well. Maple's fingers clinched his robes as he brought her close, humming a tune in her ear he remembered Verona singing to him when he was a boy.

He would worry about finding Hakan later. Right now, he had more important things to worry about.

"Everyone alright?" Kai called out. The dust was beginning to clear, allowing him to see several moving shapes among the cloud. He brushed away the blood seeping from his injured eye.

"We're good here, 'pothy," Morgan shouted. Kai spotted the sellsword helping Lucretia and Ione up from behind a pile of firewood logs they dove behind for protection. Peering to the other side, he saw two more shapes growing larger in the lingering dust. To his relief, the veil dispersed to reveal Teos and Orelia, both covered in specks of dirt.

"We're fine, too," said Orelia. Teos shared a look of frustration with Kai when he noticed their enemies were gone.

"Where in Finyt did they get to?"

"The Crest," Kai muttered. He helped Maple to her feet and turned his head towards the east, where Tapimor's Crest towered above the forest canopy. "They're probably going to reunite with their allies before the attack."

"We have to stop them," Lucretia declared. "One way or another, we must prevent them from firing that cannon!"

"You kids think you can catch them? They'll have a good head start on you, with your lady friend in her condition." Petro asked, ambling towards them with Gaspard's arm swung over his shoulder. The two men were covered in dust, though Kai was thankful they only bore a few new cuts and bruises from the explosion. Gaspard's injured shoulder was wrapped tight in crimson-stained cloth.

"We've got to," Orelia said, her lips set in a thin line that reminded Kai of Lucretia when agitated by something.

"And what do you reckon we do?" asked Maple. "I'm feeling a lot better than I was yesterday, but I doubt I can run or glide all the way to the Crest on my own."

"Say," said Morgan, eyes wide with clarity, "do you think the village stables might still have wirochs available?"

Gaspard burst into a wheezing laugh. "By the winds, boy, you might be onto something! With how fast the Hunters retreated across the river, I doubt anyone bothered to empty the stables before heading out."

"What are we waiting for, then?" Orelia exclaimed. Everyone followed Petro as he led the group towards the village center. Several stragglers racing down the roads called out to them, begging them to hurry and escape. The Hunter commander led them to a broad circular building. Kai's ears twitched, hearing the cacophony inside. There were wirochs in there, alright. And from the sound of it, they weren't happy about being left behind. Heaving the crossbar to the ground, Petro pushed the doors open and allowed the party to enter.

"How many we got?" asked Gaspard.

Kai scanned the stables, spotting over a dozen wirochs in various states of distress. All of them flailed in their pens, their beaks cutting through the air like brightly colored sickles. Doing a quick mental tally, he answered, "Looks like sixteen. Alright, crew, pick a bird and saddle up! We'll try to run those bastards down before they can reach the Crest. Petro, whichever ones are left, open the pens and cut them loose. I reckon they'll follow the villagers out of town."

"You got it, Kai," Petro said.

The party ran towards the tack closet and grabbed the essentials: saddles, stirrups, and bridles. Kai also grabbed a large sack of dried berries and fruit from the feed station before filling several pouches and handing them to every rider. Splitting up, they each chose a wiroch and, with Petro's help, got them prepped to ride.

Heavy footsteps reverberated through the stables. Kai turned to see Dekel and Montagru rushing their way.

"What in Finyt are you two doing here?" asked Kai. "You should be on the *Senberg* securing the supplies."

Montagru dropped to his knees and prostrated himself in front of Kai, to the apothecary's shock. "It's my nephew, sir. He's still locked up in the gaol. I know Yasso made a mess of things, but he's my brother's only son. I can't leave him here to die!"

"I told the damned fool we didn't have time to go after the boy, but he don't listen to me," explained Dekel. The engineer's eyes simmered with frustration as he watched Montagru plead for the party to save his nephew.

His lips curling into a frown, Kai mulled over his options. The gaol was on the southern edge of the village. He understood Montagru's plight, and regardless of Yasso's allegiances, Kai liked the older deckhand. The problem was that retrieving the traitor would take up valuable time they could use chasing down Hakan.

"Kai, we don't have time to get Yasso *and* catch up to the enemy," Teos said.

"We'll take care of it," offered Petro as he opened the pens for the remaining wirochs. He grabbed a pair and tied them to a post, giving him freedom to rest saddles on their backs. "Gaspard and I can take these two to the gaol and grab the nephew before heading back to lead the retreat.

We can stick him in your ship's brig until we're ready to hand him to the authorities. You lot get out there and stop those bastards."

Nodding to the older Hunters, Kai ordered the party to prepare themselves. It didn't take long for all to be mounted and riding out. The wirochs not being used burst through the doors with indignant squawks. Petro rode up from behind and swatted the lead bird on its flank, sending it scampering into the village. The others were quick to follow. The commander grinned at the party and wished them luck before leading his group south.

"We best be on our way," Lucretia said. "Who knows how far ahead those two have gotten since their escape."

"Right, then," said Kai as their mounts cantered towards the eastern river, "spread out but stay in line of sight. Things might get a little tight once we reach the forest, but it's nothing we haven't done before. Keep your eyes and ears open. We don't know what traps the enemy may have left for us."

The forest canopy grew the closer they got to the village edge. A pile of stone rubble, the shattered remains of the bridge, lay as a reminder of what awaited them on the other side. The river itself was perhaps thirty yards wide and flowed at a steady, gurgling pace. A line of trees stood along the opposite bank, surrounding a single winding road leading from the end of the broken bridge into the woods.

"How will we get across?" Ione asked, eyeing the river with hesitation.

"The river on this side is certainly wide, but it's not as deep as the western fork. We can walk across with no trouble. Watch," Kai said. Spurring his wiroch forward, he coaxed the bird to step into the water. To the others' visible relief, even after ten yards, the water only rose to the soles of Kai's boots. "See? We'll be fine."

His eyes met Maple's, and the merchant took a deep breath before urging her mount to follow. Her wiroch trotted into the water without hesitation, its broad feet splashing water everywhere. Maple smiled and beckoned the others forward.

With Orelia at the front, the rest of the party crossed the river at a steady pace. Kai let his wiroch rest once he made it across. Reaching into his pouch, he retrieved a handful of dried berries and allowed the bird to snap them up.

Once everyone had safely crossed, Lucretia studied a map she procured from Petro. Furrowing her eyes, she cast an uneasy glance towards the main road while pointing at a rough path to the left. "It seems our best bet is to cut through there. The main road will take us too far south of Tapimor's Crest."

"She's right," Kai added. "We've got a lot of ground to cover and not much time. Stay sharp, and we'll try to get some short rest breaks along the way. Let's go!"

Sharing a nod, the seven friends rode into the brush. The mossy scent of the forest filled Kai's nostrils, giving him a sense of calm. The trees flew past in brown and white blurs as his wiroch ran forward. More than once, he needed to duck his head down to avoid a low-hanging branch. Any sense of time felt distorted the longer they rode on; Kai had no idea how long it had been since they left Havenfall, and the treetops made it impossible to check the sun's position. So instead, they kept going, hoping to spot a glimpse of their quarry.

A soothing trill reached Kai's ears. Looking to the side, he spotted Maple vocalizing a gentle melody. The sound of her voice brought a beaming smile to his lips. After taking a quick swig from her canteen, she flashed him a grin and began singing in earnest in her native Aerian. Everyone listened as her song filled the air. The sound reverberated throughout the forest, creating an echo among the trees.

"Not that I am unappreciative of the lovely song, but should we not be quieter? What if the enemy hears us?" asked Lucretia.

"Let her sing," Orelia responded. "I think we could use some perking up. Besides, with how her voice is echoing, I doubt anyone would be able to tell our exact location."

A calming aura settled over the party. Kai allowed himself to close his eyes and let his wiroch take the lead while he focused on Maple's voice. Thoughts of her singing back in Grantide during the festival deepened his smile. No matter how bad things got, he appreciated the merchant's innate skill at calming others. She told him once that he had a soothing presence, but he felt she unequivocally outclassed him there.

"How much longer until we get there?" asked Morgan.

"We should be nearing the base," Kai answered, opening his eyes and scanning the area. The entire forest was now cloaked in the shadow of Tapimor's Crest looming overhead. "I'm not sure how we'll be able to sneak up there without alerting the enemy to our presence, though. The path is easy to spot from the plateau, and I'd wager anything they have scouts keeping an eye on it."

The blast of a horn shattered the surrounding quiet, sending the party's wirochs into a brief panic. A few tugs on the reins kept them from sprinting back towards the village, though Kai's gaze swept over the trees in search of the one responsible.

"Who's there?" he called out. "Show yourself!"

"That you, Gravebane?" a familiar voice responded. Kai's eyes shone with relief when a contingent of Royalist sailors emerged from the bushes, led by Admiral Larimanz. The Wasini officer's uniform was covered in leaves as he approached the party. His men were alert, their flintlocks primed and ready as they spread out through the trees.

"Waveweaver!" Kai exclaimed. Riding forward, he reached down and clasped Larimanz's hand in a firm handshake. "Good to see you again, my friend."

"The feeling is mutual, Gravebane. What are you lot doing out here? I assume you know the Libbies are in the area."

"We are more than aware, Admiral," Lucretia said with a deadpan expression. "In fact, we are trying to determine the best way to get to them."

"Wait, you know where they are? We've scoured the entire forest for them! Where are they hiding out?"

In unison, the party all raised their hands and pointed towards the top of Tapimor's Crest. Larimanz gazed up and swore when he spotted the tiny figures moving along the plateau's edge.

"You must be joking," he grumbled. "No wonder we couldn't find the bastards. Wait, they can't *all* be up there, right? That's impossible, given their numbers."

"In your defense, Waveweaver," Kai chuckled, "not many people think to look up. As for how many are up there, we have no idea. I reckon they probably have a few hundred at most. The rest are probably hidden nearby."

"Fair point, but now I feel like a damned fool. Wherever they are, though, they found a bloody good hiding place. We figured out they were using the river to cover their tracks. They could be anywhere within a day's ride along the bank."

A coarse voice rang out from near the cliff face, "You always *were* a damned fool, Larimanz. But maybe we can fix that today." All eyes spun towards the cliff to see Cairn slithering out from behind a veil of ivy climbing up the rocky crags.

"Father!" Larimanz gasped. He dropped his flintlock in surprise, though he was quick to retrieve it when Cairn lashed out, smacking him behind the head with his tail. "What in Finyt are you doing here? Is the den in danger from those bastards?"

"No, you durned brat, everyone is fine! I doubt those morons have any idea we're even there. Of course, this'll work in our favor for getting rid of them."

"How so?" Teos wondered. "We can't march up the path without being spotted."

Cairn gave the group a sly smirk, before beckoning everyone to follow him. He led the group to the cliff face and gestured to the ivy. "Only a simpleton would believe there's only one path to the top of the Crest. Look here." He grabbed the edge of the ivy and pulled it aside, revealing an opening in the rock that led deeper.

The party each sent a flat stare towards the elderly Wasini. "I shouldn't be surprised by this," Kai said, "but I still feel silly for never realizing this was here. I can't count how often I tramped up that path to the top of the Crest as a boy."

"Our den prefers to be left alone, so don't feel too bad. Only a few of the senior Hunters know about this path and exactly how many of us are here. If it weren't for those Libbies causing such a fuss, we wouldn't be doing this, but we'd rather have those fools off our plateau sooner rather than later. I've got several scouts searching the forest from top to bottom. We'll find the rest of 'em, one way or another."

"How many do you reckon we can fit into these caverns?"

"Enough to send the ones up there into a panic when they realize what's happening." Cairn turned and gave Larimanz a grin. "Grab a company of your best men, son. We're gonna pay our unexpected guests a visit they'll never forget."

Chapter XXX

Not for the first time, Kai was thankful for the sparkstone he kept tucked within his satchel. With it, the party had plenty of torches available to light their way as they followed Cairn through the caverns of Tapimor's Crest. Larimanz slithered alongside them, followed by two hundred of his most skilled sailors. The cave was wide enough to allow them to advance in lines of ten with adequate shoulder room.

Aromatic tika moss grew all over the uneven cavern walls, filling the air with its scent. The sight reminded Kai of the underground spring in Glimmerdale, sending an uneasy shiver through his spine. Drops of water from the ceiling dripped into puddles along the floor, forming a soothing tune alongside the crackling torches.

The craggy surface of the walls created shimmering patterns of light and shadow as the group began climbing a spiraling slope with numerous footholds dug into it. Kai allowed Maple and Orelia to each grasp one of his tails as they ascended the pathway together.

"Cairn," Maple spoke as they reached a new section of flat ground. "This might be a silly question, but why are there footholds dug into the slope? Didn't you say your den prefers to be left alone? It's almost like those were made deliberately."

"Heh, I was wondering if any of you would catch onto that," the old Wasini chuckled. "For official reasons, we dug those in for the rare times when the reigning Grand Duke or Duchess visits. After a while, we realized they're also handy for merchants interested in selling their wares here. We've made more than a few nifty deals with merchants all over the province by offering a way to reach us without having to use the outside path."

"That makes sense. I reckon the hidden path comes in handy when the weather turns foul."

"Indeed it does. Gets us on a nice discount on certain goods too, which we won't complain about."

Maple did her best to stifle her giggles, though Kai was happy to see her smile returning in full force. Looking around, he noticed the others all with various expressions on their faces. Orelia was gazing about with eyes full of wonder, her staff held limply in her other hand. Ione's eyes were darting about the cavern as she kept her dagger close. Morgan looked relaxed, a wide grin on his face and a finger sliding up and down the edge of his blade's scabbard. Lucretia's face was settled into the focused, intense gaze he was so familiar with. Teos remained vigilant, his eyes scanning everywhere with his halberd kept in a loose but prepared grip.

"Admiral," Orelia spoke up, drawing Larimanz's attention to her. "Do you think the rest of your fleet will be prepared to handle the enemy if the ones up here come barreling down the Crest all at once?"

"They'll have to be. This is our best chance to end this war. If we can deal a big enough blow to the Libbies in this fight, they'll be so demoralized the rest of the Navy can follow along and clean up the remains. They may outnumber us now, but I reckon that'll change real soon."

The group remained quiet as they continued their upwards march. The higher they climbed, the more Wasini who slinked from within alcoves hidden in the shadows to join them. Many were bedecked in armor and bearing weapons ranging from flintlocks to war hammers. Others joined the group while carrying ladders made from thick planks of wood. In the crevices, Kai could see groups of children watching with apprehension and waving farewell to the adults assimilating into the small legion.

Kai wondered if this *could* be the final battle of the war. He liked Larimanz's optimism about their chances, but his tails were coiling in anticipation, and there was a strange feeling in his gut that they were missing something.

After what felt like forever, Cairn brought the group to a halt. The Wasini rapped their tails on the ground in a steady beat, causing the sailors to glance around in confusion. The ones carrying the ramps began setting them down near specific areas of the room. Cairn smirked and pointed towards the ceiling.

Raising his torch, Kai noted dozens of circular cracks in the rock above, each roughly wide enough for a grown man. Almost like...

"They're openings. The stones are loose enough to lift them up like doors."

Cairn's toothy grin gleamed in the torchlight. "Exactly. The plateau is covered in these escape hatches we built for emergencies. You can't even tell they're there on the other side."

"Why put your emergency exits near the top?" Lucretia asked. "Would it not trap you on the plateau the same way the Liberators are now?"

"Were they anyone but Wasini, you'd be right, lass," Morgan answered. "Except Wasini ain't normal, even among faumen. Their tails let them scale cliffs and other surfaces the other tribes couldn't even attempt. I used to remember watching my grandpap do it when I was a kid. The old lunatic would slither over the beach cliffs more easily than a mountain goat."

"Ah, I get it," Orelia continued, "so the Wasini can escape to the plateau, then slide down the cliffside while their pursuers would have to use the caverns or the narrow path going down the south side of the Crest."

Ione raised a hesitant hand. "How will we lift those doors, though? The Liberators are standing right on top of them."

"Never said anything about lifting them *up* now, did we?"

A tremor went down Kai's spine at the morbid glee in Cairn's voice. "You're going to drop the hatches from underneath them," he guessed.

"Damn straight. We've got more than enough blackpowder to cave in the entire center of the plateau. These ladders will let you get up top to deal with the cannon. There should still be plenty of room along the edges once we blow the floor out from under their legs. We'll handle the Libbies who fall down here. Son, where are the rest of your men? I know you aren't foolish enough to come here with just one fleet."

"There are two others approaching as we speak. The Fourth Southern Fleet is traveling north along the river from Everstill, and the Sixth Northern is approaching from the northeast. If we're lucky, one of them will find the main body of the Libbies' army before they can attack the village."

"I doubt they'll charge into Havenfall," Morgan piped up. "They've got their cannon aimed right at it. I doubt even they're crazy enough to risk so many of their men against a weapon that powerful."

"What makes you so sure?" Cairn pressed.

The sellsword gave Cairn a solemn frown. "After the drubbing they got at Faith Hollow, they'll want to fight defensively. Able-bodied men are plentiful right now, but war has a nasty habit of changing that. Hakan's entire plan centers on using the Libbies to take out the Grand Duchess, so he'll want them to walk out of this with enough men to finish the job he's grooming them for."

A tremor of fear shot through Kai's tails, causing them to coil into a corkscrew around Maple's arm. "Bloody Nulyma," he murmured.

"What's wrong, 'pothy?"

"Hakan never intended for the Liberators to be the main force in this battle. That's why you can't find them. They're probably hidden somewhere further north, possibly in the forest a day or two's march from here. It's how they were able to get the drop on us so fast. It's way easier to move a few hundred bodies as opposed to eight thousand."

"That makes no bloody sense, Kai," Teos retorted. "Why bring so few men up here just to man one cannon? Hakan can't be that confident in it, can he?"

"He could be if he had a trump waiting in the wings. Remember how Hakan said his wealth gave him the ability to hire people to get the job done right?"

Larimanz's face paled to an unhealthy pallor. "You can't possibly think—"

"Corlati *is* renowned for the skill of its sellsword companies," Morgan admitted. "If he's got the coin to entice them, it's possible Hakan could use hired blades against Havenfall, protecting the main army from heavy losses."

"And if they happen to die off in the cannon's barrage," Lucretia added, "then Hakan saves money by not having to pay them, which he can then use to lure more sellswords into his plan."

Orelia dropped to her knees, staring at the ground in shock. "He did say the other realms of Alezon were about to get involved as well. Corlati wouldn't have a leg to stand on if it were known men waving their banner intervened in another realm's internal conflict. Galstein, Belomas, and Rodekan would all have to react, and might even turn on each other in the process. That monster is using the Federation to draw every realm on the continent into war!"

Growling, Larimanz turned to Cairn. "Father, I need your men to lead us to the nearest openings to send some hawks. We have to warn the Hunters and other fleets they're looking for the wrong enemy. They'll be blindsided!"

The tension was stifling beneath the plateau of Tapimor's Crest. Kai and the others waited with Larimanz and Cairn for word back from the fleets. Kai himself leaned against a far wall with Maple and Orelia snuggled into his sides. Both women were curling the fur of his mane around their fingers, their heads nestled into his shoulders.

The rest of the party was scattered about preparing themselves for the impending battle. Lucretia was close by, her nose once again buried in Cacovis' journal. Morgan and Teos were next to Larimanz, and if Kai was hearing them correctly, discussing strategies for handling the Liberators once their trap was sprung. He couldn't hold back a smile at the sight of Ione near the center with a group of sailors, leading them in fervent prayer.

Most of the sailors were using leather straps to secure rectangular bombs to the hatches. According to Larimanz, the plan was to use the explosives to not only bring most of the ceiling down in one swoop, but also disorient Hakan and the Liberators, leaving them vulnerable. A scout from Cairn's den confirmed not long ago that Vizent was on the plateau, accompanied by Hakan and his entire entourage, with the exception of Adalbard.

"Kai," Maple murmured, drawing his eyes down to hers, "do you think we really have a chance to end this? There's no telling what's waiting up there."

His smile grew, tightening his grip around Maple's shoulders and drawing her close. "Larimanz seems to think so, and he's been doing this a lot longer than us."

"We both know he's not truly confident in this plan. What if something happens? I don't want to think about losing you."

The apothecary's gaze turned to the Wasini admiral, who was slithering in a circle, his eyes furrowed, and a tight fist pressed against his chin. "You do have a point, but it's the best chance we have. And I already came close to losing you once; I refuse to let it happen again. We'll get through this together, like we always have."

"What if that monster is up there as well? Hemlocke is with them, after all."

Kai shook his head. "I like to hope they're keeping Grimghast elsewhere as a trump. If it were on the plateau, I can't imagine those Libbies being quiet about it."

Shrugging, Maple conceded the point and wrapped her arms around Kai. He blushed when her face nuzzled into his mane, taking a deep breath. She giggled. "You really do smell like moss."

Orelia copied the merchant's actions and inhaling deeply. She curled her arm around him, her fingers trailing along his bare stomach. "Sweet Finyt, she's right," the Vesikoi murmured.

"Maybe I should start bathing in flowers and do something about that."

A low, rumbling trill came from Maple's throat while Orelia poked him hard on the nose. "Don't even think about it," they warned in unison.

The sound of quick footfalls echoed through the cavern. Kai glanced up to see a sailor rushing towards Larimanz, a bound scroll clutched in his hands. The admiral accepted the scroll and read it, his eyes darting from one side to the other. Once he reached the end, an audible groan escaped his lips.

"Bad news, folks," he announced. Everyone's eyes spun towards him. "The Fourth Southern has spotted a large army bearing Federation flags but no other insignia. It's possible they're a sellsword company looking to stir up trouble. The Fourth is moving to engage but are still outnumbered. Lieutenant Thorne!" An Aerivolk officer with crystal bars on her epaulets approached Larimanz. "I need you to facilitate contact with the other fleets during the battle. First, contact the Sixth Northern and have them scour the area for the main Liberator force . Then, contact our own men and have some of them move to join the fight against the Corlatians. Understood?"

Thorne saluted and rushed off with parchment and quills, followed by several hawk-bearing sailors. Larimanz faced the rest of his troops and called for order. Cairn moved in front of his son and eyed the crowd with an intense scowl.

"Listen up, you fools. We don't know what's waiting up top. This plan is our best shot at taking down the Libbies' new weapon, and that's your primary mission: Stop that cannon! Use whatever force is necessary, even if we have to use our own bodies to drag it over the cliff. We cannot allow them to fire on Havenfall or the Hunters fleeing the village. Now get to your positions. This war ends today!"

Everyone raised their fists in solidarity, scattering amongst the overhead doors with a quiet determination. Larimanz directed Kai's party to a set of hatches near the corner, pointing at the ceiling.

"From what we've gathered, the cannon is directly above this corner. An unexpected smart move on their part; none of the hatches are beneath the corners. The ones above us will get you closest. Do you have a plan?"

It was Morgan who raised his hand, to the others' surprise. "Assuming the carriage is made of wood, our best option is to set it aflame with torches or a sparkstone. If not, we'll need to redirect the barrel somehow. Of course, that would mean dealing with the firing crew."

"We'll make it work," Orelia stated. Her staff was pressed tight against her chest, and she stared at the party with eyes full of hope. "I believe in every single one of us. Things may look dark, and it's true we're facing an enemy that outnumbers us. But to use Hakan's own words against him, quality will overcome quantity."

"Well put, Orelia. Now, is everyone ready?" said Lucretia as she tucked the journal back into her pack. The seven friends eyed each other in anticipation before each gave a solemn nod. Lucretia smiled and turned to Larimanz. "Give the order, Admiral."

Larimanz regarded the request with quiet dignity, not letting the emotions roiling in his eyes emerge. He turned to his men, all of whom stared back in apprehension. Raising his arm overhead, Larimanz gave a smug grin before snapping his fingers.

The crack of dozens of flintlocks roared through the cavern. Kai felt Maple's hands press down on his ears, causing him to give the merchant a grateful smile. In moments, they were surrounded by the rest of the party as they hugged the wall while the bombs shook Tapimor's Crest down to its base.

Each explosion rattled Kai's bones and pierced his ears like knives. Dust washed over them in waves, forcing the party to cover their mouths. Teos pulled a leather tarp over their bodies as a shield. Terrified screams echoed all around. Kai forced himself to flare his pupils, watching through a small opening in the tarp as scores of Liberators dropped into the cavern. Many near the edges scrambled to grip the plateau, only to fall when the cracked stone gave way under their weight.

"What in the bloody abyss is going on?!" Hakan screamed from above. Kai poked his head out and gazed upwards, spotting the forge master on the far corner, opposite the Shatterstar. His cloak was once again wrapped around his shoulders, its hood pulled up to conceal his ears. Mirabell stood at his side, her mouth hanging open. Vizent wasn't with them; Kai found him next to the Shatterstar, back on his feet and watching his men fall into the cavern with horror on his face. A small group of Liberators surrounded him, close enough to the cannon to avoid being dragged down with their comrades.

The Royalists fell upon the enemy like a swarm while the Wasini began propping the ladders against the edges of the collapsed plateau. The sounds of battle soon filled the air. Men and women alike cried in pain as flintlocks roared and blades sang, rending flesh everywhere. Cairn's den used their trunk-like tails to bat the Liberators around while they focused on tying the ladders to stakes to hold them in place. Larimanz was in the thick of battle, as was Cairn, their swords cutting enemies down with each swing.

Explosions rocked the cavern as a thin, inky mist spread through the air. Various strangled cries echoed above the din, accompanied by the sight of numerous men on both sides collapsing to the ground as the mist surrounded them.

Kai couldn't hold back a grimace. The scent coming from the mist was unmistakable. "Watch yourselves! They're carrying stonehood bombs!" he called out to the Royalists, many of whom began backing away from the cloud of pollen. Several tried clambering up the ladders on the opposite side, only to be killed when several bombs soared through the air and blew the fleeing sailors apart.

As more bodies collapsed amid the chaos, the iron tang of blood stung Kai's nostrils, and the sharp clang of steel blades stabbed his ears. He detected movement from above and watched as Vizent peered over the edge, their eyes meeting.

The general's face morphed into a vicious snarl. "You!" he growled.

Drawing his mace, Kai licked his lips and nodded. This was it. He signaled for the others to follow and threw the tarp aside, charging up a ladder before the Liberators could spot them and retaliate. All the while, Vizent barked orders for his men to load the Shatterstar.

Collapsing the plateau left a jagged edge roughly six yards wide, though the corners were seven yards square. This gave the Liberators ample space for the Shatterstar, which stood at five yards wide and six tall with a barrel eight yards long extending past the edge of the plateau. Half the men bolted behind Vizent, who advanced on the party with the rest at his side and hate blazing in his eyes.

"Take them down!" shouted Kai. Teos led the attack as everyone met the enemy charge head on. Several men were sent flying into the cavern below when Teos swung his halberd in a wide arc, sweeping them aside with little effort.

His gaze flickered to Hakan and Mirabell, who stayed back and observed from a distance. Kai hissed, certain their plan was to let the Liberators wear them out first.

A flash of movement on the farthest corner to the right had Kai spinning towards it. A curse flew from his lips when he spotted Obram and Hemlocke approaching from their rear. Kai noticed the Aerivolk's eyes filled with confusion and anger when he spotted Maple. He scanned the area but gratefully saw no sign of Grimghast.

If the Wind Saints were smiling on them at all, it would stay that way.

To his relief, he spotted Agosti down in the cavern, pinned against the wall by three sailors. What disturbed him was that the former river pirate was holding his own. Using the wall to protect his back, he blocked their attacks and countered with swings that severed limbs and spilled blood.

Morgan fell back to join Kai as Obram and Hemlocke bore down on them, skidding to a stop several yards away. Kai sent the sellsword a relieved grin.

The men with Vizent pried open a nearby crate, four of them grabbing the corners of a cloth lining. The others used ladders to load the Shatterstar's muzzle with a massive powder cartridge and wad. They lifted a sizable ball from the crate and hauled it towards the cannon at a sedate pace; an act which left Kai blinking in confusion.

What are they doing, he wondered, *they're treating that cannonball as if it'll explode in their hands.* It was when they passed through a sunbeam that Kai saw it: the ball was exuding a glittering lilac sparkle. Tiny pinpricks of purple dotted the missile's entire surface. The blood drained from his face. Now he understood why they were so careful with their payload.

It more than likely *would* explode if they were careless enough to drop it.

"Don't let them fire that thing!" Kai roared. The others looked at him in worry. "The cannonball is made out of those crystals from the Guaca mine!" Kai's friends paled just as quickly as he did, their eyes locking onto the cannonball.

An eerie laugh rang over the tumult below. Everyone on the edge turned to Hakan, who cackled with a maniacal gleam in his eyes.

"Well this is surprising. I wasn't aware you fools had encountered lekrite before."

Chapter XXXI

"Lekrite?" asked Kai. He stared at Hakan in shock, wondering how the older Norzen acquired the explosive crystals. Around him the party was dispatching the last of the attacking Liberators. "Is that what that damned rock is called? You have no idea how dangerous it is!"

"Oh I'm well acquainted with the dangers of lekrite. This entire continent has seen the devastation it's capable of firsthand."

Lucretia speared a Liberator through the chest with her rapier, slamming her boot into his gut and sending his corpse into the ongoing battle below. Turning to Hakan, she brushed her frazzled ponytail away from her eyes. "What are you talking about? Those mines have been abandoned for almost a century."

"How do you think Cacovis brought about the Desolation?" retorted Hakan, a dangerous glint in his eye.

"Wait, but then..."

"Indeed," Hakan answered, "the southern region of the Everstill Mountains, where the Desolation occurred, contained one of the biggest veins of lekrite in all Nixtral. It's said the reason so much of it formed there is because the area lies within a nexus point of the Origin ley lines beneath Nixtral's surface."

He gesticulated with his arms as he paced back and forth, reminding Kai of a priest delivering a favored sermon. Even Hemlocke and Obram stood transfixed, their attention focused on the forge master while the battle raged below them. Duarte regarded his master with silent reverence, watching the man pontificate with a half-lidded stare.

"Lekrite is dense in the magical energy of Origin, which is why it reacts so violently. It took some experimenting, and losing quite a few useless minions, but I discovered a way to process lekrite dust without losing the reactivity. That's how I could craft these special cannonballs. The wooden core is filled with enough dust to level a small mountain."

Orelia tightened her grip on her staff, eyeing Hakan with a worried expression. "If what you say is true, and lekrite was what caused the Desolation, then why go to the trouble of using it yourself? It sounds like a weapon that can pose as much a danger to yourself as your enemies."

"You may be surprised to hear this, but I consider myself an admirer of poetry." Everyone's eyes rose in confusion, even those of his allies. "My primary interest lies in the classics of pre-Rebirth Rodekan. The best poems in my mind are those of stories culminating in justice being served through ironic methods, which was often how the Empire disciplined criminals in those days."

"What does that have to do with anything?" Ione asked.

"Simple, you stupid girl." A heavy rumble echoed from Kai's chest as Maple embraced the crestfallen tavern maid. "Cacovis destroyed my ancestor's dreams using lekrite as her medium of choice. Therefore, it's only appropriate I wipe out her descendants and their homes via the same medium."

The party erupted into a furor. They raised their weapons and stood ready as Hakan and Mirabell advanced, with Duarte following close behind. Ione, Teos, and Orelia charged to meet them, with Lucretia yelling a challenge to Duarte. The scholar and monk faced each other, separate from the rest, saying nothing but raising their weapons in an solemn salute before beginning their fight.

Vizent turned and rushed for the Shatterstar, shouting orders to his soldiers.

"Be careful," warned Kai. "They've had time to rest since we last saw them, so stay vigilant." He and Morgan shared a grim stare before facing Hemlocke and Obram. "Morgan and I will deal with these two. The rest of you handle the others."

Maple cast a worried glance at Kai. "Are you sure you two will be alright?"

The apothecary answered with a confident smirk. "We'll be fine. Besides, we've got bones to settle with these bastards."

The others grimaced but nodded and braced themselves as Hakan led the enemy charge. Kai winced as the metallic clang of weapons meeting bit into his ears again, louder than ever. He felt the beginnings of a Frenzy Haze fester in his belly when his eyes met Hemlocke's. The other man twirled an iron-plated quarterstaff as tall as he was in his right hand. Both ends of the weapon were littered with small nails affixed to its metal covering.

"I don't know how you managed to heal that scruffy buzzard of yours," the white-feathered Aerivolk hissed, "but this time I'll make damn sure you watch her die!"

"You're welcome to try. Still, you want to know something, Hemlocke?" replied Kai, a cocky grin splitting his face in two. "I've met quite a few pricks in my life, but you're the first one to prove themselves a whole fucking cactus!" Despite the outward confidence, Kai sensed the Haze threatening to overtake him. He bit his tongue hard enough to draw blood, using thoughts of Maple and Orelia to keep himself grounded.

Hemlocke scowled, surging towards Kai with a bellow and aiming a swing at his temple. Kai knocked it aside but stepped back when a nail broke off, flying towards his face and slicing a tiny cut on his cheek.

The apothecary rolled his shoulders, trying to shake off the prickling sensation dancing through his arms. While the other Aerivolk was shorter than Maple, it seemed the emberona tonic gave Hemlocke a noticeable strength boost. If he hadn't blocked it, Kai was certain that blow would have left him unconscious. The two circled each other with weapons held out in front, searching for an opening. Not far away, Kai heard Morgan's heaving breaths as he clashed with Obram.

"You talk big for a weakling," Hemlocke goaded. Kai was more than willing to let the traitor prattle on; every second they talked gave him a chance to catch his breath and think. Reaching into his satchel, Kai hoped to find something he could use against Hemlocke. He cursed at having used the last of his cappara powder on Duarte back in Runegard. Instead, he felt the familiar texture of leaves, nuts, and seeds in one of the pockets. His eyes widened for a moment.

Wait...

Pinching something between his fingers, Kai ascertained what he grabbed and gave a short huff. He tightened his right hand into a fist, the nails digging deep into his palm. A drop of blood escaped from between his fingers, staining the dirt red.

He regarded Hemlocke with a look of pity. "You say I'm a weakling, Hemlocke, but you know nothing of what true strength is," said Kai as the two circled each other like predators. "Besides, you're the one hiding behind your damned monster. Where *is* Grimghast, anyway? I never would've guessed you'd let it wander too far."

"Wouldn't you like to know?" he replied with a cocky smirk. "And don't you dare talk to me about true strength; I lived in constant pain for 25 years! Whether it was my own body or my pissant of a father, all I've known in life is pain. Compared to me, you lived on a cushion, never wanting for anything. I've learned knowledge and power are the only things worth having in life, because they're the only things people listen to. We faumen know more than anyone how brutal the world is."

"I know more about pain and suffering than you think. It took the people of Havenfall years to accept me, and even now not all of them do. I was bullied and attacked by my schoolmates growing up and told I was worth less than dirt. I didn't have any friends until my adoptive sister was old enough to walk and understand what was going on. I may not know all of your physical pain, but living a life almost completely alone is just as painful to the mind."

Hemlocke scoffed, spinning his staff as he lunged forward and tried thrusting it into the apothecary's gut. Kai batted the attack aside, and saw Obram pressing Morgan back with persistent attacks, not giving the mixblood a chance to counter. He chanced a quick glance to see the others holding off Hakan's group, though they also seemed locked in a stalemate.

Thinking quick, Kai altered his path, allowing Hemlocke to push him towards the other two. Once he was close enough, Kai whistled to grab Morgan's attention.

"What do ya want, 'pothy?" Morgan growled. "I'm a bit busy, if ya can't tell!"

"I can see," Kai whispered, blocking another bone rattling hit from Hemlocke. He had to use both hands to maintain his grip on his mace. "Want to trade?"

Kai grinned when Morgan cast a baffled look at him before forming a grin himself. "Yeah, sounds like a plan."

"I don't know what you idiots are whispering about," Obram taunted as he hammered Morgan's sword with a downward slash, "but I doubt it'll save you."

"We'll see about that, won't we?" grumbled Morgan. "Now, 'pothy!"

Kai ducked underneath Hemlocke's jab towards his face and watched as it struck Morgan's neck, sliding off the sellsword's scales. Obram blinked when his sword pierced the ground when Morgan darted left. The two friends spun around each other and lashed out at their confused opponents.

In an instant, Hemlocke was knocked back as Morgan aimed an upward strike at his staff and sent it airborne. The Aerivolk's eyes followed his weapon, leaving him open to the devastating hook Morgan smashed into his cheek. The staff clattered to the ground next to him. Emitting a growling trill, Hemlocke scooped up his weapon and charged again.

Using the momentum of his spin, Kai gripped his mace in both hands and landed a heavy blow to Obram's exposed thigh. The Risbado sellsword roared in pain, jerking his sword from the dirt. Bracing himself, Kai switched to a one-handed stance and met Obram's wild attack, batting it aside. Twirling the mace like a baton, Kai pressed forward with quick, light swings to keep Obram off balance. Seeing the rage building in the sellsword's eyes, Kai took a step back.

His grin grew when Obram rushed forward, thrusting his blade at Kai's face like a rapier. Kai dodged to the side and swept his opponent's feet from underneath him. The sellsword hit the dirt with a loud groan. Kai dropped his mace and grabbed the Risbado by his bushy tail. Ignoring his pained screams, Kai spun Obram in a circle before hurling him towards Hemlocke.

"Morgan, duck!"

To Kai's relief, Morgan didn't ask questions and dropped to his belly at once, allowing Obram to fly overhead and collide with Hemlocke. Both men were left sprawled in a pile though Hemlocke raised a knee, nailing Obram in the gut.

"Get off me, you furry fuck!" he shouted.

Obram rolled off with a fiery scowl, muttering something about turning the Aerivolk into a dinner roast.

Staggering to his feet, Hemlocke rolled his eyes. "I'm amazed you know anything about cooking. I thought all you were good for was eating our rations. Go help the master, I'll take care of this."

Kai saw the two casting heated glares at each other and wondered if they would come to blows, but Obram ran towards the others with a huff. Jerking his thumb, Kai gestured for Morgan to follow.

Silently, the two shared a nod as Morgan rushed after Obram, shouting a warning to the rest of the party. Hemlocke sneered and emitted a cackling trill that unnerved Kai. In all the time Kai had known Hemlocke, he still wasn't used to hearing such a malevolent sound from the other man.

"You really think you can defeat me without your friend," the Aerivolk jeered, "or have I not beaten the reality into your skull enough?"

"Don't get too cocky. I still owe you double for what you did to Maple."

"Your stupid girl jumped into my knife on her own. But since you seem to be so attached to her, I'll get even more pleasure out of gutting her before your eyes. I can't wait to hear those delicious screams as the life leaves her eyes."

The veins of Kai's right arm pulsed as an odd sensation wriggled beneath his skin from hand to elbow. His eyes flashed, a silvery glint mixing with the stormy grey. "You'd best make peace with whatever god you kneel to, because I'm going to kill you before you even think of touching her again."

Maple evaded another of Mirabell's kunai as it clipped the edge of her hair, firing an arrow in retaliation. Her chest heaved with every dodge, but she fought the burning sensation in her lungs. She knew her body was still recovering, but she refused to let the others fight this battle without her. Kai especially.

I'm not letting him die before Orelia and I can marry him, she thought. *Bloody Nulyma, we haven't even* kissed *yet!*

A ping rang out when Ione deflected another of the assassin's blades with her pan. Mirabell growled and rushed forward, plucking the spinning kunai from midair with practiced ease. She swiped at Maple, who raised her hand on instinct and cried out when the blade bit into her palm. Snatching her hand back and cradling it to her chest, she felt the blood run through her fingers in rivulets.

Matching Ione's gaze, they nodded and spread out, hoping to make it harder for the woman to attack them at the same time.

Reaching for her quiver, Maple bit back a curse; she was out of arrows. The pain in her hand flared when the fingers curled in aggravation. Her eyes twitched to where Lucretia was doing her best to evade Duarte's axe while countering with short jabs to his exposed arms. Nearby, Teos and Orelia were having their own difficulties with Hakan, who was proving stronger than his advanced age suggested.

She was grateful that Vizent opted to assist his troops rather than join the fighting himself; there's no telling how much trouble the former Hunter would give them on top of everyone else. Seeing him drop the lekrite cannonball, wrapped in its lining, into the Shatterstar sent a chill down her spine. The shivering intensified when she saw him lowering the barrel at an angle, pointing it towards Havenfall. They needed to act fast.

"Ione, how confident are you in holding her off on your own?" Maple asked. With a wince, Ione admitted that she'd likely be overpowered in short order. "Damn. We have to do something about the cannon; they're almost ready."

A familiar bellow came from behind, prompting the two women to turn and see Obram barreling towards Ione with Morgan rushing to catch up. Rather than wait for the crazed Risbado to attack, Maple took off running towards Ione and shouted for her to duck. The tavern maid did so, yelping in fright when Maple leapt into a glide, clutching her by the shoulders and carrying her towards Mirabell.

The assassin froze at the strange tactic. Struggling against Ione's flailing arms, Maple shouted.

"Lift your feet!"

She was thankful the command got through to Ione, who raised both legs parallel to the ground in time for her boots to crash into Mirabell's chest. Ignoring the maid's muffled groans, Maple let go of her friend's shoulders and came to a running stop after several yards. A giggle escaped her lips when she saw Ione sitting on top of the frustrated Mirabell, pointing the tip of her dagger at the other woman's breast.

"Get back here!" roared Obram.

"Forget them, Obram," Hakan commanded. He and Teos were locked together by their weapons, the Soltauri using his heavier body to press the forge master to his knees. "Mirabell can handle herself. You know the plan. Don't let your target escape!"

The sellsword sputtered angrily before cutting a sharp turn and bolting for the Shatterstar, to Maple's confusion. Morgan moved to dash after his former commander, but the sound of Ione being tossed off Mirabell had him veer back to save her from being stabbed by the irate assassin. The clangs and screams from the battle below were dwindling compared to the start. Maple gazed down into the cavern and fought back the urge to vomit.

Tens of dozens of corpses littered the ground. Many had weapons protruding from their bodies, and only a few spots of the cavern floor were unstained by blood.

The Royalists seemed to have the upper hand, thanks to Cairn's den, but it was clear they still suffered heavy losses. She was stunned to see Agosti among the enemy soldiers still standing. In fact, the enraged officer looked quite healthy despite being covered in a mixture of blood and dust.

Shaking her head, Maple forced herself to face the Shatterstar, seeing Obram approaching Vizent, who regarded the sellsword with an indignant sneer. Frowning, she skirted around the other battles and snuck closer to where the Liberator general was shouting at Obram, ducking behind one of the few boulders left standing.

"What in the winds are you doing, Obram?"

"I'm only doing what my employer asked me to do. Apologies in advance."

Vizent blinked. "Huh? What in Nulyma—"

Anything else the general wanted to say was cut off when Obram landed a solid punch to his temple. Vizent yelped as he fell on his backside, though from pain or surprise was unclear. Maple gasped when the Shatterstar's firing crew rushed the sellsword, firing their flintlocks. Their aim left much to be desired, though; not one of the bullets found their mark. With a gloating laugh, Obram brandished his sword, hacking the men down. Their bodies soon lay strewn about while Vizent struggled to his feet.

"What are you doing, you idiot!?" Vizent shouted. "How are we supposed to fire the Shatterstar without a crew?"

Obram plucked the sparkstone from the hand of a dead soldier and waved it in front of Vizent's face. "It's not difficult. Even a court fool can light a fuse since you've already done the work of aiming it. I don't know why you're so worried anyway."

"And what exactly do you mean by that?" Vizent asked, his voice cracking.

From her vantage point, Maple felt a tremor of fear at the wicked smile stretched across Obram's lips. Her attention shifted when an audible thump sounded next to her.

Drops of sweat beaded down Lucretia's cheek as she avoided another swing from Duarte's axe. A quick jab to the monk's shoulder skidded off his leather cuirass. She took several steps back, eyeing her former friend with hesitance.

"I do not understand," she said, taking the brief respite to wipe the sweat from her face. "Why are you working for a monster like Hakan? The Duarte I knew would never submit to someone so vile!"

"That's just it, Lu," he replied, pointing the head of his axe towards Lucretia, "the Duarte you knew is gone. I don't know what you know of the auction houses in Corlati, but it was a horrible place. I would argue it's worse than what the Windbringer priests say about Nulyma. Disease was rampant in the barracks, and many were beaten by other slaves for their own meager rations of food and water. Each day was marked by beatings and starvation to break our spirit, and that was just for the men. The women received much worse; I'm sure you can imagine the gruesome details.

"I was only there for two moons before Master purchased me and I swore to do everything I could to avoid ever returning to the overseers. Master was kind enough to have me sent to a Cadist temple in the Empire to undergo full ordination training, as none of the temples in Corlati would accept faumen. After all the tribes have been through, perhaps it's time the humans learn what it's like to wear our boots for a change. Besides, I have done killed too many in Master's name to turn back now."

In one corner of her mind, Lucretia sympathized with Duarte. She heard many stories of how slaves were treated in the Federation, none of which were flattering. Disregarding her years-long dislike of the Norzen, the scholar felt no ill will towards the other tribes and often questioned how the Corlatians could treat them so reprehensibly.

Looking back, a sense of nausea settled in Lucretia's stomach when she considered the idea of subjecting the Norzen to the conditions Duarte just described. An image of Tuvi flashed through her mind, the young girl staring at the party in unrestrained joy. The thought of that sweet smile being forced into the horrors of an auction house threatened to drive her into a retching fit.

"No," she declared, "there has to be a better way. No one deserves to be subjected to such treatment. It is cruel and unnecessary."

"What about the Norzen? I would've thought you'd like them to suffer."

"Perhaps in the past, I would have believed such a thing. Now, though, I have learned and grown. My experiences in this war have forced me to see our world from a different perspective. I shall admit, there is a part of me which still holds onto those feelings of wrath, though the targets of my anger have shifted. I do believe there is still a piece of the Duarte that Ria and I knew from our childhood deep inside you."

Duarte chuffed, denying the statement with a snarl and another swing of his axe. Lucretia rolled underneath it, stabbing her rapier into his exposed elbow. The monk growled and pushed her back with a swing of his arm. She regarded him with a curious expression. Given Kai's description of his own fight with Duarte, Lucretia wondered why she wasn't having more difficulty.

It was when he rumbled towards her that she saw it. A misty haze hidden behind Duarte's eyes.

Stepping back to avoid his next swing, Lucretia murmured to herself, "You are wrong, old friend. Even if you cannot see it within yourself, it is plain as day to me; the old you still lives. I just need to discover a way to free him once more."

Kai flinched as sparks grazed the cut on his eye. He fought to ignore the throbbing pain in his face and right hand, focusing instead on deflecting Hemlocke's staff. The two men edged closer to the Shatterstar thanks to Kai's footwork. Every few moments, he allowed himself a quick glance at how the others were doing. He wondered why Morgan was holding off Mirabell alongside Ione for a scant moment.

Scanning the plateau, he spotted Maple watching Obram and Vizent's confrontation. The sight only brought more questions, most of which Kai couldn't think about with Hemlocke doing his best to smash the apothecary's head open.

"What's the matter, Kai? You seem occupied. Perhaps you'd be doing better if you stopped worrying about your friends. You'll all be in Cacovis' embrace soon enough."

"I already told Duarte this, but I refuse to let a mongrel like you decide when I die!" Bracing himself, Kai held firm against Hemlocke's next downward swing and pushed the weapon aside. Stepping into the Aerivolk's guard, Kai's knee shot up and folded the man in half with a heavy blow to the gut.

Two arms wrapped around him, and Kai felt the wind rush through his fur when Hemlocke lifted and threw him back. Tucking into a ball, Kai rolled along the ground. A gasp at his side told him that he maneuvered himself next to Maple.

"Kai?" she asked. Looking up, he gave her a nervous smile. "Are you hurt, love?"

"No worse than any of you. I'm glad we can fight on even footing with these bastards, but at the same time, we still can't seem to put them down for good."

A dark chuckle resonated from Hemlocke as he bore down on the couple. "How sweet, the lovebirds are together once again. You both make me want to retch."

"You're just jealous no one could love you with that void where your heart's supposed to be," snapped Maple.

Emitting a rumbling trill, Hemlocke hurled several vehement curses at the merchant in their native Aerian. "I've heard enough out of your beak, girl," he hissed. "I'm going to smear your brains all over the rock and make that damnable Norzen watch!"

Kai stood protectively in front of Maple, his stance wide and his bloody right hand clenched in a half fist. "You want her, Hemlocke, you'll have to step over my rotting corpse."

"I can arrange that."

A shout from behind piqued Kai's interest, his gaze shifting to the Shatterstar. Vizent was gesturing at Obram with his sword. The general looked infuriated and ready to stab his ally at the slightest provocation.

"Maple, I don't know what those two are doing, but see if you can distract them while I finish this."

"Be careful, Kai," she replied, giving his arm a comforting squeeze before spinning around.

The distinctive clack of talons on stone warned Kai of Hemlocke's approach. Turning back, he saw the Aerivolk charging, his staff tucked under his arm like a lance and the twin moons rising into the sky behind him. His lilac eyes were locked on Maple's back and burned with hatred, white feathers shining in the sunset. Closing his eyes, Kai focused on the pain in his arm and flexed his fingers, allowing it to spread through the entire hand.

"Maple, behind you!" he heard Orelia shout from nearby. His eyes burst open fully dilated, giving him a sharp view of Hemlocke's movements. Watching the man's arm, Kai saw it thrust forward, the staff aimed at his partner's heart.

Wait for it, Kai thought.

He had to time this just right, or he risked everything. It took all his willpower to keep his eyes focused on Hemlocke's hand, rather than the staff. The glint from the weapon's metal plating was enough of a clue to let him judge its distance.

Just a little closer...

Tightening his grip on the mace, Kai took a deep breath and prepared himself. Every muscle in his body grew tight, coiling in anticipation. Hemlocke was now close enough that Kai saw himself reflected in the man's eyes.

Now!

Launching himself forward, Kai clenched his teeth as the staff's nails tore through the shoulder of his robes. Swinging his mace, Kai batted the weapon aside and knocked the Aerivolk off-balance. With a sly grin, he lunged for Hemlocke with his right hand, matching the other man's gaze and focusing on a specific image in his mind. The pain in his arm exploded, stretching from the fingertips to his shoulder and combined with a slithering sensation that felt wholly unnatural.

Hemlocke's eyes bulged, emitting a gurgling wheeze as he stopped. Kai stared into his enemy's lilac eyes, taking in the unfettered shock as their gazes shifted down.

A woody vine covered in flat, fan-shaped blue flowers wrapped around much of Kai's hand and wrist, bursting from a bloody cut on his palm. Two branches of the vine coiled into a pointed spiral and extended from Kai's palm, piercing through Hemlocke's rib cage like a spear.

Chapter XXXII

"Wh-what the...?" Hemlocke stammered, blood dripping from the edge of his lips. "What did you *do*?" he gasped while staring at the vine in horror. He stumbled backwards, yanking the wood out with a sickening squelch. The traveler dropped to a knee while clamping both hands over the wound, trying to block the gushing blood.

Kai watched as Hemlocke staggered away, his pinion feathers now stained crimson. "I warned you about trying to hurt her," he growled. The treacherous Aerivolk snarled at Kai, swearing revenge before he turned and leapt over the cliff. Kai could only watch him spread his wings open and glide away with blood dripping from his body. It wasn't long before Hemlocke vanished into the trees.

A gasp at his side alerted him to Maple staring open-mouthed at the vines protruding from his hand. "Kai, what did you do to yourself?" she asked. Both hands trembling, she traced the wood with her fingers before giving it a hesitant tug. Kai winced at the sharp pain shooting through his arm when she pulled it.

"It seems I figured out a way to use our connection to Origin; the magic is locked within our blood somehow. I sowed wisteria seeds inside my palm and focused my thoughts on forcing the plant to grow in a spiral. It was a hell of a gamble, but it worked."

A pained shout resonated over the battlefield. Kai and Maple spun to see Vizent wobbling in place with Obram standing in front of him with fists raised, his sword lying abandoned on the ground nearby. Judging from the blood dribbling down the side of the general's face and Obram's knuckles, it was obvious the sellsword had landed a nasty punch. Obram's arm shot forward and grasped Vizent by the throat, lifting him up.

"What in the winds is he doing?" Ione asked. "Aren't they on the same side?"

Mirabell scoffed, prompting the party to turn their stares on her. "General Doulterre has outlived his usefulness, I'm afraid."

From their spot half a dozen yards away, Kai and Maple watched as Obram yanked Vizent's sword away and, to everyone's horror, stabbed the general through the chest with his own weapon.

The defiance in Vizent's eyes continued to flare as he kicked out against Obram's torso, though the blows were weak and ineffective. His eyes sought out Hakan, who only gave a malicious chuckle.

"Don't expect me to help, General. You should've seen this coming from the start, especially after your embarrassing failure at Faith Hollow. Don't worry. Your army will still serve its purpose in the end." Hakan glanced at Obram and smirked, snapping his fingers with a single order. "Finish him."

Obram gave Vizent an eerie grin before pitching him over the cliff towards Kai and Maple, the sword still jutting from his body. The couple watched in horror as Vizent flew out of reach, his eyes locked on theirs.

Acting on instinct, Kai reached out for Vizent's hand, the vine in his arm extending towards him. For a moment, Kai felt a brief spark of hope when Vizent's hand grabbed hold of the wisteria. That hope was replaced by blinding pain when Vizent began his descent, holding onto the vine for dear life. It proved unable to bear Vizent's weight, being torn from Kai's arm in a bloody mass. The apothecary collapsed to the ground with a bloodcurdling howl, cradling his arm and releasing a steady hiss as Maple rummaged through his satchel for bandages.

Glancing at his mangled hand, Kai could only watch as Vizent plummeted screaming to the forest floor, his eyes full of terror. With his mind so focused on the former Hunter, Kai almost missed the infuriated shout rising from behind.

"No!"

Kai twisted to see Agosti standing at the top of a nearby ladder, his eyes wide and fixed on the Norzen. Chest heaving, the hand gripping Agosti's sword trembled as he ran towards Kai emitting a furious bellow.

"You ruddy peltneck bastard," Agosti screamed, raising his sword high. "You murdered the general! I'll kill you!"

Before he could reach Kai and Maple, a flash of silver came from the side as Orelia slammed her staff into Agosti's cheek, knocking the officer back.

"Don't even think about it," Orelia snapped. "Kai, you alright?" Agosti skittered to a stop and assumed a stance, hurling a bevy of expletives at the priestess.

"I doubt I'm getting much use out of my right arm for a while," Kai admitted. Peering over the cliff edge, it felt as though an iron weight had settled in his stomach. Vizent was nowhere to be seen, having vanished among the trees five hundred yards below.

"Any chance he might have survived?" Maple asked.

Kai shook his head. "Not bloody likely. If getting skewered with his own weapon doesn't kill him soon enough, a fall from this height damn sure would."

"Out of my way, fish wench," Agosti spat at Orelia, "I'm going to butcher that peltneck for what he did."

Eyes blazing, the priestess feigned another strike at his head, leading Agosti to raise his arms up before Kai launched a boot into his gut. "Believe what you wish," Orelia warned, "but only a fool would trust these monsters. Their leader isn't what you think he is."

Agosti sneered at the two. "I never said I trusted the bastard, but we share a common enemy and your peltneck has caused me enough grief."

The distinctive crackle of a lit fuse prickled Kai's ears. Clenching his teeth, he spotted Obram holding a sparkstone at the Shatterstar's base. The cannon's fuse spewed multicolored sparks while the sellsword commander braced himself against the carriage.

"*Taen*!" Kai shouted.

Hakan and his crew moved to physically block the rest of the party's frantic charge towards Obram. Blades clashed and cries rang out as everyone made a desperate push to reach the cannon before it could release its deadly payload.

After wrapping Kai's ragged wound, Maple gave him an uneasy smile before grabbing a deserted sword and running to join the fray. Knowing he wouldn't be of much help in his condition, Kai peered into the cavern below and called for Larimanz. The admiral waved in response while slithering up the nearest ladder.

"Gravebane, what in the winds happened to you?"

"I'll explain later. Listen, Waveweaver, you have to help the others. If that cannonball lands, Havenfall and everything around it will be wiped out in a single shot!"

Larimanz spat a curse and threw himself into the fight. Using his tail as a shield, he blocked Mirabell from stabbing Ione through the shoulder, her kunai bouncing off his scales. At the same time, he pulled Lucretia out of the way of Duarte's axe. The ruined plateau was a free-for-all, with each side battering at the other in the hopes of striking a weak point.

Under Obram's watch, the Shatterstar's fuse neared its end. Biting back a hiss, Kai shakily returned to his feet and rushed for the cannon. Maple circled around the crowd to get closer to the Shatterstar, only to leap back to avoid being skewered by Obram. Kai increased his pace, ignoring the throbbing palpitations in his chest.

"I don't think so, chickee." Obram picked his sword back up and stalked towards Maple with a vicious grin on his face. She attempted to swing her own weapon at him, but he knocked it from her hands with a dismissive smack. "Hemlocke's gonna be right pissed at me for taking his kill, but I think it's time one of you bastards died."

Backing away, Maple tripped over a loose stone and tumbled backwards. Kai saw her chest rising from the quick, repeated gasps she was releasing. Obram raised his sword, ready to pierce her heart.

"Stay back!" Maple shrieked. Wrenching her eyes shut, Maple threw her hands up, palms out. To Kai's shock, a bright light erupted from Maple's hands. Obram stumbled back, using his sword to shield his eyes.

This proved to be a mistake when the space in front of Maple rippled, and a visible orb of air erupted from her injured hand. The force sent her flying backwards, crashing into Kai's stomach and leaving them sprawled in a heap. Wrapping his good arm around Maple's waist, he watched the orb slam into Obram. The impact carried the sellsword off the ground and into the Shatterstar's iron-plated carriage with a sonorous boom.

The cannon's barrel shifted, it's trajectory now pointing further north, towards the river fork.

It was then that the fuse ran out, and the Shatterstar exploded in an ear-rupturing crash. The lekrite cannonball shed its protective lining, soaring towards the horizon. The weapon itself was left a ruin, the end of its barrel blown open and curling back like a lily's petals. Smoke rose from the destroyed cannon and the overpowering scent of blackpowder filled the air.

Still reeling from the concussive blast, Kai held his ears down and stumbled away, with only Orelia and Maple's arms keeping him on his feet. He eased his eyes open and watched with trepidation as the missile arced through the air.

Images of his family flashed through Kai's mind. The thought of everyone in Havenfall, torn apart by the eminent explosion, filled him with an icy chill of terror. He desperately wished he could fly, if only to pursue the cannonball and block it with his own body. In his heart, he knew doing so was impossible and could only stare as the vessel of his home's destruction grew smaller with every moment.

Knowing what was coming, he forced his eyes closed and clutched the girls flush against him. Both ears flattened against his scalp as he shouted for the party to brace themselves. A solid mass hit their bodies, carrying the trio down into the cavern. He allowed himself a moment to open his eyes and saw it was Teos who collided with them. In moments, a thud nearby prompted them to look and see Ione and Lucretia on top of

Morgan's prone body; the mixblood used himself as a cushion. Larimanz landed nearby and was bellowing commands for his sailors to flee to the lower caverns.

Each passing second felt like a whole moon. Morgan and the others clambered over, and the party wrapped themselves in the discarded tarp like a protective cocoon near the wall. They ignored the remaining Liberators fleeing up the ladders to escape the Royalists. Larimanz gave the party one last look before following his men.

A hand grabbed hold of Kai's and he looked up to see Ione staring at him. They shared an uneasy smile as Ione uttered a prayer to Luopari pleading for the villagers' safety. With his partners curled against his chest, Kai joined in, offering a prayer of his own.

Then came the explosion.

Visible even through the thick tarp, a blinding flash encompassed the sky above accompanied by a thunderous boom. The party huddled closer together, surrounded by a crowd of corpses. Seconds continued to drag on, when Tapimor's Crest shook. The shockwave hit the plateau with a vengeance, nearly sending everyone to the ground.

Screams rang out when several Liberators found themselves standing too close to the cliff edge when the unforgiving gale hit them, though their cries were muffled by the howling winds. Kai glanced up through an opening and saw men disappearing over the side, careening into the abyss. He felt little sympathy for them, despite knowing they likely had little knowledge of their weapon's true destructive force.

After a while, the sound of skittering debris settled into a tense silence. A whoop of triumph came from Obram, a sound that made Kai's vision hazy. "Well I'll be damned, Hakan," the Risbado exclaimed, "that little cannonball packed a hell of a punch; the whole village is gone, even the sellswords ransacking it and the pack of Royalists trying to stop them!"

A blood-stopping frost settled over the party.

"Indeed. I must confess I overestimated the Shatterstar's ability to withstand its own ignition charge. I probably shouldn't have layered the outside of the cannonball with lekrite powder either. Regardless of the material loss, this is progress. Agosti!"

"What do you want?" the belligerent officer asked. The venom in Agosti's voice suggested he was barely constraining himself from telling the forge master exactly what he wanted to say.

"I'd suggest you gather what's left of the men and take control before the Royalists discover where the rest of your army is hidden. With General Doulterre dead, you are the most experienced and qualified warrior left to lead the Liberation Army."

Even though he couldn't see Agosti, Kai detected the raised eyebrow in his exasperated reply. "Me? I'm quite certain there are lots of higher-ranked officers who could lead the army."

"True, but their performance up till now has been mediocre at best, and none of them have the passion you carry for your cause, nor your drive to succeed. It doesn't hurt that I happen to know of your prior association with Bloodbeard. Besides, this battle showed me just how skilled you are with a blade. Let the other officers know I'm appointing you as the new General, and failure to abide my decision will result in a severe loss of provisions from my forges. My recent attempts to contact the Conclave have gone unanswered, so we must assume they've been compromised. The army needs leadership."

"I appreciate the compliment on my abilities, but I'm curious about something. Why are you putting so much effort into helping us? You know how we feel about your minions' kind. What's in this for you?" Kai blinked, wondering if Hakan was still hidden beneath his cloak, as he doubted Agosti would be so amicable if he knew the forge master's true identity.

Hakan's voice cracked just a bit as he replied, "Let's just say the Grand Duchess and certain others in her court have proven to be personal thorns in my side. Thus, you and I have a common enemy, one who I think you'd be quite happy to be rid of."

"What makes you say that?" The confusion in Agosti's voice was palpable.

"Simple. It isn't common knowledge, but I've discovered the royal family has been hiding a dark secret ever since Livoria's creation. The Ardei family is Norzen, and it always has been. This includes the sow, Fusette."

An enraged scream rose from the Liberator. "What?! The ruddy duchess is a *peltneck*? You're sure about this?"

"I'd be willing to bet my entire fortune on it. I like to think we can maintain a professional and mutually beneficial relationship once your side has usurped the throne."

"As much as I hate to admit it, you have a point. And worse, knowing that wench is a peltneck boils my skin. Bah! Fine, I'll take the job. However, I want you to come with me to deliver the news. I don't trust the other officers to not stab me in the back with everything that's happened."

Kai was surprised when Hakan conceded the point, agreeing to join Agosti. They heard the stomp of Agosti's boots as he barked orders to the surviving Liberators and marched them down the path. Once the main army was gone, a heavy silence kept the party in place, the early evening wind stinging against their wounds.

"I heard you talking to the boy about your past back at the village," Mirabell spoke up with a timid voice. "W-what was your former master like? The one who purchased you?"

"As far as masters go, he was better than most. He wasn't unnecessarily cruel, but he put me to work in ways I'd much rather forget." Kai saw Teos wince and wondered what would cause such a reaction. "It didn't help when his other slaves made it their duty to torment and ridicule me for being forced to do the things I did. This scar on my neck was from one of their more vicious punishments; the result of being slathered in boiling oil. I offered to learn how to work the forges myself as I got older, since it offered a welcome reprieve from the other slaves' vitriol and my 'duties,' as they were. So life passed me by, until the master fell ill shortly after I reached my twentieth year.

"The apothecaries never could determine what was wrong with him. The other slaves were scared, as was I to a measure. The master had no remaining family, or none who laid claim to him, and the illness addled his mind. His encroaching death would mean a return to the trading houses and their brutal overseers for all of us. It didn't take long for me to come up with a rather ingenious plan.

"During one of his less lucid episodes, I convinced him to draw up a will naming a distant nephew named Razarr the sole heir of his forge and fortune. A few fake letters later as proof of correspondence, and he signed the parchment without a single question. Once the will was in place, it was a simple matter of poisoning the master's tea and pinning the blame on the chief butler. The man was known for his pugnacity, so the constables were quick to accept the story and arrest him while I vanished into the mists the same night. Only I returned a few days later disguised as my master's nephew."

"And so you claimed his entire fortune for yourself," Mirabell finished.

"Precisely," said Hakan, chuckling. "So long as I kept the evidence of my heritage hidden, no one knew or suspected the man assuming control of my former master's business was the same Norzen he purchased so many years ago."

"What about the apothecary and his friends?" Obram asked.

"I'd be willing to guess they've fled into the caverns with the other Royalists, likely to assess the destruction." Kai bit back a snort. "We'll have to deal with them later. Despite our victory, we've taken heavy losses, at least in regards to our sellsword allies. I'll have to scrounge some more from the border. Besides, I must confess the fight was more taxing than I thought, and without Hemlocke or his pet, we'd only exhaust ourselves. Once we regroup, *then* we can hunt them down."

"If that's your decision, boss, so be it. Let's get out of here. I just wish I could see the damage up close."

Staying hidden among the shadows, Kai and the others watched as Hakan's group followed the remains of their army towards the path leading down the southern cliff face. They waited with bated breath for what seemed like an eternity. Once an eerie silence had settled over the battlefield, Kai stood and gripped his injured arm. With heavy footsteps, he ambled towards the ramp and began to climb back up to the plateau.

"Kai," Lucretia started.

"Don't try to stop me, Lucretia. Please," he begged. Turning to the party, he knew they could see the raw anguish in his eyes as he fought back tears. "I *need* to see it for myself before we go back."

His body tensed when he felt the gentle touch of two hands on his back.

A soft whisper reached his ears, soothing him. "We understand, love," Maple murmured. She wrapped her wing around him in a tender embrace. "I'm not letting you see it alone."

"None of us are," Orelia added, curling herself under Kai's arm.

More footsteps resounded from behind them before the sensation of additional hands pressed against Kai's spine. He didn't need to turn around to know the rest of his friends were at his side.

"What did I do to deserve you? Any of you?"

"You're our friend," Morgan answered. "And we know damn well you'd do the same for any of us."

"Thanks, everyone."

Without another word, the party marched to the top of the plateau and gazed across the river. Kai's breath hitched when he saw the results of Hakan's weapon.

Havenfall was no more.

Though not as extensive as he imagined it would be, only a crater remained of the proud Hunter village. Only a few scattered buildings on the village's southern side remained standing, though they were extensively damaged. Maple's shocking attack had knocked the cannon's aim off enough to send its payload into the Great Ardei River itself, judging by the crater's epicenter. Even now, the river was rushing to fill the unexpected void left in the explosion's wake. Once it was done, the space that once held Havenfall would be a small lake connecting the Great Ardei to its southernmost branches.

At his best estimate, Kai guessed the crater to be at least three thousand yards in diameter, if not more. He wondered why the damage wasn't more extensive. Hakan had said the cannonball contained enough lekrite to level a mountain, so the crater should've been much larger. Licking his lips, he pulled a spyglass from his satchel and inspected the area.

"Do you see the Hunters?" Orelia asked, her staff shaking in her hands. "Did they escape in time?"

Not wanting to answer until he knew for sure, Kai peered west, then north. He couldn't hold back the relief in his voice when he spotted a mass of people moving north.

"I think they made it. They're northwest of the crater." Everyone released stifled cheers of joy and shared a comforting hug.

"What about the *Senberg*?" Teos added. "They were supposed to be securing the village's supplies on the ship."

Glancing along the river, Kai's mouth dried at not seeing the envoy ship anywhere. A tap on his shoulder brought his attention to Maple, who pointed further south, on the western fork. He looked again before confirming that the *Senberg* was paddling back towards the crater, having fled south rather than north.

After additional inspection, Kai reported seeing the Liberators emerging from a forest well away from where the fighting occurred, fleeing to the northeast. A smaller group of Corlatian sellswords, on the other hand, were running south with a Royalist fleet heading the opposite direction, towards the remains of Havenfall.

Unable to handle the turmoil, Kai dropped to his knees. He was only partially aware of Orelia's arms encircling him.

"We need to catch up with the villagers," Ione declared. Kai noticed the tavern maid clutching at a long cut on her arm. "They're going to need help, and we need to rest and heal up."

"Agreed," Lucretia added. "Once we make a thorough accounting of what happened, then we can report to Lady Fusette. I cannot imagine she will be much pleased with what happened here today."

"No," Kai muttered, "she won't."

Maple pressed her cheek against his and gave a short sigh. "We'll cross that bridge when we get there. Besides, love, we need to have a talk once we make sure everyone else is safe and sound."

Chapter XXXIII

In the aftermath of Havenfall's destruction, Kai was never more thankful for Larimanz. His fellow Exarch, while unable to accompany the party, was willing to provide extra wirochs since theirs fled into the forest after entering Tapimor's Crest. According to Larimanz, eighty percent of the Fourth Southern Fleet had been lost in the explosion, along with a quarter of both the Marine Cavalry and the Sixth Northern who had gone to assist. His plan was to combine the rest of the Royalist forces together and head north with the hope of chasing the Liberators down and whittling away at their numbers.

Bidding the admiral farewell as he led the remains of his sailors to rejoin the Marine Cavalry and pursue their enemy, Kai and the others rode west in search of a way across the river. With Havenfall gone, it was obvious the main bridge across the western fork would be destroyed, and the western branch was significantly deeper than its eastern sibling. Kai muttered a prayer of thanks that night was setting; though the air would carry a sharp chill, the darkness would allow them to traverse the area undetected and hopefully catch up to the villagers.

It took longer than expected, but they found an intact bridge south of the crater. By the time they spotted torches indicating the survivors' camp in a clearing on the river edge, the moons were reaching their peak in the night sky. Given that it was the spring equinox, the moons were layered over one another, looking like an elongated two-toned egg. Gazing towards the water, Kai was relieved to see the *Senberg* docked near the bank as well.

"Oh, thank Finyt! You're all alive," cried Verona as the group emerged from the trees. She and Serafina both waited near the camp's edge, their eyes red and puffy. As soon as Kai dismounted, they were on top of him, pulling him into a tight embrace. Verona pulled back and stared at Kai with shock, her eyes locked on his shredded arm. "What in the winds happened to you?"

"You might not believe me, even if I told you. I'll be fine once I patch myself up. It's good to see you, Ma," Kai replied, doing his best to hug the pair back. He looked around, his eyes furrowing. "Where's Da?"

Verona released a choked sob, tightening her grip on Kai's torn robes. "He...he didn't make it, Kai. I'm sorry."

Several gasps rang out from the party as Kai's face paled. "Didn't make it," he mumbled, "but how? What happened?"

"He and Petro never made it back. The old Aerivolk from your ship was the only one to return after he and the Soltauri went looking for you."

"Dekel? Where is he?"

Serafina pointed towards the center of camp, where multiple fires cast a flickering orange haze over the area. "He and your crew are resting over there."

"Thanks. We'll talk more later, I promise, but I need to hear this myself."

"We know," Verona said, "just don't stay up too long. You lot clearly need sleep." Nodding, Kai let Serafina take the reins of his wiroch and tether it to a nearby tree. The others followed suit before trailing after Kai as he wandered into the center of the camp.

Scanning the area, Kai noted several large groups of tents bundled together in a circle around a central fire. Numerous smaller fires burned nearby with bundles of people surrounding them. For a moment, he wondered if it was safe for them to allow such large fires to burn with the enemy still lurking around. After thinking a few moments, he brushed the concern aside.

Considering what happened to their village, the Hunters would be raring to fight anyone foolish enough to come after them. And with the

Shatterstar destroyed, the enemy wouldn't have a trump on hand to stop them.

It didn't take long to spot Dekel at one of the smaller fires alongside his fire crew and the cabin girls, Kerta and Annika. To his surprise, he didn't see Montagru among them. Taking a deep breath, Kai approached the group, greeting them warmly.

"I was wondering what happened to you," the old engineer grumbled with a cheeky grin. "You look like you had a rough time of it. Pity you couldn't stop them."

Kai bit back a wince. Thinking about their failure today rankled his fur. Peering towards the new lake, Kai felt a chill reverberate through his body. The moonlight reflected off the surface of the water, exposing the broken silhouettes of the surrounding trees and headlining how far the damage stretched.

"Dekel, what happened to the others? I thought you and Montagru went with my Da and Petro after Yasso."

"I warned Monta about how dangerous it was going after that traitor, but he wouldn't hear a word of it. Well, we went and plucked the bastard from his cell, but then everything went to pot." Kai raised an eyebrow, gesturing for Dekel to continue. "Yasso jumped his uncle from behind once we reached the town square. Monta couldn't do a damned thing to stop the whelp from slitting his throat with a shard of glass."

A gasp came from the party. Kai's gaze twitched to Ione, who stared at Dekel with wide eyes and pale cheeks. "What about my Da and Petro? I doubt they would've gone down so easily."

"Nah, they both took the brat down before I could blink and yelled at me to run back while they dealt with him. I didn't wanna leave them behind, but that Petro fella was pretty persuasive. So, I left them to handle Yasso and make sure the ship cleared the danger area. I heard a boom as I was leaving, though, and looked back to see all three of them lying on the ground, twitching."

Kai muttered a curse under his breath. "Bloody Nulyma. Sounds like Yasso had one of those stonehood bombs; he must've nicked it from that

Liberator's body the night they attacked us. I appreciate you being honest, Dekel."

The engineer responded with a silent nod before offering the party space to sit and eat. Kai declined for himself, citing a desire to sleep, but told the party they were welcome to eat and recuperate before going to bed.

"We'll find Barraco and decide on a plan come morning," Kai muttered.

Leaving the others with the crew, the apothecary wandered into the trees. His mind kept repeating the events on Tapimor's Crest in a loop. They were on the back foot from the start, even when it looked like their surprise attack worked. And they had lost both Gaspard and Petro in the process...

Dropping to his knees, Kai hammered the ground with his fists as tears streamed down his cheeks. "Da," he murmured, his chest tightening. Gaspard, despite his injury, had always been an involved father and did his best to teach both Kai and Serafina the importance of compassion and balance in their lives. It was no secret he and Verona faced ridicule after bringing Kai back to Havenfall and declaring they would raise him as their own son. Regardless of the odds, or the mockery they received from the other villagers, they stood their ground and treated him the same as any other child. It was an attitude Kai took to heart as he grew older, devoting himself to proving he was more than what the villagers thought of him when he arrived.

The thought of never hearing his dad's boisterous laugh again, or tasting the delicious sweet rolls he baked every day, sent a chill throughout Kai's body penetrating to the marrow of his bones. Releasing a pained howl, he continued pounding the dirt with his knuckles, ignoring the needle-like pain shooting through his mangled arm with every blow. His energy soon left him, leaving him to pitch forward onto the ground, emitting a choked sob as his forehead left an imprint in the soft dirt.

Tiny blades of grass drifted across his cheeks as he lay there. A lump formed in his throat, weighing down on him as much as the hole in his heart left by hearing of his father's fate. Turning his head, he saw the light reflecting off the water's surface. Seeing the expansive lake reminded Kai of the battle, forcing him to bite his tongue while the shroud of a Frenzy Haze tickled the edge of his vision.

Hakan and his allies would pay for what they did. Kai knew they would not be easy to defeat, but they would find a way. He could only offer thanks to the Wind Saints that Grimghast was kept out of the battle. He was certain at least one of his friends would have died had the monster been there.

A gust of wind cut across his body, causing him to shiver. Emitting a grumble, he found a wide tree with sprawling roots and nestled against the trunk. Kai wasn't sure how well he could sleep with his mind unable to let go of those images, but he could try.

"You weren't thinking you'd be alone, did you?" a familiar voice chirped.

Despite his muddled thoughts, Kai couldn't keep a smile off his face when Maple and Orelia both settled next to him and snuggled into his side. "You're not going to eat?" he asked.

"Doubt I can hold anything down, to be honest," said Orelia. "Besides, you're more important. I'm sorry about what happened to your father."

Tears pricked at his eyes, though he brushed them away at once. "It's not your fault. I wasn't able to stop that bastard Hakan when it really counted. At least we knocked the cannon off course. What even happened, Maple?"

"Don't know," she replied, shrugging. "I reckon it's something like your crazy trick with the vine. Seems like there's more to faumen than we ever could've imagined."

Kai stared at his bandaged arm and Maple's palm, numerous questions buzzing about in his head. "The real question is why this is happening now of all times? If Lucretia is right, faumen haven't been able to do this since the Rebirth."

"Again, not too worried about it right now. You're our priority. We can talk about it after returning to Whistlevale."

"True. Thanks for putting up with me. Also, didn't you say we had something important to discuss?"

Maple's lips curved upward in a sly smile. "Yes, but it can wait. For now, I'd rather get some sleep, and being here like this brings back fond memories."

Thinking back to their watch together outside Runegard, Kai smiled and wrapped an arm around Maple's waist, pulling her tight against his side. Unwilling to leave Orelia out, he pulled her close as well and kissed both women on the forehead. "I remember that, and it still makes me smile."

"Me as well. We'll have our talk tomorrow after we've recovered. Besides, I have a feeling you'll find the topic much more pleasant than today's events."

To Kai, that sounded like music to his ears. Cleaving tight to one another, the trio soon fell into blissful slumber.

As the morning sun peeked through the trees, Kai emitted a soft groan when the light shined on his face. Rubbing his eyes, he stretched out with a sense that something was off. With a half-lidded stare, he gazed about and noticed Maple curled up next to him, head cradled within her arms. Orelia was splayed out on her back, lightly snoring with her mouth wide open.

Chuckling, Kai brushed the hair from Maple's face and ran a finger down Orelia's cheek. A loud snort startled him for a brief moment, until he looked around and realized the rest of the party surrounding them, sleeping against nearby trees. Some, like Lucretia, had small blankets providing protection from the spring winds. Others, like Morgan, opted to sprawl themselves out in the most comfortable positions they could.

Kai shook his head and gave the girls another longing glance before rising to his feet. He grabbed his satchel and left them to rest before going in search of his mother and sister. Taking a peek at the low position of the sun, Kai doubted they would be up and about yet. Instead, he wandered off in search of a quiet spot to work. The survivors would need medicine, and even though Havenfall was gone, he technically still held the title of town apothecary.

A gust of wind passed him, ruffling his mane and causing his injured arm to throb. A gentle creak broke the silence, drawing Kai's attention to a small makeshift shack just outside the camp's edge. Curiosity piqued, he approached the rickety building and pushed the door open.

His eyes lit up when he saw it was a small workshop, likely built by the Hunters ages ago to dress large animals for easier transport. A large, sturdy table stood in the middle of the shack. Several rods hung along the walls. Judging by the dark stains in the wood, Kai guessed they were for drying small cuts of meat. Setting his satchel on the ground, he removed his herbs and began working. If nothing else, focusing on preparing medicine for the sick and injured would distract him from thinking about Gaspard.

Time seemed to stand still as he attacked his tasks with vigor. Each act of crushing, grinding, chopping, and mixing all blended together, and soon there were several jars and bowls full of medicine ready for use. The cut on his palm flared in pain, forcing Kai to bind it with a thick cloth to dampen the sensation.

A gentle knock on the door stunned him for a moment before Maple invited herself in. "Hey, love. Someone told me they watched you come this way earlier, and your mom and sister are looking for ya. You want some breakfast?"

Kai's lips curved upward. "Breakfast sounds great. Sorry if I made you worry."

"I'm well aware you can take care of yourself, Sir Gravebane." As always, the way Maple purred his Brand in her alluring drawl sent shivers down Kai's spine. "But at the same time, I'd rather you not work yourself to exhaustion. Orelia is trying to rouse the others, though it's a gamble on whether she'll wake Morgan without a well-placed smack. Besides, I think we can have the discussion I mentioned now that we're alone."

Blinking, Kai twisted his hips to gaze up at the mischievous gleam in Maple's eyes. "I suppose we can talk then. What did you want—"

Anything else Kai wanted to say died on his lips as Maple curled her wings around him from the side, resting her hands on his right shoulder. He was left breathless at the look of adoration in the merchant's eyes, licking his lips instinctively as her face descended towards his. Unable to speak, Kai's grip on the knife in his hand tightened when Maple leaned in and captured his lips with hers.

He heard plenty of stories from other men on what kissing felt like, but none of what he heard could've prepared him for the reality. His lips tingled, as if an electric shock ran through him. The softness of Maple's lips was unlike anything he felt before. He knew he enjoyed holding her hand, and the feel of her skin when they danced was exhilarating, but that was nothing compared to this.

Lifting a hand to her cheek, Kai held her in place as he returned the kiss with ardor. He was aware of Maple settling into his lap, but his shock returned when he felt something wet run along his lips. Her tongue.

Kai allowed his mouth to open just a bit, and Maple took the initiative to press forward and touch her tongue to his. All of Kai's thoughts were washed away as he let go of the knife and wrapped his arms around Maple's waist, losing himself in the sensation while they kissed with feverish passion. He wasn't sure how long they sat there, engrossed with each other, but Kai knew one thing was certain.

I think I found my new favorite activity.

He couldn't hold back a blush when Maple pulled back, staring at him with a timid smile. "I love you, Kai," she whispered, pressing her forehead against his.

"I love you too, Maple," he replied. "I reckon Orelia is going to be a bit jealous when she hears about this."

She giggled and gripped a handful of his hair, tugging it back as she pressed herself closer. "She already agreed to let me have first crack at your lips, though don't be surprised if she starts chasing you before long."

The sound of rising voices reverberated from outside the shack. The couple stared at each other with raised eyebrows.

"What in the winds is going on?" Maple asked.

"No clue. We probably better check it out."

They rose to their feet and left the shack at a brisk pace. The clamor grew louder as they approached the camp. Kai squinted, seeing a crowd of Hunters shouting and shaking their fists at another group. Reaching the outer fringe of the camp's center, Kai released an exasperated groan when he recognized the dark green and red feathers of the Aerivolk at the other group's head, surrounded by armed guards as usual.

Kendela had found them.

What the pompous noble wanted with the Hunter Corps, Kai didn't know. All he knew was it couldn't be anything good, judging from the obscenities the Hunters were hurling towards Kendela. Even Barraco scowled at him with a furious expression Kai couldn't remember ever seeing on the portly man. To the noble's credit, he ignored the vitriol with an aplomb Kai didn't think he possessed.

Pushing his way forward, the apothecary demanded to know what was going on.

"You have no business here, Gravebane, so begone," snapped Kendela. "I am simply offering to sell my extra wares and supplies to the survivors of this horrible attack on our realm. It's not my fault they can't understand a good deal." Kai felt movement at his side and watched Serafina stomp past him.

She pointed an accusatory finger at the noble. "Your idea of a good deal is trail robbery, you featherbrained hack!" she shouted. Verona sidled beside him and pulled Serafina back by the shoulders. From the corner of his eye, Kai spotted the rest of the party shoving their way through the crowd towards them.

"You'd best shut your mouth, girl, if you know what's good for you," Kendela warned. Growling at the noble's threat, Kai turned to Barraco and asked for details.

"This pebblewit expects us to pay him a gold per stone for food. And his offer for fabric was seven silvers a square yard." Kai was expecting to hear an exorbitant number, but the truth made him choke on his own spit. Kendela was charging over five times the standard price!

Maple emitted a shrill chirp and shrieked at the lord, her feathers ruffled. "You're a disgrace to our profession! What kind of merchant tries to take advantage of people after their home has been destroyed?"

"Silence, woman! Any merchant with a head for business uses the opportunities life provides to earn honest coin. Although—" Kendela eyed Maple with a lecherous sneer. Kai's tail fur stood on end, wondering what was going through the lord's mind. "Perhaps we can come to a *different* kind of deal."

Maple scoffed, "And what are you proposing this time?"

"Simple. I'll lower my prices to market value for these homeless wretches, but only if you agree to marry me."

A rumbling growl rose from Kai's chest, though he was surprised when Maple erupted into peals of laughter. All eyes turned to the young woman as she collapsed against Kai's chest, thumping his mane with a closed fist with each spurt of giggles. Soon the rest of the party joined in and was leaning on each other in their amusement.

It was clear Kendela was unused to being laughed at, as his face was beginning to resemble a freshly picked tomato once more. It was a look Kai thought appropriate for the arrogant man. "What in Galen's name do you find so amusing?"

"You can't possibly think I'd agree to something so stupid, would you?"

"You will regret insulting me. Now you have two choices; marry me and accept the deal, or the price triples! You don't want these fools to starve now, do you?"

This time it was Kai who broke out into laughter, which drew Kendela's hardened glare to him. Seeing Kai's reaction sent Maple into another giggling fit, and the two held onto each other until they were left wheezing.

"Kendela, I hate to be the one to tell you this," Kai sputtered, "but your deal is not only trail robbery, but it also proves how much of an imbecile you are."

The noble's fierce expression faltered. "How dare you!"

Holding up three fingers, Kai ticked them off one at a time. "First of all, because we serve the Grand Duchess directly, your offer to Maple qualifies as attempting bribery of a royal officer."

Kendela's face turned sallow, which filled Kai with a morbid glee. The accusation alone could result in being stripped of his Margrave title, if not his entire fortune.

"Second, you picked the wrong group to try gouging. In case you've forgotten, we're Hunters. We can go catch our own damned food!"

The noble's face shifted from a sickly yellow to deep red once again as the crowd of Hunters erupted into braying laughter. Serafina fell to the ground in hysterics while Kendela's guards looked about with hesitation, unsure of how to react.

"Lastly—" Kai's voice trailed off when Maple took his hand in hers.

"I'll take this one. The fact is, *Lord* Kendela," she spat, drawing out the noble's title in blatant sarcasm, "you don't seem to know how to take no for an answer, something your parents should've taught you as a chick. Consider this my third and final official refusal. I will *never* marry you. In fact, I wouldn't marry you if you were the last man on Nixtral! There's only one man I plan on giving my hand to, and he's standing beside me."

Kendela's face colored again, this time to a mottled grey. If Kai remembered correctly, having a proposal refuted three times was a death kneel to any potential deal, whether between merchants or a man seeking marriage. To bring the matter up again invited legal retribution. His men stared at the Aerivolk woman with unbridled shock. With a smug grin, Maple pointed in the direction from which they assumed Kendela's group came, judging by the tracks in the mud.

"Now begone with you. Shoo!"

Biting on his knuckle to stifle the mirth threatening to burst from his chest, Kai gave Maple's hand a squeeze and turned to walk away. Seeing this, the Hunters followed suit and began trudging back towards the camp.

"D-don't you turn away from me!" Kendela shouted. "Get back here, you miserable bastards. As Margrave of this province, I order you to do as I say!"

Without even turning back, Kai waved a dismissive hand. "Give it up, Kendela. It's over, and we have more important things to worry about. Go home and plot your next shady Parliament deal or whatever it is you do." Kai was so exhausted from the battle, he couldn't even muster the anger needed to smack the pompous Aerivolk around like he deserved, given the headaches he'd caused. He just wanted him to leave them in peace. With Maple giving three refusals to his proposal, Kendela had no reason to continue pursuing her without stirring up more trouble.

The apothecary was so focused on putting the situation behind him, he almost missed the distinctive ring of a sword being drawn.

"You pathetic peltneck, I always get what I want!" The sounds of shifting grass and rapid footsteps reached Kai's twitching ears. His eyes pinched together.

He wouldn't dare...

He was caught by surprise when he felt Maple's feathers on his side, shoving him away. At the same time, something pulled at his belt, removing a noticeable weight. His mind flashed back to that day in Glimmerdale, when Hemlocke poisoned Maple.

No!

Twisting his body mid-fall, Kai managed to catch himself in time to hear an ominous thud, followed by a wave of gasps. His eyes looked up to see Maple pressed against Kendela, staring into his eyes with the noble holding one of his guard's swords above his head. The guards stood still as statues, their eyes resembling saucers.

Kai scrambled to his feet and moved towards the two but stumbled to a halt when he noticed a thin line of blood emerging from the corner of Kendela's mouth. Frowning, he stepped to the side and his breath hitched.

The weight he felt pulled from his belt was his harvesting sickle. The tool rested in Maple's hand, its curved blade rammed into Kendela's heart. Maple reached up and batted the sword from the noble's hands, sending it clattering to the dirt.

"Not this time," she hissed in a deadly whisper.

Lifting her talon, she kicked Kendela back towards his men where he fell to the ground, dead. His eyes were listless and empty. The guards broke into a clamor and moved to draw their own swords before skittering to a stop. Faster than they could blink, they were facing a crowd of furious Hunters, each armed and ready to fight.

Raising the bloody sickle towards the men, Maple answered their furious glares with a single word.

"Leave."

To Kai's awe, one of the guards, a burly Soltauri, grabbed Kendela's body and threw it over his shoulder before leading their entire group in running from the furious merchant. As they disappeared into the trees, Kai froze when he heard Maple drop the sickle with an audible clatter. He rushed to her side, asking if she was injured as he helped her up.

"No, love, I promise I'm fine. Just a little shaken. I wasn't expecting that bastard to try stabbing you in the back, though it shouldn't really surprise me."

Unable to hold back his tears, Kai drew her into a hug and pressed his face into her hair. "Don't you ever scare me like that again, Maple," he begged, "I thought it was Glimmerdale all over again." He felt a thump on his back as Orelia threw herself against the two, checking them both for injuries.

"You're not getting rid of me that easily," she replied.

Kai's gaze shifted. "Orelia," he started, his eyes meeting the priestess', "were you serious about what you told me before, at the dispensary?"

She gave a bright smile and nodded. "Of course."

Taking a deep breath, Kai pulled back and dropped to one knee. Maple's wings flew to her mouth, both eyes wide as he held out his mother's pendant to her.

"I know this is rather sudden, but this past moon has taught me the rivers wait for no one, and we can never predict what the future holds. I know we have other plans to consider and work out, but I'll ask you now: Will you give me the honor of being my partner in everything for the rest of eternity, even after we sail to the gardens of Finyt?

"Maplyne, will you marry me?"

The crowd watched with bated breath as Maple broke out into tears, her hands cupping the glass orb in her hands as they stared into each other's eyes. Kai refused to move or breathe, his mind pleading desperately for her to say something.

He didn't have long to wait. After a few moments, Maple threw her arms around Kai's neck with a euphoric trill, knocking them both to the ground.

"Yes, yes, a million times yes!" she screamed.

Serafina led the Hunters in jubilant cheers, all while the party helped the couple to their feet and offered their congratulations. Waving her staff to gain everyone's attention, Orelia, with tears streaming down her face, clapped her hands together and suggested they get to work.

"No time like the present, friends, and we could use some joy after everything that's happened. Let's get to work; we've got a handfasting to put on!"

Chapter XXXIV

Emitting a heavy sigh, Fusette slumped into her chair as she read the small pile of parchments littering her desk. In addition to Waveweaver's report on the Battle of Havenfall, there were also letters from Gravebane and each member of his party detailing the incident. The urge to scream rose in her chest, though a quick glance at Saredi's glowering visage stayed her hand.

"Your Grace," the Vesikoi noble uttered, his voice tight as he held up Larimanz's report, "how could something like this happen? There was no indication the Liberators had access to a weapon like this."

The sharp pinch of her nails digging into her scalp helped calm Fusette, taking her mind off the frustration. "I wish I knew, Saredi. It appears our enemy is far more vicious and prepared than we anticipated. Have you read Gravebane's report on the identity of the one responsible for orchestrating the war?"

"I have not," Saredi admitted. He accepted the sheaf of parchment from Fusette, eyes darting from side to side as he appraised the document. His gaze narrowed when he reached the end, leaning back with a pained groan. "Damnation," he muttered. "All this time, it was another Norzen pulling the Liberators' strings?"

"I'm more disturbed by the fact that this bastard Hakan appears to be related to myself and Gravebane, and is actively engaged in Blood Feud against the Cacovis line. It appears the shadows of the Desolation continue to haunt Livoria even now."

From the opposite corner, Hanblum took a draw from his pipe, eyes closed as he sank into the plush chair Fusette provided for him. "Admiral

Basner has admitted it will take time for his fleet to rest up from their march. However, they have offered their services in defending Whistlevale until they are ready to pursue the enemy. For now, the plan is to wait until the Five Realms Council convenes. Her Majesty has informed me she is eager to arrive and see you again."

A soft smile curled into place on Fusette's lips. She hadn't seen Queen Isolde since her coronation ceremony almost nine years ago. It would be good to see the older monarch in person again after so long.

The sound of Saredi slapping an open palm on the table drew the duchess' attention back to her advisor. He was staring at a shorter piece at parchment, the pale sheen of his face becoming almost translucent. Rising from her seat, Fusette strolled over and looked over the man's shoulder. She bit back a wince when she recognized Kai's familiar scrawl and realized which letter he was reading.

Damn, I should've put that one in my secret cabinet...

"What is this, Your Grace?" Saredi asked, raising the letter and waving it in front of her. His eyes were narrowed and he regarded the duchess with a disappointed frown.

Releasing an amused snort, Fusette grinned. "It appears to be a letter, Saredi. From Gravebane, judging by the handwriting."

"You know exactly what I meant. Is what he wrote in here true? Are you intending to go through with allowing him to marry someone outside of his own tribe? I know we discussed the possibility, but I never imagined you'd actually go through with it."

Hanblum shot to his talons, his eyes bulbous as he stared at Fusette. "Your Grace, what madness is Lord Saredi speaking of? You know the church forbids relations between the tribes!"

Crossing her arms, the duchess quirked an eyebrow at the man while snatching the letter from Saredi's hand. "Then I suppose it's a good thing the church's precepts have no bearing on the legality of marriage." She almost lost her composure to laughter when the Aerivolk's spectacles came within a nail's length of falling off his face.

Both the envoy and chamberlain stared at Fusette with dumbfounded expressions. "Milady," Hanblum whispered, his voice cracking, "you can't be suggesting you intend to ignore a cardinal church tenet to allow who I assume to be Gravebane to take a bride from another tribe. Such an event would cause unnecessary turmoil in the wake of the Council summit."

"As I said, while the church has considerable influence within our realms, the fact remains its precepts do not determine whether a marriage is legal and binding. As it stands, Gravebane meets all the legal and financial requirements to take a spouse. Besides, he intends to to plead his case to the Archbishop upon his return to request permission to take a second bride in a similar situation."

Staggering back as if struck, Hanblum collapsed into his seat. "A *second*?!" he choked out.

Saredi paced the room, a low grumble emanating from his throat. "I hope you know what you're doing, milady," he finally said. "This could turn the entirety of the Quorum of Bishops against you."

"My friends, I understand you are only reacting as the church has taught you," Fusette soothed. "For many of us, that's all we've ever known. However, the church, while a good teacher of morals, has remained blind in certain areas, especially in regards to us faumen." The duchess ignored Hanblum's raised eyebrow. "Ambroz came into being because his parents saw their love for what it truly was: a gift and a blessing. If we're going to fight the hatred spewed by the Liberators and their allies, then we need to send an equally strong message to counter it. And I can think of no one better suited to spreading a message of hope and love than Kai Travaldi."

Gazing at the transformed clearing, Kai couldn't help but admit the Hunters outdid themselves in proving their ingenuity. In the two days since his proposal, the villagers turned the clearing into a thing of beauty.

A rudimentary wooden arch loomed over him near the riverbank, held together with ivy vines and decorated with multicolored lilies. A small grove of trees was hacked into hundreds of yard-tall stumps to use as chairs. The villagers of Havenfall set them in a wide fanning arc split by an aisle in the center, allowing as many people to see the arch as possible while sitting. The majority stood behind the stumps with the shortest up front to the tallest in the rear.

Orelia stood beneath the arch to Kai's left, dressed in her typical vestment with the addition of a golden stole around her neck, marking her dedication to Galen. She carried two small ribbons, one red and one yellow, and a braided cord in her hands. Maple was dressing in the nearby woods with Serafina, having asked the younger girl for assistance. The rest of the party stood with Verona next to the stumps nearest the arch.

The apothecary himself was dressed in his formal wear again, the green waistcoat and brass-colored breeches contrasting against his ebony fur and pale skin. He tugged at the neckline of his shirt and glanced at Orelia with a nervous grin.

"Thank you again," he said. "I know this has to be hard for you."

"I already knew she'd be the first choice, so I'm not terribly upset," Orelia replied. "Besides, I'm more impressed you gathered the courage to ask her so suddenly. You both deserve this." Emitting a joyous squeal, she hugged Kai tight and gave him a quick peck on the cheek.

Rubbing the back of his head, Kai found himself unable to reply as his throat tightened. Instead, he stood and waited, mentally rehearsing what he wanted to say.

A rustling sound from the trees made Kai's ears twitch. His eyes followed the noise to see his sister bustling towards him. Raising her hand, Serafina snapped her fingers and rushed forward to give Kai a hug before taking her place next to Verona.

At the sound of Serafina's snap, a group of men near the front revealed a variety of instruments and began playing an upbeat processional tune with a flowing melody. For a moment, Kai questioned the odd choice in music, wondering why they didn't opt for a traditional slower wedding ballad. His thoughts shifted as the music's tempo increased, reminding him they weren't a traditional couple, and Maple was certainly not a traditional lady. More rustling came from the trees, and Kai looked over in anticipation, only for his breath to still.

Standing at the rear of the aisle, dressed in the same garb from their first dance, was Maple. The only new addition to her attire was a silver lace veil covering her face from the nose down, and his mother's pendant adorning her neck. Hands clasped at her bare belly and eyes locked on Kai, Maple strode forward at a brisk, steady pace. Her hip sash billowed at her side in the afternoon wind.

Kai emitted a soft grunt when Orelia jabbed an elbow into his ribs, reminding him to breathe. He rubbed the area tenderly, casting an unamused smirk at the priestess before returning his attention to Maple, who raised an eyebrow at him while holding back a chuckle.

Soon, she reached the arch, standing across from him on Orelia's left and fluttering her eyelashes in an amusing manner. Stifling his urge to chuckle, he returned her smile and the pair turned to face Orelia. The priestess cleared her throat and addressed the crowd, raising the cord above her head.

"Dear friends and family, we are gathered on this beautiful day to bear witness as these two before us join in the most sacred and momentous act of marriage. With the winds' blessings, it is my honor to lead this handfasting.

"Marriage is not a decision to be made lightly. Binding two paths into a single journey must be made with willful commitment, honesty, and intention. It requires an understanding of the foundations which make any relationship strong, such as loyalty, communication, and unwavering love. Love has brought us here today, and this pair stands as a testament that our ability to love and be loved is the most precious gift to be shared between two people."

Taking a breath, Orelia cast a serious gaze towards the crowd. "There are many in this world—nay, even within our very church—who would tell us these two are unable to be together simply based on appearances. I say anyone who expresses such rot knows nothing of true love, which knows no boundaries. The connection between this pair is unlike anything I have seen, and I believe with every fiber of my soul that theirs is a love which shall spring eternal."

With the party leading the crowd in crows of agreement, Kai and Maple's faces flushed red at the outpouring of support. Gesturing with her arms, Orelia invited everyone to settle down. With a warm smile, the priestess brought Kai and Maple closer and asked them to join hands.

Kai swallowed the bubble of nervousness lodged in his throat and held his hands out, palms facing up. A small bundle of heliotropes lay in his left palm. The skin of his right palm remained dark, the stitches holding his wound together standing out against the rest of his arm. His fingers twitched when Maple rested her arms in his hands, pressing the flowers between them, as they grasped each other by the wrist.

Taking her cue, Orelia threw the cord over her shoulder. She separated the smaller ribbons, tying the yellow around Kai's wrist and the red around Maple's. Next, she wrapped the braided cord around first their hands, then arms, before tying a loose knot underneath.

Placing her hands on top of theirs, Orelia continued, "We will now commence with the sharing of vows. I invite each partner to speak freely and share their innermost thoughts and feelings as they enter this union. Kai, you shall go first."

The apothecary's throat felt like a desert as he stared into Maple's eyes. Beneath the veil, he could see her tilted grin. He felt the softness of her hands squeezing his in a comforting manner, and all his fears melted away. Closing his eyes for a moment to gather his thoughts, he opened them again and met her gaze.

"Maple, you already know I'm not one for eloquent speaking, so I'll come right out and say it: you're a precious treasure beyond measure. I'll always remember seeing your eyes the day we first met, glittering brighter than polished amethyst. During our travels, I got to learn more about you and found myself fascinated. I couldn't stop thinking about this bright, honest, and vivacious woman who wandered into my life by pure chance.

The more we talked and shared on our journey, I became scared at how deeply my attachment grew. It wasn't until you asked me to dance that I realized I needed to grab hold of this with my heart and arms open and not let others' opinions plant the seeds of fear in my heart.

"I wouldn't change this for anything. I know what the church's official stance on us says, but I don't care. If loving you means we'd be cursed to Nulyma, then I say let it come. We'll simply conquer the void together. I love you, Maple. My wish is to give you the happy life you deserve, and as the heliotropes between our hands symbolize, my love for you will forever be eternal."

The crowd broke into polite applause as Kai watched a single tear escape Maple's eye. Worried he may have spoken *too* freely, he paused when her grip on his wrists tightened, her fingers stroking back and forth along his skin.

"Kai," she whispered, "every time I think you couldn't possibly be more charming, you somehow exceed my expectations." A wave of muffled laughter rose from the crowd. "Then again, you've been doing that for as long as I've known you. I'll admit, if anyone had told me as a little girl I'd be standing here today, I would've called them barking mad. I had to fend for myself for so long, I almost forgot what it was like to have friends and people who cared about me. Then you came along.

"At first, I wasn't sure what to think. My whole life, people told me to never trust a Norzen. And yet...I was intrigued by this strange man who defied every expectation I had and proved to be not only strong, but compassionate, loyal, and protective. We've shared our fears, our hopes, and our dreams, and I can say without a doubt I don't regret my decision to ask you for that dance back in Grantide. As a merchant, I'm supposed to be able to put a price on anything, but to me, your love is the most priceless gift in all Nixtral. I love you, Kai Travaldi, and I'm prepared to face the world with you beside me. Forever and always."

Another round of applause rang out as Orelia clapped her hands together and bowed her head.

"Excellent! I ask that you both take heed. This cord represents the bond you two share. However, you are bound not by this cord, but by your vows to one another. Going forward, there will be those who question your affection. Share in not only each other's pain, but your joys and triumphs. Protect one another in times of danger. Care for each other in sickness and in health. Continue to strive towards harmony and serve as a guiding wind for others to follow. Show the world love has no boundaries and can never be quelled by fear and despair. By the authority granted to me by Jovanni, Archbishop of the Order of the Windbringers, I pronounce you husband and wife."

Removing the cord from their arms, Orelia turned the couple to face the crowd, a wide smiling adorning her face.

"It is my duty and pleasure to introduce you all to Kai and Maple Travaldi!"

Everyone erupted into cheers, the party leaping to their feet and applauding with gusto. Not even Lucretia could hold back her tears.

Turning back to Maple, Kai removed the veil from her face and wrapped his arms around her hips. The merchant encircled both wings around her husband's neck with a brazen grin as she was pulled into a searing kiss. The crowd's cheering grew even more thunderous, the ground shaking with the number of people leaping in joy. Interlocking his fingers with hers, Kai led his wife towards the crowd. The musicians broke into a festive tune while many of the villagers paired off.

The new couple began twirling and spinning, joining everyone around them in laughter. Kai almost sputtered at seeing Morgan dancing with Lucretia, whirling the woman around in circles. Nearby, Teos led Ione in a steady waltz.

A lilting trill reached his ears, prompting Kai to look down at Maple as she grabbed him by the arm and led him towards the trees. Grinning, he allowed himself to be pulled away with Orelia chasing after them. Once they reached a shady spot far enough away but still within eyesight of the crowd, Maple pulled Kai's head down and kissed the edge of his mouth. She took his hand and danced to the musicians' peppy melody.

"I don't think I've ever felt so happy," Maple murmured, tittering with an open-mouthed smile. Letting Kai twirl her in place, she let go and pushed him towards Orelia. She watched them dance while moving her own body in time with the beat.

"I feel the same way," Kai replied. "I wish Da could've seen this." Tears trailed down Kai's cheeks, only for Maple to brush them away.

"He may not be here, love, but I'm sure he's watching from Finyt. I know he'd be proud of you."

"Maple's right," Orelia said. "Now we just have to decide how to approach things once we return to the capital. I doubt we can hide your marriage too long, especially from the Archbishop."

Kai quirked an eyebrow. The thought of having to explain himself and his situation to the Archbishop was nerve wracking, though required if he wished to bring his plan to fruition. Still, he refused to back down; they'd already come this far.

He was surprised to see Maple cackle and draw Orelia into a tight hug. "Oh no you don't! You're not getting out of our deal that easily."

"What deal?" His gaze pinned Orelia in place, though she said nothing, biting her lip and casting her eyes towards the grass.

Maple cupped his chin and pulled him towards her. Her eyes sparkled with mischief as she bounced around Kai in an odd dance he'd never seen before. Her feathers brushed against his skin like silk, leaving goosebumps in their wake. "The two of us made a wager on whether you'd be able to cure me, and I *may* have taken advantage of Orelia being a tiny bit drunk at the time."

Kai's face shifted into an amused smirk. "What did you do?"

Coming to a stop, Maple turned her own eyes downward and hooked her wings behind her back in apprehension. "I might have tricked Orelia into agreeing to share you," she stammered out, the words gushing forth in a jumbled mess.

Every thought in Kai's mind came to a grinding halt. His heart thrummed at a furious pace, sweat beading on his skin. "Wait a tic. Is this serious? You *both* agreed to share me? As in, you came to the decision together." He couldn't wrap his mind around the possibility of them already being in agreement on his plan without even knowing it.

Orelia nodded. "We shook hands on it and everything. Even if I was drunk, I was coherent enough to know and accept that, at least."

Stumbling back, Kai felt his back hit a tree, stopping him from going further as he slid to ground. He soon started chuckling, his mirth growing louder until he had his head thrown back crowing in laughter. "I suppose this makes things a bit easier," he finally gasped out.

"What are you talking about, love?" Maple asked.

As he took deep breaths to calm himself, Kai looked up at the two with a light pink tinge to his cheeks. "Remember how I said I couldn't imagine breaking either of your hearts?"

"Yes," the two answered in unison. Their heads tilted to the side in opposite directions, an action that made Kai hesitate with how cute he found it.

"Well...I broached the idea with Lady Fusette on whether I could be permitted to marry both of you; since we're all of different tribes, I felt it best to seek approval from the mountaintop, so to speak. Needless to say, I received a hawk with her consent in our last correspondence." As proof, he removed the letter from his satchel and held it up for them to see.

The women responded with blank stares before turning to each other. Blinking, they said nothing, which sent a tremor of nervousness through Kai. He began wondering if he overstepped in revealing his actions. His lips began curving down when they both launched themselves at him with shrieks of glee.

"You crazy, brilliant fool!" Maple exclaimed. "Are you serious?" Kai nodded, explaining that Fusette would arrange a meeting with Archbishop Jovanni, a known faumen advocate, to gain a church-based approval. There would likely need to be concessions on both sides, but the Grand Duchess had already pledged her support.

Orelia buried her face in Kai's chest, rubbing her cheeks into his fur while emitting happy squeaks. "Kai, are you really willing to go through with this?" He nodded, producing a contented sigh from the young woman.

Maple tugged her back a few paces, to Orelia's consternation, though her countenance quickly changed after the merchant whispered a few muffled words in one ear. Kai's own ears twitched, trying to hear what was being said to no avail.

He felt a shiver rumble down his spine when Orelia turned to face him, her face twisted into a sly expression suggesting more than a little playfulness. "Orelia, sweetheart...what are you doing?"

She advanced on him without a word and an enticing sway in her hips. With his back already against the tree, Kai had nowhere to run as she settled herself into his lap and hooked her arms around his neck. He was immediately reminded of Maple's expression earlier that morning, giving the Vesikoi a gentle smile before she pulled him forward and kissed him.

Unlike his experience with Maple, Kai was a bit more prepared and held Orelia by her hips, deepening the kiss while keeping them both steady. He felt her tongue brush against his lips and opened them, allowing her to explore while they clung tight to each other. The entire time, Maple watched from her place a few strides away, giggling and peering back at the celebrating crowd. A stray thought flitted across Kai's mind that no one seemed to have noticed their disappearance yet, though he doubted that would remain true for long.

The pair separated just enough to catch their breath. Orelia's smile widened to the point Kai wondered if she might hurt her jaw. "That was amazing."

"I'm glad you enjoyed it, sweetheart. Things will certainly be different going forward. The real question is: Are you willing to go through with this? If we gain the Archbishop's approval, will you marry me as well?"

Orelia nodded, pressing her lips against his nose and ruffling his hair. "If you're willing to have me, I would be delighted to be your wife."

A light chuckle had the pair turning towards Maple. "It's funny. Before, you were worried about your father's reaction if you became a mistress, but the prospect of marriage has you ready to jump into the deep end of the lake?"

"I think my concern was more how people would view Kai for taking a mistress not of his tribe, considering the grief my father gets for the same decision, but then I remembered something." Kai and Maple blinked, waiting for her to continue. "I don't give a flip what my father or anyone else thinks. I love him as any daughter should, but he can be rather set in his opinion that anyone subordinate to him must do exactly as he says. None of that ever included letting me choose what to do with my life. My main reason for joining the clergy was to stick a needle in his craw; he expected me to follow my brothers into the Navy simply because he demanded it! Besides, I like to think my husband-to-be can protect himself from a cranky old man."

Kai released a nervous chuckle. "We may encounter him sooner than you think. Fusette said he's leading the Galstan fleet sent to assist us. We'll need to bring the Hunters back to Whistlevale now and prepare for our meeting with not only Jovanni, but your father as well. I only hope Fusette can accommodate everyone."

"Oh, I'm sure Saredi will figure things out," Maple said. "The man has a plan for everything."

"You're not wrong, but at least we have each other."

"And our friends," Orelia added. "One way or another, we'll find a way to end this war. I refuse to believe those monsters can beat us."

"They won't. Unlike them, we have something worth fighting for: Our future."

Maple stroked a hand through Kai's mane, resting her other arm on his waist. "Couldn't have said it better, love. I will admit, though, I *am* looking forward to one thing after all this ruckus."

Kai tilted his head in confusion. "Oh, and what's that?"

Maple answered her husband with a steamy gaze, her fingers curling around his fur. "Our wedding night," she whispered. Orelia squeaked and cupped her head in her hands to hide the crimson blush covering her cheeks at the older woman's words.

Kai gulped, wondering just how prepared he was for what awaited him.

— THE END —

Glossary

Aerian – The native language of the Aerivolk tribe.

Aerivolk – A bird-like faumen tribe able to take running glides at high speeds. They have the strongest eyesight and are considered the most peaceful of the tribes. They are most famous for their artistry with fabrics.

Alezon (pronounced Al-a-zon) – The southern continent of Nixtral. Consists of five realms and is infamous as the origin point of the faumen tribes.

Ausrina the Wanderer – One of the Wind Saints. An Aerivolk traveler who joined the Wind Saints during the Desolation Wars. Not much is known about her. Known as the Saint of Honesty.

Belomas Highlands – An ancient Alezonian realm known as the birthplace of the faumen. They are led by a Chiefs Council, currently headed by Chief Velibor.

Berelmir – A warlord who conquered several Galstein provinces until meeting his end at the hands of the Wind Saints.

Cacovis the Shadow – One of the Wind Saints. A Norzen carpenter and village leader who became infamous for bringing about the Desolation to free the lands that would become Livoria. Also known as the Fallen Saint or the Saint of Pride.

Centric – The primary trading language of Nixtral.

The Citadel – Livoria's foremost learning academy. Located in Runegard, it was once the fortress of the warlord Berelmir and now consists of four scholar divisions that work together to accumulate and advance knowledge within Livoria.

Corlati Federation – The most technologically advanced of the five Alezonian realms. Human superiority is preached as gospel, faumen are often kept as slaves, and most inhabitants follow the teachings of the warrior monk Cadell, known collectively as Cadism. Led by President Gideon Harmod.

The Desolation – A massive explosion caused by Cacovis via triggering a massive lekrite vein, which wiped out a swath of land between Livoria, Galstein, and Corlati.

Dolmaru the Quillblade – One of the Wind Saints. A Wasini warrior scholar who joined the Wind Saints during the Desolation Wars. He was responsible for opening the Citadel and served as its first Highmaster. Known as the Saint of Courage.

Edeval the Bandit Lord – One of the Wind Saints. An Aerivolk thieving band leader who joined the Wind Saints during the Desolation Wars. Known as the Saint of Loyalty.

Exarch Knights – The most prestigious order of Livoria. Known as the duchy's most skilled protectors, they are a special class of noble given a unique epithet by the Grand Duke or Duchess called a Brand.

Faumen – Demi-humans with animal characteristics that *mostly* originated from the Belomas Highlands. There are six currently known tribes in Alezon with their own unique strengths.

Feswili (pronounced Fez-wi-lee) – The northern continent of Nixtral. Not much is known about this place other than being much colder than the other continents and is the ancestral home of the Risbado faumen tribe.

Finyt (pronounced Feh-neet) – The land of paradise, according to Windbringer doctrine. It is said to be full of gardens and rivers where no war or conflict exists.

Fullblood – A faumen of pure lineage with no intermixing among humans or other tribes.

Galen the Sage – The leader of the Wind Saints. A human warrior monk who led the resistance against the warlord Berelmir. He was known for his wisdom and sense of fairness. Known as the Saint of Justice.

Grand Duchy of Livoria – The youngest of the Alezonian realms. It was once a series of Galstan provinces conquered by Berelmir, but gained independence following the Desolation Wars. Led by the Grand Duchess, Fusette Ardei.

High Norzen – The native language of the Norzen.

Holy Queendom of Galstein – A peaceful realm located in southeastern Alezon. Galstein is the historical ally of Livoria, ruled by a matriarchal royal family and famous for the potency of its medicinal herbs. Led by Queen Isolde Graffeld.

Lekrite – A purple, energy-dense mineral found in scattered pockets throughout Nixtral. It is highly reactive to shock and will explode if mishandled. Cacovis used it in order to bring about the Desolation.

Luopari the Oracle – One of the Wind Saints. A Vesikoi soothsayer who joined the Wind Saints during the Desolation Wars. She is among the most popular of the Saints. Known as the Saint of Faith.

Mixblood – A faumen of mixed heritage, usually with one faumen and one human parent. Mixbloods of two tribes are possible, but exceedingly rare and considered taboo.

Nixtral – The planet upon which the story takes place. It encompasses four major continents, one at each cardinal direction.

Norzen – A cat-like faumen tribe known for their two tails and sensitive ears. They are ostracized for their association with Cacovis, the one who caused the Desolation. However, they are also famous for their skills in engineering and scouting.

Nulyma (pronounced Nu-lee-ma) – According to Windbringer doctrine, a hellish void made of five levels where the damned go to suffer for their sins.

Order of the Windbringers – The primary church within Livoria and Galstein that reveres the Wind Saints as heroes and protectors.

Risbado – A fox-like faumen tribe native to the northern continent, Feswili. They have thick, bushy tails and pelts of fur covering their arms and torso. Many Risbado are short and stocky compared to the Norzen, their taller, leaner historical rivals.

Rodekan Empire – The oldest of the Alezonian realms, the Rodekans were considered the premier slave traders of Nixtral for centuries until several of its provinces declared independence and formed the Corlati Federation. Currently led by Emperor Kabuji Aduleji.

Soltauri – A bovine-like faumen tribe who typically have hooves for feet and two horns atop their heads. The tallest and strongest of the tribes, they are commonly seen as guards and soldiers. Historically nomadic, they are known for their skill in farming.

Soltish – The native language of the Soltauri.

Tapimor the Lifeweaver – One of the Wind Saints. A human apothecary who joined the Wind Saints during the Desolation Wars. Now considered a patron of the healing arts and the harvest. Known as the Saint of Compassion.

Vadako the Maiden – One of the Wind Saints. A Soltauri priestess who joined the Wind Saints during the Desolation Wars. A popular Saint among young women, she was famous for her kindness and willingness to help others. Known as the Saint of Generosity.

Vesikoi – A fish-like faumen tribe noted for their mottled skin, usually pale in the front with darker shades on the back. They are primarily water-based and famous for their craftsmanship with shells and gemstones.

Voidlands – The uninhabitable wasteland where the Desolation occurred. Once a thriving forest, it was reduced to a barren desert where nothing can grow by Cacovis' use of lekrite.

Wasini – A faumen tribe who have snake-like tails covered in armored scales for their lower bodies. They are the heaviest of the faumen and historically known as both great warriors and blacksmiths.

Wind Saints – A group of eight heroes led by Galen the Sage who saved the lands that would become Livoria from the warlord Berelmir.

About the Author

Cyrus Whelchel grew up in Converse, Texas, where both his local and school libraries were his home away from home. His favorite book growing up was *The Thief Lord* by Cornelia Funke.

After hopping between various jobs in early adulthood, Cyrus re-discovered his love of books and dedicated himself to being a Children's Librarian, where he now shares his passion for stories with the next generation.

An avid reader of fantasy and mystery, Cyrus loves the challenge of anticipating the end of a good story. Inspired by the historical challenges faced by his father's Jewish ancestors, *The Faumen War Chronicles* shows the importance of accepting each other's differences, being true to oneself, and standing strong against discrimination, no matter where you may find it.

Printed in the USA
CPSIA information can be obtained
at www.ICGtesting.com
CBHW031757070824
12857CB00004B/8

9 798989 516629